THE LITTLE SHIP

Margaret Mayhew

CORGI BOOKS

LITTLE SHIP
A CORGI BOOK : 0 552 14693 5

First publication in Great Britain

PRINTING HISTORY
Corgi edition published 1999

3 5 7 9 10 8 6 4

Set in 11/12³/₄pt Sabon by Kestrel Data, Exeter, Devon.

Corgi Books are published by Transworld Publishers,
61–63 Uxbridge Road, London W5 5SA,
a division of The Random House Group Ltd,
in Australia by Random House Australia (Pty) Ltd,
20 Alfred Street, Milsons Point, Sydney, NSW 2061, Australia,
and in New Zealand by Random House New Zealand Ltd,
18 Poland Road, Glenfield, Auckland 10, New Zealand
and in South Africa by Random House (Pty) Ltd,
Endulini, 5a Jubilee Road, Parktown 2193, South Africa.

Printed and bound in Great Britain by
Mackays of Chatham plc, Chatham, Kent

Margaret Mayhew was born in London and her earliest childhood memories were of the London Blitz. She began writing in her mid- thirties and had her first novel published in 1976. She is married to American aviation author, Philip Kaplan, and lives in Gloucestershire. Her previous novels, *Bluebirds* and *The Crew*, are also published by Corgi.

Also by Margaret Mayhew

BLUEBIRDS
THE CREW

and published by Corgi Books

For Tricia and Derik

Acknowledgements

I should like to thank the following for all their kind help and advice: James McMaster, Derik Quitmann, John Allen, Stephan Stritter, Joyce and Shimon Camiel, Neal Kaplan, Kay Huffner, Diane Pearson, my editor, and, as always Philip Kaplan.

Foreword

In May, 1940, eight months after the start of the Second World War, the armies of Nazi Germany surged across North Western Europe in a surprise *Blitzkrieg*, driving the British and Allied Forces back towards the coast and encircling them at the French port of Dunkirk.

A desperate plan, code-named Operation Dynamo, was hurriedly concocted in Britain to send as many ships as possible to rescue the trapped troops. Appeals broadcast on the wireless to civilian boat-owners produced a huge response. Together with the big ships of the Royal Navy, an extraordinary and heroic armada composed of craft of all sorts and sizes emerged from the rivers and ports along England's south and south-eastern coasts and set out across the Channel: paddle-steamers, barges, lifeboats, ferries, fire floats, oyster-dredgers, drifters, motor boats, mud-hoppers, cockle boats, yachts, fishing trawlers, pleasure-excursion launches . . . some of which had never been to sea before. A number of them were manned by Royal Navy personnel, but many were taken by civilian volunteers and weekend sailors, often with little experience of maritime hazards.

Over the following ten days, under heavy bombardment from the Luftwaffe and with the German army closing in, 338,226 British and French troops were snatched from the port and beaches and transported to England. During most of the period the sea remained, quite uncharacteristically, dead calm. The episode became known as the Miracle of Dunkirk and the ships as the Little Ships.

The bungalow is called Hove-To. It stands alone at the end of a potholed track that peters out near the river. I park the car by the gate and walk up a concrete pathway past a scruffy square of lawn and a bed of straggling petunias. The place seems deserted but when I press the bell at the front door there is a shuffling sound from inside and an amorphous shape looms behind the frosted glass. The door opens.

'Mr Potter?' I ask.

He is an old man – in his mid-eighties I judge – and wearing a food-stained cardigan and maroon carpet slippers. He looks at me suspiciously.

'You collecting for something?'

I shake my head. 'No.'

'Because I don't give any more. You never know where your money's going. Into other people's pockets more often than not, I reckon. You one of those Jehovahs?'

'No.'

'Blooming nuisance they are. Used to get them where we lived before. You must be selling something, then.'

'No, nothing.'

I can see that he doesn't believe me. 'I don't want insurance. Or double glazing. Nothing like that.' He starts to shut the door.

I say quickly: 'I'm not selling anything, Mr Potter, I promise you. On the contrary, I want to buy something.'

He frowns. 'You're wasting your time. I've got nothing of any value here. No antiques, or anything like that.' He starts to close the door.

I press on. 'It's your boat I'm interested in.'

The frown deepens. 'My boat? How do you know I've got one?'

'I was told. A fourteen-foot fishing boat called Rose of England.'

'Well, she'd be no use to you, unless you want her for firewood. She's a wreck.'

'Just the same, I'd like to buy her, if you're willing to sell.'

He looks me up and down, still suspicious. 'Whatever for? You look like you could afford a lot better than her.'

'It's for sentimental reasons . . . a connection with former owners.'

He grunts. 'She's been left out in all weathers for years. Not fit to sail. She wouldn't be worth buying.'

'She would to me. Could we talk about it?'

He stared at me for a moment. 'You sure you're not selling something.'

'Quite sure.'

He shrugs. 'Better come in then, I suppose.'

I step into a narrow hallway and follow him into the living-room. The furnishings are drear, the house stale-smelling, but the view through the large picture window makes up for it. I gaze out at the river Crouch flowing beneath wide and glorious summer skies to meet the North Sea; at great white, puffy clouds piled high against blue; at mud flats glistening and greenish water sparkling; at boats sailing and sea birds flying. The tall, feathery grasses on the banks ripple in the wind. Always the wind, I remember. Always the wind. 'Wonderful view you have here.'

He grunts again, sits down in an armchair beside the gas fireplace and reaches for the pipe and tobacco pouch on the mantelpiece. 'You don't see it any more once you're used to it. The wife and I bought this place when we sold our shop in Margate and retired twenty years back. That's when I got the boat. She wasn't much to look at then but I thought she'd be nice and steady and she was cheap. I always thought the name was a bit daft for something her size. More like for one of those big ones that go across the Channel. I reckoned I'd tidy her up and do a bit of sailing. Nothing fancy – just going up and down the river. I'd done some when I was a nipper and always had a dream of having a boat of my own. Only Molly didn't take to it. She got seasick first time out and that was that.'

'What a pity.'

He begins to fill his pipe. 'Life's full of

disappointments, that's one thing I've learned. Things never work out like you've planned. We'd all sorts of ideas for our retirement but Molly passed away soon after that and none of them ever happened. I've been here on my own ever since. You work hard all your life and in the end it's for nothing.' He tamps down the tobacco with his thumb, bitterness in every jab. Finally, he scrapes a match alight and holds it to the pipe bowl, drawing hard on the stem. Clouds of smoke emerge and the tobacco glows red. He leans back, puffing away for a moment. I wait. 'And what makes you think my Rose is the one you want? Could be another one of the same name. You don't have to register boats that small.'

'I don't think so. I've traced all the owners. She's been bought and sold several times since the late Forties. In fact, the trail went stone-cold and I'd given up hope of finding her. I put advertisements in every newspaper and sailing magazine I could think of and then out of the blue I got an answer from a man who said he'd sold her to you. If she is the same boat I'll be able to tell for certain when I see her.'

'How?'

'Some carving near the bow.'

'Huh. I've never noticed anything like that.' The pipe is going well now and he puffs away at it, studying me over the bowl. He is trying hard to size me up. 'Sentimental reasons, you said?'

'Yes.'

'She's only an ordinary boat. Not much more than a dinghy. Nothing special.'

I can see I will have to tell him the whole truth, though it will probably raise the price. It might even stop him selling at all. 'She's very special, as a matter of fact. She's one of the Little Ships.'

He takes the pipe out of his mouth, staring. 'You mean she went to Dunkirk? Rubbish! She can't've done. She's only fourteen foot and she's got no power. Just oars and sails. There wouldn't've been any boats as small as that – not on their own. They were steamers, motor yachts, lifeboats, launches, ferries . . . that sort of thing. We lived at Margate then. We saw a lot of them coming back.'

'But she did.'

'Huh!' He sticks out a slippered foot. 'Try this one, it's got bells on it. I told you, they were all much bigger. Molly and I went to the pier to watch the troops coming off the boats. We stood there cheering and Molly cried her eyes out. They'd taken our lads from under the Germans' very noses. Grabbed them off the beaches and brought them safe home. Hundreds of men packed tight on those decks, not an inch to spare, some of the boats half-sinking with the weight. And the Jerry planes'd been dive-bombing them. God knows how they made it. The sea was dead calm, though: flat as a millpond. It was like a miracle. A bloody miracle.' He looks off into space for a moment, lost in the past, and then brings himself back to the present with a shake of his head. 'You've got it all wrong.'

'Well, you see, I know all about what the Rose did – the whole story.'

He says suspiciously: 'I don't believe any of this. You're spinning me some fairy tale. Trying to con me, aren't you? I don't know what your game is but I'm not selling you my boat, or anything else, so you can leave now. This very minute.'

I've handled things badly. A real con artist would laugh himself silly at the mess I've made of it. 'Would you let me tell you the story? Before you make up your mind?'

He looks at me long and hard again and gives another of his bad-tempered grunts. 'You can tell it if you want. I doubt I'll believe it.'

'It will take some time.'

'Time's one thing I've plenty of these days.'

He sticks his pipe in his mouth and leans back in his chair, eyeing me sceptically. Since he has never invited me to sit down, I am still standing by the picture window overlooking the estuary. A clinker-built sailing-dinghy with a white sail is tacking to windward, pitching her way along with the spray shooting over her bows. Probably nine foot, or so – about the same size as the Bean Goose. I watch the helmsman alter course, the boom swing over, the three figures in the boat duck. Just kids, all of them.

'I'm not sure where to start.'

'The beginning'll do.'

I lean against the window, still watching the dinghy. I'm not certain from such a distance, but *it looks like two boys and a girl. Strange, that. The long arm of coincidence. 'Well, I suppose you could say it really begins long before the war. Just a mile downstream from here, in fact. In the summer of 1934.'*

Chapter One

'Look Lizzie, there's a heron!'

Matt was pointing and she twisted round quickly in time to see the big bird skimming over the surface of the water, head drawn back, long legs tucked up behind him, arched wings beating slowly. She watched him flapping away down the creek and half stood up in the dinghy so she could see better. *Bean Goose* rocked sharply.

'Sit *down*, Lizzie. You can't come out with us again if you don't keep still.'

'Sorry, Guy.'

She sat down with a bump on the planks in the bottom of the boat. It was uncomfortable there and her skirt was wet through to her knickers from all the water slopping about, but she didn't dare to complain. Guy hadn't wanted to take her out sailing in the first place. She'd overheard him talking to Aunt Sheila.

'Do we *have* to, Mother? It'll be an awful nuisance.'

'Yes, you do, Guy. It's not fair to leave her behind on her own. She's a guest. You're supposed to entertain her.'

'She's not a proper guest. She's only a cousin. And she's only twelve. She probably can't even swim.'

'Yes, she can. Go upstream and sail round the creeks. It will be perfectly safe there.'

Guy had muttered something and she could tell he was really cross about it. 'Are you *sure* you can swim?' he'd asked her later when they were walking across the lawn towards the wooden steps leading down to the river. He was striding out fast and she'd had to hop and skip to keep up.

'Yes. I learned at the swimming-baths.'

'Well, you'll have to do *exactly* what I tell you.'

'Yes, Guy.'

Matt, on her other side, had winked at her. 'He's the captain, see. I'm just the mate. If you don't behave he'll have you keelhauled, Lizzie. Or make you walk the plank.'

She was afraid of Guy. He was nearly sixteen and already as tall as a man. She wasn't afraid of Matt. Fourteen wasn't so much older than herself and he wasn't much taller; and he didn't stride around like Guy, or order her about either. And she was sorry for him with his funny arm. Something had gone wrong when he was growing inside Aunt Sheila, Mummy had explained. His right arm hadn't finished forming so that he'd been born with an arm that only went as far as the elbow with a sort of hand on the end of it – except that it only had a thumb and one finger, a bit like a lobster's claw. Whenever she turned round in the dinghy she could see it poking out from the short sleeve of his green aertex shirt. He was using it as a hook to hold onto the rope that worked the small sail at the front and it made her feel rather sick to look at it.

The heron had gone and Lizzie sat very still where Guy had told her to sit – in the bottom of the boat towards the front. Forrard, he'd called it. Matt and Guy sat on whichever side the sail wasn't and Guy was the helmsman, which meant he moved the handle thing at the back which made the boat turn left or right and he held the rope that made the big sail do what he wanted. The little sail that Matt was working was called a jib. And ropes were called sheets – she must remember that. She was just ballast, that's all, Matt had told her, with his crooked grin: weight to keep the boat steady. Whenever Guy shouted 'ready about' and then 'lee-oh' she was to duck down so she didn't get hit on the head by the piece of wood on the bottom of the big sail as it swung across. The boom, Guy called it.

It was the first time she'd ever been sailing and she'd been scared stiff out on the main bit of river. The dinghy had kept tipping steeply to one side or the other and she'd clung on terrified she'd fall into the water. The bank was a long way away and the water wasn't nice and clear but greenish brown, like soup, so that you couldn't tell how deep it was, or what horrible things might be underneath. It was better when they sailed into the narrow creek. The tide was out and there was mud all along each side – thick, wet mud, all brown and shiny like melting milk chocolate. Underneath, though, it was black and slimy and stinky. She'd found that out when she'd trodden in it by mistake near the jetty. She went on sitting as still as she could, facing forward and watching the channel of water ahead. The wind was blowing her plaits about and she could hear it making a humming sound in the long grasses on the banks. Grey and white seagulls swooped overhead, screeching, and some birds she'd never seen before with long bills and legs were pecking about in the mud.

'You'll have a lovely time while we're away, Lizzie,' Mummy had said. 'Much better than being cooped up in London.' On the train she'd sat rigidly in a corner seat, afraid that she'd miss getting out at Burnham-on-Crouch station. Aunt Sheila had met her and they'd driven in an open car along a lane running between fields full of golden corn and past trees with long, silvery leaves blowing in the wind. They'd gone under a railway bridge and round a corner and suddenly the river had appeared, right in front of them. The road turned and went along beside it for a little way until the river began to bend to the left and the lane ended at a white five-barred gate beside a group of trees. A gravel driveway led to Tideways. She remembered the house quite well from visits in the past: the slippery wooden floors covered with fringed rugs, the staircase with the sharp turn halfway up, the blue carpet all along the landing, the smell of furniture polish and flowers, the rooms full of light and, through nearly every window, the view of the wide river flowing out to meet the sea. Uncle William was away on his ship with the Royal Navy and Guy and Matthew had gone out sailing. 'We'll go down and watch them come in,' Aunt Sheila had suggested.

Nereus the black Labrador padded after them across the lawn, past the grass tennis court and down the flight of steps to a beach that was mostly mud except for a narrow pebbly bit above the reach of the high tide. There was a slipway leading up to a boathouse at one end and a wooden jetty sticking out into the water from the steps. Aunt Sheila had pointed out the dinghy, *Bean Goose*, in the distance and Nereus had started to wag his tail and bark and run up and down the beach. Lizzie had watched the dinghy coming closer and closer, its big white sail puffed out with wind. She'd never heard of a bean goose before but Aunt Sheila had told her that they came from cold countries, like Russia, to winter on the marshes. Her cousins were leaning out on one side of the boat and she'd known which was which from a distance because Guy was fair and Matt dark. When they had come alongside the jetty Guy had waved casually, busy with the boat, but Matt had shouted out to her, grinning all over his face.

They had come to the end of the creek now and were sailing out back into the main river. 'Lee-oh,' Guy shouted, 'Ready about.' She remembered to duck down as the boom went over. *Bean Goose* was going up and down again and tilting sharply to one side, her cousins hanging far out to the other with their feet braced against the boat. Lizzie clung on for dear life, salt spray half blinding her. The wind caught hold of one of her plaits and whipped it smartly across her face like a slap. She shut her eyes and when she opened them again, to her huge relief, she could see the group of trees with two tall Scots pines in the middle that marked the bend where Tideways stood. The white walls of the house showed through the trees and she could see the jetty sticking out into the river. The dinghy was going up and down even more and if they didn't get there very soon she knew she was going to be sick. She kept swallowing the sick taste down and when Guy shouted out she didn't hear him properly. Then something whacked her hard on her head. The sail had gone over and she hadn't ducked like she'd been told to. She kept her back turned to the cousins so they wouldn't see that she was crying.

'Are you *sure* you're OK, Lizzie?' Matt caught her up near the top of the steps from the beach as soon as he'd made sure that *Bean Goose* was securely moored to the jetty. Once a bowline he'd tied had come undone and the dinghy had drifted off. Luckily the wind had blown her onshore and aground or they might have lost her. Father had made him practise tying bowlines until he could have done it in his sleep. Guy was striding on ahead, already halfway across the lawn.

'Yes, thank you.' But she kept her head turned away from him and he guessed she'd been blubbing. The boom had given her an awful crack but she hadn't made any fuss. He looked at her anxiously. The sailing couldn't have been much fun for her at all. He could see that the skirt of her cotton frock was soaked at the back where she'd been sitting in the wet and her white socks and sandals were covered in mud. Her plaits were dripping water and one of her bows had come undone; the other must have got lost.

'I was always getting caught by the boom in the beginning. You'll soon get the hang of it.' She nodded. 'So don't let it put you off.' She shook her head. 'I hope you'll come out with us again.'

'If Guy doesn't mind.'

'Why ever should he?'

'I just think he might.'

She was quite right, of course. Guy hadn't wanted her with them at all. It had meant they couldn't go downstream to the mouth of the estuary which Guy liked much better. Not that Matt was going to tell Lizzie that. She was a funny little thing, with her freckles and her long plaits and her round blue eyes. He could remember her when she was very small, visiting Tideways with Aunt Helen and Uncle Richard. She'd toddled about the place and fallen over on the terrace, grazing her knees so they bled all down her legs, but she hadn't made any fuss then, either. He'd always known that she was adopted because he and Guy had been told so from the very beginning. It was no secret. Aunt Helen and Uncle Richard hadn't had any children of their own and so they had chosen to adopt a baby instead. He had never actually talked about it to Lizzie because he wasn't absolutely sure how she would feel. In a way, he and she had something in common because they were both different from normal children. 'How long are you going to stay with us, Lizzie?'

'Till Mummy and Daddy come back from Vienna next week.'

'That's the capital of Austria. On the river Danube. We did the Empire last term and all that Hapsburg stuff. Have they gone for a holiday there, or something?'

'No, it's a doctors' meeting. A conference they call it. A big one with doctors from all different countries. For psychiatrists. Daddy's giving a lecture – about all the work he's done with patients.'

'Uncle Richard must be an awfully good doctor.'

'He doesn't actually have to cut people open, or anything, you know. He just talks to them.'

'Still, he's got to know all about how they work, hasn't he? It takes years to be a doctor of any kind. As a matter of fact, I'd rather like to be one myself one day.'

She gave him a quick sideways glance and he could see the big bump on her forehead. 'Would you? I'd hate it. When I had my tonsils out last year I thought it was horrible in hospital. The ether made me sick.'

'I don't mind hospitals. The parents used to take me to one in London when I was small – to see if they could do anything about my arm.'

'Oh . . .'

He'd stuck his left hand in the pocket of his grey shorts but the wonky right one wouldn't reach the other pocket which meant that he could never hide it properly if he wore short sleeves. He put it behind his back. He didn't know whether Lizzie minded it or not but it was best to be careful in case she did. 'They couldn't, of course, but the doctors were very decent. I sort of thought then that I'd like to be one. I don't suppose I could ever become a surgeon, but I think I could manage to be a GP all right.' *Terribly sorry, old chap, but there's nothing we can do to improve it much for you. The thing is, though, you've got a thumb and the first finger and they're the most important ones. You can do almost everything with those. Doesn't matter too much about the rest. Look.* The doctor had pressed his own thumb and forefinger together and worked them open and shut like pincers.

He'd soon discovered that it was true and began to use his right arm and hand just as much as he used his good left one; he even taught himself to write with it. He could hold the pen or pencil quite normally with the thumb and forefinger and by leaning forward so he was closer to the paper and turning his shoulders to the left, he could write as well as anybody else. One thing the doctors at the hospital hadn't warned him about was that he'd have to put up with people staring at him for all of his life. Once people got used to it, of course, they stopped staring – none of the chaps at school ever did – but strangers nearly always gawped. In trains and buses and shops he could feel their eyes fixed on his stump of an arm and on the ugly thing on the end of it. And sometimes, out of the corner of his eye, he could see them shudder and shrink away as though he was as bad as a freak in a circus. Small children often blurted something out aloud and their mothers would hush them up, so everybody got embarrassed, himself included. He'd learned to keep it covered up as much as possible but he wasn't sure if he would ever learn not to care.

They'd reached the terrace and Matt led the way round to the side door. 'We'd better take our shoes off before we go in,' he said. 'Mother's not too keen on the mud indoors.' He levered off his plimsolls at the heels and Lizzie sat down and unbuckled her sandals. 'We can give them a wash out here.' He rinsed both pairs under the outside tap and set them to dry in the sun. His old plimsolls were already permanently mud-coloured and Lizzie's sandals didn't look as though they'd ever be the same again. 'I expect your socks will have to be washed properly. I'm afraid the mud stains everything.' He wasn't sure what to do about Lizzie herself. Mother had gone shopping in Burnham and the bump was awful. 'I'll get some ice to put on that bruise,' he told her. 'It's the best thing.'

He got the ice tray out of the freezing compartment of the fridge, wrapped some lumps in a clean tea towel and made his cousin sit down at the kitchen table. 'This is what Mother always does. It's supposed to bring down the swelling.'

She kept her eyes screwed tight shut while he was holding the ice-pack against the lump with his good hand. He put the other one behind his back again in case it bothered her having it so close. After a bit the ice started to melt and run down her face and soon the front of her bodice was as wet as the back of her skirt. He took the ice-pack away and touched the lump gently with his fingertips for a moment, wishing the pain away for her, like he did sometimes with Mother's headaches. It generally worked. 'There, I think that'll've done the trick.'

She opened her eyes and felt her forehead gingerly. 'It doesn't hurt so much now. Hardly at all.'

'Good. Sorry about your frock. Perhaps you'd better go and change into something else.'

'Yes, I'd better. I'm wet all over.' At the kitchen door she turned back, still holding the lump as though she was afraid to let go. 'Thank you very much, Matt.'

'Gosh, it was nothing. Oh, Lizzie . . .'

She peered at him with one eye from under the crook of her elbow. 'Yes?'

He said hesitantly, 'If you come out sailing again, we could lend you something else to wear – so you wouldn't spoil your frocks. We've got some old shorts and things . . .'

'Oh . . . thank you, Matt. You're very kind.'

He went to refill the icetray at the kitchen sink, grinning to himself. She was awfully funny.

*   *   *

Guy was rummaging for dry clothes in the chest of drawers in his bedroom. He heard his cousin come up the stairs and go into the spare room next door and felt guilty about her. Bit of a poor show on his part, letting her get a crack like that . . . He pulled on a pair of grey flannels and an old cricketing sweater and ran a hand through his hair – a habit of his whenever something bothered him. The thing was, they shouldn't have had to take Lizzie out with them. It wasn't fair to have to keep watching out for her all the time when he was trying to concentrate on helming. He shouldn't have to play nanny to little girls. Look at the way she'd gone and stood up like that when he'd told her quite clearly to stay exactly where she was. He'd had to keep his eye on her the whole time. He thrust his feet into his gym shoes without bothering to untie the laces, wriggling the toes home. Still, she hadn't *meant* to be a nuisance, and it wasn't really her fault that Mother had made them take her. In fact, he wasn't sure she'd wanted to come at all. She'd looked pretty scared most of the time, and she'd taken a nasty whack . . . Guy pushed his fingers through his hair again. The decent thing would be to go and say he was sorry about that. She was only a kid. He ought to go and do it – right this minute.

The spare-room door was ajar and he pushed it further open. The first thing he saw was Lizzie's bare pink bottom bent over towards him. She was stepping into some knickers and wrenched frantically at them. Guy felt like laughing but he kept a straight face. 'Sorry, Lizzie. I didn't realize . . .'

She turned round, scarlet in the face. 'I was just changing. I got a bit wet.' The lump on her forehead looked awful and he felt guiltier than ever. 'So did I. Everybody does, sailing. You can't help it. Look, I came to say I'm sorry about that bash you got from the boom. It was all my fault. I hope it isn't too bad.'

'It's all right.' She had grabbed a frock off the bed and was dragging it on over her head so that her voice was muffled. Her face reappeared, still bright red. 'Matt put some ice on it. It made it better.' She put both arms behind her, buttoning up her frock.

He knew he ought to have thought of the ice. He'd been a real rotter. 'I promise I'll make sure it doesn't happen again. Next time.' He smiled at her – his best smile. 'You *will* come out with us again, won't you, Lizzie?'

'If you want.'

'Of course I want you to. And so does Matt.' She was having trouble with the buttons, fumbling clumsily behind her. 'Look, I'll give you hand with those. Turn round.' She stood obediently, head bent, while he redid the buttons. 'You'd got half of them wrong, you little idiot.' There was a sash thing hanging down on each side that he could see was meant to go in a bow at the back. 'Do you want me to tie this for you?'

'No, thank you. I can manage.'

From the stiff tone he knew she was still embarrassed. He smiled at her again. 'So, that's settled, then. You're coming out with us again next time, aren't you, Lizzie?'

'Yes, Guy.'

'Jolly good.' He went off downstairs, whistling. At least he'd done the decent thing. It'd still be a bore having her around but it wouldn't be for long. She'd be going back home soon.

Lizzie heard him calling to Matt and when she peered out of her bedroom window she could see them setting up cricket stumps in the far corner of the lawn in front of some bushes. Guy was doing the batting, Matt the bowling. She watched from behind the curtain as Matt ran up and hurled the ball with his left hand. It went skew-whiff and disappeared into the bushes. Nereus bounded after it and presently came out with it in his mouth, looking pleased with himself. He trotted over to Matt and laid it carefully at his feet. The next ball was better and Guy hit it so hard that it sailed right across the lawn and landed on the terrace, bumping and rolling over the flagstones beneath the window until it came to rest against the wall. Nereus came and fetched it again. Lizzie went on watching. She knew that Guy was in the first cricket team at school so he must be good. Poor Matt couldn't help not being so good, having to bowl left-handed. She touched the lump on her forehead again. It felt much better. And Guy had said it had been his fault and that he was sorry.

Matt shoved *Bean Goose*'s bows well clear of the jetty and the water slapped gently against her hull as the dinghy made way. The big white sail above Lizzie's head had been flapping away like a flag but now it began to fill up and bulge outwards and the wind started to push them along. They sailed downstream, towards the mouth of the river, but the water looked quite friendly this time, sparkling away calmly in the sunshine. And she trusted Guy. 'Lee-oh, Lizzie,' he shouted out very loud and clear every time he changed tack and the boom was going to go over. He turned *Bean Goose* round before they got to the sea and gave Matt a turn at the helm coming back. She could tell that Matt wasn't nearly as good at sailing from the way Guy kept giving him orders, and on one tack they got stuck on a mud bank. The dinghy suddenly stopped dead and if Guy hadn't taken up the centre board quickly and paddled the bow round so the wind blew them off they might have been there for hours. After that, Guy took over again and let her sit right beside him. He explained about the water flowing against the rudder under the boat and about moving the stick one way to go the other. 'You can make her go about, if you like, Lizzie.' He kept hold of the mainsheet and put his hand over hers on the tiller. 'Look, you push it away from you to turn the bow round towards the wind . . . and about she goes.' *Bean Goose* swung round smoothly as though by magic. Guy laughed at her. 'Well done, Lizzie, you did that all by yourself.' She hadn't really, of course. His hand had made hers do it.

Aunt Sheila took her to Burnham station to

catch the train back to London. Matt came with them but Guy was busy building a model aeroplane out of wood. When she had gone to say goodbye to him he had shown her a picture of how it would look when it was finished. 'It's a Bristol Bulldog,' he'd said. 'A Royal Air Force fighter. The pilot's got two guns, see, and they're synchronized to fire through the propellers.' She hadn't really understood what he had meant but she'd nodded as though she had. 'One day I'm going to learn to fly fighters,' he'd told her. She had believed him completely.

Matt carried her suitcase into the compartment and heaved it up onto the luggage rack, hooking his funny hand through the handle. 'There you are, Cousin Lizzie.'

'Thank you, Matt.'

'Come and stay again, won't you?'

He looked as though he really meant it. She wished Guy had said that too.

Chapter Two

'This is my daughter, Anna.'

Mama had spoken in English because the visitors were from England. If they had been French from France it would have been easy – it was one of her best subjects at school – but she only knew a few words of English: *Good morning, good night, thank you very much, my name is Anna Stein* . . . The woman from England was smiling at her and holding out her hand.

'How do you do, Anna.'

She shook the woman's hand and then the husband's afterwards. He was a doctor – a psychiatrist, like Papa. They were the first English people she had ever met and she watched them closely at the dinner table; studied them as they ate and drank and talked with Mama and Papa. They weren't Jewish, she was sure of that. They had the wrong colouring and the wrong-shaped faces and noses and they'd never eaten matzos or klops before. They were well-dressed but their clothes were boring. The woman wasn't elegant, like Mama, and she showed large front teeth when she smiled. The husband leaned across the table and asked in very bad German how old she was. His pronunciation made her want to giggle but Mama's eye was on her and she answered him politely. '*Vierzehn?* Fourteen,' he said, nodding. '*Unsere Tochter, ist zwölf Jahre alt.*'

He smiled at her and the woman smiled too. They were being friendly, she realized, but she couldn't see what them having a daughter of twelve had to do with her. After the meal was over Mama played the piano to entertain them: a Beethoven sonata, a Chopin mazurka, and a Strauss waltz. The English sat as still as statues and at the end of each piece they clapped hard – hardest for the Strauss. She could tell that they liked the waltz best.

'We will excuse you now, Anna,' Mama said. 'You may say good night to our guests.'

She went to her room, relieved to escape from a dull evening. Mama and Papa went on talking in English with the visitors. They talked on and on for a long time but whatever it was they were discussing couldn't have been very amusing because nobody laughed once. It sounded an ugly language to her. After a while she shut her door so she couldn't hear them any more, undressed and put on her cotton nightgown. It was stiflingly hot in the room and she opened the two windows as wide as she could and leaned out. The lamplight fell in golden pools on the old cobblestones of the *Wallstrasse*, and squares of light glowed from windows up and down the street. She could see straight into the Fischer family's sitting-room directly opposite. Papa Fischer was in his arm-chair reading, his wire spectacles stuck on the end of his big nose and his black beard jutting out from the end of his chin like a spade. Mama Fischer, fat as a barrel, was bent over her sewing and Jacob and Gideon were sitting at the table, studying. They were always studying, always buried in books, always so serious. Once she had asked Gideon if he ever did anything else and he had looked at her with his gentle brown eyes, all puzzled, and said exactly what sort of thing did she mean? Anna leaned a little further out of the window. It was so hot – the air as thick as soup. All of Vienna was suffocating. Not a breath of wind for days and days. Too hot to sleep. Too hot to do anything. Footsteps sounded from further along the street and two men came into one of the pools of lamplight: young men strolling along. She drew back quickly but one of them had caught sight of her. He stopped and stared upwards. '*Guten Abend, Fräulein.*' He had nice blond hair and he was handsome. A student, most probably, by the cheap clothes he was wearing – but he wore them with style, a loose black tunic slung across his shoulders. He smiled up at her. '*Es ist ein schöner Abend, und Sie sind ein schönes Mädchen.*' She was used to men smiling at her – men of all ages – and paying her compliments, telling her she was beautiful. Because he was handsome she smiled back. After all, she was perfectly safe where she was. '*Guten Abend, mein Herr.*'

The young man bowed and flourished one

hand. '*Dieter Rach. Ich stehe zu ihren Diensten, liebes Fräulein. Wie heissen Sie, wenn ich fragen darf?*' Naturally, she had no intention of telling him her name. Mama would be very angry if she knew she had spoken to him at all, especially in her nightdress. He stepped closer, still smiling, teeth gleaming, eyes shining in the lamplight. His companion tugged his arm impatiently. 'Come, Dieter, what are you thinking? You don't want anything to do with her. She's a Jewess, can't you tell? They're all dirty Jews in this street.'

The smile faded and vanished. He stared up at her. '*Ach . . . natürlich*. Of course, I see now. So she is. Stupid of me.'

They strolled on down the *Wallstrasse*. Anna would have thrown something at them if there had been anything to hand. Cretins! *Pigs!* She stuck out her tongue as far as it would go. How dare they speak of dirty Jews! How *dare* they! It was *they* who were dirty to speak in such a way. She was trembling with outrage. Well, that was nothing new either. On her first day at school she had discovered that to be Jewish was to be hated and despised. The other girls had either teased her or snubbed her and the teachers had picked on her. Mina, her one true friend there, was Jewish, too, and neither of them was ever invited to Gentile homes. Nobody could explain properly why it was so – not Papa or Mama, or Grandmama, or Aunt Liesel or Aunt Sybille, or Uncle Joseph or Uncle Julius . . . nobody. The Jews had always been blamed for things, was all they said, driven out, hounded, and that was why they kept together. It was safer and better. Mama's mother and father had fled from persecution in Russia and come to Vienna where, it seemed, nobody much wanted them either. Grandpapa had died long ago and she couldn't remember him at all but how could anyone hate Grandmama who was always helping the poor and doing good works?

The heat was worse, the bedroom like an oven. She switched out the lamp and collapsed on the bed, fanning herself with a book. The English were leaving. She listened to them making their polite farewells in the hallway, the door closing after them, their steps ringing on the stone stairway and then in the street below, walking away in the same direction as the two young men. After a while she heard her mother playing the piano – something slow and quiet. Liszt? Or perhaps it was Schubert? Yes, definitely Schubert – his last sonata, the one in B flat. Mama loved Schubert. The notes hung on the air, each one separate, like pearls on a string. Mama is sad tonight, she thought. *Very* sad. Something is wrong. After a time the playing stopped. She heard Papa going to their bedroom and then the soft click of her own door as Mama opened it a little way.

'Anna . . . are you asleep?'

'It's too hot, Mama. How can I sleep when it's like this?'

'You must try, or you will be tired tomorrow.'

'What does it matter? It's the holidays.'

'There is still your piano practice – you need to work hard on that Impromptu – it's very ragged.

And there is studying that you should do if you want to do well in school.'

'I *hate* that school. All the girls are horrible, except Mina.'

Mama came into the room and sat on the end of her bed. Anna could only see the shape of her in the darkness, not her face, but she knew for sure that she was sad. She sat up, hugging her knees. She loved the chats she sometimes had with Mama – just the two of them, talking about all sorts of things together. Perhaps Mama would tell her what had made her feel sad.

'How would you like to go to another school, Anna? A very different one?'

'With all Jewish girls?'

'No . . .'

'Then it wouldn't be any different, would it? They'd still hate me.'

'Papa and I were thinking of a school in England.'

'In *England*! What are you talking about, Mama? Is it a joke?'

'No, it's not a joke. What would you think of going there to school – just for a while?'

'I wouldn't go. What a strange idea, Mama.'

'Papa and I have our reasons. We have been talking about it with the English guests.'

'With them? What has it to do with them?'

'They have been telling us all about England and the schools there. Their daughter goes to an excellent one in London, they say. A private day school, like yours. We think, Papa and I, that it would be good if you went there – for a time.

Frau Ellis has been most kind and said she would have you to live with them. You could come home in the holidays.'

It wasn't a joke. Mama was quite serious. They'd been plotting to send her away. Planning it all behind her back with the English visitors, talking away in English so she wouldn't understand. They'd arranged it all and that was why Mama was sad. She felt sick with horror. 'I refuse to go. I won't, I won't, I *won't*! I'd sooner die. I *will* die if you make me go . . . I'll kill myself!'

'Sssh, Anna. That will do. Please, control yourself and listen to what I have to say.'

'I don't care what you have to say. I'm not going. How could you be so cruel, Mama!'

'Please, Anna, you must understand that Papa and I are only concerned with what is best for you. Best and safest.'

'Safest? What do you mean, *safest*? Those stupid girls at school can't do me any harm.'

'I'm not talking about schoolgirls; there are others who might. You know how it is for all Jewish people – you have experienced it yourself – and lately it has been getting worse. People are turning against us. Papa has fewer and fewer patients. They do not want to be treated by a Jew. Old patients have left, new ones do not come. It is the same for other Jews in other professions and trades. And Papa believes that it will get even worse. Much, much worse.'

'I don't mind if we're poor.'

'If that were all, Anna, we would not be worrying like this. We should endure, just as Jews

41

have done for centuries and been made all the stronger. But there is more. Think of the terrible assassination of our Chancellor – brutally murdered by the Nazis, the very people who most hate us. The Nazi Party is in power in Germany. They parade through the streets with burning torches, and they chant and shout like men possessed by the devil. Their *Führer*, Adolf Hitler, detests the Jews. He burns books by Jews, his soldiers beat and kick Jews. Jews are forbidden to work for the civil service. Forbidden entry to places. All kinds of difficulties are put in their way. The Nazis are our deadly enemies.'

'But that's in Germany.'

'Many people believe that Austria may soon unite again with Germany and become Nazi as well. If that happens every Jew here will be in danger too. It is impossible for us to hide ourselves; impossible to conceal what we are. We can never be only Austrian; we will always be Jews as well.'

'How do you mean, danger? What sort of danger?'

'We don't know exactly . . .'

'What could they do? They can't put us in prison if we have done nothing. It would be against the law. There is no crime in being Jewish.'

'The law is not saving the Jews in Germany from persecution. It did not save them in Russia and it will not save us here. That is why we want you to go to England – just for a while, at least, until we can be more sure of things. We don't want you growing up where there is such hatred.'

'I won't go. I won't leave you. If there is danger, then what about you and Papa?'

'It is not so easy for us to leave. Papa's work is here in Vienna and my place is here with him. But we will come and visit you whenever we can and perhaps we will try to come to live in England as well. Papa was talking with the English doctor this evening and he thinks it may be possible for Papa to work there. Did you like them – our English guests?'

She shrugged. 'They were all right. Very dull, though. I think all the English must be dull. And wear dowdy clothes.'

'Nonsense, Anna, that's not so. They are a very civilized people and their country is one of the most beautiful in the world.'

'One of the girls at school went there once. She said it rained every single day and that it was all grey.'

'Perhaps in winter, but they have nice summers.'

'How do you know? You've never been there.'

'From what I've heard. Anyway, the weather is not important. They have good schools – that is well known – and you will be able to go with their daughter. She is called Elizabeth, but I believe they call her Lizzie.'

'She's only twelve.'

'She'll be thirteen in January.'

'She's still a baby. I'd *hate* being with her. And

43

I'd *hate* going to England. I don't speak any English. I wouldn't understand a word.'

'You'd very soon learn, and it's a wonderful, rich language. The language of William Shakespeare.'

'It sounds stupid. And ugly. And when that Englishwoman laughed it was like a horse neighing. Her teeth were like a horse's, too.'

'*Anna!* That will do. You're being extremely rude and very silly. Frau Ellis is a charming person and it is most kind of her to offer to have you.'

'They're not Jews, though, are they?'

'No . . .'

'So, they won't know about us, will they? They won't understand.'

'The English are very understanding and tolerant people. Many, many refugees have made their homes there. Your faith will be respected.'

How could they even *think* of doing this to her? Sending her off like a parcel to live with strangers. *Foreigners.* They must want to get rid of her. They couldn't love her or they would never want her to go. Mama was still talking, still trying to win her over. '. . . it will be a wonderful new experience for you. You will learn a new language, make new friends, see another country—'

'*Stop it!* I don't want to hear any more. I won't listen to another word. It's all lies . . .' She stuffed her fingers in her ears and flung herself face down on the pillow, sobbing. Mama stroked her hair but she buried her face the deeper. After a while, the stroking stopped and she knew that Mama had gone away, leaving her alone. She cried into her pillow until she could cry no more and lay exhausted in the darkness. Outside in the *Wallstrasse* there were footsteps again – the sound of heavy boots on the cobblestones and men's voices, harsh and mocking. And then, suddenly, the sound of breaking glass. Anna jumped off the bed and ran to look out. A group of soldiers were throwing stones up at the Fischers' lighted sitting-room window and there was a big hole in the broken pane. Papa Fischer had leapt to his feet, his book fallen from his hand, the wire spectacles from his nose. She saw Frau Fischer's shocked and frightened face, sewing clutched to her bosom, and Jacob and Gideon looking up from their books with mouths agape. There was another stone thrown and another hole in the glass. Herr Fischer grabbed at the wall switch and the light went out.

'*Schmutzige Juden, schmutzige Juden.*' The soldiers chanted as they moved off down the street. 'Dirty Jews, dirty Jews . . .'

'Papa, you don't really mean to send me away to England, do you? Not if I don't want to go?'

Her father looked up from his writing-desk. He took off his spectacles and laid them beside him. 'We don't want you to go either, Anna, but we think it's wise. Mama told you why.'

She sat down in a chair beside the desk. 'And I still don't understand. What does it matter if a few people don't like us here?'

He smiled at her. 'Why should you understand, Anna? You are much too young, too trusting, too innocent. You have not yet encountered real evil, so, of course, you don't believe that it actually exists. Do you remember when I went on that visit to Hamburg last month? To meet with some other doctors?'

'Yes, of course.'

'The German Chancellor, Adolf Hitler, paid a visit to the city while I was there. I walked out into the streets to see for myself how they received him. The pavements were lined with thousands cheering him all along the route, waving Nazi flags, applauding . . . When he spoke later from the balcony at the *Rathaus* the square in front was packed with people. You could hardly move for the numbers. They listened to him speaking of the new and mighty Germany that was being born again, of how he would lead them to greatness once more.'

'But that has nothing to do with us.'

'I'm afraid it has. He began to rant and rave against the Jews. To blame Jews and Jewish financiers for defeat in the last war and for everything else that has gone wrong for Germany since. He is making us his target. His scapegoat. He spoke of Jews as parasites, feeding on the blood of industrious Germans; of the need to expel the Jewish bacillus out of the national bloodstream, and all around me people were nodding in agreement. At the end they cheered and clapped as though he were a great prophet. Their saviour.'

She said curiously, 'What was he like? Did you see him close up?'

'He passed very near in his car and I could see him easily when he was on the town hall balcony. He is small, dark and very ordinary-looking. You wouldn't glance at him twice in a crowd. And yet he has this extraordinary power over people. They believe what he says and they believe in him. And hatred for Jews is spreading all over Germany. I saw placards being carried in the streets telling people not to buy from the Jews. *Deutsche kauft nicht bei Juden!* Shops owned by Jews are boycotted, Jews dismissed from their jobs, and in many occupations proof of Aryan ancestry is demanded. I was told of Jews being attacked and beaten by ordinary citizens; of towns in parts of Germany with signs saying *Jews enter this place at their own risk* and where there are notices posted outside restaurants and hotels: *Jews Not Wanted Here, Entry Forbidden to Jews*. They speak of being *judenrein* – Jew free.'

'But Adolf Hitler has no power in Austria. He can't harm us here.'

'Not yet. But my doctor friends in Hamburg believe that he would like to take over our country too. To reunite us with Germany. There are many people here in Austria who would be sympathetic to that.'

'If he's so wicked why isn't anybody trying to stop him?'

'Some brave people are, but the Nazis get rid of anybody who speaks against the Party. Anyone merely suspected of being opposed to them is threatened and some are arrested by the *Sturm Abteilung*, the Nazi troops, and put in prison or in special camps.' Papa shook his head. 'I have said enough, Anna. We do not want you to be frightened. We only want you to be safe – to go to England for a while – where such things do not happen.'

'We'll put Anna in the empty bedroom next to you, Lizzie, and I think it would be a good idea to make the old playroom into a sort of sitting-room for you both. You won't mind that, will you?'

She *did* mind – rather a lot – but it seemed awfully mean to object. It had all been explained to her, after all. This girl, Anna Stein, was coming to stay for a while because it wasn't very safe for her in her own country. She was Jewish, and some people in Austria didn't like Jews. It sounded very peculiar but that was how it was.

'What is she like, Mummy?'

'I only saw her for a short while, when we went to dinner at the Steins' apartment in Vienna, and she hardly speaks any English. Her parents are delightful. Charming. The father is a psychiatrist, just like Daddy, and Frau Stein teaches the piano. She plays brilliantly herself. I expect Anna plays too.'

She was probably brilliant as well. 'What does she *look* like?'

'Very pretty. Green eyes and long dark hair.'

'In plaits?'

'No, she wears it loose. But then she's two

years older than you, Lizzie. She seems rather more than that, in fact, but I'm sure you'll both get on very well. It may be a bit difficult, at first, because of her not knowing English, but she'll soon pick it up and I know you'll help her to learn quickly. Her French is very good, apparently, so that will help.'

'Mine's not very good.'

'Well, you know quite a lot of words and how to say simple things, so you can try speaking it sometimes. It will be excellent practice for you.'

The more she heard about Anna Stein, the less she liked the idea of her coming to live with them. 'When will she be here?'

'Not until the autumn – in time for the new term.'

'How long will she stay?'

'We don't know that yet. If things settle down in Austria she may go home quite soon.'

'If they don't, though?'

'Then she might be here for a long time. Several years, even. Daddy and I hope she will be company for you, Lizzie. Like having a sister.'

A *sister*? How could she ever be that? A foreigner who didn't even speak English? Lizzie was used to being an only child. A special child because she had been adopted, she had always been told: specially chosen. 'Why don't her parents leave Austria as well, if it's so horrid there for them? Couldn't they all go and live somewhere else together?'

'It's not as simple as that. You can't just go and live and work in other countries without

49

permission. But Anna will be allowed to come to school here. Of course, they will miss her very much. It's a great sacrifice on their part.'

It is for me, too, Lizzie thought. I don't want a stranger here all the time. Not one bit.

'Does she *have* to come and live with us?'

'We promised that we would take care of her. Her parents are very worried.'

'I don't understand why people would want to harm them – just because they're Jewish. What's wrong with them?'

'Nothing is wrong with them. I don't understand, either, Lizzie, but some people in other countries – wicked people – try to make out that there is. Daddy and I felt that we should help the Steins. We're very lucky to live in a country like England, you know. Very lucky indeed.'

She couldn't see what that had to do with it. All she could see was that everything was going to change and that it would probably never ever be the same again.

'Oh, Anna, how terrible!' Mina was staring at her, appalled. '*England*! But *why*?'

'Mama and Papa don't think it's safe for Jews here any more. And the other night some soldiers threw stones up at the Fischers' window opposite us and broke it, so they're really panicking now.'

'*Stones!* How dreadful!'

'The soldiers were probably drunk, that's all.'

'My parents don't seem to worry.'

'Lucky you, Mina. They won't try to send you away. I've told mine I refuse to go.'

'They'll make you. You'll have to do what they say.'

'Then they'll have to carry me onto the train.'

'Oh, Anna . . . Do you remember in French class when Mademoiselle Deuchars said that the English were barbarians? *Ils sont barbares*. She said they were dirty and drunken and behaved like savages. Whatever will you do?'

'Not go.'

'You'll have to.' Mina's face was tragic now. 'And I'll miss you so much, Anna. I won't have a single friend at school. You know how all the other girls despise us. I'll be so *miserable*.'

'I told you,' Anna said fiercely. 'I'm not going.'

Matt unhitched *Bean Goose*'s painter and shoved her bow sideways away from the jetty so that she came round at right angles to the wind. He settled himself with his wonky hand on the tiller and grasped the mainsheet with his good hand. As he was on his own, he hadn't put the jib up. He let the mainsail out and kept his course steady, steering for a distant marker upstream on the far bank – a tall tree. He was doing everything pretty well right so far. If Guy had been here he'd probably have told him he wasn't, but Guy was on his way to the dentist in London with Mother to have his front tooth mended so, for once, he was out on his own. It didn't happen often – not that that was Guy's fault. He could take the dinghy out alone any time he wanted, but the truth was that he had to screw up the nerve to do it. He didn't sail nearly as well as

Guy. Guy knew by instinct what to do, whereas he often got it wrong. On his own, he always went upstream because it was much easier. It was OK pootling along up there and going round the creeks, but downstream, where the river became hugely wide and the great mass of water surged out to the North Sea, scared him. He'd never admitted it to a soul – least of all to Guy who was never afraid of anything – but he hated the sea. There was nothing kind about it, he thought. The sea was out to get you if it could and drown you in its freezing depths. *The mighty ocean deep*. The very words gave him the shivers. When he'd been learning to swim in the prep-school swimming-baths he'd almost drowned. The instructor's idea of teaching had been to make you jump straight into the deep end when he blew a whistle. *Swim or sink, boys. You'll soon get the hang of it. Quickest way to learn*. He'd sunk all right – gone down like a stone to the bottom and as soon as he'd come up he'd gone down again. And then up and down again. With only one good hand he couldn't do proper strokes and with all the splashing and kicking from the others going on around him, nobody had noticed until it had almost been too late. He could never forget the terror of it: the frantic struggle to breathe, the way he'd clawed and fought and kicked. Then someone had grabbed hold of him and they'd hauled him out, choking and spluttering. The instructor had been furious with him. *Stupid boy. You should have stayed near the side*. He'd learned to swim soon after that – found a way to use his right arm that worked pretty well, though he wasn't as fast as most of them.

He sailed on steadily, keeping the dinghy's bow in line with his tree marker on the bank. The sun had gone in and some dark clouds were gathering. *Bean Goose* heeled as the wind freshened but he counterbalanced it all right by moving towards the windward side and easing the mainsheet. As he drew near to his tree he went about, pushing the tiller away from him so that the bow swung through the wind. The sail flapped loudly above his head and then filled again on the other side. He brought the tiller back to the centre and settled *Bean Goose* on her new course, sailing to windward. He hauled in the mainsheet, flattening the sails, and began beating steadily towards the mouth of the river. And the open sea.

Guy sat in the dentist's chair, mouth open, wishing the fellow would get a move on and finish the job. He'd been fiddling about for ages. The whole thing was a bore and Mother had made a big fuss over it. Chaps were always getting teeth broken and chipped at school, or knocked out completely. It was usually a cricket ball, or playing rugger, or bashing up against the side of the swimming-baths, or going over bike handlebars like he'd done. If he hadn't turned quite so sharply and been going a bit slower, he'd have made that corner OK.

'Open a little wider, please.'

He stretched his aching jaw further and stared at the ceiling and the eighteen plaster rosettes along the edge – he'd been counting them on every visit since he was five. The third from the end on the right had a big chip out of it, like his tooth. Or like his tooth had been before old Payne had got to work on it. Rather a joke a dentist having a name like that; people must pull his leg about it no end.

'You may close now. All done.'

Mr P. was washing his hands fussily at the basin in the corner and then drying them on a towel. It amused Guy that he was much taller than the dentist now. He'd looked up to him on every visit for years and years until one summer hols when he'd walked into the room for his appointment and found he was looking *down* instead.

'Don't bite on it for a few hours. And try not to knock it again, if you can help it. If you're careful it should last for years.'

In the waiting-room his mother was sunk in the corner of a sofa, reading *The Illustrated London News*. 'Let me see, darling? Heavens, that looks wonderful. You'd never know.'

He glanced in the mirror over the fireplace, baring his teeth. Behind him some rather glamorous woman in a red dress was watching him over her *Tatler*. He caught her eye and she smiled. He smiled back before he looked away from the mirror. 'Good as new. Can we go and have some lunch? I'm famished.' Striding down Harley Street towards Wigmore Street beside his mother, he found himself playing bears and stepping over pavement lines like he and Matt used to do. At the Orange Tree restaurant, where they always went after the dentist, he forgot about not biting on the front tooth but it didn't seem to matter anyway as the fried plaice didn't need much chewing, nor did the vanilla ice-cream. His mother looked at her wrist-watch.

'We've got more than two hours before the next train. I'd like to go and see Aunt Helen, darling, if you don't mind.'

That was OK by him. Wimpole Street was only round the corner and Mother's sister was pretty decent. She fussed much less than Mother so she wouldn't make a drama over the tooth. The house was actually rather grand. Uncle Richard's consulting-room and his secretary's office were on the ground floor but the rest of it was a normal home. The manservant, Hodges, opened the door and Aunt Helen appeared, all smiles. Cousin Lizzie, hovered in the background like a timid little mouse. His aunt drew her forward.

'Do show Guy your paintings, Lizzie. He'd like to see them, wouldn't you, Guy?'

He wouldn't in the least, but he agreed graciously, seeing that his mother and aunt obviously wanted to have one of their sisterly chin-wags. There was a time limit for catching the train so it was no great sacrifice. He followed his cousin up three floors and then on up a steep and narrow flight of uncarpeted stairs to the very top of the house. Lizzie opened a door and beckoned him in. The attic room was surprisingly light and spacious and there was even a small fireplace. The only furniture was a wooden table and a couple of old kitchen chairs. He could see an open box of water-colour paints on the table, beside a pad and a jamjar full of cloudy water. Another jamjar held brushes. He said teasingly, 'Is this your artist's studio, then, Lizzie?' She went pink in the face, like the time he'd caught her without her knickers. 'It isn't really a studio. I just pretend it is. The maid sleeps in the other room up here but this one was empty so Mummy said I could use it.'

'It's jolly nice.' He went to the open window where there was a cooling breeze and looked out over the parapet and across the rooftops of London. There were hundreds of chimney-pots. Rows and rows of them, all shapes and sizes, sticking up jauntily as far as the eye could see. 'I like your view.'

'It should be north,' she said solemnly. 'But it's east, so the light's not really right for painting.'

That tickled him even more but he didn't show it. 'Well, come on, let's see these pictures of yours.'

'You don't have to look at them – not if you don't want to.'

He realized that she was just as reluctant to show them as he was to see them. 'May as well, Lizzie, now we've come all the way up here.'

She edged aside so that he could see the water-colour of a sailing-dinghy with two figures on board. He looked at it in surprise. He'd expected infantile pictures – toytown houses, cotton-wool clouds, yellow suns with rays like bicycle spokes . . . all that sort of stuff – but she'd got the water and the sky rather well and the boat wasn't bad either. 'Is this meant to be *Bean Goose*?' She nodded. 'I don't think I've got it quite right. I couldn't remember exactly.'

'Well, you've got the sail wrong – it's too small – and you've forgotten the standing rigging for the mast. Otherwise it's OK. Is that Matt and I?' She nodded again. 'Why aren't you there, too? You came with us.'

'I never do myself. I don't really know what I look like.'

He tweaked one of her plaits. 'You should look in the mirror and do a self-portrait. All the great artists did that. Rembrandt and van Gogh, and all that lot. Where're the others you've done, then?'

'There's some underneath.'

He picked up the pad and flicked over the pages. The more he turned, the more it dawned on him that Lizzie was actually rather good. The subjects were quite grown-up – the view over the rooftops, some fruit in a bowl, a likeness of his aunt sitting in a chair . . . 'I say, these really aren't bad, Lizzie.'

'Oh . . . ' She stared at him, her blue eyes round as marbles. 'Do you really think so? *Honestly*, Guy?'

'Yes, I do. *Honestly*.' He turned more pages. 'I think they're jolly good. Are you going to be a real artist when you grow up?'

'Gosh, no, I shouldn't think so. You have to be brilliant.'

'If you carry on like this, you might turn out to

be. Perhaps you inherited it from your other mother and father.' It was OK to say that, he reckoned, because everyone knew she was adopted, and she knew that they knew. Uncle Richard and Aunt Helen thought it was better. Maybe Lizzie's real parents had both been artists and pretty casual about how they lived, which explained how they'd come to have Lizzie and then given her away. Rather intriguing. He put the pad down on the table. 'It must be nice having this room up here all to yourself. You can pretend as much as you like when you're alone.'

She pulled a face. 'I won't be alone much longer. There's somebody coming to live with us in September. I expect she'll want to come up here as well.'

He wasn't very interested. 'Oh, who's that?'

'Some girl. Mummy and Daddy met her parents in Vienna. She's Jewish. That's why she's got to come and live here. Mummy says they hate them there.'

'Sounds a bit rum. Why?'

'I don't know really.'

He said carelessly, 'Actually, I've never met anybody Jewish. Can't say I know much about them – except that they don't believe in Jesus Christ. Perhaps that's the problem – why some people don't like them.' He glanced at his wrist-watch. 'Time Mother and I got a taxi or we'll miss the train.' On the way downstairs he said over his shoulder, 'What's her name, this Jewish girl?'

'Anna. Anna Stein.'

'Well, bad luck about it, anyway.'

They caught the train from Liverpool Street station with only a minute to spare. Guy watched the sooty buildings and the slum backyards sliding past and wondered how people could live in such hideous places. The carriage was full and two old women nattered non-stop to each other most of the way. To make matters worse, his tooth had started aching. By the time they arrived at Burnham station he was in a foul mood, not improved by the fact that it was pouring with rain and the soft top of the Alvis leaked like a sieve. 'You ought to get it repaired, Mother.'

'I know, darling, but it would cost such a lot. It will have to wait.'

He never thought much about money unless the lack of it prevented him from having something he really wanted – like a bigger and better boat or a decent bike. Father didn't get paid a fortune in the Navy, he knew, but he had shares, or something, and Mother had some money of her own, so things were fairly comfortable. There just wasn't enough to splash it around. When he'd finished with school and university he was going to make sure he earned enough to own three things: a thirty-foot sailing-yacht, a sports car and an aeroplane.

When they reached home he went up to the bathroom and hunted for some aspirin in the cabinet. He took two tablets and went into Matt's room, expecting to find him with his nose in a book, but he wasn't there. He wasn't downstairs either and as it was raining cats and dogs he wouldn't be outside in the garden. Maybe he'd gone off somewhere on his bike and was sheltering. Nereus was lying on the rug in the hall. 'Where is he, Nereus? Where's Matt?' The Labrador lifted his head and thumped his tail and then lowered his head on his paws again. 'Not telling, eh? Useless dog.'

He stuck his head round the kitchen door. The cook was peering at something in the oven. 'Seen Matt anywhere, Mrs Woodgate?' She straightened up creakily, her moon face shiny red from the heat. 'Not all afternoon, Master Guy. He's not been in here – not like he usually does when I've been baking.'

'What's for supper?'

'Fish pie. And there's no call for you to make that face. It's good fresh cod, caught today. I've made a treacle tart for pudding. And I've baked some of those almond biscuits you like.'

'Can I have one now?'

She huffed and puffed but she gave him one. She always did. He went off, munching the biscuit, wandered into the drawing-room and stood at the French windows. The rain was worse than ever, the wind gusting hard and whipping up the river's surface. From the look of the sky there was plenty more bad weather to come, which would put the kibosh on any sailing tomorrow. Still, he could do some more work on the Fokker D-7 – finish off the fuselage so he could start putting the whole thing together and get the Hun markings on. He looked at his wrist-watch. Where the hell *was* Matt? Where on earth would the idiot have gone? He was still eating the biscuit and watching the rain and the river when he suddenly guessed what his brother had done.

Matt knew that he was going to drown. He had been swimming and floating alternately for what seemed like hours and all he could see around him were waves – grey-green waves with white crests, rising and falling in endless motion. He rose and fell with them and every so often one would break over his head. He knew the waves were playing a game – taunting and teasing him, biding their time. When *Bean Goose* had capsized she'd reared up suddenly like a horse and the next thing he'd known he was in the water, caught under her hull. He'd seen the dark shape of the dinghy above him and her mast pointing downwards towards the bottom and felt ropes dangling all round him. When he'd dived down to get clear of the hull he'd come up under the sail which was spread wide over the surface. His life-jacket had forced him hard up against the canvas so that he'd been trapped. It was the choking nightmare of the school swimming-baths all over again, only this time it had been even more terrible because there was nobody near who could help him. He'd tried diving down again and got tangled up with some rope. Somehow he'd managed to free himself and to dive down yet again to try and get clear of the sail. Once more he'd come up still trapped underneath it but on the third try, lungs bursting and with the last of his strength, he'd swum deeper and further and shot up to the surface and to air. The first breath had been agony. His lungs hadn't worked properly and he'd had to made a great effort to go on breathing. For a long while he'd been too weak to do anything but breathe and float. His limbs had terrible pins and needles and were useless. Eventually, he had started swimming – slow, feeble strokes. *Bean Goose* was only a few yards away, bobbing along upside down, but the force of the tide was carrying her from him much faster than he could swim. And even if he could have reached her, he knew he'd never have been able to right her on his own. All he could have done was cling on and probably be carried further and further out to sea. Better to try and swim in the direction of the land. He'd set off and soon discovered that he was making no headway against the tide. He floated again for a while, dazed with shock and cold and fear. He'd been a complete fool and this was all his own fault. He'd seen the bad weather coming, felt the wind's strength increasing, and yet instead of turning back to safety he'd gone on doggedly, driven by the stupid idea of overcoming his fear of the open sea and of proving that he could sail *Bean Goose* as well as Guy. Guy would never have got himself into a mess like this. When things had got hairy and *Bean Goose* had started to heel over he'd have eased the mainsheet and shifted his weight to windward. That's what *he* should have done himself – only his brain had turned to jelly and he'd sat there like a fool, clinging on to the mainsheet for dear life, legs braced hard against the steepening tilt, until, of course, she'd gone over.

Another wave broke over his head, and then another, making him choke and retch. The salt water burned his throat and nostrils and made his eyes smart, and his teeth were chattering violently. The rain was driving down so hard now that he could hardly see. How much longer would he last before he drowned? There was no hope of rescue. Mother and Guy were in London and even when they got home, it could be ages before they found that he'd taken the dinghy. And when they did, they wouldn't realize, at first, that he was in any serious trouble – not until he didn't come back. And then they wouldn't know in which direction he'd gone. He could have gone aground on any of the mud-banks and in any of the creeks. Out to sea was the last place they'd think of. A bigger wave lifted him up high and, through the rain, he caught a glimpse of the shore in the distance, further away than ever – no more than a thin dark line. Useless to try to swim for it; his crabwise stroke hadn't the power to fight against the tide and the currents. Guy might have done it. Guy had won cups for swimming at school and broken the crawl record. But he wasn't Guy. And he was going to drown. Choke to death as the water filled his lungs. His body would be washed ashore or maybe never found at all. The sea that he had always secretly feared would get him and keep him. Matt began to sob with terror.

'They'll find him, Mother. He can't have gone far.' She was sitting on the sofa, staring down at her hands in her lap. She hadn't cried or had hysterics, but she kept on kneading her hands together, as though she was washing them, over and over again. It was driving him mad. 'He's not as good a sailor as you, Guy. Not nearly. He'd never manage on his own in this weather.'

'He's OK. He knows enough not to get into any serious trouble. He'll be all right.'

She stopped the hand-kneading and lifted her head; he was shocked at her expression – at the way she was looking at him accusingly, as though it was all *his* fault.

'You know why he did this, don't you, Guy? Why he went off alone?'

'I've no idea. He's been on his own plenty of times before, anyway.'

'Never out to sea. Not alone. He wanted to prove he could do it. Are you too self-centred to see that? Haven't you ever realized how Matt must feel?'

'If you mean about his arm, then you're wrong, Mother. He's never let it stop him trying anything. Nobody ever notices it or talks about it. He's got nothing to feel upset about.'

She went on staring at him. 'You've got a lot of very good points, Guy. You're handsome, clever and charming, strong and brave . . . but you're insensitive to others. You don't really think or care about anybody but yourself. Maybe you'll learn better one day – when you're older. I hope so.'

The words wounded him deeply. So did the sudden suspicion – something that had never occurred to him before in his life – that his mother loved Matt better than himself. She'd sooner it was *me* out there, he thought, stunned. If she could have chosen between us, she'd sooner lose me.

'That's not fair, Mother. It wouldn't do Matt any favours to mollycoddle him – it's the last thing he'd want. He wants to be treated just like everybody else, that's the whole point. And I'm just as worried about him as you, as it happens.'

Her face changed suddenly. 'Yes . . . I know you are, Guy. And I'm sorry I spoke so harshly, darling. I'm afraid I'm in a bit of a state . . . overwrought. Forget what I said. I didn't mean any of it.'

He said stiffly, 'That's all right.' But she *had* meant it. And he doubted that he'd ever forget. The telephone shrilled suddenly from the hall and his mother jumped to her feet and rushed to answer it. He stayed where he was, holding his breath. From the sound of her voice and the words he could catch, he knew that the news was good. When she'd replaced the receiver she came to the drawing-room doorway.

'They've found him?'

She nodded, her eyes brilliant. 'The lifeboat picked him up five miles off Foulness Point. Apparently the dinghy had capsized . . . he's been in the water for hours. They've taken him to hospital suffering from hypothermia, but otherwise he's fine. Oh, Guy, thank God. *Thank God!*' She moved blindly towards him and he put his arms around her. She wept on his shoulder.

'What a complete ass you were, Matt. An absolute cretin.'

'I know.' He was grateful to Guy for acting normally, after all the drama of being carried off the lifeboat on a stretcher, Mother in tears, the nurses fussing round, the newspaper reporter wanting a story. '*How do you feel after being snatched from the jaws of death, young sir?*' Actually, he felt a complete fool and mortifyingly embarrassed at the trouble he'd caused everyone. It was a relief to be able to talk to Guy alone while Mother was with the ward sister. 'How did you know where I'd gone?'

'We didn't.' Guy sat down on the chair beside the bed. 'Not at first, anyway. I looked all over the place for you when we got back from London and then I suddenly guessed what you might have done. I went down to the jetty and found *Bean Goose* had gone. I thought at first you'd be bound to have taken her upstream and Mother and I took the car out to see if we could see you. When we couldn't, we phoned the coastguard and the police. You were bloody lucky, you chump.'

'I know,' he said again. 'I thought I'd had it.' He heard himself sounding terribly casual and knew he'd never be able to tell a soul what a snivelling coward he'd been. 'Sorry about all the fuss and bother.'

'Well, you can imagine how Mother flapped . . . What on earth happened?'

He told Guy about *Bean Goose* capsizing. 'I just sat there like a dummy instead of easing the mainsheet—'

'You could have let it go completely, you know, and the tiller, too. She'd've looked after herself. Don't you remember that time last year when we nearly went over? I just let go. The sail made a most frightful racket but she got herself right again.'

He remembered how scared he'd been. They'd been sailing round the mouth of the estuary in a roughish sea with *Bean Goose* thumping along, sending the spray flying, and a sudden squall had caught her. Guy had stayed cool as a cucumber, doing all the right things, while he'd clung on for dear life till the dinghy had got back on an even keel.

He started to shake again. He'd gone on shaking for ages after they'd picked him up out of the sea; couldn't seem to stop himself. Guy was watching him.

'You OK?'

He clenched his left hand under the bedcover, trying to stop the shakes. 'Yes, fine, thanks. Bit cold still. I don't suppose *Bean Goose*'s been found, has she?'

'Not much chance of that, I'd say. She'll probably drift around and then sink eventually.'

'I'm terribly sorry, Guy.'

67

Guy smiled. 'Actually, it'll probably turn out to be a blessing in disguise. We could do with a bigger boat and if Father collects on the insurance maybe we'll be able to have one. Something really decent to do some proper ocean sailing.'

Matt swallowed. 'Yes, that'd be jolly good.'

They kept him in hospital for another day before he was allowed home. There were only two weeks left before the autumn term started and, much to his relief, no question of getting another boat before then. He wasn't sure he'd ever be able to go in one again.

'Shall I open the window a little more, Grandmama? It's very hot in here.'

'If you wish, Anna. But not too wide. It lets in all the dust and dirt from the street.'

Grandmama's salon was so crammed with furniture and knick-knacks and old photographs of people dressed in funny, old-fashioned clothes that there was hardly space for one more thing. In winter, when the fire was lit in the grate and the curtains drawn, the room was very cosy but in summer it was too stuffy. Still, she always liked visiting Grandmama. She could talk to her about anything she wanted and Grandmama always listened. Sometimes Grandmama did the talking and told stories about her childhood in Russia where she had lived until she was eighteen. She still spoke German with a Russian accent and would often use Russian words, mixed up with German ones. On some visits, for a change, they spoke only French because they both liked the language. Grandmama would read aloud from French books – poetry and stories and collections of letters – and Anna would sit and listen. Sometimes she read too and Grandmama would correct her pronunciation.

'*Respirer. Tu n'as pas bien prononcé r. Rrrrespirrrer. En français la r est très important.*'

She loved hearing about Russia. Grandmama's father had been a banker and they had lived in a large house in Grodno near the border of Poland. She and her three sisters had had a governess and her brother a tutor, and a music teacher had come to the house to teach them all the piano and the violin. 'He was Polish and very poor,' Grandmama told her. 'I remember that there were holes in his shoes and patches in his sleeves. My eldest sister, Natalia, fell in love with him and he with her.'

'How romantic!'

'But then Mama discovered them together and there were no more music lessons with the Polish teacher. We had a very old and ugly man instead. Not even Natalia could fall in love with *him*.'

'Tell me about your count, Grandmama.'

'*Again?* I've told you about him so many times.'

'But I like to hear it. How you met him in the park.'

'You know already.'

'Tell me again.'

Grandmama sighed. 'We had a little dog – a spaniel called Pushkin – and I used to take him to

69

the park near the house in the afternoon. Then one winter's day—'

'It was snowing, don't you remember?'

'Yes, it was snowing – quite hard. There was a lot of snow on the ground and the lake was frozen. The winters were always very cold in Russia – much worse than here. My hands were so numb that by mistake I let go of Pushkin's lead and he ran away from me – he was a very disobedient dog sometimes, you see. Very naughty. I ran after him, of course, but I couldn't catch him; as soon as I got near he ran away again. And then a young man in the uniform of a cavalry officer came along and when he saw what was happening he called to Pushkin in a very firm voice and Pushkin stopped running at once and let him take hold of the lead.'

'And he brought him to you and bowed and said: "I believe this is your little dog. Permit me to restore him to you." '

'I really do not see why you want me to tell the story again, when you know it so well.'

'I shan't interrupt any more, I promise. What did you say then?'

'I thanked him, of course.'

'And then?'

'He asked if he could walk a little way with me – just in case Pushkin ran off again. So we walked together, and talked together.'

'What did he look like?'

'He was tall and broad-shouldered with dark hair and deep blue eyes and he had a beautiful voice – so low and musical. I can hear it still. He was very handsome in his soldier's uniform.'

'And after that you met often in the park? Secretly.'

'Almost every day. At first I did not know that he was a count. And it would not have mattered to me what he was. He was Alexis, that is all.'

'How old was he?'

'Twenty-two. And I was sixteen. Just two years older than you, Anna, and a lot more foolish. I fell so in love with him.'

'And he with you.'

'And he with me.'

'No wonder. I can see from the photographs how beautiful you were.'

'Natalia was much the best-looking of us.'

'Did the count ever kiss you?'

'Only with his eyes. Anything more would have been most improper. He wrote me letters and gave them to me when we met. I hid them away and read them in secret when I was alone. He wanted us to be married and live together for always . . . Of course it was impossible. Quite impossible. We were from two different worlds: he an aristocrat and me a Jewish girl. Our families would never have permitted such a marriage. Neither his nor mine.'

'You could have run away with him.'

'I might have done, if I had found the courage. But then our secret was discovered. A friend of my mother's saw us together in the park and the letters were found and destroyed. Of course I was not allowed to go out alone any more, and not so long after that we left Grodno to come and live in Vienna. I never saw him again.'

'Were you very sad?'

'At first I thought my heart would break, but, with time, it mended, and I understood how wrong it would have been. And then, of course, three years later I met your grandfather.'

Anna could remember very little about Grandpapa but she had a feeling that he had never quite measured up to the count.

'Grandmama, why must Jewish people always marry each other?'

'We must keep faith with ourselves. It is very important to our people. And the home is sacred to us. It is where we first encounter the laws that govern our lives, and it is from our parents that we learn the language of Jewish spirituality. It is where most of our great religious rituals take place. To have a Jewish home, both mother and father must share the faith. Natalia, you know, married a Gentile. It was a great mistake.'

'The Polish piano teacher?'

'Oh, no, not him.'

'Who was it, then?'

'But I've told you about her before.'

'Tell me all over again.'

'Well, she fell in love many times after that. She was always in love with somebody. Finally, she met a Roman Catholic artist just as poor as the piano teacher and ran away with him. Our parents were so distraught that they sat *shiva* – mourned her as though she were dead. I remember my mother weeping for days and days. They would have nothing to do with her again.'

'How cruel of them!'

'They weren't really cruel. They truly believed that she was lost to them. Poor Natalia! She went to live in Paris with her artist and died in childbirth a year later. We did not know what had happened to her for a long time.'

'That's so sad.'

'Yes. I was very unhappy for her. She was my favourite sister.'

'I've forgotten what happened to the others – my other great-aunts?'

'Tania emigrated to America with her husband and I never saw her again. She died a few years ago. Sophia never married and she died of tuberculosis when she was only thirty. My brother, Peter, drank himself to death before he was fifty.'

'Did he marry?'

'Yes. A Jewish girl, of course, but without a brain in her head. I imagine she drove him to the drink. They went to live in France too and never came to Vienna. Of the five of us I am the only one left now.'

'Do you mind that?'

'Sometimes very much. There is no-one to share all the childhood memories . . . But I have you and your dear mother and your good father. And your uncles on your father's side and their children, your cousins. We are a good Jewish family.'

'Why does everybody hate us, Grandmama?'

'You have asked that question before, Anna. I

do not know the answer but, in any case, not everybody does.'

'Well, it feels like it.'

'There are some Christians, especially Roman Catholics, who blame us for the killing of Jesus Christ. Others who do not like the fact that in our bible we are called the chosen people. But we were not chosen because we were superior, but to carry a specially heavy burden of faithfulness to God. And so it has proved. And perhaps our own strict rules and rituals set us apart. People do not always understand us and they often fear what they do not understand, and what they fear they can also hate – if they are ignorant and bigoted. My family left Russia because Jews were being murdered and nobody tried to stop it. My mother and father were so sure it would be better in Vienna – that we would be able to live here undisturbed and in peace. Now, that may no longer be so. There are signs that it is becoming dangerous, just as it was in Russia. Which is why you must go and live in England, Anna – for a while.'

'I won't go, Grandmama. I will *not* go and live far away in that uncivilized country.'

'It is not uncivilized, Anna.'

'They are barbarians. Mademoiselle Deuchars says so.'

'And who is she, pray?'

'Our French teacher. She says England is a horrible country and so are the English. She says they are dirty, dull and stupid.'

'What nonsense! How can she say this?'

'She lived there for a year. The English people that Papa and Mama want to send me to are not at all elegant. I saw that when they came to dinner.'

'One does not have to be elegant to be civilized, Anna. It is extremely kind of these English to offer to take you into their home, and extremely ungrateful of you to reject them.'

'I won't leave Mama and Papa. Nor you. If it is so dangerous, then why are you staying? You don't have any work here – not like Papa.'

'I have a great deal of work here, Anna. There are many families in need of help. The Talmud instructs us that in a city where there are both Jews and non-Jews we should feed the poor of both, visit the sick of both, bury their dead and comfort the mourners. For the sake of peace. We must always remember our duty and perform it without complaint. In any case, I am too old to uproot myself all over again. But *you* are not. You are young with your whole life ahead of you and you *must* go. Go for one year. If you hate it so much after that time, then I promise that I will persuade your mama and papa to bring you home. They will listen to me.'

This was perfectly true. Grandmama was the head of the family. Everybody listened to her and everybody did as she counselled. Papa might be a clever doctor and Mama a wonderful musician, but they still paid attention to Grandmama.

'And you will learn English while you are there. That will be good.'

'It's a hideous language.'

'It may not be as pleasant to the ear as Russian or French but it is a very useful language to be able to speak.' The old glass-domed clock on the mantelpiece chimed the hour with its sweet notes. Grandmama raised a hand to signal the end of the conversation. 'And now it is time for some tea so we will not discuss this any more.'

The tea, poured from a beautiful silver teapot, was dark as ink, with a thin slice of lemon floating on the top, and there was a honey *kuchen* full of nuts and filbert macaroons. After-noon tea was always safe with Grandmama, unlike other meals. She kept strict kosher and sometimes the food served was horrible – chopped chicken livers, cabbage beef, boiled gefilte fish. But tea was always delicious and there was no boring *kiddush* like on Friday even-ings when the wine and bread had to be blessed with the long Hebrew grace. Papa or Uncle Jacob always had to start off and they had to join in. On and on it went.

After tea Anna played to Grandmama. Like almost everything in the apartment, the piano had come all the way from Russia and was very old and very beautiful, with two heavy silver sconces to hold four candles.

'A little Chopin, I think, please, Anna. Some-thing pretty and light-hearted. Perhaps the "*Grand Valse*" . . .'

"It's too difficult. Too fast.'

'Very well. Play me a Nocturne – the one in E flat.'

Grandmama sat very still as she listened, her

head, with its crown of soft snow-white hair, resting against the chair back and her hands lying along its padded arms. When Anna came to the end it was a few moments before Grandmama moved or spoke. At last she said quietly, 'That was delightful, Anna. I shall miss your playing very much. When you are in England, you must be sure to continue your musical studies and to practise the piano as much as you can.'

'I shall be miserable if I go, Grandmama. Nobody cares how unhappy I should be. I should *die* of unhappiness.'

'We *all* care, Anna. And it is because we care so much about you that we are sending you away. Don't you see?'

She shook her head vehemently. 'No, I don't. You just want to be rid of me.'

'*Rid of you*? Oh, Anna . . . how could you even think such a thing? We will miss you every hour of every day and I shall probably miss you most of all.'

She started to cry then and Grandmama came and put her arms around her. 'This will not do, child. There must be no sadness, only bravery. We must all be very brave. Dry your tears and play me something else. You can choose this time, but nothing sad.'

She wiped her eyes and sniffed hard as she turned the pages of the music book. Grandmama stayed beside her, one hand touching her shoulder. 'This one?'

'An excellent choice. Play it very boldly.'

The brisk notes of the Polonaise filled the

salon and floated out of the open window into the Viennese street.

The whole family went with her to the *Bahnhof*: Mama and Papa, Aunt Liesel, Uncle Joseph, Uncle Julius, Aunt Sybille, the little cousins Shimon and Esther, Rachel and Daniel and, naturally, Grandmama. Mina came too and started crying almost at once which made it even harder not to cry herself. 'No tears,' Grandmama had whispered in her ear. 'Show me how brave you are going to be. Make me very proud of you.'

When it came to saying goodbye to them each in turn, to the kissing and hugging and the last words, she couldn't speak for the lump in her throat. She climbed up into the carriage and stood by the open door, looking down at them all. The engine was making too much noise for her to hear what they were saying but she could see the tears running down Mama's cheeks, Papa comforting her, the aunts dabbing away with their handkerchiefs, Mina sobbing, the little cousins looking anxious. Grandmama, alone, was smiling at her. When the train started off and glided along the platform they all waved: a little forest of hands and handkerchiefs fluttering together, getting smaller and smaller as she was carried away.

Mr Potter shifts in his armchair. 'I don't see what all this has to do with my boat. Jews in Vienna. Those children in that other dinghy . . .'

'I told you it would take a while to tell the story.'

'Huh.' He grunts and puffs at his pipe. 'I can remember some Jews coming to live round the corner from our shop just before the war started. Polish Jews, they were. Could hardly speak a word of English. Nobody took to them much. Molly and I thought they were a bit odd, to tell the truth. Strange ways, and habits. We didn't fancy them. Hard workers, though, I'll give them that. They lived over an old bakery and the wife used to cook pies and pastry things and sell them in the front of the shop while the husband did tailoring at the back. It couldn't have been easy for them. You couldn't get the ingredients, or the cloth, or anything. We tried one of the pies once but it had a funny taste and Molly threw it away.' He puffs out more smoke. 'They only had the one kid – a small girl, but you hardly ever saw her. They sold up and went away after the war

79

finished. I wonder what happened to them . . .'
He puffs again. 'That Jewish girl, Anna – there
were lots of them like her, weren't there? They
used to send them over on special trains, smuggle
them out – the lucky ones. She ought to have
been grateful instead of making such a song and
dance about it.'

'She didn't understand the danger. Not then.
Not at that stage. Her parents were among the
few who did.'

'We took too many refugees in, if you ask me.
Enough mouths to feed without all that lot as
well.' He smokes some more for a moment. 'The
boy with the deformed arm puts me in mind of a
lad at my old school. He was missing a hand –
lost it in an accident. We used to tease him about
it. Called him Hook. And one day he says to us,
the next one calls me Hook, I'll knock his block
off. He was as good as his word. Punched a
boy so hard he went down like a ninepin. Nobody ever called him Hook again, not after that.
Funny, I haven't thought about him for more
than sixty years . . .' He waves his pipe at me.
'Well, come on, let's hear some more.'

Chapter Three

'This is her train, Lizzie. Keep your eyes peeled so we don't miss her.'

'I don't know what she looks like.'

'I told you, darling. She has long dark hair.'

Perhaps she won't come, Lizzie thought hopefully. Perhaps they'll have changed their minds at the last moment and decided to keep her in Austria. We'll stand here waiting until everyone's gone and then Mummy and I can go home by ourselves and everything will be just as it's always been. The engine slowed to a halt and clouds of white steam hissed out. The doors started opening, passengers appearing, porters wheeling their trolleys forward, people streaming down the platform towards the barrier. Her mother stood on tiptoe, craning her neck. 'I can't see her yet . . .'

'Mind yourself, miss.' A porter steered his laden trolley past her. More trolleys trundled by and more and more people. Her mother was still on tiptoe, searching. After a while, the stream became a trickle and then ceased altogether. Her mother looked worried. 'She must have missed the connection at Harwich. That's what's happened. Oh, dear.'

'No, she didn't.'

Someone had got out of the very last carriage at the very end of the train and was standing all alone at the far end of the platform. Even at that distance Lizzie knew it was her.

They had to buy platform tickets and walk the whole way down because the girl didn't move, and even when they got quite close she still went on standing there, a suitcase at her feet. Lizzie's mother hurried up.

'Hallo, Anna. Do you remember me? Welcome to England. *Willkommen.*'

She was more than pretty; she was beautiful. Her hair was long and so dark it was almost black, her skin pale, her eyes green with thick lashes. And she was tall – much taller than Lizzie – and dressed in a grown-up coat of blue wool cloth. She neither smiled nor spoke, but simply stared. I'm going to hate her, Lizzie thought in despair. She's stuck-up and horrible.

'This is my daughter, Elizabeth.' Her mother was shouting very slowly, as though the girl were stone-deaf. 'Have you got some more luggage? *Une autre valise?*'

'*Ein Schrankkoffer . . .*'

'Of course, a trunk. It will be in the luggage van. Don't worry, we'll go and find it now.'

The trunk was a huge brown thing with metal bands. The porter struggled to heave it onto his trolley and then into the luggage space beside the taxi-driver where it stuck out. Lizzie sat on one of the tip-up seats inside, facing her mother and the girl. Her mother was speaking very distinctly and pointing as they drove along. 'This is the old City of London, Anna. In some places you can still see the wall that the Romans built round it when they were here . . . look how narrow some of the streets are. There was a big fire in the seventeenth century and nearly all the houses were burned down because they were made of wood and built so close together . . .' The girl stared blankly out of the window as though she hadn't understood a word. ' . . . and this is Oxford Street – a famous shopping street in London. Look, there is one of our policemen – over there, in the dark blue uniform and helmet.' Lizzie knew her mother was trying to be kind and jolly but she wished that she would stop. The girl wasn't interested; she didn't care one bit about any of it. When they got home there was another struggle to get the trunk into the hall with the taxi-driver muttering things under his breath. Then Hodges stomped up from the base-ment and started muttering too as he took over. Her father came out of his consulting-room and started spouting away in German but the girl didn't seem to understand whatever it was he was trying to say. There was an awkward pause. Her mother said brightly, 'Lizzie will show you to your room, Anna – won't you, Lizzie? Lizzie speaks a little French. *Elle parle un petit peu le français.*'

The girl followed her up the stairs to the third floor without a word. Lizzie opened the door.

'*Votre chambre à coucher.*' She could manage that all right. '*J'espère que vous l'aimez.*' Her mother had spent ages making it nice, so she'd better like it. They'd had the walls repainted and had new curtains made and bought a new dressing-table from Heal's and a new cover for the bed. Actually, it was much nicer than her own. The girl didn't speak or look a bit impressed. Lizzie opened the next door to the old nursery, except that it wasn't the nursery any more There was a new sofa and a new carpet on the floor. Her old toys had all been stored away in the cupboard, the doll's house shoved into a corner and a cloth put over the table.

'*Bitte, wo ist das Badezimmer?*'

What on earth was she saying? Something in German . . . 'I don't understand. *Je ne comprend pas.*'

'*La salle de bain. La toilette.*'

Light dawned: she wanted the lavatory. Lizzie showed her where the bathroom was and went into her own room, not knowing what to do next. She sat on the bed and put her head in her hands. It was going to be awful. *Awful.*

How was she going to endure it? This dreadful country, these strangers shouting at her in their hideous language or, worse, murdering her own? The mother had gone on and on in the taxi until she had thought she would scream. As for the daughter, she had looked at her as though she wished she'd never come. Well, she wished it too. She felt sick: sick in her stomach from the sea-crossing and sick in her soul from missing Mama and Papa and Grandmama and home. What a dreary country this England was! Everything so drab and dirty – the port, the railway stations, the train carriage, the streets. Even the countryside which Mama had said was supposed to be so beautiful had looked flat and dull from the train window. And, of course, the skies were all grey. Everything was grey. Grey, grey, grey. She washed her hands at the basin and stared into the mirror, scarcely recognizing herself. She was looking at a stranger. Someone with a dead white face and lifeless eyes whom she didn't know. Her real self had stayed behind in Vienna. There was knocking at the door. Tap, tap, tap. The mother's voice sounded from the other side. 'Are you all right, Anna?' Why couldn't they leave her alone?

'Anna? *Tout va bien?*'

'*Oui, madame.*'

'We just wondered because you've been in there such a long time. There's some tea downstairs. Come down as soon as you're ready. *Descendez au premier étage quand vous êtes prête.*'

What a terrible French accent she had. She spoke it as though she was speaking English. No proper French rs at all. Grandmama would be horrified. 'Anna?'

'*Oui, madame. Sofort.*'

She would have to go downstairs and do as the mother said and sit and be very polite, when all she wanted was to be alone. She dried her hands and went down the stairs. The mother was there waiting at the first floor and baring her teeth in her horse smile. 'We're in the sitting-room at the back, Anna. *Le petit salon*. We always have tea in there.'

The soft furnishings were all in flowery patterns, not a bit like at home where everything was elegant. The mother and daughter were sitting on the flowery sofa but, luckily, the father wasn't there so she wouldn't have to try to understand his dreadful German. A maid in a white apron and frilled cap was just leaving the room and stared at her as though she were a curiosity. The mother was pouring tea from a china pot, not a beautiful silver one like Grandmama's. 'Do you take sugar, Anna? *Du sucre?*'

She shook her head. Sugar in tea? She had never heard of such a thing.

'Pass it to Anna, will you, Lizzie.'

The daughter got up and brought the cup and saucer over to her. The china had flowers all over it, too, like the chair covers and curtains. 'A cucumber sandwich, Anna?' The mother was holding out a plate. She shook her head; she couldn't have managed a crumb.

'A cake, then, perhaps?' Another plate with lumplike things on it was offered. She thought of Grandmama's honey *kuchen, blitz torte, mandelchen* . . .

'*Nein, danke.*'

The mother smiled at her. 'No, thank you. That's what you would say in English. No, thank you.'

She lifted her teacup, drank and retched. Whatever she had swallowed it wasn't proper tea. They had put milk in it and it tasted disgusting. She clapped her hand to her mouth.

'*Entschuldigen . . . Excusez-moi.*' Hand over her mouth, she rushed from the room.

'Chuck me over the glue, Matt. This bit hasn't stuck properly.'

Matt picked up the tube and handed it over. He watched Guy putting a tiny dab of glue on the end of the wing rib and easing it carefully back into place. The ceiling in Guy's bedroom was festooned with model aeroplanes. Suspended from fishing-line, they climbed and dived and swooped at all angles. This was the latest.

'What's this one?'

'A Hawker Super-Fury.'

'Looks jolly fast.'

'It's the fastest interceptor fighter in the world. Top speed of two hundred and seventy-three miles an hour. But that's nothing to what fighters will do in the future. And they'll all have one wing, not two. Biplanes'll look old hat.' He sanded part of the balsa-wood fuselage and blew on it. 'The Americans have got one or two monoplanes already and so have the French, and they'll soon make one that goes faster than the Fury. We'll have to watch out we don't get left behind.'

Matt glanced up at the seaplane soaring over his head. 'Well, we won the Schneider trophy with that one up there, didn't we, so we must have some pretty good designers.'

'The Supermarine's just a racer, not a fighter. Not the same thing. Still, they'll learn from it. By the time I get to fly there'll probably be some terrific new fighter.'

Guy was always talking about learning to fly. He'd got it all worked out. When he went up to Oxford in three years' time he'd join the University Air Squadron and then the Royal Air Force. Father wanted him to go into the Navy, of course, but even though Guy liked sailing and ships a lot, he liked aeroplanes better. Next to the Supermarine was a plane marked with black German crosses, a red heart, a green laurel wreath and a white cross with arms bent at right angles. 'What's that one?'

'An Albatross. It was flown by a Hun ace called Werner Voss; those are his actual markings. There was a piece all about him in one of the model mags. The cross is a good-luck symbol – a swastika. He shot down forty-eight RFC planes in ten months. One of our chaps got him in the end, though, in a Spad.'

'The Germans aren't allowed to build planes now, are they? Not since the Great War ended.'

'Only ones for flying clubs and passengers. Nothing military. Just as well for us. Father always says you can never trust the Huns.'

Matt went on watching Guy working on the fuselage, sanding and blowing by turn as he smoothed it to a sleek, rounded surface. *Bean Goose* had never been found – not even a trace of her, so she must have gone to the bottom. It made him wretched to think of her, rotting away on her own down in the darkness – all because of him. Father was still waiting to hear from the insurance people about the claim. Perhaps it would be refused, in which case they wouldn't be able to get another boat. Perhaps he'd never have to go sailing again. He wasn't sure if he'd have the guts to do it. Yesterday he'd walked down to the jetty by himself and stood looking at the river and his stomach had started churning in fear just at the sight of the water. Anyway, they were going back to school tomorrow so he needn't think about it. Not for weeks and weeks.

'This is the drawing-room.' Lizzie stood aside so the girl could see into the room. Overlooking Wimpole Street, at the front of the first floor, it was the biggest room and ran the whole width of the house. The tall windows stretched almost from ceiling to floor, and there was a huge marble fireplace and two beautiful sparkling glass chandeliers. The furnishings were blue and cream and gold and Lizzie thought it looked lovely. What on earth was drawing-room in French? She hadn't a clue. Still, the girl could see for herself what it was, though she didn't look very interested. Lizzie pointed towards the grand piano at the far end of the room. 'Do you play the piano? *Est-ce que vous jouez le piano?*' No, that wasn't right. It was *du* piano. The girl shook her head anyway. She showed her the dining-room at the back of the house, next to the little sitting-room, and then went on down the staircase where it swept round and widened out rather grandly onto the black and white marble hall floor. 'The ladies used to come down here in their crinolines – that's why it's so wide.' She pointed to the way the wrought-iron balustrade curved outwards but the girl didn't seem to understand and it would be hopeless trying to explain in French. 'My father has his consulting-rooms on the ground floor, so we can't go into any of them. *Mon père travaille ici*.' Miss Cobb, the ancient secretary, who'd been around for years and years, was pounding away on her typewriter behind her office door next to the waiting-room. The consulting-room door was closed. Her father would be seeing patients until evening. She would show the girl that bit later on. 'Do you want to see the kitchens down in the basement?' She opened the door that gave onto the basement stairway. '*Voulez-vous voir la cuisine?*' The girl shook her head so she took her back upstairs again and paused at the second floor. 'My parents' bedroom is on this floor and two spare rooms for if anyone stays and two bathrooms. We're on the floor above this, of course, and there's another floor up above us – *un autre étage*. Just attics.' She wasn't going to mention the studio. 'That's where the maid sleeps. *La bonne*. Elsie. You saw her at teatime. Well, that's it. *C'est tout*. Unless you want to see the garden. *Le jardin?*' The girl shook her head again. '*Ich bin sehr mude*.' She was holding onto the banister and looked as pale as a ghost, as though she was going to faint. 'I am very tired. Please, I sleep now.'

She didn't come down to supper and when Lizzie was sent up to see if she wanted anything to eat the bedroom door was firmly shut. She was just going to tiptoe away when she heard a faint sob, and then another. When she tapped on the door the noise stopped at once. 'Do you want anything to eat? *Avez-vous faim?*' There was no answer. She opened the door a crack. Supposing she was ill, or something? The curtains were drawn, the room in darkness, the girl a hump under the eiderdown. 'I say, are you all right?'

Anna answered then, all in German – a long stream of it. Lizzie shut the door hurriedly and went away.

Liebe Mina,

I do not know how I am going to survive. I have been here for six weeks and it seems like a year. I am so homesick I could die. You would hate this country as much as I. The sun hardly ever shines and it has rained for the last five days without stopping. London is nothing like as beautiful as Vienna and Mademoiselle Deuchars was quite right about most of the English. They are dull and dowdy and they shout at me when they speak. I cannot understand their stupid language and nobody speaks German and if they speak any French it's so bad I can hardly understand that either.

The house where I am living is big and quite

old. It would be very nice except that it is always freezing cold. I don't think the English feel the cold because they don't seem to mind at all. The food is always cold too. The kitchens are down in the basement and everything has to be carried all the way up to the dining-room on the first floor. Of course, by the time it gets there it's not hot any more. Not that it would have been much better before. English food has no taste at all.

The father is a psychiatrist like Papa. He looks at me sometimes as though he knows how unhappy I am and talks at me in very bad German. The mother tries to be nice to me all the time, but I can't understand what she's saying. The English all speak their words as though they were eating them. As for the daughter, Lizzie, well, she tries hard to be nice, too, but I can tell that she hates my coming here. She hides away somewhere in the house to avoid me. On Saturdays the mother and father drive me to the nearest synagogue and wait outside. Grandmama would be very upset but they don't understand that we are not supposed to go anywhere by car on the sabbath. I shan't tell them.

The daughter and I walk to the school which is nearby. It's a girls' day-school, like ours in Vienna, and some of the girls are just as horrible. We wear a hideous grey uniform with felt hats and ugly black shoes and I have to tie my hair back. They've put me in the same form as Lizzie because I don't speak English, so all the others are two years younger and act like babies. At first they tried to talk to me but I couldn't understand them so they gave up. Now they leave me alone and I sit at my desk, saying nothing at all. I think I'm the only Jewish girl in the school. They are all Christians but not Roman Catholics. They belong to something they call the Church of England. We have prayers every morning before lessons. We all march in and stand in rows in the assembly hall and somebody reads from the Bible and then we sing a hymn. Jesus is mentioned all the time. Of course, I don't sing. I just open and shut my mouth and pretend. The teachers are all old except our French teacher, Mademoiselle Gilbert. She's not elegant like Mademoiselle Deuchars but she is *très sympathique* and she and I talk a lot together. She says I will soon learn English because I have an ear for languages but I don't want even to try. They don't teach them any German at the school and most of the girls are very bad at French. And they are very clumsy. They barge about and slouch at the table. Grandmama would be upset about that too.

I haven't played the piano since I came here. I lied and told them that I had given it up. I don't know why but I don't feel like playing here at all. I don't feel like doing anything. All I want is to come home. I am so envious of you, Mina. You are so lucky to be in Vienna. If I could only come back I would never grumble about anything again. I write to Mama and Papa every week and beg them to let me return but they say I must stay here for the time being. I shall die of homesickness and then perhaps they will be sorry. Please write to me often, Mina, and tell me everything that you are doing. It will make me even sadder but at least I won't feel so very far away.

Deine Anna.

'Anna Stein, why haven't you eaten your sausages?'

'They are of pigs, Miss Mitchell. I am not permitted.'

'What do you mean, not permitted?'

'We must not eat the flesh of pigs.'

'I never heard such nonsense. Who says so?'

'It is commanded in the Torah. It is not kosher.'

'Not what?'

'It is not clean.'

'Are you having the impertinence to suggest that the school kitchens are dirty?'

Miss Mitchell was glaring at her from the end of the table. The other girls were turning round to stare, some giggling, some sneering. 'No, Miss Mitchell.'

'Then eat your sausages at once. No food is to be left on plates.'

'I regret that I cannot.'

'*Cannot?* Of course you can. You'll sit there at table until you finish every scrap of them.'

She went on sitting there. Pudding was served

to everyone else – a suet roll with currants that they called *dead baby* because that was exactly what it looked like, and, of course, the bright yellow custard that was always poured over everything. The two sausages sat side by side in a congealing puddle of grease at the edge of her plate. They had hard, shiny skins and one of them had burst so that she could see pinkish-grey stuff poking out. She kept her eyes fixed on the plate while the chattering and clattering went on around her. Chairs scraped the floor and grace was said. *For what we have received may the Lord make us truly thankful. Amen.* How could they be thankful for pigs' innards and dead babies? Miss Mitchell paused on her way out. 'You will remain there, Anna, until you have eaten your sausages. You must learn that good food is not to be wasted.' The maids came to clear the tables and giggled at her. She ignored them completely. The big clock on the wall ticked on. She could hear the bell being rung for the beginning and end of each lesson. After the final bell for end of school, a prefect put her head round the door.

'You're to go and see Miss Foster in her study at once.' She looked at her scornfully. 'Honestly, what a *fuss* to make. I thought Germans ate sausages all the time. Sausages and sauerkraut.'

'I am not German. I am Austrian.'

'It's the same thing, isn't it? You all speak German.'

'No, it is not the same at all. And I am Jewish as well so I cannot eat pig.'

'*Pork*, you mean. Why on earth not? We all do. You're in England now so you should jolly well do what we do. And you'd better get a move on. Miss Foster's waiting. *At once*, she said.'

She knocked at the study door and heard the headmistress's sharp '*Enter*'. Miss Foster, so bony and gaunt, was sitting ramrod straight at her desk. 'I am waiting for your explanation for this wilful disobedience, Anna. Miss Mitchell tells me that you refused to eat your lunch.'

'Jewish people are commanded not to eat pig's flesh.'

'I am quite aware of that, thank you, but this happens to be a Christian school, founded for Christian girls, strictly in conformity with the principles of the Church of England. I am afraid that you must conform to our rules and traditions. You can't expect us to cater differently for you and you alone. Do you consider yourself special in some way?'

She could not understand everything that the old woman was saying; she spoke too fast. 'I cannot eat pig. It is a *mitzvot*.'

'Speak only in English, please. I accepted you in our school against my better judgement and so far the experiment has proved a signal failure. You have been here for more than half a term, Anna, yet you appear to have made minimal progress in the English language. Until you do so you will be unable to progress in any other direction. My staff report that you make very little effort. What have you to say about that?'

What was she saying? Something about her English. 'I do not understand.'

'Then it's high time that you did. I shall arrange for you to have extra tuition in English for the remainder of this term. As for this nonsense about pork, as long as you attend this school you will abide by its rules in every respect. If you do not then you will have to leave. You may go now.'

When she went to get her coat and hat and change into her outdoor shoes she found Lizzie was waiting for her in the cloakroom. 'Did you get blown up?'

'What is that?'

'Was Miss Foster angry?' Lizzie looked at her anxiously. 'She can be absolutely beastly.'

'She was not nice. But I do not care.'

'What about the sausages? Did you eat them?'

'I did not eat them, no. I will *never* eat pig. Never.'

'Well, we'd better go home. They'll wonder where we are.'

They walked back to the house in Wimpole Street. She never called it home or thought of it as that. Home was hundreds of miles away in the cobbled *Wallstrasse* in Vienna. *Vien, mein liebes Vien* . . . Home was Mama and Papa. Home was Mama playing the piano and Papa listening and beating his hand gently in time. It was the red velvets of the *salon* and the soft gleam of crystal and gilt. It was the street lamplight slanting through the shutters into her bedroom at night. It was the gardenia scent that Mama

always wore, and the rich aroma of Papa's cigars.
Home was eating lovely food. Home was talking
in German: understanding and being understood.
It was not, and never, never could or would be,
the house in Wimpole Street.

Chapter Four

'Open wider, please.'

Guy opened his jaws as wide as they would go. Old Payne had been drilling away like a roadmender and it was hurting a lot; once or twice he'd winced in spite of himself. He started the old trick of counting the plaster rosettes along the ceiling and when he got to ten a searing stab of pain made him grip the chair arm hard.

'Bit tender, is it?'

He shook his head firmly. He was blowed if he'd let Mr P. have the pleasure of knowing it. The chap was a sadist. Had to be, to be a dentist at all. *Eleven, twelve, thirteen, fourteen, fifteen* . . . the third rosette from the end still had that chip out of it . . . *sixteen, seventeen, eighteen. Christ, it was agony* . . . Start all over again, quick. *One, two, three, four, five, six, seven, eight* . . .

'That's the drilling done, then. Quite a bit of decay there, I'm afraid. Not as fortunate with your teeth as your brother, are you?'

Matt had never had a filling in his life, the lucky so-and-so. He'd been in and out in a jiffy, as usual, and now he'd be going through all the *Punches* in the waiting-room, which was the only decent part about going to the dentist. Guy probed gingerly with his tongue round his back tooth; the drilled-out hole felt like a crater. The nurse had come in and was grinding up the filling stuff in a glass dish. He peered sideways and saw that she wasn't the usual old frump. This one was quite young and not bad-looking. Must be new. As his mouth was now full of cotton wool and the bubbling hookah thing, he smiled at her with his eyes. She smiled back and went on grinding away.

'Open wide again, please.'

Payne started dumping in the filling and packing it all down, prodding and scraping and prodding. Guy didn't care, now that the drilling was over. This part was easy.

'Take a rinse.'

He sloshed around his mouth with the pink water and spat out the silver bits into the basin where they swirled away. Thank God that was over. The nurse had gone but he passed her in the hall on his way to the waiting-room and this time gave her a proper smile. Matt looked up from *Punch*.

'You were ages.'

'Three fillings. One whopper.'

'Bad luck. Mother went off to Debenham & Freebody to do some shopping. She says she'll meet us at Aunt Helen's.'

Guy groaned. 'That's fatal. They'll start jawing away and we'll be there for ever.'

'We can talk to Lizzie.'

'What about?'

'Well, I'd like to see those paintings of hers. You said they were good.'

'Not bad for a kid her age.'

They walked from the dentist's in Harley Street round to Wimpole Street. Guy banged the knocker and Hodges opened the door. Their aunt was out shopping as well, apparently. 'But Miss Elizabeth is at home. And Miss Anna.'

'Miss Anna?'

'The Austrian young lady. She is living here at the moment.'

Guy had forgotten all about her. 'We'll go and find them.' He caught a strong whiff of drink from the manservant as they passed him. When he wasn't lugging coal around or polishing the silver or answering the door or Mrs Hodges's bidding, it was a known fact that Hodges spent his time in the wine cellar. Uncle Richard would have sacked him years ago if it hadn't meant sacking Mrs Hodges too, which, according to Aunt Helen, was unthinkable. The first-floor sitting-room was empty and Guy was about to give a yell up the stairs to Lizzie when he heard the sound of the piano being played in the drawing-room. He beckoned to Matt and the two of them listened for a moment outside the closed door. 'That's not Lizzie,' Matt whispered. 'I heard her practising once. She can't play anything like as well as that.'

Guy turned the handle gently and opened the door. A girl was sitting at the grand piano over by the window, her back half-turned to them. He could see her long dark hair but not her face. He made a sign to Matt to keep quiet and they went on watching and listening from the doorway. He'd no idea what the piece was; something mournful by one of those chaps like Chopin or Liszt. He watched the way the girl swayed as though she was playing with her whole body, not just her hands. When she came to the end he and Matt both started clapping. The piano lid fell down with a crash as she leaped to her feet and whirled round to face them. She said something in a foreign language and, though he couldn't understand a word, it was clear that she was pretty angry.

He stepped forward, both hands raised in mock surrender. 'Terribly sorry if we startled you. I'm Guy and this is my brother, Matt. We're Lizzie's cousins. You must be Anna. Anna from Vienna.' She was quite tall and older than he had expected. He'd imagined some little girl of Lizzie's age but this one must be fourteen or fifteen. And she was beautiful – in a dark, foreign sort of way. Well, she was Austrian *and* Jewish, which made her doubly foreign, of course. 'I am sorry,' he said again, loudly and clearly. Perhaps she didn't speak much English. 'We did not mean to frighten you.' He smiled at her – his very best smile.

'I am not deaf.' She didn't smile back. 'You spy on me. You and him.'

'No. Not at all. We heard the music and wondered who it was. You're most awfully good.'

'I do not play.'

'But we just heard you. Didn't we, Matt?'

'I don't think she wants us to know,' Matt muttered.

'Why ever not?'

'Don't know. But we'd better make ourselves scarce.'

'Hang on a minute.' Guy turned to the girl again. 'Where is Lizzie?'

'She is up in her studio. She is painting there. It is private. Do not disturb.'

Damn cheek, he thought, Lizzie was *their* cousin. He said over his shoulder, 'Go and tell Lizzie we're here, Matt. It's the room on the right at the top of the attic staircase.' When his brother had gone he folded his arms across his chest, confronting the girl. She had the most amazing green eyes he'd ever seen. And she really was incredibly beautiful. He tried another smile. 'Well, how are you liking it here, in England?'

'I detest it.'

He was shocked. How could anybody hate England? It was the best country in the world. 'It's not so bad, surely?'

'I think so.'

'You don't know it, so you can't possibly judge. Not after such a short time. You don't even speak the language. Not properly.'

'It is not necessary to speak the language to know what a country is like.'

He found himself getting enraged. 'I happen to think it is.'

'Can you speak German?'

'No, actually I can't.'

'If you went to my country, you would know what you thought of it without speaking a word of German.'

He said coldly, 'I've no intention of going. It can't be such a marvellous place if you've had to leave it.' The look on her face showed that she had understood him perfectly and that his arrow had found its mark. He was rather ashamed of himself. The girl was a refugee, after all, and bound to be a bit homesick. He uncrossed his arms and ran a hand through his hair. 'Look, I'm sorry I said that and I'm sorry if we interrupted your piano-playing. You carry on.'

'I do not play.'

'For heaven's sake, we heard you, and saw you.'

'I do not play again in England.'

She walked past him and out of the room. Guy ran his hand through his hair again. Dash it all, he'd only tried to be friendly and decent to a foreigner and she'd been bloody rude.

Matt found the steep stairway that led from the third floor to the attics. He knocked on the door at the top on the right. After a moment, it opened a crack and half of Lizzie's face appeared round the edge. '*Matt!* What are you doing here?'

'Guy and I have just been to the dentist. We're supposed to meet Mother here. Can I come in?'

'Yes, of course.'

She opened the door wider. He'd never seen the

attics before. 'I say, this is fun up here. What a perfect place for a studio.'

'The light's not very good really.'

'It looks OK to me, but then I'm no artist. Guy says you paint jolly well.'

'I think he was just being nice.'

'Guy wouldn't be nice about something like that. He wouldn't say anything much at all. Can I see what you're doing?'

'If you like.'

It was a water-colour of the vase of chrysanthemums standing on the table. The vase was dark green glass, the flowers golden yellow; he thought it looked wonderful and said so. 'Still life, isn't that what you call it? How did you make the glass look transparent like that, so you can see the stalks?'

'I don't know, really.'

'I never knew you could paint like this, Lizzie. You've never talked about it, or about this place up here. Is it some sort of secret?'

'Not exactly.'

'We met that girl, Anna, downstairs. She said you were up here. She didn't want us to disturb you.'

'I used to come here to get away from her when she first arrived. When she found out about it, I was afraid she'd want to keep coming up here, but she never does. She's always writing letters home in her room.' Lizzie fiddled with a paintbrush. 'What did you think of her?'

'I'm not sure. She was a bit angry with Guy and me.'

'Whatever for?'

'Well, we overheard her playing the piano in the drawing-room and she didn't like that. Aunt Helen's out and you're up here, so she must have thought she was all alone.'

Lizzie stared at him. 'But she doesn't play. She told us she'd given it up ages ago because she wasn't any good.'

'Well, she does and she's brilliant.'

'That's odd.'

'Yes, Guy and I couldn't see why she got so het up about it, but still. Perhaps it's a bit like your painting – she wants to keep it quiet. She doesn't speak English very well, does she?'

'She doesn't try. She won't try with anything. They've got fed up with her at school. Miss Foster, the headmistress, told Mummy that if she didn't pull her socks up she couldn't keep her. And there was an awful row over the pork sausages.'

'Pork sausages?'

'She can't eat them because she's Jewish. It's against their religion. They mustn't eat any sort of pig – not bacon, or ham, or sausages, or anything. It's not clean, or something. They kept trying to make Anna eat sausages but she wouldn't.'

'If it's her religion, they shouldn't have done that. It'd be like trying to make Catholics eat meat on Fridays.' Matt grinned. 'It wouldn't matter much with us, would it? But I expect the Jews are a lot stricter.'

'Well, Daddy got the rabbi at the synagogue to

write to Miss Foster and ask special permission for Anna to leave anything that comes from pigs. Miss Foster was livid about it all, but she agreed in the end. She told Anna that it was only because she'd decided it was her Christian duty to be charitable to a refugee, but that if she didn't do better in class next term she'd be expelled, sausages or no sausages.'

'Oh, lord.'

'Perhaps she'll go back to Vienna if that happens,' Lizzie was looking at him hopefully.

'Perhaps she will.'

He heard Guy shouting from below and went down. His brother was pacing about the hall. 'That foreign girl's impossible. I'm sorry for Lizzie, having her around. I hope we never have to see her again.'

Mother broke the news in the taxi on the way to the station. 'I've asked them to come to us for Christmas. Aunt Helen and I thought it would be nice for Anna to get away from London and see some more of the country.'

'Well, it won't be nice for us.'

'Don't be difficult about it, Guy.'

'I'm not being difficult. She's awful and I don't fancy the idea of having her like a skeleton at the feast. It won't even be Christmas for her, will it? Jews don't believe in it.'

'That doesn't matter. She needn't come to church.'

'She'll go and spoil it for the rest of us.'

'Of course she won't. Really, Guy, you're being

extremely selfish. Matt has no objection, do you, Matt?'

Guy dug him hard in the ribs but he thought of the headmistress and the sausages and what it must be like to be far away from home in a strange country. 'No, not really.' Another sharper dig from Guy. Matt shifted out of range. Guy was probably right, though: having Anna there could spoil everything.

It was almost dark on Christmas Eve when they arrived by car at Tideways. Lizzie's feet felt frozen from the journey even though she'd had them stuck in a footmuff, with a rug wrapped round her as well. Aunt Sheila and Uncle William came to the door, with Nereus, to welcome them and when Uncle William kissed her his sailor's beard prickled her face. Inside the house everything was warm and bright. The hall was hung with holly and ivy, a log fire burned in the grate and carols were being sung on the wireless. Guy and Matt were decorating a huge Christmas tree at the foot of the stairs – Guy up a stepladder, arranging the lights. 'Come and help us,' Matt called out. He gave her a beautiful glass angel with outstretched wings.

'Where shall I hang it?'

'Anywhere you like,' Matt told her. 'You choose. Here, Anna. Would you like to do one?' He held out a plaster snowman to her with his good hand but Anna shook her head.

'*Nein . . . danke.*'

Lizzie hooked the angel carefully over a

branch. She hung some coloured glass balls here and there, the sharp needles pricking her hands. Guy had finished the lights and climbed down. 'It needs some more round the back, Lizzie. Here.' He passed over two more ornaments and held one out to Anna. 'Come on, we need some help.' When she made no move to take it, he tried to force it into her hand. She stepped back and the golden glass bell fell to the floor between them and shattered.

'For God's sake . . .'

'I am very sorry.'

Matt gathered up the fragments quickly. 'Doesn't matter a bit, Anna. There're masses more.' Guy went on hanging ornaments grimly. He doesn't like her, Lizzie thought. He doesn't want her here. And I don't either. She felt very guilty, but she couldn't help it. They gave her the star to put at the very top of the tree. She had to climb up to the highest step of the ladder to reach out to fix it on while Guy held the ladder steady and Matt hung onto her ankles. When it was all finished Guy turned on the lights and the tree came to life magically, twinkling and glittering gold and silver, red, blue and green.

She was sharing one of the spare rooms with Anna. 'Which bed would you like?'

Anna shrugged. 'I do not care.'

They were changing for the special Christmas Eve dinner. Lizzie pulled her brown velvet frock over her head, did up the buttons at the back and tied the sash in a bow. It was a babyish frock but it was her best. She fastened her string of coral beads round her neck and instead of plaiting her hair she left it loose and wore her velvet hairband. Anna was standing in her petticoat. 'Please, would you help me?' She had taken a frock out of her suitcase. It was made of rose-coloured silky material, with a round neck, long sleeves and tiny pearl buttons all down the back. 'My mother gives this to me when I leave *Wien* but I never wear it before.' She put it on and Lizzie did up all the buttons for her which took ages because they had to go through little loops, not ordinary buttonholes. They were the last ones downstairs and when they went into the drawing-room everybody turned round. Lizzie saw how they all stared at Anna in her beautiful dress – Uncle William, Aunt Sheila, Daddy and Mummy, Matt . . . and even Guy.

After dinner they put presents under the Christmas tree and Aunt Sheila gave everybody a long red woollen stocking. 'This one is yours, Anna.'

'I must wear it?'

Aunt Sheila laughed. 'No, it's an old custom, dear. We hang stockings up by the hall fireplace so that Father Christmas can leave presents in them when he comes down the chimney tonight.'

Guy groaned. 'For heaven's sake, Mother. She doesn't know what on earth you're talking about.'

Anna turned on him. 'But I understand your mother very well. We have this person in Austria. He is coming down our chimneys also. Not in our house, of course, but in others. We do not have Christmas. We have Hanukkah. It is for eight days and we give presents, too. One for each day, and each day we light one more candle on the menorah. We call it the Feast of Lights.'

There was a brief silence. Aunt Sheila said brightly, 'Yes, of course, Anna. I hope you don't mind joining in our Christmas?'

'No. My mother and father would wish it.'

Anna hung up her stocking between Lizzie's and Matt's. Afterwards, in the bedroom, she said to Lizzie, 'I do not know what to do. I have no presents to give, only chocolates that my mother has sent. I give those, you think?'

'Golly, yes. That'd be quite all right.'

'They are Viennese chocolates. Very special.'

'Gosh. Super.'

When the light was out Anna spoke again out of the darkness. 'Why is the arm and hand of Matt not good? What has happened?'

'He was born like that. I don't know why.'

'*Ach* . . . poor Matt. He is always hiding it from me. I must tell him that it is not necessary. I do not mind it. He is a very nice, kind boy.'

'Yes, he is.'

Anna turned over in bed. 'His brother, Guy, is not so nice.'

That wasn't fair, Lizzie thought to herself. Guy *was* nice. He could be very kind, too. As kind as Matt sometimes. Just as kind, but in a different way.

Anna was dreaming that she was in Vienna. It was snowing and it was dark. She was walking down a cobbled street – not the *Wallstrasse* but another that she didn't recognize. There were houses on each side with lighted windows but the windows were too high for her to see inside. The snow had covered the cobblestones but she could feel the bumps beneath her feet and her feet were cold – cold as ice – because she was not wearing shoes. Her hands were cold because she was not wearing gloves either. She knew that she must find the *Wallstrasse* and home soon but the street went on and on: more and more houses and then a lot of shops like in the *Karntnerstrasse*, but not quite the same. A woman in grey was coming towards her and when she asked her the way the woman answered in English and she saw that it was Miss Foster. Her face was all grey, too, even her thin lips. 'You must try harder, Anna Stein. Or you will never find your way.' She passed another window, lower down, and inside she could see the Fischer family, all sitting round. Herr Fischer with his book, Frau Fischer with her sewing, Gideon and Jacob studying hard. When she rapped on the window Herr Fischer came to open it, his spectacles on the end of his nose. 'What are you doing here, Anna? You are not supposed to be here. It is no use to look for your home. It is not there any more.' He banged the window shut and went back to his book. She was crying now and she was colder than ever and the street went on and on . . .

'Are you all right?' Lizzie was standing by the bed in her striped pyjamas. 'You were making funny noises. I thought you might be having a nightmare.' It was day, not night, and it was raining, not snowing. And she was not in Vienna, but in England – staying with the aunt and uncle of Lizzie. She could feel the tears on her cheeks and wiped them away quickly.

'Happy Christmas,' Lizzie said.

'Oh . . . Happy Christmas. What is the time?'

'It's eight o'clock but there's no need to get up yet if you don't feel like it. Your eiderdown's fallen off.' Lizzie picked it up off the floor and then climbed back into her own bed. Anna pulled the eiderdown up round her shoulders. It was made of slippery satin and immediately started to slither off again. She was cold – as cold as in her dream. Why did the English not have bedclothes that stayed put and why did they not heat their houses properly? At dinner, the evening before, there had been an icy draught at her back and she had been frozen in her thin dress. The meal had gone on for ever and the effort of trying to understand what everyone was saying and what was going on had exhausted her. She had sat on the uncle's left at the end of the table and when he spoke to her most of his words seemed to get caught up in his beard. The beard didn't jut from the end of his chin like Herr Fischer's black spade but went all round his lower jaw to his ears.

'How are you enjoying England, Anna?'

She must be polite. He was the host. Mama would expect her to show very good manners. 'I enjoy it very much, thank you.'

'Jolly good. I expect it's a bit different from Austria?'

'Yes, it is different.'

'Do you sail?'

What was he asking? 'I do not know what is *sail*.'

'Go in a small boat. With a sail. With the wind.' He had held up his white napkin and blown hard at a corner so that it fluttered. Anna had stared in panic. Was he mad? Or was it some sort of English joke? They were always laughing at things that she didn't understand or find at all funny. Then Lizzie's father had called down the table. '*Zur See gehen . . . in Segelboot*.'

'Oh . . . *Nein*. No. I never do this.' Did they even know where Vienna was? The sea was miles and miles away. She had only seen it twice in her life: once on a trip to Venice and the second time when she had voyaged to England. Across the table, the cousin, Guy, had looked at her as if she had failed some test. Did everyone go in sailboats on this island? The uncle had leaned towards her again, speaking even louder than before. 'You must come and stay here in the summer and go sailing. Matt sank the last boat we had but we'll be getting another by then.'

She had understood sunk: *versunken*. 'I do not think I enjoy this . . . '

'Oh, don't worry, Guy will be in charge. Won't you, Guy?'

'Yes, sir.'

'Matt's coming along, but he's not quite so experienced yet. Are you, Matt?'

'No, sir.'

They had answered their father as though they were on board his ship, being issued orders.

'Guy will take you out. Matt can crew. You'll enjoy it. Jolly good fun.'

He had turned away to speak to Lizzie's mother on his other side. Matt, on Anna's left, had whispered quickly in her ear. 'Don't worry, you don't have to come if you don't want to.'

At half-past eight she and Lizzie got up and dressed and went downstairs for breakfast. The red stockings hanging by the fireplace were bulging. The aunt, Frau Ransome, came up to her, smiling. 'Happy Christmas, Anna. Father Christmas visited us in the night. He's left you a few little presents.'

Her stocking was full of a strange assortment of things: a velvet hair ribbon, a diary, a tortoise-shell comb, a box of pencils, a pencil-sharpener, a pink sugar mouse, a string bag full of nuts, and, at the very bottom, in the stocking's toe, an orange. Everybody had different things but they all had an orange. She saw that it was another strange English custom. They were to open their other presents under the tree after lunch, Lizzie explained. And after breakfast they would all go to church. 'But, of course, you needn't come – unless you want to.'

'No, I do not come. Thank you.'

The church was within walking distance and she watched them go off, wrapped up in hats and coats and scarves and gloves. It had stopped raining but the sky was still dull and grey. She went into the drawing-room. There was a grand piano in one corner – a Bechstein – but she didn't touch it. Instead she sat and flicked through some magazines. Some of them were full of photographs of people hunting on horses, or standing around at cocktail parties or dancing at dances, the rest were about sailing and sailing-boats. She put them back on the side-table and went to look out of the long windows at the river. The Danube was not really blue, as Johann Strauss had pretended, but it never looked so cold and bleak as this English river. She watched it for a while. They had told her last night that the sea was very near – the *Nord See* – and the river must be going there. She had travelled across that sea to come here. On the other side of it was Germany, and beyond Germany was Austria. This river was a link with home. She decided to put on her coat and go and take a closer look. The black dog with the curious name followed her out of the house and, as though he knew where she wanted to go, led the way across the lawn and down some wooden steps leading to a wooden jetty built out over the water. She walked out onto it. This must be where they sailed their boat from – the one that the uncle had been talking about and that Matt had sunk. What had happened? Had he hit a rock? But there were no rocks in sight – just banks of wet mud. The wind was coming from downstream and it blew her long hair about her face. She could smell the salt smell of the sea, and the grey and white birds wheeling and calling overhead were sea birds. She stayed there for a long while, hands thrust in her coat pockets, gazing out over water, the black dog sitting quietly beside her, his nose lifted to scent the wind.

'Anna! *Anna!*' Somebody was shouting at her, breaking into her thoughts. She turned and saw Matt at the top of the steps. He waved. 'Are you coming? It's lunch-time.' The dog bounded off to meet him. 'Sorry,' he called, patting the dog. 'But they sent me to find you.'

She walked back along the jetty. 'I look at the water.'

'Be careful you don't fall in. It's quite deep there at high tide and the river runs fast.'

'It is dangerous?'

'It can be. Can you swim?'

She understood easily. *Schwimmen.* She couldn't but she didn't want to admit it. The English would probably think it very strange. 'Yes, of course.' She started up the steps. 'How did you sinken the boat?'

His face changed and coloured. 'Oh, it wasn't here. It was out at sea. I let her capsize. All my fault.'

'Capsize?'

He tilted his good hand. 'Go over.'

'Then *you* must swim when this happens?'

He nodded. 'Yes. For rather a long time. The lifeboat picked me up. I was jolly lucky.' He looked over her shoulder at the river and she watched him. He is perhaps a little afraid of it now, she thought. I am not afraid, but I do not much like it. 'We ought to get back,' he said. 'Father's carving. You know, cutting up the goose. It's sink, by the way, not sinken,' he added as they walked across the lawn. 'Just thought I ought to tell you.'

They were all sitting down, waiting for her, except the sailor uncle who was standing at a sideboard, brandishing a big knife and fork. The table was decorated with holly and the candles had been lit. She sat down in her place beside Matt. In front of each person was a cylinder of red crêpe paper frilled at each end. 'What is this?' she whispered to him.

'It's a cracker.'

Guy, sitting opposite, would be watching for her to make some stupid mistake. 'It is for what?'

'We pull them at the end.'

'Which end?'

Matt grinned. 'Both ends. But I meant the end of the lunch. When we've finished eating. We pull them apart and they make a big bang.'

Another English madness, she thought. The goose was good, though – the best thing she had ever eaten in England – and afterwards there was a steamed plum pudding and little pastry pies filled with sweet and spicy currants. She wasn't sure what any of it had to do with the Jesus Christ they all believed in and were supposed to be celebrating. His name had not been mentioned once. The uncle, at the head of the table, had not said any kind of *kiddush*. Now he took hold of the paper cylinder in front of her and thrust it at her. 'Grab that end, Anna, and give it a jolly good tug. Hard as you can.' The cylinder split into two pieces with a loud crack that made her jump. The uncle picked up the largest piece and handed it to her. 'You won. Well done. Good show.'

They all started pulling the crackers with each other and poor Nereus ran out of the room with his tail down. Anna saw, with astonishment, that they were putting on paper hats shaped like crowns and Matt, beside her, was blowing a tin whistle. 'Is this a Christmas custom?' she asked.

'Rather.'

'It is to do with Jesus Christ? The paper crowns?'

'Gosh, no, nothing like that.' He tore open her part of the cracker. 'Look, you've got a hat, as well, and a present.' He dropped a silver thimble into her palm. 'Jolly useful that. And there's a motto, too.'

'*Bitte?*'

'Well, actually, it's a sort of quiz thing. Not really a motto. You have to guess the answer.' He smoothed out the curl of paper. 'When is a door not a door?'

'I do not know.'

'When it's a jar. See – ajar. Ajar means half-open. When it's *two* words it's a jar. Gosh, sorry, that's too difficult for you.' He unfurled a roll of green paper that turned into another crown and set it on her head. 'There you are. Queen Anna!' They *are* mad, she decided. Completely mad.

After the lunch it was time to open the presents. The aunt came to her holding several of the beribboned parcels in her arms. 'These are all for you, Anna.'

'For *me*? These?'

'Yes. For you, my dear.'

'I do not expect this.'

'Oh, but you have presents too. Of course you do. Sit down and open them.'

They had all given her something: the Kapitan and Frau Ransome, the Herr Doktor and Frau Ellis, Lizzie, Matt, and Guy. She unwrapped each one: a manicure set in a leather case from the aunt and uncle, a fountain-pen from Lizzie's parents, an embroidered handkerchief from Lizzie, lavender bath salts from Matt, and, from Guy, an English-German dictionary small enough to fit in her pocket. They had all done this, even Guy. She sat and stared at the things on her lap. Then she went upstairs and fetched the big golden box of Viennese chocolates that Mama had sent and presented it to her hostess. 'I am very sorry that I have nothing more to give.'

Frau Ransome smiled at her. 'What beautiful chocolates, Anna. But not just for me. You must give some to everybody.'

She went round, offering the open box and thanking them for their presents. '*Danke, danke, vielen dank . . .*'

The uncle stood up and clapped his hands together loudly. 'Right. Charades now, everyone. We'll divide into two teams: I'll be captain of one, Uncle Richard the other. I'll have Aunt Helen, Matt and Lizzie in my team; Richard, you take Sheila, Guy and Anna. We'll toss for first to bat.'

'It's a word game,' Lizzie told her. 'Each team has to choose a word of three or more syllables and then act each syllable and then the whole word. The others have to guess what the word is. Uncle William won the toss so we go first.'

The Kapitan and Frau Ellis, Lizzie and Matt went outside the room and then Lizzie came in again. She knelt down and started licking her fingers and wiping her ears. 'That's easy,' someone shouted. 'It's cat.' Lizzie went out and the Kapitan came in crawling on all fours, like an animal, while Matt prodded him along with a walking-stick. Everybody laughed, except Anna who was shocked. She watched, bewildered, as Lizzie and Matt ran round and round in a circle. When they stopped, Frau Ellis came in and shook Matt's hand and handed him something invisible. 'We've got it,' Guy called out. 'No need to do the whole word. Cat-ass-trophy. It's catastrophe.'

Frau Ransome turned to her. 'Our turn now, Anna. We have to go out of the room and think of a word to act.'

'Please, I cannot do this.'

'It's just a game, Anna. You don't have to act properly, or anything. Nobody minds. It's only a game.'

It was the stupidest game she had ever seen, with grown-up people behaving like children. 'I do not wish to play.'

'Then you don't have to, of course.'

'Yes, she jolly well has to, Mother. We'll be one short in our team.'

'That hardly matters, Guy. We can manage perfectly well without her.'

'She's just being a spoilsport.'

'You're forgetting that Anna isn't used to our ways.'

'She won't even try.'

'That will *do*, Guy.'

'Ask her to play the piano instead, then. See what she says to that.'

Frau Ransome turned to her. 'Can you play, Anna?'

'Yes, she can. She can play very well. I've heard her.'

'How nice. Perhaps you'll play for us later, then, dear. That would be lovely.'

Guy had trapped her. She could not refuse – not after the aunt had been so kind and after all the presents they had given her. Mama would have been very angry if she had not agreed, Grandmama shocked at such ingratitude. After they had finished the rest of the stupid game she sat down at the Bechstein in the drawing-room and played a Strauss polka, Lehar's 'Vilja', and then the Blue Danube because she remembered that the English liked waltzes.

The old man nods. 'I should think so. After all they'd done for her. Can't abide ingratitude. Not at any price. We had a son like that. Our only child. Gave him everything, we did. Spent every spare penny on sending him to a decent school, buying him whatever he wanted. Molly doted on him. Couldn't do wrong in her eyes. Soon as he could he left home. Never settled to anything steady. Job after job, and all dead ends. When I told him what I thought about it he said it was all our fault because we'd tried to push him. We didn't see him after that. Molly went on sending him money, on the quiet, but I wouldn't have him in the house.' He reaches for the matches from the mantelpiece. 'They got another boat, then? Instead of the one that was lost?'

'Yes, they got another one. A second-hand fishing boat.'

'I'd've thought that boy, Guy, would've wanted something a bit fancier, by the sound of him.'

'Guy didn't always get what he wanted.'

'Good job too, if you ask me. Look what it did to our boy.'

'His father bought the boat when he was home on leave the following spring. She'd belonged to a fisherman who used to go out with a trawl net. You could take the centre thwart out and have enough room for five men to stand to haul the net in.'

He grunts in his gruff way. 'Sounds a bit like mine. You can do that with her.'

'And she had the same name. Rose of England. The fisherman was very patriotic.'

'I'm like that myself. Best country in the world, this is. I don't know what that Jewish girl had against it. Nowhere to touch it.'

'She was very homesick. Later on she felt differently.'

'I should think so,' he repeats. 'Blooming foreigners. They come over here and start complaining. Demanding this and that. If they don't like it here they ought to go back to their own country, that's what I say.' He lights another match and touches it to the pipe bowl, drawing hard. When it's going well he looks across at me. 'Well, what happened next? Did that girl go back to Vienna?'

'Her mother and father visited her in England but they were still afraid to let Anna return.'

'Lucky for her they had the sense, though I don't suppose she appreciated it.' He resettles himself comfortably. 'Go on, then.'

I pause for a moment, collecting my thoughts

and sorting the chronology of events in my mind. 'Lizzie and Anna didn't go to Tideways again until the next summer, in August 1935. They all went out sailing then. It was a beautiful day.'

Chapter Five

Rose of England moved away from the jetty, making no sound until she found some wind and the water began to slap against her bows. Guy let out the main sheet and put the helm up. The boom swung out and the boat wallowed round sluggishly to head upstream. He'd been bitterly disappointed when he'd first set eyes on her: a fourteen-foot, clinker-built, gaff-rigged, broad-beamed open fishing boat with a straight stern like a Viking ship; solidly built to withstand wind and weather. She had been sadly neglected and was scarred by hard usage: her varnish rubbed to bare wood in places, her rust-red sails patched. And she sailed like a fishing boat, butting her way through the water. Unlike the smaller *Bean Goose* she had no centreboard to make her go better against the wind; she was meant for negotiating shallow seas and estuaries with treacherous sandbanks. A plodding workhorse. A joke – as far as Guy was concerned. Even her name sounded ridiculous and old-fashioned. It was the sort of thing you'd call a paddle-steamer or some old river barge. He'd so hoped for something with sleek lines, modern and faster and a whole lot racier, but he knew better than to say so and be reprimanded for looking a gift horse in the mouth. 'Nice old thing,' Father had said firmly. 'Good and solid. Matt'll have a job tipping *her* over.'

He and Matt had done a lot of work on her in the Easter holidays, scraping and scrubbing her hull free of weed and sanding off all the old varnish before they revarnished her inside and out. They'd cleared the bow and stern lockers, chucking out an accumulation of empty tobacco tins, broken lamps, glass floats and fouled netting – even the skeletal remains of long-dead fish. They'd sanded and revarnished her long, heavy oars and Guy had repainted the name in white on her bow. He might not be able to take any pride in her lines or her performance but he was blowed if he was going to take out a badly kept boat and add to the humiliation.

The breeze was freshening and their wake lengthened out behind them. He held *Rose* on a steady course, letting her run before the wind with the boom broad off. He kept a close eye on the burgee fluttering at the masthead, watching for any wind shift that could cause a standing gybe. Anna, sitting with Lizzie on the centre thwart, was hanging out over the port side, trailing one hand in the water. She was wearing a white dress made of thin stuff, like muslin, and a wide-brimmed straw hat tied on with a red ribbon. All right in a punt, he supposed, but it looked ridiculous in a tub like the *Rose*. When he'd suggested she should go and change into something more practical, like Lizzie's flannel shorts and aertex shirt, she'd said she hadn't got anything like that and wouldn't wear it if she had.

'Anna, can you sit down properly, please.'

She turned to make a face at him. 'So strict, Guy! We are not the Royal Navy.'

'You're upsetting the balance.'

'Does it matter so much?'

'Yes, it does actually.'

She pulled herself back in, but unwillingly. If it had been Lizzie she would have done what he told her instantly. Anna, on the other hand, took very little notice of him at all. He hadn't seen either of them for more than seven months, not since Christmas. Lizzie had grown a bit taller but she was still just a kid, still in awe of him and easy to boss around. Anna, of course, always immediately did the exact opposite of anything he said. She was even more beautiful – he'd seen that at a glance, though he was very careful not to look at her too often. Over the next couple of days he'd discovered that her English was now pretty fluent. He listened to her chatting away to Matt – she was always talking to him – and there were hardly any mistakes. She spoke with an accent and sometimes said things in a foreign way, but it wasn't bad.

Rose sailed on steadily up the river, round Black Point and on to Raypits Reach. Guy kept a lookout for a good place for the picnic they'd planned. With the midday sun beating down, they needed to find a spot with some shade and there weren't many trees around. Matt pointed ahead to a clump at the edge of a field beyond the next bend, which might do if there was somewhere they could land and make the *Rose* safe.

'Ready to gybe.'

Lizzie instantly crouched down.

'*Anna*, get your head *down*.'

'You said before that we are not to move.'

'Just do as I say, unless you want a crack on the head. Gybe-oh!' The *Rose* heeled in stately fashion and Guy and Matt ducked under the boom and changed sides as it swung over. Guy eased the mainsheet as they rounded the bend into the wind. There was a patch of shingle at the foot of the bank by the field and some wooden fencing that looked as though it would serve as a mooring. Approaching the spot, he let go of the sails and drifted gently against the shore, side-on. He'd got it smack on right, which pleased him though it went unnoticed by either of the girls. Matt was over the side in a jiffy, splashing in up to his knees, and grabbing hold of the forestay.

'OK, you two girls can get out now.'

'But it is water, Guy.'

'Of course it's *water*, Anna. This is a river. There's no jetty so you'll have to damn well get your feet wet.' Lizzie was already taking off her socks and her brown leather sandals but Anna was making yet another face; he was sick of her faces. He watched her unbuckle her flimsy red shoes and slither reluctantly over the side of the boat. He waited for the moaning when she landed in the mud.

'*Ugh!* What is *this*?'

'Mud,' he said, pleased at her discomfort. 'Don't you have it in Austria?' It was beastly, squelchy, slimy stuff and he didn't much like the feel of it himself. 'It won't kill you.' She waded ashore, her white muslin skirts bunched up high in one hand, the red shoes clutched in the other. He let down the sails and took off the rudder and got out himself, carrying the picnic basket and rug. Then he and Matt hauled the boat up onto the shingle and made the painter fast round the fence with a bowline. Anna and Lizzie were splashing around in the shallows, trying to wash the mud off their feet – Anna still grizzling, of course. They walked across to the clump of trees. It wasn't as good a spot as he'd thought. The ground had been well trampled by cattle who had also left several cowpats. There were flies buzzing around. Anna held her nose.

'This is horrible. We cannot stay here.'

He dumped the picnic hamper down. 'It's shady.'

'It is also smelly. And we cannot eat with these flies.'

He knew she was right which didn't make it any better. He was angry with himself for picking such a rotten place and furious with her for kicking up a fuss. She was a guest, after all, not family. She should jolly well say nothing. That would have been the decent, English sort of thing to do. But, of course, a foreigner wouldn't have a clue about that. He started to open the hamper, tugging at the leather straps. 'Well, we're here now and it's too late to move. You'll just have to put up with it.'

She pointed to a single oak tree standing at the very far end of the field. 'We could go there. It is much nicer.'

'It's miles away.'

'I do not mind. Do you, Lizzie? Do you, Matt? It will be away from the flies and cows' messes.'

He slammed the hamper lid down. 'All right, *you* carry all this if you're so keen.'

'Matt will help me.' She took one handle, Matt the other and walked off barefoot through the grass, her red shoes dangling from her other hand. Guy followed with the rug, fuming, Lizzie anxiously bringing up the rear. Of course, the place Anna had found *was* much better, which did nothing to improve his temper. He opened up the hamper again while Lizzie spread out the rug. Mrs Woodgate had done her usual stuff: egg and tomato sandwiches with cress, sausage rolls, fruit cake, ginger beer. All pretty good. He handed the Bakelite boxes to Lizzie who set them out on the rug, together with the picnic plates. 'Dig in everybody.' He was ravenously hungry and shoved the sausage rolls under Anna's nose. 'Come on, then. Take one.'

'What are these?'

'You can see what they are. Sausage rolls.'

'She can't eat them,' Lizzie said. 'Not if the sausages are pork.'

'Why on earth not?'

'They're not allowed to.'

Matt took one. 'Jewish people are forbidden to eat pork. It's in their religion.' He chewed away. 'Not sure what these are made of, I'm afraid, Anna. Better not risk it.'

'For heaven's sake . . . does it really *matter*?'

'It does to her, Guy. Have a sandwich instead, Anna.'

'Perhaps she's not allowed to eat eggs,' he said sarcastically. 'Or tomatoes. Or cress.' He knew he was behaving badly, but he couldn't help it. He flung himself down on the grass, at a distance from the rug, out in the sun. Thank God he was Church of England and there was none of that sort of nonsense. He stretched out on his back and chewed on a sausage roll. The others were jabbering away – Lizzie's voice high and clear as a bell, Matt's all croaky because it was breaking, Anna's huskily foreign. They were talking about school food but he only half-listened. He was looking up into the clear blue sky and thinking about flying. One day he'd be up there, soaring about in a machine that would climb like an eagle and dive like one, too: plummet straight down from a great height onto its prey. He'd be eighteen next year and taking his Oxford Entrance. He'd go up the following autumn in 1937 when he was nineteen and join the University Air Squadron straight away. Train on something like a de Havilland Moth, most probably. Bound to be rather boring to start with but, later on, when he'd joined the Royal Air Force, he'd go on to something really wizard. Even better than the Hawker Super Fury. Even faster. Even more powerful. Two-winged like the eagle . . .

'Would you like a sandwich, Guy?' Lizzie was standing above him, thin legs streaked with dried mud. She was holding out an open Bakelite box.

He sat up. 'Thanks. Sorry, I was being jolly unsociable.'

'We've already started on Mrs Woodgate's fruit cake, I'm afraid. It's awfully good. Would you like some?'

'I'd sooner have a sandwich first.'

'Shall I get you some ginger beer?'

'Yes, thanks.' Funny little Lizzie, he thought; always so anxious to please. If he'd had a sister he'd have liked her to be just like Lizzie. When she brought him the sandwich and the ginger beer, holding the beaker carefully so it didn't spill, he asked her if she'd been doing any of her painting lately. She shook her head.

'Not much, actually. We had end-of-term exams, so it's been a bit busy. Then we came here.'

'Did you get good marks?'

'Not specially. Anna did, though. She was top in French and Scripture.'

'*Scripture?*'

'Well, she knows the Old Testament awfully well, you see. Much better than any of us. She was second in Maths, too, and tied third in Geography. They're going to move her up two forms next term so she'll be with her own age. Now that she speaks English all right.'

'When on earth is she going back to Austria?'

'I don't know. Her parents came to England to

see her a few months ago and she tried awfully hard to get them to take her home with them, but they wouldn't. She was dreadfully upset.'

He chewed on the sandwich. 'Well, it seems a lot of fuss over nothing to me.' He didn't want to talk any more about Anna. 'You must do some painting while you're here, Lizzie.'

'I did bring my paints,' she said.

'There you are, then. Make sure you use them.'

She knelt down on the grass beside him. 'Anna wanted to know if we could go down the river to the sea. I said I'd ask you.'

'She can ask me herself.'

'She doesn't think you'll say yes – not if *she* asks.'

'That's rubbish,' he said, nettled. It made him sound a real ogre. 'We can't today, actually, because I promised Mother I'd stay upstream. She worries – ever since, Matt, you know . . . But, if the weather stays OK, she might say it's all right to take you.'

'Anna wants to see the North Sea again, that's the thing.'

'What for? It can get jolly rough out there.'

'She came over that way. From the Continent.'

'Yes, she would have done. But it's tricky sailing with all the sandbanks and the tides and everything. It's OK with me and Matt, but I wouldn't want to risk getting into any difficulties with you girls. I don't think you'd like it much, Lizzie. You'd get scared.'

'Not with you.'

He was rather chuffed by the solemn way she

said that: as though he were infallible. Not true, of course, but he still liked to hear it. He smiled at her. 'Well we could probably go a little way out and she could take a look. I'll ask Mother.' There was a loud peal of laughter from Anna who was talking to Matt. He added sourly, 'But I doubt she'll enjoy it.'

Matt was hunting for a knife. 'Have some more cake Anna.' She couldn't eat the sausage rolls and he could tell she hadn't much liked the egg and tomato sandwiches which had gone all soggy, but she'd had two bits of cake.

'Thank you.' She watched him cutting. 'You are very clever with your hand, Matt. You manage so well with just the thumb and finger.'

He went red; he'd meant to use his good left hand and forgotten. 'Lots of practice, I suppose.'

'You do not mind my saying this?'

'No, of course not.'

'You are just as quick as anybody. And so quick in the boat, with ropes and things.'

'Not quick enough sometimes.'

'Ah, when you turned over . . . what was the word?'

'Capsized.'

'Yes, capsized. Was it frightening?'

'It was rather.'

'*I* should have been very frightened. And the sea so cold. And uneven.'

'Rough,' he corrected. 'We say rough.'

'I must remember – rough. When I came

135

to England on the boat it was rough, even in summer, and I was very sick. I felt so ill. Very, very ill. I wanted to die.'

'The North Sea's often like that, I'm afraid. And it's always cold.' He suppressed a shudder.

'But still I would like to go to see it again,' Anna said. 'I should feel closer to my home. Can you understand?'

'Yes, I can. I expect I'd feel the same if I was on the other side of it.'

'I knew that you would. Oh, no! There is an insect on this cake, Matt.'

'It's only an ant.' He flicked it away for her.

'Better than a fly.' She said it loud enough for Guy to hear, and laughed. 'Do you know, Matt, I have never had a picnic before.'

'*Never?*' He was astonished.

'Never.' She wriggled her bare toes. 'I think it is a very English sort of thing. To sit on the earth outside and eat food with insects on it.'

He grinned. 'I suppose it is. A bit mad.'

'When I first came to this country, I thought all the English were mad. Now I know that is not true. Only some of them. You are a very nice people. Very kind. But I still miss my home and my own country.'

'It must be awful, having to be away so long. Won't your parents let you go back soon?'

'They say not yet. Always, it is *not yet*. They are still afraid.'

It seemed extraordinary to him. He couldn't imagine having to stay away from England. 'What's Vienna like?'

She sighed. 'How to tell you, Matt . . . Vienna is a most romantic city. We have the most beautiful old buildings – some of them very grand like the *Hofburg*, the *Staatsoper*, the *Kunsthistorisches* Museum and, of course, the *Stephansdom* – that is the great cathedral in the very middle. And there are beautiful parks where you can walk, and long streets with many wonderful shops, and cafés where you can sit and listen to an orchestra playing the music of Vienna while you eat chocolate *sachertorte*. Everywhere there is music. *Great* music. Haydn, Mozart, Beethoven, Schubert all lived there. So did Brahms and Bruckner and Mahler and the Strausses. It is a magic city—'

Guy had got to his feet. 'Well, let's get on, if you two have quite finished yacking.'

Anna saluted him. 'Yes, Captain.'

'It's aye, aye, actually, Anna, if you want to get it right.'

'Eye? Why eye?'

'Not eye – aye. A-Y-E. It means yes.'

'And you say it twice? Yes, yes.'

'Oh, forget it.'

She was mocking Guy, of course, and he knew it. Matt saw him practically grinding his teeth. They packed up the picnic things and Matt and Guy carried the basket back across the field, the girls trailing along behind.

'She gives me the pip, that girl. Miss Clever Clogs.'

'Well, actually she *is* rather clever. Lizzie told me. She says she's brilliant at school now.'

Guy stopped and glowered at him. 'Whose side are you on, anyway, Matt?'

'I'm not on anyone's.'

'I thought you didn't like her either.'

'I didn't much at first, but now I like her rather a lot.'

Guy strode on. 'Well, as far as I'm concerned the sooner she goes back to Vienna the better.'

'She can't, Guy. That's what's so awful for her. Her parents won't let her because they're still afraid. They must really have it in for the Jews over there.'

'I expect it's their own fault. They probably get everyone's goat, like she does.'

They'd reached the spot where the *Rose* waited. The falling tide had left her several yards from the water. 'Untie her, Matt. The girls can jolly well help shove.' It took all four of them to get the heavy boat back into the river, stern first. Anna, of course, couldn't push and hold her skirts up at the same time. She stood knee-deep in the water with white muslin floating round her.

'I am *soaking* now, Guy.'

'You'll dry off soon enough. Next time wear something more sensible, like Lizzie.'

'I have not smalls.'

'Shorts you mean.'

'*Ja*, shorts.'

'Then you'd better get some. You can't wear that frock again.' Guy swung himself on board. Matt held onto the forestay keeping *Rose* to wind while Guy put the rudder back and then hauled away on the halyard. The red sail rode up the

138

mast and when it was at the top he made the halyard fast on the cleats under the thwart. 'Come on, you two, get on, unless you want to be left behind.'

'Our feet are full of mud. It is horrible. It smells.'

'Just shut up and get on board, Anna, will you. Or I *will* leave you behind. OK, Matt, push her off.'

Matt shoved hard on the bows and scrambled aboard. They sailed back downstream, against the wind, short-tacking from one bank to the other. Anna ostentatiously wrung her skirts out over the side and Guy, just as pointedly, ignored her.

Liebe Mina,

I am writing this at the cousins' home by the sea. You remember my telling you about Guy (the one who is so pleased with himself) and Matt, the younger one? I am sitting in a deck-chair on the terrace at the back of the house in the sun, which is shining for once. Lizzie has gone to do some painting by the river – she's very good at painting, by the way, though she doesn't believe it when you tell her so. The cousins are practising playing the English game, cricket, on the grass. It is a very dull game indeed. Somebody throws a ball at you and you hit it with a wooden bat and then run backwards and forwards. That's all that seems to happen. Guy is meant to be wonderful at it and he has just hit the ball so hard it has

139

gone into the middle of some bushes so poor Matt has had to go off and find it. The dog has gone to help him, too. Did I tell you about the black dog? He has a strange name, Nereus. Matt told me that it's the Greek name for some wise old man of the sea. The father is a sailor in the Navy and he chose it.

Yesterday we went out in their boat – the cousins and Lizzie and me. It is a funny old thing meant for catching fish and not at all beautiful, but it feels very safe. I think Guy is ashamed of it because he would like to sail something much smarter and better. He is like that. The weather was very hot and it would have been fun except for Guy ordering everybody about. We took a picnic with us (the English love picnics) and ate it in a field by the river. Matt asked me about Vienna but it was so difficult to describe it to him and it made me sad even to speak of it. How I miss home, Mina! I try so hard to be happy here but whenever I start to think of Vienna I am just as homesick as ever. The cousins' mother has said we can take the boat down the river as far as the sea tomorrow, so long as the weather stays good. It's the North Sea and it will make me feel closer to you all just to look at it. If only I knew how to sail a boat I think I should just steal the cousins' one and sail across and find my way home, whatever Mama and Papa said.

Matt is hitting the ball now. He has a crippled right arm which means he can't do as well as Guy, which is bad luck for him. I like him much better, though. You would like him, too. He is gentle and kind and he has the nicest eyes and smile.

Will you go and see Grandmama for me? She writes to me and says that everything is well with her but I should like to be sure of it. Would you go and see for yourself?

Matt has just hit the ball into the bushes so that Guy has to go and hunt for it now. I clapped very loudly. I hope it takes him a long time to find it.

I will write again next week when we are back in London.

Deine Anna.

The fear had come back. He'd been quite all right up until the moment when they'd reached the point where the estuary merged with the sea. The wind had suddenly freshened and the wavelet crests began breaking into glassy foam, and *Rose* had started to pitch and roll. The fear began with small shivers inside him and then welled up into a blind panic that made him physically shake all over so that he could hardly hold onto the jib sheet. Matt fought it down. There was *nothing* to be afraid of. No gremlins of the deep waiting. Nothing evil. Treat the sea with respect, Father always said, and she'll respect you. He'd nearly drowned with *Bean Goose* because he'd been stupid, not for any other reason. It had all been his fault. After a bit the shaking stopped and he felt better. Nobody seemed to have noticed. Guy was too busy helming and poor

Lizzie was feeling very sick and had her head stuck over the side. Anna, sitting athwart, had her eyes fixed straight ahead. She had borrowed an old pair of Guy's navy rugger shorts and a green and navy striped rugger jersey. They were too big for her but Matt thought they suited her terrifically well.

They were sailing with the tide and the *Rose* had charged downstream as though she wanted to get to the open sea as fast as she could. Matt fancied that she was remembering her fishing days and a greater freedom than the river. He could almost believe that ships had souls, which was why he hated to think of poor *Bean Goose*.

They were nearing the end of a starboard tack. 'Ready about.' Guy yelled it loud and clear. '*Anna, get your head down.*' She was still gazing ahead and didn't seem to have heard so Matt reached out and grabbed her. 'Lee-oh.' The boom and the red sail swung over and filled again on the other side. The *Rose* heeled and wallowed to port as she changed tack and spray flew up. Lizzie, crouched miserably over the gunwale, got drenched. Anna, ignoring the spray, pointed to a group of seals lying on a mud-bank.

'*Seehund!* What are they in English?'

'Seals,' Matt told her.

'I have never seen these except in a zoo.' She turned to watch them flopping about. 'They are so funny.'

They sailed down the Whitaker channel between Buxey Sand and Foulness Sand. The wavelets grew bigger and sprouted white horses.

The *Rose* was pitching and rolling much more strongly now, water sloshing over her bows, the spray slapping them in the face. Lizzie was clinging to the gunwale for dear life.

'I'll take her round the Whitaker buoy,' Guy shouted. 'Then we'll head back.'

Anna looked at him over her shoulder. 'Oh, please, can we go further?'

'No, we can't.'

'*Please*, Guy.'

'Lizzie's seasick, in case you hadn't noticed.'

'Oh . . . poor Lizzie. I did not see. I am sorry.'

Anna was neither seasick nor afraid. She went on gazing longingly out to sea and kept looking back as they rounded the beacon and sailed back towards the mouth of the river. Now they were against the tide and *Rose* had to battle her way upstream. It was nearly low water and the flats on each side were uncovered, curlews walking about and plunging their curved bills deep into the wet mud. The water surface was calmer and Lizzie had stopped hanging over the side and sat chalk-faced. Matt tried to jolly her up. 'Look, Lizzie, there's another heron.' She turned to watch it flap downstream and managed a smile. Anna hadn't seemed to notice the bird. She hadn't said a word for ages and was staring out over the mud-flats. 'Did you see the heron, Anna?'

She turned her head. 'What, Matt?'

'The heron? That big bird that just flew over. Didn't you see it?'

'No, I did not see it.'

She looked awfully sad and he tried to jolly her up too. 'They've got long legs and beaks so they can stand in the water and catch fish. You probably have them in Austria.'

'*Ja* . . . perhaps.'

'Those black and white birds over there with orange beaks are oyster-catchers.'

'*Ach so* . . .'

'And the little ones running about are called stints.'

'You're supposed to be keeping a watch out, Matt,' Guy said sharply. 'I don't want us going aground.'

With the water so murky it was hard to gauge the depth at all. Sometimes, if it turned a lighter colour, there was a bit of warning, but mostly it was impossible to tell until it was too late. They were on port tack, rounding a bend, when the *Rose* lurched to a halt. Anna turned her head. 'Why have we stopped, Guy?'

'Because we're on a mud-bank, that's why. Matt, I *said* to keep a lookout.'

'It is not Matt's fault. You cannot see anything under the water. How could he tell? You look so cross, Guy. What does it matter?'

'It matters because we could be stuck here for ages.'

She started to laugh. 'We look so funny, sitting here in the middle of the river, not moving at all.'

'There's nothing funny about it. Unless you find the prospect of sitting here for hours until the tide comes in amusing.'

'*I* don't mind. Lizzie doesn't mind, either, do you? She's not feeling sick any more.' Lizzie was giggling and then stopped when she saw Guy's face.

Another sailing-boat came fast up the river with two aboard and Matt recognized the Chilver brothers, Tom and Harry, who lived upstream from Tideways. They were in their brand-new *Grey Heron* – a sleek twenty-foot thoroughbred from Pettigrews that Matt knew Guy would have given his eye-teeth for. The elder one, Tom, cupped a hand round his mouth and shouted across. 'I say, awfully bad luck, Guy! Anything we can do?'

Guy flushed and yelled back. 'No, thanks, Tom. We're fine. We'll be off in a jiffy.'

'They are laughing,' Anna said. 'They think it is funny too.' She waved at the brothers who waved back, grinning.

Guy looked even crosser. 'If you don't mind being some help for a change, Anna, you and Lizzie can come back aft, out of our way, and keep your heads down. We'll try and push her off at the bow with the oars, Matt.' The patched red sail flapped loosely and the boom swung free as they wielded the heavy oars like punt poles against the mud. The wind had blown *Rose* side-on to the bank and she was clinging to it affectionately. The wet oar kept slipping in Matt's grasp. He couldn't get a good grip on it with his wonky hand to put enough pressure on the shove.

'Come *on*, Matt. Harder!'

'He is trying his hardest, Guy. You are very unkind.'

'Shut up, Anna.'

'I can help Matt.'

'You're to stay where you are,' Guy yelled at her. 'You'll only get in the way. And keep your head *down* unless you want the boom to catch it. OK, Matt, let's try again.'

'I think she's moving,' Lizzie said. 'Yes, she *is*.'

Rose's bows swung slowly out into the river and Matt scrambled down to the stern to push off there with his oar while Guy took the helm.

'We were not there for long,' Anna remarked. 'You need not have worried so much, Guy.'

Further upstream they overtook *Grey Heron* aground on another mud-bank. Guy cupped his hand.

'Bad luck, Tom! Need any help?'

'We're perfectly all right, thanks.'

Anna waved at them graciously as the *Rose* ploughed by. 'They are not laughing this time,' she said.

'I have come to say goodbye, Guy.'

He put down the balsa-wood wing that he was sanding. 'Didn't realize you were off already.'

'Oh yes, your mother is taking us to the station very soon to catch the train to London. Lizzie is just finishing her packing.' Anna nodded at the table. 'What is it that you are making?'

'A plane.'

'I can see that it is a plane. I meant what kind?'

'You wouldn't know it.'

She looked round the room and up at the ceiling. 'So many aeroplanes. You must like them very much.'

'I do, as a matter of fact.'

'Matt says you want to be a pilot one day. To join – what is it called – the air army?'

'The Royal Air Force. Possibly.'

'At least there are no mud-banks in the sky.'

He picked up the wing and started sanding again. 'We got off all right, anyway.'

'I meant to *joke*, Guy. I know that you are a very good sailor. And I am sure you will be a very good pilot.' She watched him working for a moment. 'Why do you want so much to be one?'

He frowned. 'No idea, really. I had an uncle who flew with the Royal Flying Corps in the Great War but I never met him. He was killed before I was born. Some of these models are ones he made. He left them to Father and Father gave them to me. I suppose it started then.'

'How sad that he was killed.'

He blew on the wing. 'He was shot down by von Richthofen.'

'Who?'

'The German ace. Haven't you heard of him?'

'I do not think so.'

'Surely you've heard of him? He was on your side?'

'My side?'

147

'Well Austria fought with Germany against us, didn't they?'

'I was not alive. It is not my fault.'

'I didn't say it was. Von Richthofen was one of their highest-scoring pilots. He had eighty kills. That's a model of his plane up above your head. The red one with three wings.'

'Such a funny-looking thing.'

'The men he shot down didn't think so.'

'Why could they not shoot *him*?'

'One did, in the end.'

'So he was not lucky any more.' She stopped looking at the triplane. 'I came to thank you, too, as well as to say goodbye.'

He glanced up suspiciously but she looked quite serious. 'What for?'

'For taking me to the North Sea.'

'Oh. That's OK.'

'I wanted very much to go.'

'Yes, Lizzie told me. You could have asked me yourself.'

'I was afraid.'

'Afraid? *You?*'

'I was afraid that you would say no. You like Lizzie, but you do not like me.'

'I'd've said the feeling was pretty mutual, wouldn't you? Anyway, I wouldn't have done. I'm not that mean, whatever you think.' He carried on sanding busily, smoothing the wood. She'd spent the whole visit putting his back up and now she expected him to be all sweetness and light.

'So . . . I wish you a good term at school. You

will be the *schulsprecher*, Matt says. The chief boy.'

'Head boy.'

'I can imagine you as that. Giving the orders.'

He ignored her, blowing hard, and went on sanding. When he looked up again, she had gone.

Chapter Six

'Anna Stein, will you see me after class, please.'

The girl sitting in front of her turned round with a smirk on her face. 'You're for it.'

What could she have done wrong? Her marks were always either A plus or A and her spoken French easily the best in class. When the bell rang for the end of the lesson she went to the desk where Mademoiselle Gilbert was gathering her books together. The teacher spoke to her in French.

'You have been helping Elizabeth Ellis with her homework, isn't that so? No use denying it, Anna. The French language is not Elizabeth's strong subject and suddenly she is giving me perfect translations and a composition that I know very well she could not have written by herself. I wonder how this can be and then I remember that you live with Monsieur and Madame Ellis and, *voilà*, I have my answer.'

'I may have helped a little.'

'More than a little, that is certain. And it does *not* help Elizabeth. No doubt you meant well, but she will not learn if she does not need to do the work. You must not do it all for her. Do you understand?'

'*Oui, mademoiselle.*'

Mademoiselle Gilbert picked up her books. 'Good, then we need talk of it no more. Instead, I want to speak of a different matter. My mother is visiting me from Lille in France for a few weeks. She speaks no English and is extremely bored with only myself for company. It would be a great kindness if you would come to visit one day and she could converse with you in French.'

'Of course.'

'Thank you, Anna. Shall we say tomorrow, immediately after school? You need not stay long.'

Guy knocked on the door of the Head's study. 'You wanted to see me, sir?'

'Ah yes, Ransome. Come in and sit down. There's something I wish to discuss with you.'

What bee had old Simpkins got in his bonnet now? Guy sat down in the chair in front of the desk and waited warily while the headmaster searched around in one of the drawers.

'I have received this letter from a Herr von Reichenau in Berlin.' Throat-clearing went on, spectacles readjusted. 'It seems that he is to take up some special post at the German Embassy in London. He expects to remain in this country for some time.'

'Really, sir?' Guy looked suitably interested.

'Herr von Reichenau has a son of approximately

your age, Ransome, and he would like him to attend this school. He has been told, quite correctly, that it is one of the best schools in the country. As head boy, I'd appreciate hearing your views.'

'My views, sir? On what, exactly?'

'On how the other boys would take to having a German in their midst.'

'I'm not sure, sir. Of course, the war's been over a long time, hasn't it?' There was a sharp intake of breath. He'd obviously said the wrong thing.

'It may seem so to your generation, Ransome, but for some of us the memories remain very clear. Indelible, I might say.'

Any moment now I'm going to hear about the trenches, Guy thought. The thousands dead, the mud, the wire, the gas, the rats, all the grisly horrors. The Head's history classes frequently had a way of winding up on the Somme and refighting the battle. He said cautiously, 'Some of the boys' fathers were killed in the war, sir. I don't know how they'd feel about it.'

'I appreciate that. I lost two brothers myself.'

'I'm very sorry to hear that, sir.'

'However, it is part of our Christian teaching that we should forgive our enemies.'

'Yes, sir.'

'Only savages hold grudges for ever.'

'Oh, absolutely, sir.'

'Nothing against the German nation yourself, I take it?'

'Not specially, sir. My father fought against

them in the war, of course, but he doesn't talk about it much.'

'Naval man, isn't he? Not quite like the trenches.' Father had actually been sunk by a German U-boat and spent two days on a life-raft in the Atlantic before being picked up, but there was no sense in mentioning the fact. 'A generation virtually wiped out,' Simpkins was saying. 'My generation. Hard to forgive and forget sometimes, I must admit.'

'Yes, sir.'

'Even so, I am of a mind to accept this boy. Show to the world that this school is capable of magnanimity. Set an example to others.'

'Yes, sir.'

'Provided, naturally, that he passes an entrance examination satisfactorily. He would be joining us next term. I understand that his English is already excellent. According to his father he is of well above average intelligence. He may even contribute something to the school. A better understanding between our two countries. We must try to look forward, not back. Put the past behind us.'

'Yes, indeed, sir.'

'I should expect you, as head boy, to keep an eye on him and make sure that there are no unpleasant incidents which might reach the ears of the press. Nothing that would reflect badly on the school. We pride ourselves on being English gentlemen, isn't that so, Ransome? Tolerance, decency, decorum.'

'Absolutely, sir.'

'Very well. You may pass the word round. It's probably as well to give everyone plenty of time to become accustomed to the idea.'

Guy left the study, groaning inwardly. He'd been wrong: there *was* something to worry about: having to play wet-nurse to some Hun and stop him getting punched up. Damn silly idea of the Head's. He would have told him so outright only it would have been a waste of breath. The old boy had already made up his mind. He was determined to show what a good, forgiving Christian he was and never mind the consequences.

Mademoiselle Gilbert's apartment was in the basement of a house in South Kensington with the entrance door at the bottom of an iron staircase leading down from the pavement. The sitting-room, with windows below the level of the street and a fireplace big enough to take a range, had once been the kitchen. It was the same as the kitchen in the house in Wimpole Street, only much smaller. The woman sitting in the gloom was old, like Grandmama, but ugly not beautiful, and her hair was grey, not white, and coiled tightly in the pattern of a snail's shell. Anna greeted her in her best French.

The woman nodded. 'Very good. You have been well taught by my daughter.'

'Not by me,' Mademoiselle Gilbert corrected. 'Anna already spoke excellent French before she came to the school. She had been taught in Vienna. By a Frenchwoman, isn't that so, Anna?'

'What is she doing in England?'

'She has been sent here.'

'Whatever for? What is wrong with the schools in Austria?'

Anna said, 'It is because my family are Jewish, madame. There is trouble for the Jews in Austria.'

The mother stared at her with eyes as dark as coal. 'There is always trouble for the Jews . . . So, they sent you away to be safe.'

'Also to learn English.'

'I have never desired to learn English, and I never shall. I do not know how you can live in this country, Janine. You should return to Lille and France where you belong.'

'For what, *Maman*? I have a very good post here and I enjoy my teaching. What should I do in Lille?'

The old woman lifted her hands in exaggerated supplication, mouth pursed. 'She has deserted me – my only daughter. Abandoned her mother. But she does not care. Not the smallest bit.' She was still staring at Anna with those coal eyes. 'I can see that you are a Jewess, mademoiselle. It always shows in the nose, and the skin colour and the way the hair grows . . . The Jews can never hide themselves.'

'We do not wish to, madame.'

'Oh, yes, sometimes you do. Sometimes it is very politic not to be Jewish. To flee. To disappear. History is full of such times. Like now, in Germany. And in your country, too, it seems. The Austrians have never liked the Jews. Do you play cards?'

'I play bezique sometimes with my grandmother. And patience.'

'You have a grandmother in Vienna?'

'Yes, madame.'

'Does she live with your mother?'

'No, but not far away.'

'Then she is more fortunate than I. *Her* daughter has not deserted her. Janine, fetch the cards.'

She sat and played bezique with the old woman, but it was nothing like the fun it was with Grandmama. For one thing, Madame Gilbert did not like to lose and for another, she cheated. At the end of the game Anna escaped. Mademoiselle came to the basement door with her.

'Thank you, Anna, for entertaining her.'

'It was nothing.'

'I am sorry for some of the things she says. She has been a widow for ten years and finds it hard to be on her own. It has made her bitter and often very tactless.'

'I understand.' But Anna didn't understand at all. Grandmama had been a widow for even longer and it hadn't turned her sour like bad milk.

'Perhaps you will come again? It would help infinitely.'

'If you wish.' She didn't want to in the least, but she liked Mademoiselle Gilbert and she had been kind to her at school from the very beginning when the other teachers had not. As Grandmama repeatedly insisted, debts must always be repaid and obligations met.

'It is all arranged, Otto. You are to start at the school in January, immediately after we arrive in England.'

'Very well, Father.'

'It will be a valuable experience for you. You will perfect your English and make advantageous contacts among the sons of prominent families. See that you use the opportunity well.'

'Naturally, Father.' He would have much preferred to remain in Berlin and finish his education there, but it was pointless to argue. He was not looking forward to living in a country that had been the enemy of his own and a party to its humiliation at Versailles. From all that he knew of the British they were a degenerate, disorderly race, as well as slightly crazed. He despised them. They had not deserved their victory, nor the power it had given them to destroy the dignity and glory of the Fatherland; a glory that was only now being restored, thanks to the Führer.

His father gave him a thin smile, as though he could read his thoughts. 'You are very intelligent, Otto. You should have no difficulty in running rings round them.'

Mr Potter frowns. 'I wouldn't have had a German in the place. Arrogant lot. Nothing but trouble. We never learn, though, do we? Never. What year are you talking about?'

'Otto started at the school at the beginning of 1936.'

'Huh. The King died that January – I remember it well. Molly was all upset; cried for days, she did. Then we had that good-for-nothing Edward and his fancy American piece thinking she could be Queen of England. Good riddance to him, I said at the time, though Molly was upset about that too. She thought he was Prince Charming before it all happened. His brother did a much better job and gave us a proper Queen.' He fingers his unshaven chin. 'Let's see, now. 1936 . . . A lot happened that year. I used to keep news cuttings in those days – pasted them all into a scrapbook. Must have it still, somewhere. Mr Baldwin was Prime Minister, as I recall. There was that civil war in Spain going on and Hitler walked into the Rhineland, cool as you please and never mind the Versailles Treaty. They showed it on the Pathé news at the pictures: all those German troops strutting along and the people cheering and waving and swastikas everywhere. Of course we didn't do a blessed thing about it. Missed the only chance we had of getting rid of him. I remember how he lorded it over everybody at the Olympic Games in Berlin just afterwards, like he was some sort of god. Didn't like it when that black man won the gold medal, though, did he? A real poke in the eye for him. What else? The Crystal Palace burned down and the Queen Mary did her maiden voyage and won the Blue Riband. And, if I'm not mistaken, the first Spitfire flew. Yes, it was quite a year.' The pipe has gone out but he doesn't seem to notice. He is lost in the past again. 'We weren't thinking about war then. It was unthinkable after the last lot. We were living in a fool's paradise, while the Jerries were getting ready on the sly. Right up to the last. No wonder they took us for a pushover.' He shakes his head. 'No, we were none of us expecting another war then. Not in 1936.'

Chapter Seven

'Come in, Ransome. I'd like you to meet Herr von Reichenau and our new pupil, Otto.'

The Head was in his jovial mood – a fairly rare occurrence that Guy had learned to treat with extreme caution. 'Thank you, sir.' He advanced into the study with his politest manners at the ready, prepared to play the game of giving a warm welcome to the Huns. There were two of them sitting on the sofa strictly reserved for VIP visitors and they both stood up at his approach. The father was tall and thin – a silver-haired man with the sort of long, cadaverous face given to joke Germans in comics, drawn complete with duelling scars and monocles. His handshake had a grip like steel. The son, as tall but of slightly heavier build, had almost blond hair and pale blue eyes. He clicked his heels and half bowed before he shook hands. Guy disliked him on sight.

'I've been telling Herr von Reichenau about the school – our aims and aspirations, and so forth . . . The way we strive for the highest level of achievement, both academic and in our personal development.' Simpkins was making it sound as though he went through the mill himself. 'Great emphasis is placed on the formation of sound character and backbone to equip us for the rigours and temptations of life when the time comes for us to go out into the world, isn't that so, Ransome?'

'Yes, indeed, sir.'

'And, of course, we consider it vital to foster a healthy team spirit in our sports activities. To learn to pull together for the common good. Right, Ransome?'

'Rather, sir.'

'I gather our new pupil is something of an oarsman, so we should be able to make good use of that. Do you play rugger, von Reichenau?'

'I regret I do not, sir.' The English was very correct, the accent like Anna's.

'Never mind. You'll soon learn. How about cricket?'

'Cricket? No.'

'I suppose you wouldn't . . . typical English game, of course. Good swimmer, are you?'

'Very good. I am very fast at the crawl stroke.'

Old Simpkins looked taken aback at this trumpet-blowing, then rallied. Guy could see him mentally making allowances. 'That's splendid.'

'I am playing tennis very well too.'

'Excellent.'

'And I am a good fencer.'

'Ah . . . we don't carry fencing in our prospectus, I fear.'

The father spoke. 'It is not important. Otto is

also a first-class shot. Do you shoot here?'

'Certainly. We send a team to Bisley every year. And, of course, there is the School Cadet Corps. Drill, PT, orienteering, camping, assault courses, field exercises . . . all that sort of thing. We have a former sergeant-major in charge. Healthy, character-building activities and lots of opportunity to develop leadership skills. Quite a number of our boys go into the Army. It's something of a school tradition. We rather pride ourselves on it.'

'That is very good. Otto will go into the army when he has finished his education.' Herr von Reichenau smiled deprecatingly. 'The German army, of course – such as we are permitted since the Versailles Treaty. His great-grandfather and grandfather both served with much distinction. I myself spent some time in the same regiment. It is a tradition also in our family.'

'Splendid!' If it had dawned on Simpkins that Herr von Reichenau had probably been taking pot-shots at him from a trench on the other side of No Man's Land, he didn't show it. 'Well, Ransome, perhaps you'd take von Reichenau on a tour of the school. Familiarize him with the geography and our rules and regulations, eh?'

'Yes, sir.'

The German boy followed him from the Head's study. Guy started off the tour at the quad in the centre of the cluster of creeper-covered buildings. 'Rule Number One: only staff and prefects are allowed to walk across the grass; everyone else has to keep to the path going round.'

'Why is this?'

'Because the grass would get mucked up if too many people walked on it.'

The German nodded. 'I see. This is a good reason. And you are this thing . . . a prefect?'

'Actually, I'm the head boy – the head prefect.'

'*Ach* . . . *der schulsprecher*. I myself should have been this if I had stayed at my school in Berlin.'

Anna had used the same word. What a bloody awful-sounding lingo it was: like hawking and spitting all the time. Anyone could say that, Guy thought, though Otto von Reichenau looked as though he might well have been speaking the truth. He led the way in through a door. 'Most of the classrooms are in this part except the science block which is in a separate place – in case someone blows up the whole school.' It was a joke but von Reichenau didn't smile.

'It is possible somebody might do this?'

'Lord no, not really. Some chaps are always mixing things together to see what happens but we're not allowed to touch any dangerous stuff unsupervised.'

'In Germany we do not play at science. We are thinking it is very important. Very serious.'

'We do too, but we don't make a meal of it.'

'*Bitte?* What does this mean? I do not understand.'

He couldn't be fagged to explain. Some upper fourth were coming down the corridor, two of them scuffling together. They stopped as soon as they caught sight of him. He ticked them off and told another to take his hands out of his pockets.

The German said, 'This is not permitted either – the hands in the pockets?'

'Only upper sixth. You're in that, so you can.'

'But I must not walk on the grass?'

'That's right.'

He nodded. 'Rules are necessary, I think. In my school in Berlin we have many rules too. We are very strict. It is better for everyone.'

Guy opened the door to the gymnasium. There was a class in progress – a line of boys waiting to take their turn at vaulting the horse, others climbing ropes. Von Reichenau watched for a moment. 'We have better equipment. And we are very good. More advanced than these pupils.'

'They're only fourth-formers.'

'But they are already fourteen years old or so, I think? In Germany they would be taught much more difficult things. Physical fitness is very important to us. We do many exercises and train our bodies very well.'

'That's the general idea here,' Guy said drily, 'but we're not quite so keen as you.'

'That is a pity. I like to exercise. In the gymnasium and to run. Do you run?'

'Me? Sort of. We do cross-country and athletics in the summer term.' Guy was pretty good at running and specially good at hurdling but naturally he wasn't going to say so.

'*Ach* yes . . . athletics. My best distance is one hundred metres. What is yours?'

'Ours are in yards.'

'Of course. Perhaps we shall race against each other?'

'Possibly. Do you want to see the swimming-pool?'

'Certainly. I like very much to swim.'

The glass-roofed indoor pool lay empty, drained of all water, mildewy, slimy and unappetizing. Guy's voice echoed round the green tiled walls. 'We only swim in the summer term.'

'That is a pity. Why?'

'Well, for one thing we do other sports in the winter and the water isn't heated so it's freezing even in summer.'

'We do not mind cold water. We take cold showers. And we swim in winter.'

The chap was a complete pain. Boasting about everything in Germany, as though anybody gave a row of beans about what they did over there. 'Well, bully for you.'

Otto von Reichenau was studying the empty pool. 'At school ours was longer. Like I told Herr Simpkins, I am very fast at the crawl stroke. I have won silver cups. Also for diving. Here the diving-board is not so high. It will not be possible to make a good dive.'

'The water's not so deep either,' Guy said coolly. 'So I shouldn't try if I were you. The last chap to do a swallow broke his neck.'

They continued on the tour: the science block, the school chapel, the library, the art studios, the dining-hall. With the exception of the chapel, a vast Victorian monstrosity known as the Mausoleum, everything, according to Otto von Reichenau, was bigger and better in Germany. Guy's patience finally ran out. 'Look, nobody here's going to care about how bloody marvellous things are in Germany, so I suggest you shut up about it. And it's not the done thing to go round bragging.'

'Bragging? I do not know this word.'

'Saying how good you are at things – boasting about your swimming and running, and so on. In this country nobody talks like that.'

'Ah, the modest English . . . always very un-assuming. I have heard this. But to be superior it is necessary to be very confident. To *know* that one is the best and not to be afraid to say so. You will never win if you do not care about losing.'

'I didn't say we didn't care,' Guy said curtly.

'But you do not make a meal of it, *ja*?' Otto von Reichenau smiled suddenly. 'That is perhaps your mistake.'

Lizzie added a squeeze of burnt sienna to the splodge of crimson lake on her palette and mixed it together. The colour still wasn't right for the sail – she'd gone and made it too brown now. She put another dab of crimson lake and mixed it some more. The attic smelled wonderfully of oil paints and she felt like a real artist. The hard part was to paint like one. She hadn't really got the hang of oils yet and it wasn't going very well. The sky was all right but the sea was all wrong. She'd spent hours in the National Gallery studying and sketching seascapes but her sea was nothing like a real sea. She couldn't get the subtle, shifting colours, the trick of light on water, the translucent curl of the waves. There was a knock at the door. Lizzie sighed. Real artists weren't interrupted in their work. Nobody would have barged in on Rembrandt or Monet or van Gogh. Anna stuck her head round the door.

'I am very sorry, Lizzie, but can I come in? I have such good news that I must tell you at once.'

She had never seen Anna look so happy. She danced into the room, clutching a letter in her hand. 'I have received this from Mama and guess what? I am to go home for *Pesach*. Mama says that I may. She and Papa want me to be with them and the whole family for the festival. It is so wonderful that I cannot believe it.'

'*Pesach?*'

'Passover in English. It is one of our three pilgrim festivals – *Pesach*, *Shavuot* and *Sukkot*. They are very important. At *Pesach* we celebrate the coming out of Egypt from slavery to freedom in the promised land.'

'When does it happen? This festival?'

'In April. It is near when you have your Easter. I am to go to Vienna for the whole holidays.'

'That's wonderful, Anna. I'm really glad for you.'

'I knew that you would be.' Anna came closer and looked at the canvas. 'This is Guy and Matt's boat?'

Lizzie nodded. 'Supposed to be. I did some sketches when we were there last summer.'

'It is very good . . . and these figures are Guy and Matt?'

'Yes. They're only rough so far.'

'And this other person here is me?'

'I'm going to put you in the white dress and hat that you were wearing the day we went for the picnic.'

'But where are you?'

'I can't paint myself very well.'

'But you must, Lizzie, or it will not be true. You were there, too, so you must be in the picture, sitting next to me. Is that colour that you are making now for the sail?'

'When I get it right.'

'It is more red, not quite so brown.'

'I know.'

'Do you remember that day? Guy was so cross with me about everything. I wore the wrong clothes and I did not behave as he wished. I never pay enough respect to show how clever and wonderful he is. Not like you.'

'He's actually pretty decent, you know.'

'You are very loyal. You always defend him. Perhaps you love him? I hope not because he could break your heart. If I were you, I would love Matt instead.' Anna rubbed her forearms. 'It is very cold up here. How can you bear it?'

'I don't notice it – not when I'm working.'

'Then you must be a real artist. I am frozen already. I think I shall go downstairs and leave you in peace, dear Lizzie.'

She went on mixing the oil paints and thought about Anna. At the beginning, she had hated her, and then she had felt sorry for her, and then she had sort of got used to her. Now, the weird thing was that she was going to miss her.

Matt swung his arms to work some warmth into his body. Another ten minutes to go before the final whistle blew. Cheering on the school team in an at-home match usually meant a miserably cold afternoon on the sidelines, but as the school was winning by five points so far at least there was something to cheer about. Guy had scored one of the tries – a brilliant bit of passing between the forwards with Guy, the winger, taking the ball last of all and streaking down the pitch and across the line before the other team could nab him.

'You are Guy Ransome's brother, I think?' He turned to find the new German boy standing beside him. 'You are Matthew Ransome?'

'That's right.'

'You do not resemble him at all. I should not have known unless I had been told. I am Otto von Reichenau.' Matt knew who he was all right. He was Otto, the Hun, or just The Hun – behind his back. Nobody liked him. He was too jolly pleased with himself. 'Your brother plays at rugger well. I do not play this game at all. Perhaps I will learn.'

They'd half-kill him, Matt thought. Sit on him so hard they'd squash him. 'It's a pretty rough game.'

'Yes, I see this but I do not mind. I am used to such things. You do not play in a team?'

'No. Not good enough.' Or heavy enough

either. He had the speed OK but his arm let him down. He couldn't always make a clean catch of the ball.

'I play in teams at my school in Berlin. We play a lot of sport. Also, we must work at our lessons for very long hours. Here, it is not so difficult. I am finding it quite easy.'

There was a sudden roar from the spectators as Guy broke free with the ball but he was tackled by three of the other side before he could go more than a few yards. They brought him down in a crashing fall and when Guy struggled free he was bleeding from the nose. He wiped the blood away and carried on playing. Otto von Reichenau said thoughtfully, 'Yes, he is tough, your brother.'

Matt saw Guy after the match. 'I've been talking to The Hun. He's a bit much, isn't he?'

'He's a damned pain in the neck. Puts everyone's backs up. I'm supposed to keep an eye on him for Simpkins but if he doesn't watch out someone's going to punch him in the nose. Trouble is I'll get the blame for it.'

The weekly Army Cadet Corps was compulsory for all boys. They dressed up in old Great War uniforms – high-buttoned tunics, hard peaked hats, puttees – and a retired Guards sergeant-major drilled them out on an asphalt square near the rugger pitches. Matt enjoyed it though the arms drill was tricky for him. Once he'd gone and dropped the rifle completely and been torn off a strip. Marching was easier. They marched and countermarched up and down the square, marked time, turned left and right, wheeled about, saluted – all to the music of Sergeant-Major Maclean's foghorn voice. For target practice they used .22 rifles and Matt found that if he supported the gun with his left arm, cradling it tight against his shoulder, he could reach the trigger with the forefinger on his wonky arm. In fact, he was a better shot than Guy. The *only* thing he did better. He was even better than The Hun. He beat his score several times and he could tell that von Reichenau was surprised and annoyed that somebody with a crippled arm could do that. 'I am used to win,' he told Matt. 'Perhaps you are lucky.'

'Probably,' Matt agreed. 'Just a fluke.'

Guy had been right about him getting punched sooner or later. The Hun was given a black eye and a bloody nose and Jennings, the puncher, was gated for the rest of the term. The story was that von Reichenau had been bragging about his grandfather who had been a general in the German Army and Jennings, whose father had been killed at Passchendaele, had gone for him in a blind rage. Simpkins gave the whole school a long lecture on being Christian English gentlemen and everybody hated The Hun more than ever.

Chapter Eight

There were fifteen of them round the table for the *Pesach Seder* at Grandmama's: Grandmama, Mama and Papa, Uncle Joseph, Aunt Liesel, Uncle Julius, Aunt Sybille, the little cousins, Shimon, Esther, Rachel and Daniel, Frau Neumann, the crabby old mother of Aunt Sybille, two grown-up spinster second cousins, Miriam and Elisabeth. And herself. They were all dressed in their finest clothes. Grandmama very *grande dame* in black silk with pendant earrings and a choker of pearls, the rings on her hands glinting and gleaming in the candlelight; Mama very beautiful in wine red, and the aunts not so beautiful but looking nice. Nothing could ever have made Frau Neumann beautiful, or the spinster cousins, but they had done their best.

Uncle Joseph, as the oldest man in the family, had said the *kiddush* over the wine and had read from the Hagaddah. Anna had listened intently to the old story of the Exodus from Egypt and to Daniel, the youngest, asking the four questions in Hebrew in his piping little voice: Why is this night different from any other night? Why do we dip the bitter herbs twice? Why do we eat un-leavened bread? Why do we lean on our elbows to the left? The first of the four little glasses of wine that they would each drink had been filled and Uncle Joseph had blessed them. They had eaten the bitter herbs dipped in salt water to remember the tears shed by their ancestors as slaves, and the sandwich of *matzah* with the sweet *charoset* in the middle, to celebrate their freedom. Uncle Joseph had folded the other half of his sandwich in a napkin and told the little cousins to shut their eyes while he hid it behind the cushions on his chair. And, as they sipped from the first glass of wine, they had all leaned on their elbows to show that they could drink and eat like free men, as the Romans had done on their couches. The feast was served in Grand-mama's special *Pesach* crockery, brought out and washed thoroughly once a year: the lamb shankbone that symbolized the lambs' blood smeared on the doorposts so that a first-born son might be spared, the chicken soup and *knaidlach*, the fried *gefilte* fish, the roast beef, the carrots and potatoes, the green vegetables to show new growth and the roasted egg . . . Grandmama had made *matzos torte* with almonds and apples, and prunes and poppy seeds, and a honey *kuchen* made from *matzah* meal. Before the long meal could finish there was the hunt for the *afikoman* – the piece of *matzah* that Uncle Joseph had hidden. When she had been much smaller she had always looked forward to joining in this part; now she watched as Daniel, Rachel, Shimon and Esther flung themselves at Uncle Joseph's chair, hurling the cushions aside to be the first to find the *matzah* and to be given the coins as a reward.

And then the singing began. Mama sat down at the piano and they all joined in the old Jewish songs, even Frau Neumann who was deaf as a post and yowled like a tom-cat. Anna caught Grandmama's eye on her and they exchanged private smiles. Grandmama knew exactly how she was feeling. She was home again – back among her family where she belonged – speaking in her own language, eating her own kind of food, acting out the rituals of her own people: all the things she knew and understood. She felt safe and warm and blessed.

The lamplight cast the same golden pools on the cobblestones of the *Wallstrasse* as she remembered. Anna stood in the darkness by her bedroom window. Everything was just the same, except that the shutters had been closed across the Fischers' sitting-room window opposite, leaving only glimmers of light through the louvres. Papa Fischer, Gideon and Jacob would be all dressed up in their best suits for the *Pesach Seder* and Mama Fischer crammed into one of her shiny frocks, tight on her as the skin of a sausage. In the morning she would go and visit them and Frau Fischer would clasp her to her vast bosom and go on about how beautiful she was, just as she had always done since Anna was small.

Mama came and sat on the end of her bed and they talked together like in the old times.

'I want you to let me stay, Mama. I don't want to go back to England again.'

'We told you that it was only for a visit, Anna. But we may all be together again soon. Papa has decided that we should definitely try to come to England and live there. We are going to apply to the English authorities for permission.'

'Leave Vienna? How could you bear to?'

'I should not be in the least sorry to go, Anna. All kinds of terrible things have been happening in Vienna. Jews have been arrested for nothing. Permits have been taken away, shops looted . . . poor Herr Fischer's shop had its windows broken one night and everything was stolen. Many Jews are leaving, emigrating, if they can, to England and America and France. Anywhere that will take them and where they can be safe. This evening at the *Seder* you listened again to the old story of our flight from Egypt under Moses. We have nobody to lead us now so we must each do as we think best. You know that Germany has taken over the Rhineland, don't you? Adolf Hitler just walked in. He does what he wants. Takes what he wants. And the Nazis get more and more powerful. They have great influence here.'

'But what about Grandmama? You couldn't possibly leave her.'

'We are trying to persuade her to come to England with us.'

'What does Uncle Joseph say?'

'He and Aunt Liesel are going to stay here, but

they have no children so it's different for them. Uncle Julius and Aunt Sybille are going to try and go to America with the little ones – if they can. It is not easy to be accepted anywhere. Nobody wants us. It costs money and it takes a lot of time to get the necessary emigration papers. But Aunt Sybille has a sister already in Detroit, so it may help. As for us, the good and kind Herr Ellis has promised that he will do all he can for us in England. If there is the possibility of work there for Papa then it may be much easier. It will mean leaving many treasures behind and starting all over again but it would be worth it.' Mama put her hand on her arm. 'We should all be together in London, Anna. Think how good that would be.'

'We should be foreigners – out of place.'

'All Jews are out of place, Anna. We are out of place here in Vienna. That is the curse of our people. But it is also our strength because it binds us together.'

Mina came to the apartment. She was taller and thinner and her hair had been cut short. She was also wearing lipstick.

'Where did you get it?'

'I bought it in a shop. Mama said I can wear it sometimes, now that I'm sixteen.' The bright red was like a gash in Mina'a face.

'I'm not allowed to wear any yet. I have to wait till I'm eighteen.'

'You can try mine, if you like.'

They went into the bedroom and Anna sat

down before her dressing-table mirror and un-screwed the gilt tube, drawing the lipstick carefully round her mouth.

'Now you rub your lips together, like this,' Mina told her. 'Mama showed me that. It spreads it around.' Anna stared at her reflection. The lipstick made her look quite different. She lifted her hair off her shoulders and twisted it into a knot on the top of her head. Mina gasped. 'You look really grown-up, Anna.'

'Where did you buy the lipstick?'

'In the *Karntnerstrasse*. I can show you the shop, if you like. They've got all sorts of colours.'

'It must be kept a secret. Mama would not approve.'

Mina sat on the bed. 'I have a secret, too.'

Anna watched her in the glass. 'Let me guess.'

'Only three tries.'

'You've fallen in love.'

Mina looked crestfallen. 'How did you know?'

'Because of the lipstick. And because of the stars in your eyes.'

'Are there really? Does it show? I'm so happy, you see. Everything is so *wonderful*.'

'Who is he?'

'His name is Felix. He is the son of friends of Mama and Papa. A student at the university. Twenty years old. He came to our apartment one evening and as soon as I saw him I fell in love – at very first sight. He is so handsome, so clever, so sophisticated.'

'Is he also so Jewish?'

'Oh yes, of course. All Mama and Papa's friends are.'

'And did he fall in love with you?'

'Well, I think he likes me . . . he paid me a lot of attention all evening. I wasn't wearing the lipstick then. I bought it since. I shall wear it next time we meet. We are to visit his parents at their home next week. I think they are quite rich.'

'Then when you marry Felix you will be able to buy lots of lipsticks.'

'Don't tease, Anna. I may never marry him, but I think I shall always love him. Wait until you fall in love – if you haven't already. Perhaps there is some English boy?'

'English boys don't notice girls. They are too busy playing cricket.'

Mina giggled. 'But they must notice *you*. What about the cousins of Lizzie that you wrote about: Guy and Matt? Are they handsome?'

'Guy is very handsome – and he knows it. Matt is not really handsome but sweet-looking, only he doesn't know it.'

'Will you see them again, when you go back?'

'*If* I go back. I argue about it with Papa and Mama every day. They are going to try to emigrate to England and I want to stay here until they do. They say I can't because it's not safe. Is it really getting so bad for us, Mina?'

'Well, people keep calling us names . . . that sort of thing. And Frau Schwartz's pickle shop was broken into and all the food spoiled – barrels of cucumbers and herrings and cabbage, all tipped into the gutters and mixed up together.

You never saw such a mess. But I don't know if that was because she's Jewish or because she's such a mean old witch. Anyway, don't let's talk about things like that, Anna. It's so dull. Let's go out and buy your lipstick and then go and have tea with lots and lots of lovely cream cakes.'

'Something by Chopin, please, Anna. Something quiet and reflective. We have need of that.'

Anna searched through the pile of sheet music on top of the piano. 'The D Flat Prelude?'

'Perfect.' Grandmama sat in her chair, resting her hands along the arms. The daylight slanting through the window illuminated one side of her face, leaving the other in shadow. She sat very straight and very still, like a painted portrait. Others had grown in Anna's absence, but Grandmama had shrunk. Her bones were more prominent, her skin looser and her beautiful white hair sparser. She had been overdoing it, Mama had said: wearing herself out with her soup kitchen and her visiting and her work at the hospital. They had been quite worried about her and begged her not to take on so much but, of course, she wouldn't listen.

Anna began to play. At first, she stumbled over some of the notes. But she had known the piece well once upon a time and, as she went on, it came back to her and there were no more mistakes. At the end, Grandmama nodded her approval.

'You still play beautifully. A little rusty,

perhaps, but that is all. Have you been practising properly in England?'

'Not at first.'

'But why not?'

'I didn't feel like it.'

'Foolish child.'

'But then I did. And I have been having lessons at the school in England. I wrote to tell you that.'

'I was glad to hear of it. Is your teacher good?'

'She's all right.'

'What does she think of your playing?'

'She says I have talent.'

'And so you have.'

'She said I should go to a music college to study.'

'Is there a good one in London?'

'I'd only want to study here, in Vienna. How could there be anywhere better in the world to study music?'

'That is very true. But it may not be possible. We shall have to see.'

'I know you are going to tell me that I must go back to England. I can tell it by your face, Grandmama. I thought you would help me. You *promised* me that you would persuade Mama and Papa to let me come home after one year and it's much more than that.'

'I said if you still hated it there. I don't believe that you do. You would prefer to be at home, of course, but from your letters I can tell that you have become quite used to the English and their ways. Your first letters were blotted with tearstains; but no longer. England is not so bad as you feared, is it? There are some good things about it.'

'A few perhaps. But I love Vienna so much more, Grandmama. Please make Mama and Papa let me stay.'

'I cannot do that, Anna.'

'Why not?'

'Because what they are doing for you is right.'

She said sulkily, 'How can you be so sure? Mina's parents don't make such a fuss. Her father says that there is nothing to worry about.'

'He is wrong.'

'Mama told me that she and Papa are going to try to live in England. Did you know that?'

'Certainly. They consulted me.'

'And that Uncle Julius and Aunt Sybille might go to America.'

'I think it is very wise.'

'I think it's silly to run away.'

'You are too young to understand, Anna. At sixteen all you see is what you want to see. How you would wish everything to be. It's natural. But life is seldom how we want, as you will learn.'

'Anyway, they can't leave you, so they can't go.'

'Nonsense. Of course they must go, if they can.'

'*You'd* never leave, though, would you?'

'I told you before, I'm too old to start all over again somewhere else. And I can be useful here.' The glass-domed clock on the mantelpiece struck four. 'We shall not discuss this any further, Anna. We shall take tea in a civilized manner and talk of other things. And we shall now speak in French.'

The tea was poured from the magnificent Russian silver pot, the thin slice of lemon floated on the top. There were *lebkuchen* with cinnamon and nuts and *teiglach* sprinkled with ginger. Grandmama was impressed by her French.

'You have made a great deal of progress. Your pronunciation is quite perfect now. Who is your teacher at school?'

'Mademoiselle Gilbert. She's very nice. I sometimes go to tea with her and we speak French all the time, of course. She has lent me some books to read – Baudelaire, Proust, Maupassant, Stendhal . . .'

'Excellent.'

'Well, some of them can be a bit boring.'

'I dare say, but in time you will learn to appreciate them better. Now, tell me all about England. The house in London, the Herr Doktor and Frau Ellis, Elizabeth, the food, the weather . . . everything you can think of. I want to know all about it.'

They talked for a long time and the clock had struck six before Grandmama rose from her chair. 'Before you go, I have something to give you.' She left the room and returned holding a flat, crescent-shaped box. 'This is for you to take with you to England. You must hide it where it will not be found and stolen. Open it.'

The box was covered with dark red velvet, old and worn, the clasp golden filigree. Inside it was lined with creamy satin and on the satin lay a necklace of precious stones set in delicate tiers of gold with a single large jewel suspended at the centre. 'Emeralds and diamonds,' Grandmama said. 'It belonged to my dear grandmother and my mother brought it to Vienna with her from Russia. Once it belonged to a grand duchess. They are very fine stones, especially the largest emerald. It is worth a great deal of money. Let me see how it looks on you, child.' She lifted it out of the box, fastened it round Anna's neck and stepped back. 'Go and see yourself in the mirror.'

Anna imagined herself wearing it at a ball at the *Staatsoper*, dressed in a beautiful, full-skirted long gown with long white gloves . . . she swept her hair up on the top of her head as she had done with Mina.

Grandmama smiled. 'Exquisite. I knew how it would be.' She undid the necklace, put it back in the velvet box and snapped the clasp shut. 'Take it with you and keep it very safe.'

'But what would I do with such a treasure?'

'You may wear it one day. Who knows? Meantime it is for you to keep safe and to sell if you should ever need money.' Grandmama placed the box into her hands. 'It is yours, Anna.'

'They're making me go back, Mina.'

'Oh, Anna . . .'

'You'll write to me, won't you. All about Felix.'

'Of course I will.'

'Long letters, telling me everything I'm missing.'

'I promise.'

Mama and Papa took her to the *Hauptbahnhof*. She had said goodbye to everybody else in the family the night before. The aunts had dabbed their eyes with their handkerchiefs but Grandmama had not shed a single tear. 'I shall expect you to work hard at your studies, and to practise your piano constantly.' She had laid a hand on Anna's cheek briefly. 'And to be a credit to us always.'

There were soldiers in the station, milling about and making a nuisance of themselves. Some of them leered at her and passed stupid remarks. The train was very full and she took the last empty seat in her carriage. As before, she stood at the open door, looking down on Mama and Papa and waiting to wave goodbye. How can they do this to me, she thought bitterly. Why can't they be like Mina's parents? A guard was walking along the platform, slamming doors shut.

A dark-haired woman came hurrying down the platform, carrying a small child in her arms. Tears were running down her cheeks. '*Fräulein, fahren Sie nach England?*'

'*Ja.*'

'*Nach Harwich?*'

'*Ja, aber . . .*'

'Please, will you look after my son? Take him to England with you? He has a ticket, papers . . . a letter from my sister to show that she will have him to live with her. It is all arranged.'

'But—'

The woman was lifting the boy up. 'The English will allow a child . . . he will be safe. Tell my sister that I am coming too, as soon as I can. *Please.*' The child was clinging tightly to his mother who tore his hands away from round her neck and thrust him at Anna. 'Here are the tickets for him.' The guard had reached them now. He pushed the woman aside and the train door slammed shut. The mother went on mouthing words that Anna could not hear, and the little boy screamed and struggled wildly, beating at her with his small fists. '*Mami, Mami, Mami.*' The train had started and was gathering speed. She couldn't wave to Mama and Papa and the struggling child blocked her last view of them.

She put the boy down and tried to comfort him but he went on sobbing and screaming for his mother. After a while, she picked him up again and carried him into the compartment and sat down with him on her lap. The other occupants of the compartment glared with disapproval. A fat woman sitting opposite leaned across. 'You shouldn't let him behave so badly. He is causing a disturbance. Can't you stop him?'

'No, I can't,' Anna snapped. 'He's very upset, can't you see? He's just left his mother.'

The woman raised her voice above the rattle of the train. 'Are you his sister?'

'No. I'm no relation at all. I don't even know his name. The mother asked me to look after him on the journey.'

The woman looked shocked. 'The nerve of it! A child of that age . . . What on earth did she think she was doing? Where is he supposed to be going?'

'To England.'

'*England?* All that way without his mother? Crazy!' The woman sat back, studying the small boy with hard eyes. 'Perhaps he is Jewish, and that is why she is sending him away. It is better so. There are too many Jews in Vienna. They have fingers in too many pies. Yes, he looks Jewish . . .'

The child's wails and sobs stopped at last and he lay heavily against Anna, making small hiccups, tears still trembling on the end of his lashes. He was dressed in a brown coat and peaked cap and brown leather shoes. The fat woman was still staring. 'He is well-cared for. Good clothes and the shoes are new. The Jews always have money to spend. You should ask him his name. Make him tell you.'

'Later.'

'You should ask him *now*.' The woman leaned forward again and tugged sharply at the boy's coat sleeve. 'What is your name, eh? You must tell us. *Wie ist dein Name?*'

The boy turned his face away and buried it in Anna's coat. She clasped her arms around him. 'Leave him alone. He's exhausted.'

The woman shrugged. 'As you please, but you need to find out. Has he papers? He will need papers at the frontier.'

'Yes, he has papers.' The mother had said so, but where were they? She looked at the tickets in her hand which seemed in order, both for the train and the sea crossing. Tickets for a child under twelve. How old would he be? Three or four, perhaps? The fat woman seemed to read her thoughts. 'He is four years old, I think. My grandson is that age. Once they are five they grow up very fast. This one is still like a baby.'

The middle-aged man sitting next to her had been watching all the time. 'They are spawning a whole new generation of Jews. Soon we will be overrun by them. They took my custom away from me. My business was ruined. The Germans are right. We should get rid of them before it is too late.'

'They murdered Our Lord.' The woman in the corner seat spoke up. She was dressed in black, a heavy silver cross hanging from her neck. She fingered it reverently. 'The Jews are stained with the blood of Christ. They denied Him. Betrayed Him.' Her eyes accused Anna. '*You* are one of them, too, aren't you? That is why the mother chose you. She could tell.'

They were all staring at her and the boy, every one of them, and the compartment was full of hatred. She had never felt such hate before nor seen it written on people's faces. The boy had seen it, too, and he began to whimper and bury himself against her. She held him tightly. 'Have *you* papers yourself?' the fat woman demanded. 'When we cross into Germany they will want to see that they are all in order. They are very strict. As for the child, I shall report that he is not authorized.'

Anna lifted the boy off her lap and dragged her

suitcase down from the rack. The compartment door had stuck and none of them moved to help her open it. At last the catch gave and she wrenched the door open. Out in the corridor she steadied herself against the rocking of the train and holding the child by one hand, the suitcase in the other, made her way down the carriage. The boy was crying again, whimpering and wailing, but she gripped hold of his hand and pulled him on. She could not have stayed in that compartment with those people, not for one more moment. Every compartment that she passed was full and whenever a face turned to look at her through the glass she imagined in it the same hatred as in the others. She had almost reached the end of the train before she found a compartment with vacant seats. The only occupants were an elderly couple, both fast asleep, propped up against each other, and a nun who glanced up from her book and smiled at her. She slid the door open and tugged the boy in after her. When she had put the suitcase up on the rack she sat down in the corner by the window and took him on her lap again and cradled him until at last he stopped whimpering and fell asleep. The nun watched her. She had a nice face but she was wearing a heavy crucifix on her breast with the dead Jesus hanging by his nailed hands. She will be just like that other woman, Anna thought, if she suspects what we are. The train rattled on and Anna leant her head back against the seat and closed her eyes. After a while, rocked by the train's motion, she, too, slept.

She awoke later with a start and found that she had been asleep for over an hour. The nun smiled at her again. 'You have been fast asleep; the little one, too. You must both have been tired.' She spoke in German but with a strong French accent. Anna said, in French, 'Where are we?'

'We have left Linz. We will be at the German border quite soon.'

The boy was still asleep, his head lolling against her. She must find the papers before they reached the frontier. The brown coat had two small pockets at the front but they were both empty. She unbuttoned the coat and searched carefully but there were no more pockets and no papers. The nun leaned forward. 'You are in trouble, my child? Can I help you?'

She was old, Anna saw. The light from the window showed up all the lines and wrinkles; under the starched wimple her hair must be white, like Grandmama's. Her eyes were kind and nothing like the eyes of the people in the other compartment. 'He is supposed to have papers . . . a letter, a passport, something . . . I can't find anything.'

'He is your little brother?'

'No. He's nothing to do with me. I've never seen him before. His mother gave him to me at the station at Vienna and asked me to look after him on the journey to England. I have his tickets but there is nothing else.'

'Have you looked underneath his clothes? Perhaps something is sewn in or tied to him?'

She lifted the woollen jumper and unbuttoned

the shirt. Underneath was a vest and underneath the vest was a leather pouch attached to the child by a cord round his neck. Inside there was some paper money, rolled and tied with an elastic band, a folded piece of paper and a photograph. The photograph was of the woman on the platform, the mother. She was dressed in a flowered frock and smiling happily at whoever had held the camera; on the back were two words, written in ink. *Deine Mami*. Anna opened out the letter. There was an address at the top – somewhere in Essex in England. The letter had been written in German and then repeated in English. She read it through quickly. *To whom it may concern, this is to state that I, Vera Heine will take my sister's child, Daniel Isler into the home of my husband and myself and care for him as one of our family and be responsible for his welfare and maintenance in all respects . . .* She looked inside the pouch once more but there was nothing else. 'There is no passport. Nothing official. Just a letter . . .'

'Let me see.' The nun took it from her. 'I do not read English, but the German is clear to me.' She took some spectacles from the folds of her habit. After a moment she said, 'I am afraid this may not be enough. They may not let him pass.'

'What would they do?'

'Send him back to Vienna.'

'But his mother will think he's on his way to England. And there is no way to find her – except for a photograph with no name.' The train was starting to slow down; they would soon be stopping at the German border. 'If they can't send him back then they may have to keep him,' the nun said. 'Enquiries will need to be made.'

'I can't let that happen. He's Jewish. Jews are not safe in Germany.'

The nun nodded. 'Then we must think of a way . . .' The elderly couple were stirring, smoothing their clothing, finding their passports. The train was coming into the station, slowing to a stop. Doors began to open and a uniformed figure passed the compartment door. 'Give the child to me,' the nun said. '*Quickly.*' She took him on her lap and when he began to wake up, stroked his head and spoke to him softly. 'You must be very good, my little one, and keep very quiet. Do not speak a word.'

The door slid back and the German frontier guard stood there. 'Your passes, please.' He took his time over the elderly couple's documents, while the man and woman watched him anxiously. Then his eyes moved on to her. 'Yours, Fräulein.' She waited while he examined her passport, comparing the photograph carefully with her, turning more pages slowly. 'What is your destination, Fräulein?'

'I am going to London.'

'Why?'

'I am at school there.'

'*So* . . .' he turned. 'You are not staying in Germany?'

'No.'

He stared at her a moment and then returned the passport to her. 'Sister, if you please.'

The nun produced her French passport and he looked it over. 'And the child?'

'He is in my charge.'

'He has a passport? Papers?'

'No. He is an orphan. I am taking him to our convent near Regensburg to be cared for there. It was his mother's last wish before she died. She entrusted him to me, and to God.'

'That's all very well but he must have a correct pass. I cannot allow him to proceed without that.'

The nun smiled her gentle smile. 'I am sure that you are a kind and understanding man. This poor little innocent has just lost his mother, as well as his father. He is completely alone in the world and should not be distressed further. I shall say a special prayer for you and God will certainly bless and reward you for your compassion.'

Anna held her breath. After a moment the man grunted. 'Very well. But see that he does not travel again without the correct papers.' He slammed the door shut and moved on to the next compartment. The nun made the sign of the cross. 'I have to leave the train at Regensburg. When you reach the Dutch border I should tell them that the child is an orphan and you are taking him to his aunt in England. It is near the truth and you can show the letter . . . Smile at the guard and flatter him, and if that does not work, then weep.'

Anna took the little boy along to the dining-car for some supper but he had no interest in food. She tried to tempt him with some of the soup, holding a spoonful to his mouth, but he turned his head away, shaking it fiercely. 'Come, Daniel.' At least she knew his name now. 'Try to eat a little bit.' He looked at her bleakly. 'Wo ist Mami?'

'You will see her again very soon. You are just going to stay with your Aunt Vera for a little holiday. You remember your Aunt Vera?' He shook his head again. She offered the soup once more. 'Just one spoonful, Daniel, for Mami . . .'

She found her reserved sleeping compartment, partly undressed the boy and put him down in the single bunk, tucking him in. He fell asleep almost at once. There was no room to lie beside him without risking disturbing him and so she curled up uncomfortably at the end of the bunk with a blanket wrapped round her shoulders. The train pounded on through the night across Germany.

She woke from a fitful sleep with a stiff neck, and pins and needles down one leg. The train had stopped at another station and she raised the blind and peered out. She could see the illuminated sign: FRANKFURT. The platform was empty except for two uniformed men standing nearby. They were dressed in black caps with high shiny peaks, knee-high black boots and badges sewn on their left sleeves showing a black, hooked cross. A young man carrying a suitcase came into view, wanting to board the train, and they moved to bar his way. He was wearing a Jewish yarmulke on his head, and looked very like gentle Gideon of the Fischer family. He put down his battered suitcase, fumbled in his coat pockets for papers and stood meekly while they were examined. Instead of returning the papers, the two men began to ask questions. She could not hear what they were saying but she could see that the young man was frightened. They stood over him, like bullies, while he grew more and more bewildered, shrugging his shoulders and shaking his head. They were still asking him questions and he was still trying to answer them as the train pulled out.

It was daylight when they crossed the border into Holland at Venlo. A dull, grey dawn. The child had woken and she was washing his hands and face at the basin when the Dutch official rapped and entered the sleeping compartment. Smile at him, the nun had said, and if that doesn't work, weep. The man was quite young, tall and nice-looking. She smiled dazzlingly at him and explained that the little boy was an orphan going to his aunt in England. His father had been killed in an accident and his mother had just died of a terrible disease. It was unbearably sad. The child had been alone for three days before he had been discovered beside his mother's body, clinging to her. They had had to prise his fingers free, to tear him away . . . She showed the letter and, for good measure, let her eyes fill with tears. He looked at the letter and then down at her. She knew that he was admiring her and moved a step closer to gaze pleadingly up into his face, a tear running down one cheek. 'It would be such a kindness if you would let him pass.'

'Is your own passport in order?'

'Yes, indeed.'

He turned pages. 'I am sorry about the little boy. I lost my own mother when I was a small child.'

'How dreadful for you! Then you will understand how it is for him?'

'Oh, yes.'

'I should always be grateful. Always.' Another tear spilled over.

He handed back her passport. 'You can dry your tears, Fräulein, the boy can pass.' As he closed the door again he said, with a small smile, 'And I shall remember your undying gratitude, in case we ever meet again.'

She coaxed Daniel to eat some breakfast – a piece of bread with a slice of sausage and a cup of milk. He looked deathly pale and listless and she wondered anxiously if he was ill. He had stopped asking for his mother and hardly spoke a word.

At the Dutch port the train took them close to the ship. She was rehearsing her story again, with embellishments, but at the gangplank they were waved on board among a crowd of other passengers. She stood with the child at the deck rails, holding his hand and watching as the sailors untied the ropes and the ship began to move away from the quayside. The gap widened and became a gulf. Beside her, the child had started to cry again and call for his mother. In comforting him, she forgot her own misery.

Out to sea, it was cold and rough and the ship began to roll horribly. She took the boy below to sit in a saloon but the motion was worse there and after a while he began to retch. She hurried him back up on deck and took him to the rail where he vomited up what little breakfast he had eaten. Soon after she was sick herself. She found a bench in the lee of one of the funnels and held the child on her lap, trying to keep him warm. They were both shivering violently but the fresh air was better than the stuffiness of below decks. We are in the same boat, she thought – literally and otherwise. Both sent away from our country and neither of us wanting to go. Supposing the English authorities would not allow him to land? Would he be sent back again and have to travel through Germany once more where men in black uniforms patrolled stations interrogating Jews? Surely they would let him stay and Lizzie's mother would know what to do once she got him to London. She would find the aunt in Essex. She took the letter out of her shoulder-bag to look at the address again. The wind made it flap and flutter wildly and, as she unfolded it, snatched it from her hands and whirled it away down the deck and over the rails into the sea.

'You say there was a letter, miss?'

'Yes. A letter from his aunt, promising that she would take care of him. It was lost on the boat. The wind blew it away.'

'I see.' The English immigration officer stared at her. He was a very ordinary-looking man, short, and with a small moustache the colour of dry sand and gooseberry eyes that had no expression at all. She knew that smiling at him would be a complete waste of time. He would not be impressed; it might even set him against her. 'And how did you come to be in charge of the boy?'

'I told you. At the station at Vienna. I was asked to look after him for the journey.'

'By whom?'

She had been going to spin the orphan story again but her instinct told her that this was a time for the truth. 'His mother came up to me just as the train was leaving. There was no chance to refuse. She just gave me the child and his tickets and then the train left.'

'What was her name?'

'It must be Isler – like the boy. His name is Daniel. She never said her first name – there was no time. The aunt's name is Vera Heine. She promised that she would look after him at her home.' She put her arm protectively round the child's shoulders. She could tell that he was terrified by the man.

'This aunt, where does she live?' He was as bad as the two bullies at Frankfurt, barking his questions.

'I can't remember. The address was on the letter. Now it is gone. It was somewhere in Essex. The town began with the letter C, I think. There is a photograph of the mother . . .' She had to unbutton the child's coat and then undo more buttons to reach the leather pouch. She spoke to him soothingly in German. 'It's all right, Daniel, there's nothing to be afraid of.' She handed over the photograph to the man. 'Here it is. That was the woman at the station in Vienna.'

'This is no help, I'm afraid. It could be anyone. It's no proof of his identity, no proof of the aunt's existence. No proof of anything at all.'

She stared at him coldly, hating him and his gooseberry eyes and his nasty little ginger moustache. 'I thought the English were supposed to be civilized. This child is Jewish. I am Jewish, too. Do you know what they are doing to Jewish people in Germany and now in Austria? They are persecuting them. That is why Daniel's mother wanted him to come here – to be safe from persecution. The English will take a child, she said to me. She believed that, but she was wrong. You are not good at all. You don't care. It's nothing to you what happens to him. You are going to turn him away just because there are no silly papers and because you will not believe what I have told you.' Her voice had risen hysterically and heads were turning.

The immigration officer said mildly, 'Calm yourself, Miss Stein. As a matter of fact, I do believe you. And we're not such a bad lot, you know. I think you'll find that Daniel will be able to stay.'

'Did they let him?' Lizzie had been listening to the whole story. 'What happened.'

'In the end, they were very kind and I was sorry for what I said. They found out that the aunt lived in Colchester not so far from Harwich and they telephoned her and arranged for her to fetch Daniel. There were forms to be filled in, of course, and everything of that sort, but I'm sure they were going to let him stay.'

'So you left him with them.'

'They promised they would look after him. There was a woman officer there – very motherly – and she promised to take good care of him until the aunt arrived. There was nothing more I could do. Perhaps one day I may go and see him. I have the address.'

'He was lucky his mother chose you. Someone else might have not bothered so much.'

Anna was silent for a moment. 'I never really believed my parents about the hatred for the Jews, you know, until I saw the faces of those people on the train, Lizzie. I was afraid. Really *afraid*. It was evil. And then when I saw the men at Frankfurt questioning that poor Jewish boy, stopping him from getting on the train, I was even more frightened. Until then I had thought that Mama and Papa were making a big fuss over nothing. But now I know that they are right.'

'Ease the jib, Matt.' Guy yelled it at him above the wind. 'OK,' he yelled back. He eased the sheet a little. The tide had swept them out from the wide mouth of the river estuary into the open sea. Waves thudded against the boat's hull, water breaking high over her bows and sloshing around in the bilge. The *Rose* ploughed on steadily. Foulness Point was a mile astern when they hit a sudden rain-squall that blotted out the fast receding coastline. Matt was half blinded by rain and spray as they beat their way to windward through the squall.

When Guy had suggested the trip he'd gone along with the idea at once, faking keenness. In his guts, he'd been gripped by the same old terror. The river was one thing; the sea another. Guy, poring happily over charts, hadn't a clue how he felt, of course. And that was the way he wanted it: he'd fight his demons alone. He was deeply ashamed of his fear. It was pathetic and weak. Guy would be sympathetic, but mystified; Father appalled that a son of his could possibly be scared stiff of going to sea. Mother would worry for him and she'd probably try to stop him sailing at all. But he'd never conquer the fear unless he carried on.

The further away from land, the worse his terror became and he started to get the shakes again. The jib sheet kept slipping from his grasp.

'Matt . . . for God's sake, wake up! What the hell's the matter with you? Can't you keep the sheet in tight?'

'Sorry.' He pulled it in hurriedly.

The Rose butted her way northerly. They were still beating to wind and Guy began hauling in the mainsheet, ready to tack. The instant the boom went over, he let it out all the way. He looked in his element at the helm. Completely at home. No fears or doubts at all. Matt would have given anything to be like Guy.

The weather worsened and they were making little headway and taking a real buffeting. It took them almost two hours to get within sight of

West Mersea at the mouth of the river Black-water. To Matt's relief, Guy decided against trying to go any further. 'Better go about,' he shouted. 'Let's put in a reef before we head for home. Lower the main halyard, will you, Matt.' The *Rose* wallowed heavily, her canvas flapping and cracking like pistol shots. The manoeuvre seemed to take for ever. 'Like to take her now, Matt?' Guy was offering him the tiller and mainsheet. He shook his head. 'It's OK, thanks.' Coward, he thought, wretchedly. *Coward.*

Chapter Nine

'The English play at their sports, I think. They do not take them seriously.' Herr von Reichenau watched a group of fourth-formers waiting to take part in a swimming race, laughing and jostling each other.

Otto said, 'I thought so too. But when they stop playing the fool they try as hard as we do.'

'But they will not win unless they prepare. A school sports day would be very different in our country.' Herr von Reichenau looked around at the other visitors strolling across the lawns: the summer frocks and shady hats, the blazers and panamas, the old school ties. 'This is a social event, that's all. However, it is very pleasant. All very English. You must introduce me to some of your friends.'

Otto opened his mouth to say that he had no friends at the school and then shut it again. His father would view it as a serious failure on his part – the failure to make useful contacts. He checked his watch. 'My race will start in approximately thirty-five minutes.'

'Approximately?'

'Sometimes they are late.'

'I am not very surprised. What race is this?'

'The crawl. We do six lengths. We have already done the heats and this is the final for the cup.'

His father nodded. 'See that you win.'

It was Guy that he must beat. The other four would be easy – his time was much faster than theirs – but Guy had only been two seconds slower. Otto lined up at the shallow end of the pool, ready for a racing start. His heart was pounding furiously. He wanted to win. He *must* win. Not just to please his father, but for himself. If he could not make friends, at least he could win at sports. They would have to take note of him, congratulate him and clap him on the back, like they did with others. 'Well done, Otto,' they would say. 'Jolly good show!'

The whistle blew and he launched his body, fully outstretched, into the air. It hit the water flat with a stinging crack and he was into his stride at once, churning arm-over-arm down the length of the pool. At the end, he flipped into a fast turn and set off again. By the end of the third length he knew that he was ahead with only one other swimmer anywhere near him. And he could tell that it was Guy. He could hear the shouts and screams of encouragement from the spectators and knew they were for Guy, not him. He turned again for the fourth length but still he could not increase his lead and on the fifth he knew that Guy was closing the gap. As they turned for the final length they were almost level and the shouts for Guy roared in his ears. They drove him on. Made him fight the harder and swim as he had never swum before. When he flung his arm out to touch the end of the pool he was not sure, at first, which of them had won – until he heard the groans and the half-hearted claps and saw the disappointed faces looking down on him. Guy was holding out his hand across the water and he shook it firmly. Neither of them had the breath left to speak.

'Bad luck, old chap. He just pipped you at the post. You swam like blazes.'

Guy forced a smile. He'd won the cup for the past four years and he was sick as hell to have lost it this last summer term before he left the school. His father, though, would expect him to take defeat sportingly and act as though he didn't mind. To lose the cup was bad enough but to lose it to von Reichenau was the end. 'There's still the hurdling,' he said casually. 'I might pick up a cup there.'

'Do your best, Guy. You can't do more.'

The final of the hurdling was the last sports event of the day. Once again, he would be racing against von Reichenau and, once again, he knew that the race would be decided between the two of them. Warming up before the start he avoided looking at the German, who would be running three lanes away. He could sense the expectation among the spectators, hear the buzz of excitement. The school prided itself on its athletics, and the hurdling cup was specially prized. He would be expected to win. Everyone would be willing him to do so. If von Reichenau beat him it would be unpleasant for both of them. In spite of his deep disappointment over the swimming race he had felt embarrassed at the obvious favouritism shown. They should have applauded von Reichenau decently.

He positioned himself carefully, head down, the tips of his fingers touching the grass, toes dug in, his whole body poised ready. When the starting pistol fired he took off like a rocket. The rest were somewhere behind him, except for von Reichenau on his right. He forced himself faster, hurtling over hurdle after hurdle, and streaking towards the finish. When he flung himself across the line there was a storm of cheering and clapping and people ran up and slapped him on the back as he bent over, gasping for breath. He knew that he must have won, but that it had been a pretty close thing. When he'd recovered he looked round for von Reichenau but he was nowhere to be seen.

'You let him beat you, Otto. That was a pity.'

'He is very fast. I was tired after the swimming.'

'No excuses, please. You must be getting soft and out of condition. You are starting to be like the English. Perhaps it was not such a good idea for you to come here. When you join the German army you will need to be much tougher. Disciplined. Dedicated. Defeat is not a consideration – in any sphere. You understand that?'

'Yes, of course, Father.'

'What is the name of the youth who beat you?'

'Ransome. Guy Ransome.'

'What is his father? What work does he do?'

'He is in the Royal Navy, I believe.'

'Indeed? Is the son a friend of yours?'

'Not precisely.'

'Nevertheless, I should like to meet his father very much. Please introduce me at the first opportunity.'

The sports prize-giving took place in the marquee. When Otto went up to receive his swimming cup, the applause was merely polite. When Guy went to collect his for the hurdling everybody cheered and clapped loudly. So much for the famous English sense of fairness, Otto thought bitterly. So much for doing the decent thing that they talked about so much.

After the prize-giving tea was served: trays of soggy sandwiches and terrible cakes. Otto went in search of his father and found him talking with a bearded man and a woman in blue.

'Ah, Otto, there you are. I have had the pleasure of meeting Captain and Mrs Ransome – the parents of Guy. You will wish to congratulate them, of course, on his fine victory over the hurdles. Allow me to present my son, Otto.'

He shook their hands, bowing and clicking his heels smartly. 'Splendid race you ran,' the father said. 'Gave Guy something to think about.' The mother smiled at him. She was wearing the sort of floppy straw hat that seemed typical of English women. 'You certainly did. It was quite a change for Guy. Congratulations on the swimming cup. You're a superb swimmer.'

'Thank you.' He could see, to his surprise, that she genuinely meant what she said. But he was still bitter with the English.

She looked up at him from under the floppy brim. 'How do you like being at school in England?'

He said politely, 'I enjoy it very much, of course.'

'It must be difficult for you, though . . . sometimes.'

He realized that she understood, and he was grateful. He glanced towards his father who was deep in conversation with the captain. 'I am the . . . what do you say?'

'Odd man out. That will change, given time.'

'I do not think so.'

'I'm sure it will. You're a new boy still, aren't you? They always give them a hard time to start with. It's part of a silly tradition.'

'Yes, the English love their traditions,' he said. 'We have traditions in Germany, too. But they are different.' He did not add that most English traditions that he had come across appeared extremely stupid and pointless.

'I expect we seem quite childish sometimes. Hard to understand. In Germany, you apparently take things more seriously.'

'Our country has suffered much,' he said. 'There has been much to be serious about. It is only now that we begin our recovery under our Führer.'

'We've all suffered, Otto. But don't let's speak of that. It's all in the past. Tell me about your family. Do you have brothers and sisters?'

'No. I am the only child.'

'Is your mother in Germany?'

'My mother is dead.'

'I'm so sorry.'

'She died many years ago.' He could hardly remember her at all – just a vague impression of some woman holding him. It had always been his father who had counted in his life.

'Are you going back to Berlin for the summer holidays?'

'I think we are to remain in England. My father has not said yet.'

'Well, if you do, you must come and stay with us for a while. Guy would like to have you, I'm sure. Someone of his own age.'

And I am very sure that he would not, he thought. 'You are most kind.'

'Do you sail?'

'Yes. We have a boat.'

She looked surprised. 'Berlin is a long way from the sea.'

'We keep it at Schleswig in the north. We sail in the Baltic. In summer, that is. It is very enjoyable there. Very beautiful.'

She nodded. 'I'm sure it must be. We live very close to the sea – the North Sea – right on an estuary. We have a boat, too. She's just an old fishing boat – nothing grand at all – but the boys seem to have fun with her. My husband's in the Royal Navy.'

He glanced, again, at his father still talking with the Captain. 'Yes, Guy told me.'

'What does your father do?'

'He is a diplomat. At the moment he is attached to the German Embassy in London – on liaison work.'

'How interesting.' She looked away from him. 'Here are Guy and Matt.' Otto watched while she embraced her sons. He wondered whether his own mother would have embraced him like that. To Guy Frau Ransome said, 'I've just been chatting to your friend Otto. We must have him to stay with us in the holidays. He loves sailing. We can ask Lizzie and Anna, too. It will be great fun for you all.'

Afterwards, his father drew him aside. 'Frau Ransome would like you to stay with them in August. You will go, of course. I have to return to Berlin then, myself.'

'I should much rather come to Berlin, Father.'

'Later on in the holidays. It is more useful that you go to the Ransomes. You will make yourself agreeable to them. Be very charming to everyone, especially to the mother, and keep your eyes and ears open at all times. Remember anything that anybody remarks about Germany. And listen to everything that the captain says. Ask about his ship, about other ships in the Royal Navy. And take photographs of the place where they live – the estuary, the approaches from the sea, the coastline. Take as many as you can, but without attracting attention.'

'What is all this for?'

'It is for the Fatherland, Otto. For our beloved country.'

Liebe Mina,

Thank you for your letter and for sending me the photograph of Felix. I can see that he is very handsome.

The school term is nearly finished here and everybody else is excited about the summer holidays. I am the only one who is not. Lizzie and I have been invited to stay with the Ransomes again. It will be very nice to see Matt, but not Guy.

Mama and Papa are still waiting for their emigration papers. Everybody tells them that it will take time and that they must be patient. Once I wanted them to stay in Vienna, but now I want them to leave as soon as they can. If you had been with me on that railway journey, Mina, you would feel the same. I went to Colchester to see the little boy, Daniel, the other day. The aunt is very kind and married to a good man. They have two children of their own and I am sure that they will take good care of Daniel. He remembered me and I think he was happy to see me again. The aunt says his mother is trying to get emigration papers but she is still waiting, too, just like Mama and Papa. Her husband died in an accident so she is all alone, poor creature. They were very grateful to me for bringing Daniel to England and asked me to visit them again. I shall try to do so whenever I can.

Yesterday, I cut off Lizzie's plaits. She asked me to do it and so we borrowed the kitchen scissors from Mrs Hodges, the cook. There was a big row when Frau Ellis first saw Lizzie with short hair but it was all right in the end. I think it suits Lizzie. After all, she's fourteen now. I haven't worn the lipstick yet. Perhaps I'll take it to Tideways and wear it there.

Please write again very soon.

Deine Anna.

Chapter Ten

Aunt Sheila met them at Burnham station in the open Alvis. 'My goodness, Lizzie, I hardly recognized you. You look very grown-up.' Lizzie fingered her short hair self-consciously. She was rather sorry now that she'd got rid of the plaits. Anna sat in the front seat, beside Aunt Sheila, and her long hair blew around her like a thick dark veil. They drove out of Burnham and along the lane that led to Tideways. The hedge-rows had the dry and dusty look of late summer and some of the cornfields had already been harvested. In one of them a reaping machine drawn by two big shire horses was cutting a steady swathe through the crop. The car dipped under the railway bridge and the lane came out at the river's edge. The tide was high and several ships were on the water, sails bellied out with wind. 'Guy and Matt have gone out,' Aunt Sheila said. 'But they'll be back soon. We have a boy from their school staying with us for a while. He was at a bit of a loose end for the holidays, poor chap, so we asked him here and they've taken him sailing with them.'

They went along by the river then turned in through the white gateway, past the clump of trees with the two tall Scots pines and up the gravel driveway to the front door. Nereus came out to greet them. He looked fatter and there were grey hairs round his muzzle that hadn't been there the previous summer, and he moved more slowly. Lizzie and Anna were sharing the same bedroom as before and Lizzie went to look out of the open window at the view of the river. Among the boats she caught sight of one in the distance with a red sail. 'I think I can see the *Rose*. Shall we go down to the jetty and wait for her to come in?'

Anna had flopped onto her bed. 'It's too hot. You go, if you like.' Lizzie went downstairs and Nereus, who was lying in the hall, rose stiffly to his feet to follow her through the drawing-room and out onto the terrace and across the lawn. She walked down the wooden steps at the far end and out onto the jetty. The river was shimmering in the evening sunlight and she had to shade her eyes to see the *Rose* again, much closer now, coming steadily towards her. Guy was at the helm, Matt beside him, and she could see a third figure as well. Matt waved and she waved back. She stood watching and waiting as Guy brought the boat in. The mainsail came tumbling down and she drifted gently alongside. Matt hopped out with the painter, grinning. 'I wasn't sure if it was you at first, Lizzie.' He tied the rope securely. 'What've you done with your plaits?'

'Cut them off.'

He was a lot taller, though still not as tall as Guy. He's sixteen now, she calculated. He and Anna are the same age. Guy was still messing about in the boat but the third figure had sprung out onto the jetty. 'This is Otto,' Matt said. 'He's staying with us. He's from Germany.'

'I am very pleased to make your acquaintance.' The boy stepped forward to shake her hand very formally. He was just as tall as Guy with hair so fair that it looked bleached, and very pale blue eyes. Guy had jumped out, looking irritated. 'That damned halyard keeps slipping . . . Oh, hallo, Lizzie. How are you?' He didn't seem to notice her new hair at all.

They walked up to the house and went round to the side entrance to clean up at the tap. As they all went through from the kitchen passageway into the hall, Anna was coming down the stairs. She had changed into a different frock – a new one that she had brought back from Vienna. And she was wearing lipstick. She stopped when she saw them, one hand on the banister, and there was a moment's dead silence before Guy spoke.

'Hallo, Anna.'

'Hallo, Guy.' She smiled at Matt. 'Hallo, darling Matt.' She came down the rest of the stairs.

Matt said, 'I'm taller than you at last, Annie.'

'So you are.'

'This is Otto von Reichenau. From Berlin.'

Otto bowed and clicked his heels. '*Wie geht es Ihnen, es ist schon Sie kennenzulernen.*'

Anna froze. She looked at him coldly with her

214

beautiful green eyes. 'If you do not mind, I prefer to speak in English.'

Otto was up by six o'clock. His father had always insisted on early rising and the habit had become so ingrained that he could never sleep late. He had taken to going for a walk before the others came down for breakfast. The old black dog was lying on a rug in the hall and thumped his tail. Otto could hear the cook at work in the kitchen as he let himself quietly out of the side door. Outside he stopped for a moment. It was a beautiful morning. The sun already felt quite warm and the birds were singing loudly. He could never remember hearing such birdsong in Germany. He skirted the lawn, his feet marking the dew. The croquet hoops and stumps were still there from the evening before and the memory of his humiliating defeat still rankled. He had never played the game before but that gave him no excuse to have finished last. The girl, Anna, had not played fairly. She had kept knocking his ball out of the way so that he had had no chance of making progress. Guy had won, Matt had been second, Lizzie third, Anna fourth and himself the very last of all. They had stood waiting for him to finish, watching him, and he had been so furious that he had missed the final hoop five times before he had managed to hit the ball through. They had all found it very amusing. 'Bad luck!' Guy had said casually. 'You'll soon get the hang of it. How about some tennis?' But in his anger, he had refused.

He had watched them play a doubles – Matt and Anna against Guy and Lizzie – and nobody took that seriously either. The grass court was full of bumps and holes so that they kept getting bad bounces, and the chalk lines were not clear in some places. He noticed several wrong calls and tried to correct them. 'Your serve was out, Lizzie. It crossed the line.' Guy had flapped a hand. 'Doesn't matter, Otto. Matt took it.' Anna hit the ball so hard and so wildly that it kept going out and he had to go and retrieve it like a dog. He had begun to wonder whether she was doing it on purpose. Matt managed well with his crippled arm but he was no match for Guy. Otto pitied him. Physical imperfection was a grave misfortune. Ideally, the human race should be bred for perfection, just as racehorses were bred to eliminate all faults. A teacher at school had pointed this out to them. Otto had watched Guy's tennis and seen that he was good. Of course he wasn't playing anything like his best. He had been letting Lizzie do most of her own shots, but Otto noticed that he had poached just enough to make sure that they won in the end. By then it was no longer light enough to continue playing, otherwise he would have liked to take on Guy and make up for the croquet humiliation. He had studied his strokes carefully. Guy's forehand was very strong, but his backhand was erratic and his second serve always fell too short. He was sure that he could beat him.

Otto walked on down to the jetty. The river was flat calm, sea birds pecking about in the mud and seaweed at its edges. He had brought his camera so that he could take some more photographs, as his father had instructed. The scenery looked drab and featureless to him. He didn't think any of it was a patch on the Schlei at Schleswig or that the North Sea was anything like as pleasant for sailing as the tideless Baltic. The Baltic was one of the most beautiful places he knew. Deep and clear and cold fiords. Sheltered inlets. Water shining between folds of hills. Green pastures and woods on the lower slopes with scattered farms and white cottages. Nothing he had seen in this corner of England could compare. As for the Ransomes' boat, he had barely been able to conceal his scorn. He looked her over now, tied up at the jetty. *Rose of England!* Such a ridiculously grand name for an old tub. The contrast with his father's yacht could not have been greater. Under sail or power, *Nixe* cut effortlessly through the water; she was graceful, responsive, elegant – a water-nymph like her name. She had three sails, a foredeck, a roomy cockpit and, below, a well-appointed saloon and cabin. And she towed her own dinghy. The Ransomes' boat had no engine, two tiny lockers, and was clearly designed to wallow round the shoals taking on netloads of stinking fish.

He watched the sea birds for a while, and the gradual creep of the incoming tide over the wet mud. The girl, Anna, was very beautiful, of course. When he had first seen her standing on the stairs he had been quite struck . . . so struck that he had almost been unable to speak. And then, in a little while, he had realized that she was a Jewess. There had been several families of Jews living in the same building as his father's apartment in Berlin – until they had all moved away. His father had always been at pains to point them out and had forbidden him to have anything to do with them. So he had learned to recognize a Jew easily. And Berlin was full of things mocking Jews – cartoon posters of ugly, avaricious old money-lenders, crude slogans daubed on walls, boycotting banners carried in streets, books in shops . . . he had seen a children's book called *The Poisoned Mushroom* all about how to detect the poisoned mushrooms – the Jews. They had only themselves to blame, his father said. The Jews had taken over too much for their own good: banks, stores, businesses, professions. They were everywhere. And all the time they grew richer and more powerful, trampling over the backs of the Aryan people. Jews were not Germans. They were foreigners, breeding like cuckoos in borrowed nests. It was time to be rid of them. To purge the Fatherland. Germany must be cleansed. The Führer himself had preached it at the big rally that Otto had gone to with his father in Berlin last year. Above the Führer's head a great banner had proclaimed: *The Jews are our misfortune*. His father would not be pleased if he knew that the Ransomes had invited a Jewess; it would be wiser not to tell him.

He walked along the edge of the shore for some distance, taking photographs. At dinner the evening before, he had brought up the subject of the Royal Navy with the captain, but his polite questions had been met with only the vaguest answers and the captain, far from seeming proud of his country's fleet, had said something about 'a few old buckets still managing to stay afloat'. Otto thought that he would never understand the English. Whenever they had something that they had reason to be proud of, they acted as though it was nothing special at all.

By the time he had returned to the house, curtains had been drawn back at windows and there was a tantalizing aroma of frying bacon when he let himself in through the side entrance. He felt ravenously hungry. Captain and Frau Ransome were seated at the dining-room table and Guy was helping himself from the silver dishes on the sideboard. Frau Ransome smiled at him. 'Good morning, Otto. They say on the wireless that it's going to be lovely today. I've suggested to Guy that you all go off in the *Rose* with a picnic. Would you like to do that?'

'Of course.' He would have preferred to challenge Guy to a tennis match but he had been taught to defer to a hostess. 'I should like that very much.'

'Like to take the helm, Otto?'

'Oh . . . thank you.'

Matt, holding the jib sheet, watched The Hun scramble aft and take over the mainsheet and tiller from Guy. He seemed astonished at being invited to do so. The patched mainsail filled with wind and *Rose* swung round obligingly and headed upstream. Otto looked every bit as competent as Guy and Matt guessed that, like Guy, he must think the boat something of a joke. He had told them about sailing in the Baltic and all about his father's wonderful yacht. Poor old *Rose* couldn't compete. But Matt liked her. He felt safer and more confident with her than he had ever done with *Bean Goose*. There was something kindly about the way she responded and she was far more forgiving of mistakes. If any boat could ever cure him of his fear of the sea, *Rose* might do it.

'Are you going to choose the picnic place, Guy? Because if so, I hope there will not be flies.'

'You can choose it, Anna.'

'You are in a very generous mood. What is the matter with you?'

'What do you mean, what's the matter with me?'

'Well, it is most unusual. In general, you want to do everything.'

'Rubbish.' Guy turned his head. 'I'd go about pretty soon, Otto.'

'OK. Ready about. Lee-oh,' Otto said in his very correct English. He put the helm over and *Rose* heeled very gently; they all ducked their heads under the boom as it went over. He hauled in the mainsheet and Matt trimmed the jib. There was just enough wind to carry them along at a slow and stately pace. Anna stood up, shielding her eyes against the sun.

'We must find a nice field with no cows. I think I can see one.'

'Sit down, Anna.'

'I cannot see unless I stand up, Guy.' She stood on tiptoe, making the *Rose* rock. 'Yes, there is one further on, on the left side.'

'Port, Anna. Not left. How about somewhere to land?'

'I cannot see that yet.'

'We have to have a decent place to put the boat safely. We can't just stop and get out, you know. This isn't a bus.'

Guy and Anna went on wrangling over it. The first spot turned out to be no good.

'What is wrong with it?'

'Not enough room for a boat.'

The one after that wasn't right either.

'Why not?'

'It was all mud, Anna. *Rose* would get completely bogged down. We'd have a frightful time pushing her off again.'

'We could leave her in the water.'

'There was nothing to tie her to, and we don't happen to carry an anchor, in case you hadn't noticed.'

Luckily the third was all right. There was a bit of firm beach – just wide enough to take the *Rose* – and Otto timed everything perfectly, bringing her in side-on, sails down, to drift to a stop. They dragged her up onto the shore by the forestay and the shroud, unloaded the picnic and carried it across to a shady spot under a tree.

'Satisfied, Anna?'

'The grass is not so good, but at least there are no flies.'

'If I hear you grumbling about a single thing, I'm going to throw you in the river. That's a promise.'

'You would not dare to, Guy.'

'Try me.'

'Supposing I can't swim?'

'You said you could. I presume you were telling the truth about a thing like that.'

'Of course I was.'

'Then you'd better watch out.'

The rug was spread out and the girls unpacked the picnic and everything was fine, Matt thought, until Otto started to talk about Berlin. To hear him, you'd think there was no other city in the world to touch it. The streets, the squares, the monuments and buildings were magnificent, the stadium for the Olympic Games the greatest ever built. They all listened politely, except for Anna who suddenly said, 'But you have Adolf Hitler and he is not magnificent at all.'

Otto flushed. He said something sharply in German and Anna answered him in German too. Then she said, in English, 'Otto believes Adolf Hitler to be a very great man. I said I thought that he is not very great, but very evil.'

'Anna knows nothing of our Führer and yet she insults him.'

'Shut up, Anna,' Guy said lazily. He leaned on his elbow and took another bite of his sandwich. 'Don't be rude about Otto's Führer.'

'It is not a joke this time, Guy.'

'Oh, for heaven's sake . . . this is supposed to be a picnic.'

'Have another sandwich, Otto,' Lizzie said quickly. 'The cucumber ones are awfully good.'

'Thank you. I apologize. I forget myself.'

Anna had turned her back on him and he still looked very upset. Matt couldn't imagine getting upset about somebody saying things against Mr Chamberlain. Actually, they said them all the time. Lizzie was offering the sandwiches round again. He was rather sorry about the plaits; they'd been so much a part of her. Guy was lighting one of his cigarettes and there was another argument with Anna who wanted to try one.

'You're too young.'

'That's silly. You're only eighteen.'

'And you're only sixteen. Your parents wouldn't approve.'

'They are not here so they cannot know.'

'You won't like it. It'll make you sick.'

'How can you know? You don't know everything, Guy.'

In the end, he let her take a puff and laughed heartlessly when she started coughing. 'I told you so.' He offered one to Otto who shook his head.

'I think it is not very healthy, but thank you.'

He was a rum sort of chap, Matt thought. He hardly ever smiled and he didn't think he'd ever seen him laugh. Not once.

On the way back from the picnic, Anna was allowed to take the helm, once they were out in midstream. Guy sat right beside her showing her what to do.

'There is no need to tell me three times, Guy.'

'Well, you didn't do it properly the first or second. And if you don't keep her to windward you'll be in trouble. Look at the burgee.'

'The what?'

'The little flag at the top of the mast. That'll tell you what the wind's doing.'

'I cannot look at everything at once.'

They were rounding the bend after Shortpole Reach when the Chilvers' *Grey Heron* came into view, Tom and Harry waving. Anna let go of the tiller to wave back so that Guy had to make a grab for it. The two boats passed within a few yards of each other and Tom yelled across.

'Come over tomorrow afternoon for some tennis, all of you.'

The Chilvers lived two miles upstream from the Ransomes, on the opposite bank. Guy, who had learned to drive during the Easter holidays, borrowed the Alvis and Otto sat in the front passenger seat with Anna, Matt and Lizzie in the back. They had the top down and Guy drove fast, roaring along and changing gear with a flourish. The house was older than Tideways, and a lot grander, too. 'They've got bags of loot,' Guy commented drily as they spun up the long drive. 'As you can see.'

The brothers were outside, knocking up on an immaculate court. No bad bounces like at Tideways, Lizzie thought; the grass was so smooth you could have played billiards on it. Tom and Harry came over, dressed in equally immaculate tennis whites. They were both fair and good-looking – Harry a younger and slightly smaller version of Tom.

'How about some mixed doubles?' Tom suggested. 'OK with you two girls?' He was looking at Anna as he spoke. She was dressed in a long white cotton skirt and a yellow silk blouse – not proper tennis things at all – and she had borrowed an old pair of Matt's outgrown gym shoes. She shrugged. 'We are not at all good, are we, Lizzie?'

Tom smiled. 'That doesn't matter a bit. It's only a game. How about you and I taking on Lizzie and a partner? Just for a set. Her to choose.'

'If you like. You had better choose well, Lizzie.'

She chose Matt because she didn't want him left out of things and because Guy was too good. She suspected that Otto was, also. She felt all right with Matt. He wouldn't mind in the least if they lost – which they did. Two games to six. Tom had aimed lots of his shots at her which meant, of course, that they kept losing the point. The balls came whizzing at her over the net, very fast and low, and often she couldn't hit them at all. 'Sorry, Matt,' she said, as they came off the court. 'I played awfully badly.' 'No you didn't, Lizzie, you were brilliant. I went and let you down.' He winked at her. 'Still, as Tom says, it's only a game.'

The next match wasn't a game at all.

'OK, Guy. Harry and I challenge you and Otto. Best of three sets.' Tom was smiling but Lizzie knew it was going to be a serious contest. She and Matt and Anna went and sat on the grass bank by the court. 'Wake me up when they have finished,' Anna said. She lay back and put her straw hat over her eyes.

Lizzie had been right about Otto. He was just as good as Guy. In fact, his serve was better, she thought – very hard and very fast indeed and his backhand across the court was like lightning. Harry kept missing it which annoyed Tom. The score reached four all. 'It's going to be close,' Matt whispered. At five four to Guy and Otto, with Otto serving and within a point for the set, there was an argument over whether Tom's return shot was in or out. Tom maintained that it was in.

'I saw the chalk go up. Didn't you, Harry?'

'Yes, definitely.'

Guy said easily, 'Actually, I'm pretty sure it was out, Tom. I had a fairly good view from here.'

'The ball was out. I also see very well. It was beyond the line.' Otto looked at Tom coldly. 'You are mistaken.'

'I saw the chalk go up, old chap, like I said. That means it was in.'

'You suggest that I lie?'

'I'm just saying you didn't see it properly. Harry and I know this court pretty well.'

Guy called up, 'What do you lot think?'

'I think it was out,' Matt told him. 'Lizzie's not sure and Anna didn't see it at all.'

'Oh, well. We'd better play it again, Tom.' He wiped the sweat off his forehead.

'It was out and Tom knows it,' Matt muttered.

They replayed the point and Otto, who was clearly furious, smashed the ball over the net and double-faulted. The Chilvers went on to take the game and then the set. Guy and Otto won the next set, though, by six games to three. Lizzie crossed her fingers. One each. Whoever got the next would win.

At five games all, Anna sat up. 'What is happening?'

'They're even,' Matt told her. 'One of them needs to get two games ahead now.'

'Has Tom cheated again?'

'Well, there've been a couple of doubtful points.'

'He wants very much to win. But I think they will lose and it will serve him right.' She lay down again and replaced the straw hat.

Otto delivered the shot that won the match – one of his bullet-like backhands that went down the tramlines, straight past Tom who threw his racket at it in vain. Tom and Harry forced smiles as they shook hands all round and Guy clapped Otto on the back.

Tea was served on the lawn, wheeled out by a butler, and Mrs Chilver appeared, shading herself under a parasol. She was charming to everyone, and especially charming to Guy and Otto. Tom and Harry came out to see them off in the Alvis and Tom climbed on the running-board to peer in at the dashboard. 'How fast does this thing go? Oh, not that much.' He hopped off. 'I say, how about a sailing race next? *Grey Heron* against that old tub of yours. What do you say?'

Guy pressed the button and the engine burst into life. 'If you like.'

'We'll give you a good start. Make it fair.'

'No need for that.'

Tom grinned. 'Suit yourself, then. You won't have much of a hope, old chap.'

They sped away down the drive, spurting gravel. 'We can't possibly win, of course,' Guy said. 'There's not much point in taking them up on it. We haven't a chance.'

'How do you know that? You cannot be so sure.'

'I'm being realistic, Anna.'

'You are being a coward.'

'You don't know the first thing about sailing, so you can keep quiet. *Rose* simply can't match *Grey Heron* for speed and that's that. We're going to look complete fools.'

'Is that all you care about?'

'I'd sooner not give the Chilvers the chance to crow over us, as a matter of fact.'

'Crow? What is this?' Otto translated into German for her. 'Well, they will crow very much if you do not do this race. 'Won't they, Matt?'

'I'm afraid so.'

'Perhaps *you'd* like to sail her then, Matt?'

'Do not be so mean, Guy. I think we should *all* sail her. All of us against those cheats.'

'I told you you didn't know anything about sailing, Anna. If we all go, then *Grey Heron* will have finished by the time we're halfway. The more people, the slower *Rose*'ll be able to sail. And she's slow enough already.'

'All right. Then you and Otto must take her. It is because you two won the tennis match that they want this race. They believe they will win, so you must make them wrong.'

Tom telephoned in the evening. 'Kick-off at ten hundred, Guy? We'll come down to you and we can start from there. Down to the Whitaker buoy, round and back. First to cross level with your jetty wins. OK?'

'OK.' He heard Harry laughing in the background before Tom had put down the receiver.

Otto sat in the London train, staring out of the window. The English countryside could be very beautiful in some places, it was true. He had always believed that Germany had the best scenery, the most beautiful old towns, the best architecture, the best art, the best music, naturally . . . but some things in England were not so bad. He had enjoyed his visit to the Ransomes' home far more than he had expected. Of course, they hadn't really wanted him there, but they had hidden it carefully. They had been very polite. Taken him everywhere, shown him everything, included him as though he were one of the family. Captain Ransome had not talked much about the Royal Navy, though he had tried several times to encourage him to do so, but he had always been civil, and Mrs Ransome had always been kind. He liked her. He liked Lizzie very much, too. She was not so different from a girl he knew in Berlin – Martha, the younger sister of his friend, Karl. Lizzie was *liebenswert* sweet, the English would say. He had not really known Matt before the visit; because he was two forms lower in the school, he seldom saw him. Now he knew him better, he liked him too and pitied him even more for being a cripple. Deformity was a dreadful affliction. He prided himself on his own body; it was important to exercise constantly, to make sure that he kept it in perfect condition. Guy, of course, had a good physique, though he did not seem to care much about it. To smoke was bad for the lungs. If one smoked, one could not run so fast. It was a pity that there might be no chance to run another race against Guy; it was always a good competition between them. There would be no athletics in the one remaining term at the English school. Winter would begin and there would be only rugger – a game he did not care for. In any case, he was to take the examination for English university and so there would not be much time to spare. He wanted to go to the university in Berlin but his father kept insisting that he stay longer in England.

The train plunged suddenly into a long dark tunnel and then emerged, just as sudddnly, into sunlight once more. Otto no longer noticed the scenery; he was thinking about Anna. He must be careful. He should not see her again. His father would be very angry if he knew that he had found a Jewess attractive; that he had spent the whole visit watching her whenever he could. Fortunately, she had not been aware of it. He must put her out of his mind. He must remember all that his father had told him about the Jews and how dangerous they were. He must forget Anna and her bewitching beauty: forget her voice, her smile – never, ever turned on him – and her lovely hair that he had wanted many times to reach out and touch. She must be banished ruthlessly from his thoughts, for what she was – an impurity, a canker.

Otto stared at the passing fields but without seeing them. He saw only Anna's face. Just for a moment he would allow himself to think again about his last evening at Tideways when she had played for them after dinner. Mrs Ransome had requested it and she had gone to the grand piano in the drawing-room and sat down and played for over an hour. He had had no idea that she was such an accomplished pianist and he had stood on the terrace, just outside the open French windows, where he could watch her all the time unobserved while he had listened entranced. She had played Liszt and Schubert and Chopin and then a string of Strauss waltzes, her fingers dancing across the keys. His father preferred the music of Wagner. At home, the apartment walls trembled to recordings of his operas. They were soul-stirring, uplifting, electrifying, of course, but the playing of Anna was like a balm; it had soothed him as much as it had delighted him.

Otto stopped himself. He must think no more about her. In two days he would be back in Berlin for the remainder of the holidays. There would be friends to see and plenty of things to occupy his mind. He would be attending a big rally of the *Hitler Jugend* at the Lustgarten and they would march with banners and bands through the streets of Berlin. The Führer himself was expected to attend to receive their salute and to address them. It would be a great occasion.

In his luggage, on the rack above his head, were the rolls of film taken during his stay at Tideways. Most of it was of the coastline, the estuary, the river, but there would be some of the Ransomes and of Lizzie and Anna. He would destroy any negatives of Anna and keep only the ones of the others and of the house and of the old boat. He smiled to himself. The big joke was that they had won the race against *Grey Heron*. Not because they had sailed any faster or better, but because the Chilver brothers had been over-confident and gone too close to a sandbank after rounding the estuary buoy. *Grey Heron* had gone aground and *Rose of England* who had been crawling along behind, like a tortoise after a hare, had sailed majestically past and gone on to finish to loud cheers from the jetty, while her rival was still stuck fast. It had been very amusing and they had all laughed, himself included. Guy had clapped him on the back once again, like after they'd won the tennis match. Sweet Lizzie had flung her arms round him and kissed him on the cheek in her excitement. To celebrate the victory and *Rose*'s triumph they had all carved their initials on her port bow. He had hung back at first, not sure whether he was included, but Matt had handed him the penknife. 'Your turn, Otto.' He had carved his next to Anna's.

He looked at the gold wrist-watch that he had been given for his eighteenth birthday – one of the best that money could buy. The train would be arriving in London within twenty minutes. It was time to collect himself and restore sense and order to his thoughts. *Rose* winning was not so wonderful. It had been what the English would call a fluke – *ein dusel* – and nothing to be proud about. *Grey Heron*, the far superior boat, should have won. To champion the undeserving underdog was typical of the sentimental English and if he was not very careful he would start to think and behave like they did. They were a degenerate nation, he reminded himself. They befriended Jews. England was no longer the great Empire that she had once been, but a declining power, while Germany was in the ascendant with a glorious future. She had been ground into the dust by her conquerors but she had risen up despite them and nobody could stop her now.

'They'd got them brain washed – all the young people.' The old man is looking indignant. 'The Hitler Youth. I've read about it since. All boys and girls from six to eighteen years old had to join and they marched them up and down Germany and taught them to be little Nazis.'

My throat feels dry. 'I wonder if I could have a glass of water . . .'

'You can have a cup of tea, if you like.' He puts his pipe on the mantelpiece and heaves himself stiffly out of his armchair. 'Won't be a minute.'

I wait by the window, looking out at the river, and wonder if I am completely mad to take all this trouble. The boat is evidently a wreck – she'll probably fall apart if she's moved. Is it worth the effort? It happened a long time ago and a whole new generation has grown up which knows almost nothing of Dunkirk, and cares less. And then I think of what the Rose of England did. Of what they all did. Of what it meant and how it turned the tide of history. And I know that I am not so mad after all.

The old man comes back, carrying a tin tray with two mugs on it and a plate of plain biscuits. He hands me the mug with A PRESENT FROM SOUTHEND written on it and offers a biscuit. I'm not hungry, only thirsty, but I take one to be polite. 'You'd better sit down, then.' He points at the sofa and lowers himself creakily into his armchair again. 'Can't get used to doing for myself,' he says. 'Molly always saw to everything. So I don't bother much. Not much point just for one, anyway.' The tea is oversweetened dishwater, the biscuit stale, but none of it matters. What matters to me is whether I am going to be able to persuade him. 'Shall I go on?'

'If you like.' He leans back in his chair, head against the antimacassar. 'What happened with the parents – the Jewish ones in Vienna? They needed to get a move on with it, if they wanted to get out in time.'

'They had a lot of trouble with the necessary papers. It could take a long time . . . months, years even. By the spring of 1937 they were still waiting. And then the grandmother fell ill and there was no question of them leaving until she was better.' I'm very thirsty so I drink some more dishwater and then see that he is looking at me expectantly, waiting for me to go on. 'Guy passed his exams for Oxford and went up in the autumn of that year. So did Otto. He was accepted by the same college.'

'That father of his would have been some sort of spy. Sent to find out everything he could about us. Anything useful to the Germans. Worming his

way into places to see who might be on their side. Some people here were all for the Nazis, you know. There were high-up folks who were pally with Hitler. It makes me sick to think of it.' He bites into one of the stale biscuits. *'Did Guy fly, then? Like he always wanted?'*

'Yes, he did. He joined the University Air Squadron and learned to fly on Tiger Moths.'

'I always rather fancied the idea of being a pilot, myself. Used to watch them coming over in their Hurricanes and Spitfires. Of course I was too old by then, and my eyesight wouldn't have been good enough, anyway. They wouldn't have me in the army either. Not for anything. Molly was glad about that, but I always felt . . . well, left out of it all. Did my bit with the ARP, of course, but it wasn't the same. Another biscuit?'

'No, thank you. Shall I carry on?'

'May as well.'

Chapter Eleven

When he looked down from the Tiger Moth's open cockpit Guy could see the winter-brown quilt of Oxfordshire fields spread out below him. When he looked up he saw infinite space – all his to explore and conquer. He was going to be able to climb and dive and soar through the skies just as he had always planned. It was a dizzying thought. For now, though, the instructor had been annoyingly specific. 'Take off, do one circuit at a thousand feet, then come in and land. Take off again and go round again to do a second landing. Not more than ten minutes in the air. We'll see what sort of a mess you make of it on your own, Mr Ransome.'

The take-off had been easy. He'd taxied the biplane to the downwind side of the airfield, leaning over one side of the cockpit to see his way, swung the nose into the wind, tested the rudders, opened the throttle and gone. The Tiger Moth had raced across the grass, lifted her tail, hopped into the air and climbed steadily up-wards. The exhilaration had been tremendous. At a thousand feet he'd levelled off. He was on his own with the plane, actually flying it solo for the first time. It climbed, it banked, it turned, all to his will. It was bloody fantastic! He made one circuit and nearing the final approach did a gliding bank, bringing the Moth down in a smooth descent towards the airfield and in low over the boundary hedge. The trick was to get the angle just right. She touched down OK but with quite a few bounces. He let her run on for a short way before taking her off again. Next time he'd do it perfectly. The second landing was only slightly better so he went off again, determined to make a perfect landing. He thought the third one was pretty good and, pleased with himself, taxied back to the boundary where his instructor was waiting.

'I thought I said *two* circuits only, Mr Ransome, not three. And you've been in the air for twenty minutes, not ten. What the bloody hell did you think you were playing at?'

'Sorry. I wanted to get the landing right.'

'You'll never get it right if you don't do what you're told. You lost a hundred feet on down-wind, you ignored another plane over your shoulder on base leg and all three landings were bloody awful. You'll never make a decent pilot.'

Guy walked away, furious. Back in his rooms at Trinity he tried to settle down to some reading but the instructor's contemptuous verdict rankled. Damn and blast the chap! He'd got his knife into him, for some reason. He'd flown perfectly well and the landings hadn't been bad at all. Of course he'd make a decent pilot. He was going to be a bloody good pilot. He was a natural, for God's sake. He'd known that today as soon as he took off solo. He'd always known it. And what's more he wouldn't always be flying slow old biplanes, like the Moth, but a fast monoplane. And he wouldn't be tootling about on pleasure trips if the rumours were anything to go by. A lot of the chaps thought there was going to be another war with Germany. They'd talked about it late into the night, discussing the chances and what they'd all do. A couple of them had said they'd probably join the Navy, another the Army, one was an out-and-out pacifist and another chap had said he was blowed if he was going to fight for King and Country at all – why should he get himself killed because of a lot of bungling old fools in the Government. Guy knew he would join the RAF, but as a means to an end, and that end was to become a fighter pilot. If it meant killing Germans as well, then so be it. In the middle of the discussion, at some stage, Otto had come into the room. They hadn't noticed him at first and when they did there had been an awkward silence, broken by somebody saying casually, 'Just talking about whether we're going to have to put the brakes on you lot again.' Otto's English was damn good, but he hadn't understood the idiom until it was explained to him. 'Go to war with Germany all over again, old chum.'

He had said stiffly, 'Why should that be necessary?'

'Your people can't seem to stick to the Versailles Treaty.'

'If you are referring to the Rhineland, the people there have long wished to be a part of Germany once more. They are our people. They welcomed us back.' He had looked round the gathering. 'The Führer has no wish to make war with anybody.'

'Well, he's got a bloody funny way of showing it. You've been building up your army and navy on the q.t., haven't you? Most probably your air force, too, for all we know. Troops marching around, waving those swastika banners and armed to the teeth. Doesn't look too friendly to us.'

'The Führer only wishes peace. He says so frequently in his public speeches.'

'Ah, but what does he say in private, that's what we all want to know? Can you find out for us, Otto, old chap?'

They'd all laughed – except Otto, of course. He'd taken it all dead seriously. That was one of the great pleasures of Oxford, Guy had quickly discovered. Nothing need be taken too seriously. The three years up at university were for having as much fun as possible while doing only enough work to get a decent degree. There were so many things to do and enjoy: so many clubs and societies, so much sport.

He never really knew what to make of Otto and nobody else was quite sure either. He was always around, standing on the edge of groups, sitting in on discussions, listening and watching, rather than taking part. English humour escaped him – he took everything so bloody literally – but he had stopped blowing his own trumpet long ago. And he was spectacularly successful with girls, it had to be said – probably because he was foreign and also had plenty of money to spend on them. An irresistible combination to some. Not that Guy found he had any trouble himself. At parties girls always clustered round him, which was a very satisfactory state of affairs. He would stand there, drink in one hand, cigarette in the other, and wait for them to come up and make the overtures. He had three of them on the go at the moment. The most satisfactory thing of all had been the brief encounter with the wife of a history don who was a notorious nympho-maniac and dedicated to relieving as many under-graduates as possible of their virginity. His turn had come when the don was away in London giving a lecture on Oliver Cromwell, and the experience had been highly enjoyable. She'd been quite complimentary too.

All in all, Guy felt pretty pleased with life and with himself. Or had done until today's little episode with the flying instructor. He snapped the book shut and lit a cigarette. No point brooding about it. In a couple of weeks he'd be going down for the Christmas vac. He'd do a bit of work on the *Rose* perhaps. Matt would be home from school later on and he could give him a hand. Spruce her up ready for the next season. He'd got rather fond of the old girl since she'd beaten *Grey Heron*. Tom and Harry had been livid and it still made him laugh to think of it. Whenever he saw Tom around Oxford, he pulled his leg about it.

'There's a young gentleman asking for you, Miss Elizabeth.' Hodges had struggled all the way up to the attic and stood in the doorway, panting like a mountaineer short of oxygen. 'A Mr Rikenow. A foreigner. He's waiting in the hall.'

'I don't know anybody of that name, Hodges. What on earth does he want?'

'To see you.' Hodges winked. 'Asked for you specially.'

Lizzie put down her brush. 'I suppose I'd better come and see, though I can't imagine who it could be.' She followed Hodges and a waft of alcohol down the several flights of stairs. Otto von Reichenau was standing in the hall.

'Please forgive this intrusion, Lizzie. I am returned to London now from Oxford and I thought to call to see you and Anna at your home. I hope I do not disturb you.' He was wearing a suit – a very expensive one, she could tell that, and the shirt and tie were expensive too. It made him look much older and quite different. 'No, not at all, Otto.' He was the same age as Guy, of course. Twenty. A man, not a boy.

'It is more than a year since we met at Tideways, but I always remember the visit very well. I thought it would be good to renew our acquaintance.'

She was very surprised; he hadn't been in touch since. 'How did you know where I lived?'

'I remember that your father is a doctor and that you live in Wimpole Street, so I walk and look at every door until I see the brass plate with his name on it.' He smiled at her. 'It was not so very difficult. I do not need to be Sherlock Holmes.'

'Actually, he was round the corner in Baker Street.'

He smiled again. 'I know this. Number 221b. I enjoy the books very much.'

'Of course he didn't actually exist, but lots of people really believe he did.' She wasn't sure what to say next. 'I'm afraid Anna isn't here. She's gone to have tea with someone. My father is working and my mother is out, too. There's just me. Would you like some tea?'

'Oh, no, please . . . I do not wish to trouble you. You are busy, I am sure.'

'Just doing a bit of painting, that's all.'

'Ah, yes, you are an artist. You were making sketches at Tideways when we were there. They were very good. May I see your work?'

She said doubtfully, 'If you want to.'

'Oh, yes, I should like that very much.'

'It's right at the top of the house, if you don't mind.' She led the way up to her studio. He followed her and, as everyone did, admired her attic studio and the view. He looked at the still life that she was working on. 'This is excellent. You are most talented.'

'Not really.'

'The English are very modest. I know this now. They never admit to being good at anything. They always deny it. May I see more?'

She showed him the paintings stacked against the wall and he admired those too. 'Very good. You should make a career of this.'

'Well, I'm hoping to go to art college, when I leave school next year. If they'll have me.'

'I am sure that they will.' He went on looking at the paintings, crouched on his haunches. 'And Anna, what does she hope to do with her life?'

'I think she might study music at one of the colleges in London . . .'

'Yes, of course, I heard her play when I was last at Tideways. She has a great talent. She will not return to Vienna to study there, then?'

'Well, it's not very safe, is it?'

He went on looking at the canvases. 'Because she is Jewish, you mean?'

'Well, yes. Her parents are trying to come and live in England as well, only her grandmother's been very ill so they can't leave yet. Anna went to see them last holidays. She's terribly worried about them.'

He held up one of her oils – a still life that she was rather pleased with – studying it at arm's length. 'It would be better for her not to return again at all to Vienna.'

'It really could be dangerous?'

'I think so, yes.'

'But why? What have people got against Jewish people there, Otto? What are they supposed to have done?'

He stood up. 'You would not understand, Lizzie. And I cannot explain to you. I'm sorry but it is better that we do not discuss this matter.' He moved on to examine one of the paintings that she had hung on the wall. 'This is Guy and Matt sailing? But it is a different boat and they are much younger.'

'I did that one nearly three years ago. That was *Bean Goose* – the one they had before *Rose of England*. The one next along is the *Rose*. I did that the first summer that Anna went to stay at Tideways. She wore that long white dress and Guy got furious with her because it was hopeless for sailing.'

'But the dress looks very beautiful. And this is you, next to Anna, of course. Your hair is different. You have it long and tied in – what do you call them in English?'

'Plaits. I cut them off last year.'

'So you go from little girl to young lady, in one step.' He turned to smile at her and she smiled back uncertainly. He had the strangest eyes – such a pale blue that it was like looking into glass. Something about him had always disturbed her. She had felt sorry for him at Tideways because he had seemed so alone – to stand apart from everybody else, always like an outsider looking on. It was impossible to tell what he was thinking.

'You're in the same college as Guy, aren't you? I expect you see a lot of him.'

'Not so much. He is always very busy. Did you know that Tom is also at Oxford – the one who sailed *Grey Heron* with his brother? I sat beside him once at a lecture but he did not wish to be reminded of that occasion when we last met.'

Lizzie laughed. 'I don't suppose he did. The Chilvers don't like losing.'

'I do not like to lose either. I am trying to learn to be what you English call a good sport but I am not very successful. I have to pretend that I do not mind but it is hard for me.' He went on to the next painting – her portrait of Anna – and stopped. 'When did you do this?'

'A few months ago. I've never done a portrait before and I haven't got her very well, I'm afraid. She's difficult to catch. And she's much more beautiful than that, of course.'

He stared at it for a while in silence. 'You have her eyes, and the hair . . . but she would be very difficult to capture completely. To paint a portrait must be very hard. You must show not only the features but also the spirit. The soul of a person.'

'I don't think I really know Anna well enough to do that.'

'Not even after so long?'

'No, not even now. There's a part of her that she doesn't let you know – that she keeps to herself.'

He nodded as though he understood. 'Many of us do that. But even so, the portrait is good.'

'You'll recognize this next to it.' It was the one she'd done of *Rose* coming in triumphantly at the end of the race against *Grey Heron* with Guy and Otto on board and Matt, Anna and herself small figures waving from the jetty. 'That's you, or meant to be. I had to do you from memory, of course.'

He looked amused. 'You know, I have never had a picture painted of me before.'

'Well, you're only in the distance, I'm afraid. Wasn't it wonderful when she won?'

'Yes, of course,' he said slowly. 'It was wonderful.'

She remembered that he had seemed just as pleased as the rest of them and how he had laughed with them and how she had thrown her arms round him and kissed him on the cheek. She blushed about that part but he didn't notice. He was still looking at the painting intently. 'I like this very much.'

She said, on impulse, 'Would you like to have it, Otto? As a sort of souvenir.'

'Oh, no, please . . . I did not mean that, Lizzie.'

'Honestly, I'd like you to have it.' She took it off the wall and placed it firmly into his hands. 'There. You can't refuse now. It's a present for you.'

He said gravely, 'Then I thank you, Lizzie. It will be a good memory for me. And thank you for showing me your excellent work. And your studio. It is a very nice place. But I must not keep you longer. I am sorry to miss Anna. Would you please give her my good wishes when she returns.'

She went downstairs to see him out and at the door he paused. 'My father is away in Berlin at the moment; he does not return until next week.

Would you and Anna come and have dinner with me one evening? I am very bored with my own company.' Seeing her hesitation, he went on, 'Anna, of course, may not wish to. You will let me know. Here is my telephone number.' He handed her an engraved white card. 'Perhaps on Thursday, if you are free.'

She closed the front door after him, feeling uneasy.

The old mother was sitting in the corner of the basement room, as before, with her snail's-shell hair and her coal eyes. Anna greeted her politely. The woman looked up at her. 'I remember you. You are the one who speaks French so well. The pupil of Janine. The Jewess.'

Mademoiselle Gilbert said, 'Anna has come to take tea with us, *Maman*. You will be able to converse with her.'

'Perhaps I may not wish to.'

'She is very difficult,' Mademoiselle Gilbert had warned her. 'Worse than before. Her mind wanders and she can be very rude. Please excuse her. It is the curse of old age.'

Anna sat down. 'How are you, madame?'

'Terrible. I am very ill. Full of aches and pains. But Janine does not care. If she cared she would return to Lille, not force me to come to this dreadful place. She wants me to remain here with her, you know. As if I would! I visit, that is all. Next week I go home.'

She was incapable of living on her own, Mademoiselle Gilbert had said. There had been no alternative but to bring her to England for the time being. Eventually she would have to give up her teaching post and return to France because her mother would undoubtedly be miserable in England. She would be miserable anywhere, Anna decided. She's a horrible, selfish old woman. She thought of Grandmama lying in the hospital in Vienna, in great pain after the operation but uncomplaining and trying so hard to persuade Mama and Papa to leave her. Naturally, they wouldn't. How could they? Grandmama was as much in need of looking after as Madame Gilbert. They could not desert her and go to England. Uncle Julius and Aunt Sybille and the little ones had already gone to America, to live with the sister in Detroit. And although Uncle Joseph had offered to look after Grandmama, Aunt Liesel had not been well either. The doctors said that Grandmama would need to convalesce for several months when she came out of hospital. Then Anna's parents hoped to bring her to England with them.

Mademoiselle Gilbert had gone to the kitchen to fetch the tea. Left alone with the old mother, Anna proposed a game of cards.

'I do not play any more. I cannot see well enough.' The black eyes looked perfectly sharp. 'Janine tells me that your mother and father want to come and live in this country.'

'Yes.'

'They are mad. Who would want to live in such a place? But of course, they must leave because they are Jewish. They have no choice.

Jews are fleeing like rats. There are many who are trying to come and live in France. They are not welcome. We do not wish them to come to France. They will make too much money for themselves out of good, honest French people. They will be everywhere, in every place—'

'Here is our tea, *Maman*.' Mademoiselle Gilbert set the tray down. She lowered her voice. 'Please pay no attention, Anna. She has no idea what she is saying.'

'She knew exactly what she was saying, Lizzie. She is a spiteful, wicked old hag. It was only for the sake of Mademoiselle Gilbert that I was not very rude back to her. I am very sorry that I went at all.'

'Well, guess who called while you were out.'

'How can I guess? I have no idea.'

'Otto.'

'Otto?'

'The German boy who was at Tideways the summer before last. Surely you remember him.'

'Oh, the Nazi.'

'He's not like that, Anna.'

'Yes, he is. They are all Nazis. Well, what did he want?'

'He's invited us to dinner, next Thursday. If we want to go.'

'Of course I do not want to go. How could you think I would, Lizzie?'

'He's on his own in London. I think he's lonely.'

'You go, if you want to. You can listen to him talking about the great new Fatherland.'

'I felt sorry for him, Anna. I think we should go.'

'You are much too kind-hearted, Lizzie. If we did, I should not be so kind. I should ask him questions about his wonderful Führer and annoy him very much.' Anna paused and then nodded. 'It might be worth it just for that.'

Otto telephoned his father in Berlin to make certain that he would not be returning to London until the following week. His father was safely occupied on important affairs. There were military and diplomatic meetings and discussions, and, apparently, an audience with the Führer. There was no prospect of him arriving back sooner. It had been a great surprise to Otto to hear Lizzie's voice on the telephone, accepting his invitation. He had fully expected it to be refused because of Anna. Anna, of course, saw him as an enemy of her people – he was well aware of that. It was unjustified in his eyes. He himself had never done any Jew any harm of any kind, though it was true that he had listened to and accepted many things that were taught about them.

It was a big risk that he was taking. The servants who staffed the rented house had been hand-picked. They not only served, but watched and listened. Everything would be noted and reported to his father, including their assessment of his guests. He had vetted the menu carefully.

No pork, of course. Nothing that might be unacceptable to Anna. A rich chocolate dessert that he hoped would please Lizzie. The long dining-room table, usually seating twenty or more when his father entertained, looked absurd laid only for three, but everything was highly polished and the flowers were fresh. He himself had dressed formally and put on the heavy gold cuff-links inherited from his grandfather, bearing the von Reichenau crest. All was ready.

He went into the drawing-room. The curtains were drawn against the dark, the fire lit. He stood for a moment looking down into the flames, watching them burn brightly, feeling their heat and thinking of the great conflagrations that must surely lie ahead. He disliked the thought of war but he knew it must come. And that when it did, he would do his duty to the utmost. He was to serve in the army, his father had dictated. Perhaps one of the Panzer regiments. Colonel General von Rundstedt was a personal friend and would arrange for an immediate commission. Tanks were going to be of crucial importance. So, too, were the planes of the Luftwaffe, assembled in secret for years. Once Otto had tentatively suggested that he might go into the Luftwaffe – he had rather envied Guy his flying – but this had been instantly quashed. Von Reichenaus had always served in the army. But, his father had promised, there would be no more long-drawn-out trench warfare. No more digging in and fighting for months to gain a few metres of ground. Instead the Wehrmacht would sweep across Europe to conquer any country the Führer chose. And on the seas the U-boats would roam and kill like wolves.

He had fought a long, hard, private battle of his own to evict Anna from his heart but her image had haunted him since that summer of 1936. He had taken out girl after girl, hoping that one of them would erase her memory, but all to no avail. She had always come back just as he had thought he had succeeded. The only way out, he had finally decided, was to arrange somehow to see her again, to meet and talk with her face to face so that he could recognize and dismiss her for what she was – a crazy aberration on his part. An absurd fascination with forbidden fruit. That was the only cure.

But when she walked into the room with Lizzie he stood rooted to the spot, unable either to move or speak. He recovered in time to act the good host, welcoming them and offering them drinks. Lizzie asked for orange squash, Anna a dry martini. Anna produced a small silver case from her handbag, took out a cigarette and fitted it into an ebony holder. He fetched a table lighter quickly. He had not expected her to drink cocktails, or to smoke. Older English girls did both, of course, but no German girls he knew of her age did either and they were innocent of make-up or guile. Anna was wearing a dress of soft blue material that displayed every curve of her figure. Her long hair was caught back with combs on each side of her head, her full lips painted with scarlet lipstick. He forced himself to look away and pay attention to Lizzie who was being polite about the room.

'This house is rented only. It is not ours, of course.' Everything had been carefully chosen to impress, he knew. Paintings brought from Germany, including a portrait of the Führer.

'Well, it's very nice. Awfully grand. Isn't it, Anna?'

She was looking round. 'So much gold . . . so much glitter.'

He said carefully, 'As a matter of fact, it is not to my taste. But we did not choose the furnishings.'

'Whoever painted these horrible pictures?'

'They are all by German artists.' He did not actually care for them much either. They were supposed to depict the many and varied glories of the Fatherland but, privately, he considered them rather overblown and vulgar; not even very well painted.

Anna had walked across to the large, full-length portrait over the fireplace. She blew a stream of smoke casually in its direction. 'So this is your wonderful Führer, Otto? He looks just like Charlie Chaplin.'

She was goading him, of course. He would not rise to the bait. 'It is always hard to capture the inner being of a person in paint. Is that not so, Lizzie? You will agree? We discussed this.' Lizzie nodded, looking uncomfortable.

The drinks were brought in on a silver tray and he invited them to sit down. It was all very formal and very different from at Tideways where they had lounged around in casual clothes, chatting idly. Anna sipped at the martini and smoked her cigarette. 'What exactly does your father do, Otto?' She was still needling him.

'He was appointed to our embassy here to do special liaison work.'

'Oh, what sort of liaising?'

'Fostering interests of all kinds between this country and Germany. Promoting the relationship between us. The Führer much admires Great Britain.' They were his father's very words, used to smooth over many awkward enquiries.

'And have you ever met Herr Hitler?'

'I had the honour, once, yes.'

'The *honour*?'

'I considered it so.' He met her eyes in appeal. In German he said quickly, 'Please, Anna, let us not talk like this. Can we speak of other things?'

'Lizzie does not understand German,' she replied in English. 'Nor does she understand Germans. Do you, Lizzie? She does not understand what they are doing. She really has no idea. You should tell her more about your so-marvellous Führer, Otto. About his *Sturm Abteilung* and his charming *Schutz Staffel* and most especially about his kind and delightful secret police, the Gestapo.'

'Lizzie does not wish to hear these things.'

'I do not blame her. I wish I had not heard of them myself.'

'Oh, Anna, don't . . .' Lizzie was pink with embarrassment, almost in tears. 'Don't let's spoil the evening. *Please*.'

Anna hesitated and then shrugged. 'All right. For your sake, Lizzie, we shall talk about nice, safe things, if you want. Just as though nothing at all was happening. We will all play let's pretend.'

She kept her word and he was as charming as he knew how to be. He even risked some small jokes. He was especially complimentary about England and the English, about Oxford and about his visit to Tideways. They talked about the *Rose of England* and the race, and the tennis match, and about anything that he could think of that was pleasant and pleasing. He talked to Lizzie more than he talked to Anna because it was safer, and she chattered away to him. He could tell that she was anxious to make amends for Anna's behaviour and he was grateful. Sometimes he felt that he loved her, too, but it was the love of an older brother for a younger sister. It was not the same as he felt about Anna. Whenever he dared, he looked at Anna. He watched her speak and laugh and smile. He watched her drink her wine and eat her food. He watched her smoke the cigarettes that he had lit for her. And, as he did so, he knew that his strategy had failed hopelessly.

His father returned from Berlin a week later. He was exultant about his audience with the Führer. 'Everything is good, Otto. All danger, all obstacles have been eliminated. The way ahead is clear for the *stufenplan*. The Wehrmacht now has a million men. Germany will become a great power, step by step. First in Europe, and when this is achieved, overseas.' His father walked excitedly about the room. 'We are to expand first to the East. Austria and Czechoslovakia will be annexed as soon as possible. The groundwork has been well laid in Vienna and very soon the Austrian government will have no choice but to accede—'

'I thought there was to be a plebiscite.'

'The Führer has persuaded Dr von Schuschnigg to cancel it. What could be more natural than for Germany and Austria to be joined? We shall be welcomed there with open ams. The Führer will drive through the streets of Vienna in triumph, you wait and see. After that, it will be the turn of the Czechs.'

'And will nobody oppose us?'

'Oh, Great Britain and France may squeak and squeal and throw up their hands in mock horror, but they will do nothing. They want only to avoid another war. Peace at any price. We have both seen this for ourselves, Otto. You have told me how the young men at Oxford joke about a war. They do not take it seriously. They are not prepared. Some of them do not even wish to fight for their country. We have seen the way they play the fool; how slack and sloppy they have become. Once Great Britain *was* great; now her people are slothful, careless, weak . . . We shall have no difficulty at all. Herr von Ribbentrop says the same and he knows the English well. He has the ear of those who count.' His father paused and glanced at him. 'Naturally, you will not breathe one word of this conversation to a living soul.'

'Naturally not.'

His father resumed his pacing. 'The Führer always wished great Britain to become our ally, but he knows now that he cannot count on this. So he desires her to remain neutral instead. When Lord Halifax visited the Berchtesgaden, the Führer was told that Great Britain considers Germany as a bulwark against the Bolsheviks. She will turn a blind eye so long as we do not interfere with her Empire. Mr Chamberlain is anxious to appease us at all costs. Nothing could be better. The way is clear.' His father stared out of the window for a moment and then turned round smiling. 'I hear that you had guests to dine here in my absence. Two charming young ladies.'

'That is correct.'

'Who were they?'

'One is a cousin of Guy and Matthew Ransome. The other is a friend of hers. They were both also visiting the Ransomes' home when I stayed there. It was agreeable company for me.'

'Of course, Otto, it is quite natural for you to wish to entertain young ladies . . . Remember, however, that any serious attachment to a foreigner is unacceptable. You will be expected to make your choice, when the time comes, from among your own people. The British have some excellent qualities but they are a mongrel race. I should not wish my grandchildren to come other than from pure German stock.'

Thank God he had no suspicion. None at all. The servants had not identified Anna. Thank God for the mongrel race, where as many were dark as fair. Otto listened to his father talking on again about the great future that lay ahead. *Austria* . . . to be annexed as soon as possible. Anna's family in Vienna. The SS . . . There was, of course, nothing that he could do.

Anna heard her name being called as she walked down Wimpole Street. Otto von Reichenau came up behind her and spoke in German. 'Excuse me, Anna, may I come a short way with you?' He didn't wait for her agreement but started walking along beside her. 'You're going shopping, perhaps?' He looked strange. Very pale and tense. She wondered if he had been ill.

She said coolly, 'Yes, I am, as a matter of fact.' What was he doing here? What was his game?

'I hope you enjoyed the dinner the other evening?'

She hadn't enjoyed it a bit: the place had reeked of Nazis, and the portrait of Adolf Hitler had sickened her. He had looked down on her with his cruel stare – a silly little man all puffed up in a fine uniform with eagle badges and an iron cross and a big black swastika patch on his left sleeve. His moustache looked as though it had been gummed onto his upper lip and his hair cowlicked across his forehead. How could people pay so much attention to such a creature? How could they believe all his lies and his crazed rantings? How could they not see the evil?

Otto went on, 'It was a great pleasure for me but I realize that it may not have been so for you.'

'No, it wasn't pleasant for me to sit and eat in a Nazi household. But Lizzie enjoyed it. She feels sorry for you, you know. I can't imagine why.'

'She has a kind heart.'

'I know. She's too trusting. I'm not.'

He walked in silence for a while, staring ahead, not looking at her. 'I wanted to speak to you again, if you don't mind. Just for a moment.'

'What about?'

'Lizzie told me that your mother and father still live in Vienna. That they wish to come and live here in England?'

'They don't *wish* it. They'd much sooner stay in Vienna, which is their home. I should much sooner be there myself. But they are afraid of your precious Führer and what may happen.'

She quickened her pace. They had reached Wigmore Street and crossed to Cavendish Square.

'He only wishes the good of the German people.'

'And what does he wish *my* people?'

'I believe it's thought better that they should find somewhere else of their own to live.'

She said angrily, 'How is that possible? We are driven out from everywhere.'

'That is regrettable—'

'*Regrettable!*' She whirled round to face him. 'Is that all you have to say to me, Otto?'

He was even paler. Ashen. 'No.'

'What else then?'

'I want to warn you that you should tell your father and mother to leave Vienna and Austria as quickly as possible. They should not delay.'

'They can't leave at the moment. My grandmother's ill.'

'Is it impossible for her to travel?'

'It wouldn't be easy.'

'Nevertheless, tell them that they must go immediately. Somehow they must find a way. It's imperative. And on no account should you return to Vienna yourself.' He looked at her gravely. 'Please do as I say.'

She didn't trust him. 'What do you know about it?'

'I hear things.'

'*What* things?'

'I'm sorry but I can't tell you.'

'Why should I listen to you? Why should you care? We're only dirty Jews to you.'

'No, Anna,' he said. 'You're not.'

Before she could speak again, he had turned quickly on his heel and walked away. She stared after him, but he didn't look back.

'Waltzed into Austria in the March, didn't they? I remember Molly saying to me: if we don't watch out they'll try and do the same to us one day. Of course, I didn't believe her at the time. Nobody lifted a finger to stop them. Not us, not the French – nobody. Mark you, most of the Austrians didn't mind too much. Like that German bloke said, it was a walk-over. They'd already got Nazis in their own government, and they were in a mess themselves, so they made it easy for Hitler. It was a joyride for him.' Mr Potter reaches for his pipe and tobacco pouch from the mantelpiece, knocks out the ash into the fireplace and begins to fill it again. 'They put the Welcome mat out when he went to Vienna.'

'Oh, yes.'

'Did the daughter warn her family, like that German boy told her?'

'She tried, but her grandmother was too ill to move. Anna's parents stayed to look after her until she died the following October. By the time they were free to leave, they were told that their papers were no longer in order. The Nazi regime had set up a special office in Vienna that sold emigration permits to Jews. At a price.'

He strikes a match and applies it. The pipe bowl glows red and clouds of smoke rise into the air. 'The daughter must have been a bit worried.'

'She was desperate. Her friend, Mina, wrote to her and told her how badly the Nazis were treating the Jews. That they were making them scrub the streets of Vienna on their hands and knees. That she and her mother had been forced to wash buildings and pavements and that crowds had jeered at them and the Nazi soldiers urinated on them.'

He looks disgusted. 'Did that happen to Anna's parents?'

'If it did, they never told her. They wrote that they would soon be coming to England. They had sold jewellery, furniture – everything they could – and expected to be given their new papers any day. Anna went on waiting. And hoping.'

He puffs out more smoke. 'Then it was Munich, I remember. The Czechs were trying to hold out against the Nazis and we let them down. Sold them out for a worthless piece of paper with Hitler's name on it. I remember Chamberlain coming back from the Munich Conference waving it. He thought he'd stopped a war. Soon found out he'd done nothing of the sort.' He nods at me. 'Carry on, then.'

I collect my thoughts. 'Munich was in September 1938. Guy was just starting his second year at Oxford by then. Anna had gone to the Royal Academy of Music in London, to study *the piano and violin. Matt had started as a medical student at St Thomas's Hospital in London, living in digs, and Lizzie had been allowed to leave school and go to art college. In November the violence against the Jews all over Germany suddenly exploded on Kristallnacht when the Nazis burned thousands of synagogues and smashed the shopfront glass of Jewish stores. They killed a hundred Jews and marched thirty thousand more to concentration camps. All in one night. Goebbels, the Propaganda Minister, orchestrated it.'*

He grunts. 'Nasty piece of work, Goebbels. And Himmler. And Goering. The whole pack of them. Was that young German, Otto, over here then?'

'Yes, he was still at Oxford, in the spring of 1939. His father hadn't yet been recalled.'

'Should've been kicked out long before. We're fools the way we let these people into the country – spies, terorists, lunatics . . . foreigners all plotting against us and we let them stay. Like I say, we never learn.'

Chapter Twelve

Matt stuck his head round the studio door. 'Hodges let me in. He said I'd find you up here. Hope you don't mind, Lizzie. I can see you're at work.'

She put down her brush. 'I'm only messing about.'

He came into the room, grinning at her. 'Just been to the dentist. No fillings to do and time to spare, so I thought I'd pop by and see if you and Anna were around.'

'Anna's not back from the Academy yet. She's practising for some concert. Playing the violin in one of their orchestras.'

She hadn't seen him for more than six months, not since last summer when she and Anna had gone to Tideways again. He'd changed a lot. He was taller and broader and his features had altered subtly. But the grin was just the same. 'How are you, Lizzie? How's art college?'

'Fine, thanks. How about you? How are you getting on at St Thomas's?'

'Nose to the grindstone for the next six years. Still, it'll be worth it.'

'I remember you telling me ages ago that you wanted to be a doctor.'

'Did I?'

'It was when I first came to stay on my own. We'd been out sailing – in the *Bean Goose* – and I'd got an awful crack on the head from the boom. We were walking back to the house and you said you wanted to be a doctor one day. You were very kind about my lump on the head and put ice all over it.'

'I remember that bit. There was a huge egg on your forehead and you were very brave. You wouldn't let us see that you were crying.'

'I thought then that you'd make an awfully good doctor. You had healing hands.'

He held up his left arm. 'Hand, actually.' The tweed jacket concealed his deformed right arm completely. She had noticed how he always kept it out of sight now. 'Mother always used to tell me the same. I could cure her headaches just by touching her. Or so she said. I even got rid of Mrs Woodgate's neuralgia once and that was no mean feat. Still, they haven't let us loose on real people yet. It's all books and labs so far. But I think I might make a reasonable GP if I don't frighten my patients to death.' He moved forward and admired the painting that she was working on. 'I say, that's terrific.'

She didn't think it was at all. To her, the fruit looked as though it was made of wax. She couldn't get the bloom on the grapes, or the texture of the orange skin or the subtle colours in the pear. At college she was discovering what a lot she had to learn.

Matt wandered about the studio, looking at things. 'How's Anna?'

'Frantic about her parents. They're still in Vienna, waiting for their emigration papers.'

He frowned. 'That's bad news. Especially now Hitler's grabbed Austria. We might have to go to war with Germany and they'll get stuck there.'

'Do you think it's going to come to that?'

'It could do, easily.'

'I thought the last war was supposed to end all wars.'

'It was. But they didn't reckon on Hitler.' Matt stood looking out of the attic window, his back to her. 'Anyway, I hope to God they'll let me fight in it. Guy's OK, lucky blighter. He'll go straight into the RAF and fly fighters. I won't be a doctor for years and I bet they'll count me out for anything else because of my bloody arm.'

She had never heard him speak about it like that before. He sounded full of bitterness and quite wretched. Not a bit like Matt. But in the next moment he shrugged and turned to smile at her. 'Oh well, I expect there'll be something I can do.'

'I have come to say goodbye.'

Guy, lounging sideways across an armchair, looked up from his book. Otto was standing in the doorway, all togged up in a suit and tie. 'What? Are you off somewhere?'

'I have to return to Berlin.'

'Now? What about the rest of term?'

'My father has to leave at once and I am to go with him. He insists.'

'That's rather bad luck. You'll miss the Commem.'

'I know, but unfortunately my father does not consider a college summer ball to be of the first importance.'

'Couldn't you twist his arm? It's always such a good bash.'

'Yes, last year I enjoyed it very much. This year I'm afraid it's not possible.'

'Well, see you next term, then. In October.'

Otto shook his head. 'I don't think so. I'm to join the army immediately on my return. A tank regiment.'

There was a short silence. Christ, Guy thought, I know what that's about. And he knows it too. He put the book down, swung his legs to the ground and stood up slowly. He ran his fingers through his hair. What the blazes was he supposed to say next? They were probably going to be fighting each other, on opposite sides. There was nothing in the etiquette books to cover this particular one. He held out his hand. 'Well, good luck in the army.'

Otto stepped forward to shake it. 'I wish you good luck as well. In the Royal Air Force.'

'Perhaps we'll meet again.'

'Yes, perhaps. I very much hope so.'

Guy said drily: 'Let us know if you're ever thinking of coming to England.'

A faint smile flickered across Otto's face. 'Of course. Goodbye, Guy.'

He sat down and picked up his book again. Ludicrous, he thought – wishing each other good luck. Bloody absurd. He lit a cigarette and smoked it thoughtfully for a moment. Damned shame that there had to be wars.

'Otto came here while you were out, Anna. He wanted to say goodbye. He's going back to Germany.'

'That's very good news.'

'He asked me to say goodbye to you for him.'

'I am glad that he couldn't say it for himself.'

'He has to go back to join the German army. He seemed quite upset about it.'

Anna looked at her. 'I believe that you *still* feel sorry for him, Lizzie. Don't you realize that he is going back to get ready to fight against your country? The Germans *know* that there will be war soon. Everybody knows it. Just now, when I went to see Mademoiselle Gilbert she was packing everything ready to go home to France. She is taking her mother back there as soon as the school term is finished. France will be fighting together with England against Germany and they must go home to look after their apartment in Lille.'

'It might not happen,' Lizzie said stubbornly. 'It might not.'

'I wish I believed that too. But I don't. And I have made a plan, Lizzie.'

'What sort of plan?'

'Today Mademoiselle Gilbert told me that she has heard of an organization in France which can arrange for Jews to escape from Germany and Austria to Switzerland. They provide papers, passports – everything necessary – and transport them to the Swiss border. There is a man in Lille who is in touch with them and who has helped the daughter of a friend of Mademoiselle to leave Berlin. I am going to go to Lille to see this man myself. And I shall pay whatever is necessary. I don't care how much it costs. I have my money in the bank here and I can get more, if need be. A whole lot more.'

'Where from?'

'I will show you.' Anna went away and returned with a red velvet box in her hands. She fumbled with the little gold catch and opened the lid. Lizzie blinked. 'Emeralds and diamonds. It once belonged to a grand duchess in Russia and then to my great-great-grandmother. My grandmother gave it to me. She said I was to sell it if I ever needed some money.'

'It must be worth a fortune.'

'I hope so.' Anna lifted the necklace out of its case and dangled it round her neck. 'I'm going to wear it just once – because that would have pleased Grandmama. A man that I met at that silly party I went to last week has invited me to a ball at Oxford. I shall wear Grandmama's necklace in her memory. And then I shall sell it – in France.'

*   *   *

Guy finished tying his white tie and studied his reflection critically in the looking-glass. The tails were hired, but he thought they fitted pretty well. He tweaked at the stiff wing collar, adjusted the silk handkerchief in his breast pocket, gave his white waistcoat a final tug and shot his cuffs. The gold cuff-links had been a twenty-first birthday present from his parents, together with the pearl shirt studs. Aunt Helen and Uncle Richard had given him a silver cigarette case, engraved with his initials, and his godmother had given him a silver lighter. His godfather had stumped up a gold wrist-watch from Aspreys. They all compensated for the hired tails. He filled up his cigarette case and checked his lighter for fuel.

The Commem. promised well. The dinner party first up in the rooms and then dancing down in the marquee in the quad until dawn and breakfast. After a good deal of deliberation between half a dozen possibilities he had settled on inviting Cynthia, a deb he'd taken out once or twice, and two hours earlier he'd met her at the station off the London train and taken her to the Randolph where he'd booked a room. She was rather boring to listen to but very pretty to look at. He planned to take her punting from Magdalen Bridge in the early hours and to persuade her to go further than the last time he'd taken her out, when she'd suddenly refused at the final fence. He strolled into the large room he shared with Lewis where the table was set for ten. Their scout, Baxter, had done an excellent job getting everything organized and the dinner menu was a good one: iced cucumber soup, cold salmon, new potatoes and asparagus, strawberries and cream. Dry martinis to kick off with, followed by some first-class wines – a different one for each course – and champagne with the strawberries.

Lewis was still getting dressed up in his finery; Guy could hear him whistling loudly in his bedroom, next door. Interesting to see who he'd asked. Some girl he'd met in London: foreign, apparently, and a knockout, according to Lewis who prided himself on his high standards and had the lucre and a Lagonda to support them. Guy, on a strict allowance from his father and only a bicycle, found it stuck in his craw at times, but Lewis was a decent chap and good company. They'd worked out a pretty fair system for clearing out when the other was entertaining a girl, with an unwritten, sacred rule never to poach. He'd added a couple more to the history don's wife and with any luck he'd increase his tally with Cynthia tonight.'

He cranked up Lewis's gramophone and picked a record from the tottering pile. Essential aids to seduction, Lewis termed them, and invested heavily in any he thought conducive to that subtle art. This one had been worn thin: 'Blue Moon'. Guy lit a cigarette and listened to the familiar tune while he looked out of the open window at the quadrangle. A big marquee had been erected in the centre and the ancient brick and stonework of the surrounding college buildings were bathed in the golden light of a summer's evening. He admired the scene. It'd been a fantastic term – marvellous weather, not too much work and plenty of cricket and tennis and rowing and parties. Maybe he'd do a spot of travelling on the Continent in the long vac before the war put a stop to it. France most probably. He'd like to see Paris. Spend a bit of time there. It seemed most unlikely that he'd be able to finish his three years up at Oxford. The general consensus was that war was bound to break out by the end of the year. In one way it was a damned nuisance but in another he couldn't wait for it to start because it would mean getting to fly a fighter. Trundling about in a Moth was all very well, but he was itching to get his hands on something a lot faster. He hadn't thought much about killing some other chap, but the idea didn't worry him especially. Fighter combat seemed a pretty civilized form of individual warfare. You either killed or were killed. A duel in the skies. Good, clean stuff and nothing like the gruesome carnage in the trenches that Simpkins had always harped on about. The needle had reached the end of the record and he stopped it.

Lewis came out of his room, sporting an out-size red rose in his buttonhole, topaz studs glinting down his boiled shirt, curly hair watered under control. He rubbed his hands, beaming. 'All set for a bloody good evening, old boy? Wait till you see my eye-popper.'

He might have known that it would be Anna.

All heads turned at her entrance and all conversation stopped. She put every other woman present into the shade, including Cynthia. Her long white evening gown was devoid of frills or fuss and she'd pinned her hair up on her head. She looked sensational. Round her neck she wore an extraordinary necklace that might have been something belonging to the Crown Jewels. Guy, pouring martinis, watched in amusement as Lewis made the introductions. The men's eyes duly popped and the women's snapped.

'This is Guy Ransome. We share rooms.'

'We've already met,' he said. 'Hallo, Anna.'

'I didn't know this was your college.'

He handed her a martini. 'And I didn't know you were coming this evening. How on earth did you come across a scoundrel like Lewis?'

'A cocktail party in London. I scarcely know him. But I was curious to see Oxford. Have you a cigarette, please?'

He offered his new case and she fitted the cigarette into a long holder. He flicked his lighter into life and as she bent towards the flame the jewels round her neck flashed green fire. 'Where on earth did you get that incredible necklace?'

'From my grandmother. She gave it to me.'

'It must be worth a king's ransom.'

'I am hoping so. But not for a king. Isn't that one of the *Grey Heron* brothers over there?'

'Tom Chilver? Yes, he's in a different college but he's a pretty good friend of Lewis's, so we asked him. He's got almost as much money as Lewis, you know. In case you're interested.'

'I am not.'

He smiled. 'How did you get here?'

'Lewis has a car. He drove me in it from London today. Very fast.'

'Are you staying at the Randolph?'

'I believe that was the name.'

'You want to watch out for Lewis, by the way.'

'I can take care of myself, thank you, Guy.'

Lewis swooped and removed her with a hissed aside: 'Hands off, old boy.'

'Do you know that girl?' Cynthia pouted up at him.

'I've known her for years. She lives with my aunt and uncle.'

'Is she French?'

He lit a cigarette. 'No, she's Austrian. She comes from Vienna.'

'Oh. Is she a sort of refugee, or something?'

'I suppose you could say that.'

'How odd. Well, she certainly looks awfully foreign.'

At dinner, Anna was seated at the other end of the table, but diagonally so that he could see her easily. From time to time he glanced across, but she never looked his way. Cynthia, beside him, prattled on about a cookery course that she was doing. He half-listened to her talking but his eyes kept returning to Anna. He thought about the first time he'd seen her, playing the piano in the drawing-room at Wimpole Street; she would have been about fourteen and he'd been pretty much bowled over. Poleaxed, actually. She'd made it clear from the start, though, how little she thought of him and how much she preferred Matt. He'd long since given up trying to impress her.

'. . . the meringues turned out to be a complete *disaster*. They'd gone all flat, just like cow-pats.' Cynthia giggled. 'It was an absolute *scream*.' She giggled again. He was beginning to regret having asked her; the giggling got on his nerves. Her cheeks were very flushed and she was getting squiffy which might have been to his advantage except that he had a feeling it was only going to be an infernal nuisance. She'd probably throw up by the end of the evening. He glanced across at Anna again and this time he managed to catch her eye. She smiled.

'Where have you been all my life, Anna?'

'In Vienna and in London, Lewis.' She brushed his hand off her knee for the twentieth time. He was quite drunk already, which was going to be very tiresome. Sober, he was rather amusing; drunk he would be a bore. She might need Guy to rescue her eventually. It had been a big mistake to accept the invitation. She could hear a dance orchestra playing somewhere and she was not in the mood for dancing. How could she dance when Mama and Papa were in such trouble? How could she sit with all these people stuffing themselves with food, drinking and joking and laughing, as though everything in the world were perfectly all right? It was a travesty. She looked at the faces around her. Had they no idea what was going on? Were they aware of the monster spreading its hideous tentacles over the Continent? Of course, the English didn't care. If they cared they would have tried to stop it; to slay it before it could grow and grow. If they were not very careful the tentacles would reach out as far as their own smug little island. She picked up her glass and drank more wine.

It was late in the evening by the time they went down to dance in a stiflingly hot marquee. She had drunk far more than she had ever done in her life and the kaleidoscope of couples on the dance floor made her feel nauseated. Lewis tried to hold her too close and she had to keep pushing him away. She danced next with Tom Chilver who was not so drunk but still a nuisance.

'I bet you don't remember me.'

'I remember you very well. You are the one who lost the sailing race.'

He laughed. 'I'm still jolly miffed about that. We would have beaten that old tub of Guy's easily if we hadn't had that bit of bad luck.'

'It was not bad luck, it was bad steering; you got stuck in the mud.'

'It can happen to anybody in those waters. Very tricky, you know.' He spun her round in a dizzy-making turn. 'I say, you look absolutely stunning tonight. An absolute knockout. Best-looking girl here.' Another whirling turn, the other way. 'Tell me, where are you living now?'

'I am still with Lizzie's family.'

'Wimpole Street, isn't it? I come to London quite a bit, as a matter of fact. We've got a place in Knightsbridge. I'll give you a buzz when I'm next in town. Maybe we could have dinner?'

After that she danced with another man who also wanted to take her out to dinner. He trod on her toes while asking for her telephone number which she gave, putting the numbers in the wrong order. Then it was Lewis again, who had become even drunker and grasped her with sweaty hands. She escaped to powder her nose and spent a long time redoing her hair at the mirror and wishing that the evening would end. The necklace winked at her in sympathy. When she returned to the table Guy stood up and asked her to dance.

'You don't look very happy.'

'I'm not. Lewis is drunk, and so am I. Or nearly. I have had much too much wine and champagne. My head is spinning round and round. Please dance very slowly.' She leaned against him. The band was playing something smooth and quiet; after a while she closed her eyes. When the music stopped, Guy took her outside into blessed fresh air. They walked away from the marquee along a piece of lawn and she could feel the dew seeping through the thin soles of her evening shoes. She took a deep breath. 'I feel better now.'

'Sure?'

'Yes. Thank you. Can we sit down somewhere?'

They sat on a stone step in the darkness. The dance music still reached them. 'Cigarette?' Guy offered his case, but she shook her head. 'I'm not yet that much better.' Guy was lighting his cigarette. 'Lewis will be searching high and low for you.'

'No. He will be very happy drinking even more champagne. But the girl you were with . . .'

'Cynthia.'

'She will wonder where you are.'

'She's fairly smashed, too.'

'Then perhaps they can both drink together. And they will not miss us at all.'

'The only snag is she's not really Lewis's type.'

'What is his type?'

'Someone like you. Exceptionally beautiful.'

'Are you drunk, too, Guy?'

'No.'

'Well, you've never told me any compliment before.'

'Paid. You *pay* compliments. You should know that by now.'

'You have never *paid* me one, then.'

'Well, you've never exactly encouraged me to, have you, Anna?'

'Perhaps not.'

'You know damn well you haven't. *Why* – that's what I'd like to know? What have you got against me?'

She shivered, rubbing her arms. 'It's cold out here. We should go back inside the tent. But then I will have to dance with Lewis again.'

'We could go up to my rooms,' he said. 'It'll be quiet there.'

Baxter had cleared away the debris from the dinner party but left the bottles and glasses. Guy picked up a half-empty one of champagne. 'Want some?'

'No, thank you.' She looked round. 'I like this room. You share it with Lewis?'

'This one, yes. We each have a bedroom that leads off it. Lewis's is through there, mine's this door.' He wondered whether there was any remote chance of getting Anna through it. He poured some champagne and sipped it, watching her as she moved about looking at books in the crammed bookcase, at Lewis's nude French bather on the wall, at his own framed print of Gloster Gladiators flying in close formation at the Hendon Pageant against a stormy sky.

'Do you still make models of aeroplanes, Guy?'

'Not lately. Not enough time. Too much else to do here. There's a hell of a lot going on at Oxford.'

She nodded. 'And if a war starts, I suppose you will have to leave all this?'

'I imagine so. But I'll be able to come back when it's over. I shouldn't think it will take long. The French will be on our side and they're supposed to have a first-class army.'

'The Germans may have one even better.'

'I wouldn't put it past them. Otto's gone off to join up, you know.'

'Yes, Lizzie told me. He came to the house to say goodbye. Fortunately I was out.' She turned to look at him. 'The Germans have tanks and planes and guns and many, many men, Guy. Everything that they need. What does England have?'

'We'll manage all right – if we have to.'

The dance-band music reached them clearly through the open window: 'Blue Moon'. Something of a coincidence. He reached across to switch off a lamp, leaving only one on – the low-wattage one. Another of the essential aids. 'Anyway, don't let's talk any more about that tonight. Dance?'

'If you like.' She moved into his arms. He didn't make the mistake of trying to hold her too near at first. Instead he engineered it very gradually, by degrees. She was wearing some kind of marvellous perfume and her hair felt like silk against his cheek.

The door crashed open, the overhead light snapped on and glared down. Lewis stood there, swaying belligerently. 'So there you two are. What the bloody hell do you think you're doing?'

'You've missed your breakfast, Mr Ransome. I'm sorry but I can't serve it after eight and it's nearly eleven. I left you to sleep, seeing as it's a Sunday.'

Matt's landlady was standing at the bottom of the stairs. She had taken out her curlers and was wearing what he knew to be her best: a plum-coloured silk dress and a matching hat decorated at the side with a very large black feather – origin uncertain. Crow? Rook? He had often wondered. A black cloth coat would go over the dress for church. 'It was a nice kipper, too.'

'Sorry, Mrs Honeywell.'

'Won't be quite so nice tomorrow.'

The kippers were never nice, whatever day they were served. They were desiccated, jaundiced creatures with papery skins and a thousand little bones. Even so, the one he had missed would have been something to eat, as opposed to nothing, and he was starving. He'd been swotting up anatomy until late. This term it would be his turn for a leg. Last term it had been an arm. He was looking forward to dissecting the foot. Like the hand, the foot was an amazingly beautiful piece of mechanism. Brilliantly designed. The organ of locomotion of invertebrates. The knee was another wondrous thing, too, of course. Without knees locomotion would be pretty tricky. Come to that, the whole human body was nothing less than a miracle. Mrs Honeywell was still at the bottom of the stairs. Funny she hadn't yet left for church.

'If you want to listen in the front room, Mr Ransome, you're quite welcome.'

'Listen?'

'To Mr Chamberlain speaking on the wireless. Quarter-past eleven. He's going to tell us if there's going to be a war. They made a special announcement early this morning. I shan't be going to church today. If Mr Hitler doesn't promise by eleven o'clock to get out of Poland, then it means there's going to be one.'

By eleven o'clock! Nobody would expect them to, of course. The Germans hadn't invaded Poland and dropped bombs all over the place just to turn round and go tamely home again because Mr Chamberlain had told them to. Mrs

Honeywell's long-case clock started clunking and whirring in its dark corner of the hall. Matt and his landlady stayed glued to where they were, one at the top of the stairs, the other at the bottom, listening for the first strike. They waited until the eleventh one had died away and went on standing in an uncertain silence for a few more moments. 'Well that's that, then,' Mrs Honeywell said emphatically, as though she had been expecting a personal telephone call from Hitler. 'We'd better switch on the wireless.'

He followed her into her front room. It was the first time he had been invited to cross the threshold. The door was always kept shut and, previously, he had only had brief glimpses when Mrs Honeywell entered or exited. It was a gloomy room: mottled wallpaper, brown armchairs, dark red patterned carpet, aspidistras in pots and fading sepia photographs of the late Mr Honeywell who had been gassed in the last war. Mrs Honeywell's large tabby cat was curled up on the most comfortable-looking of the armchairs and opened one malevolent green eye at him.

'You can sit down if you like, Mr Ransome.' She had switched on the wireless. 'We'll just let it warm up. Then I'll find the Home Service.' He perched on the edge of an armchair, waiting while she twirled the knob and the wireless crackled and gabbled. Father was away somewhere at sea but Mother would be listening at Tideways. Guy was in Paris, having some fun before the balloon went up – as he'd put it. He might not know a thing about it. Mrs Honeywell had tuned in successfully and lowered herself onto one of the other chairs. She sat bolt upright, hands clasped in her lap; he realized that she was wearing her hat in recognition of the solemnity of the occasion. Due to some oversight, she was also wearing her bedroom slippers.

Presently Mr Chamberlain's dry, metallic voice began. *'I am speaking to you from the Cabinet Room at ten Downing Street. This morning the British Ambassador in Berlin handed the German government a final note stating that unless we heard from them by eleven o'clock that they are prepared at once to withdraw their troops from Poland a state of war would exist between us. I have to tell you now that no such undertaking has been received and that consequently this country is at war with Germany.'* Mrs Honeywell got up to switch off the wireless. 'It's happening all over again,' she said heavily. 'All over again. All you young men'll be going off to war, just like before. Just like my Cedric.'

The sudden noise of a siren made them both jump. It wailed and shrieked, rising and falling. Mrs Honeywell seized hold of the cat who struggled indignantly. 'That's the air-raid warning. We must go to the Anderson at once, Mr Ransome. The Germans are coming to bomb us.' She hurried out of the room with the cat clawing and spitting in her arms.

Matt went out into the street and stood listening to the siren's howl and looking up at the sky. There was no sign of any enemy planes. People ran past him on their way to the nearest public shelter: a mother pushing a pram, dragging a small child who was howling with fright; an old woman being hustled along by a young one. 'Come on, Gran, for God's sake. We've got to get a move on.' A white-faced couple – the wife with a tiny baby wrapped in a shawl in her arms. A policeman called out as he hurried by. 'Get to a shelter, sir. Quick as you can.'

All you young men'll be going off to war. He touched his right sleeve. What bloody use was he going to be?

'I know how he felt,' the old man says. 'Felt just the same myself. What use am I going to be? I remember that day like yesterday. The whole country'd been waiting for it to happen for months. We'd been digging trenches and building shelters and filling sandbags . . . I'd already put an Anderson shelter at the bottom of the garden that summer and they'd given out the gas masks long before. Most of us'd not been too sorry about what happened at Munich – what were the Czechs to us? We didn't know a thing about them. But then I reckon we started to feel a bit ashamed of selling them out, so when we finally did something, it was a relief. Mind you, it wasn't so much fighting for the Czechs or the Poles, but that we were fighting against Hitler, at last. Molly and me sat and listened to the wireless together and when Mr Chamberlain had finished she says to me, "You needn't think you're going to go off and join up and get yourself killed, because they won't have you." She was right, of course.' He sighs. 'I remember you couldn't get blinds for the blackout for love nor money, or

*drawing-pins or brown paper. We made do some-
how with old curtains and cardboard and I
put that sticky tape criss-cross across the shop
windows. It was pitch black after dark. Nearly
broke my neck the first night, falling down some
steps.'*

*'And then nothing happened. Not for a long
while.'*

*He nods. 'That's right. No bombs, no enemy
planes, nothing. Our forces went off to France
and Belgium and sat around waiting for Jerry
to do something. The Phoney War, we called
it. The Bore War. Some people thought it'd be
over before it'd begun. Different at sea, though.
The U-boats were already after our merchant
ships – and they got the Royal Oak, didn't
they? Sneaked into Scapa Flow and sank her at
anchor. But then we got the Graf Spee, so we
were even. I don't know what the RAF were
doing. Dropping propaganda leaflets, I think,
that's all. What happened to Guy? Did he get
into the RAF?'*

*'He'd received his call-up papers within
two weeks of the outbreak of war and when
he reported to the Aircrew Receiving Centre at
Oxford they took him in the Volunteer Reserve.
He did initial training and then got a commission
almost at once because of his time in the University Air Squadron. He was sent to another
training centre for a fortnight for drill and
lectures and then, finally, he was posted up to a
flying training school on the north-east coast of
Scotland where he learned to fly Harvards. After*

287

that, he was sent to an Operational Training Unit near Wales to train on Hurricanes.'

Mr Potter sighs again. *'He was lucky. I'd like to have done something like that. Not just the ARP. How about the girl, Anna? Did she have any luck getting her parents out in time?'*

'She went to stay with Mademoiselle Gilbert and her mother in Lille and made contact with the organization, but when war broke out she still hadn't had any news of them.'

He shakes his head. *'They went and left it too late.'*

Chapter Thirteen

The sparkling white walls of the cloud canyon soared up like tall cliffs and its cotton-wool floor stretched far ahead. Above the perspex of the cockpit, beyond the white cliffs, the sky was pure azure blue. Guy flew the Hurricane very fast straight down the centre. He could see the shadow of the fighter flitting alongside him, like a ghostly companion. At the end of the corridor he burst out from the canyon into clear, sunlit sky and went into a long, slow barrel roll. He felt drunk with exaltation. The speed, the power, the sheer freedom were the most incredible things that he had ever experienced. He felt as though he had thrown off iron shackles. As though he could do anything.

And he remembered the bridge.

He banked and took the Hurricane down in a long, shallow dive until he could see it spanning the river. One or two of the other chaps in the Mess had bragged about flying under it and he'd been impressed but not sure he was capable of it. Now, he knew that he could. He brought the fighter down low and followed the river's course upstream for a way before turning back. As the bridge loomed ahead he came down still lower to within a few feet of the water, skimming its surface. There was quite a bit of cross-wind and the archway ahead looked impossibly small but he held the stick very steady. *Come on, girl. We can do it. We can do anything, you and I. Anything.* For a split second he thought they were going to hit and then they shot into the narrow opening and were through and out on the other side. Guy pulled back hard on the stick and he and the Hurricane rocketed up into the skies. He shouted aloud in triumph.

'I congratulate you, Leutnant von Reichenau. An excellent day's manoeuvres. The Panzer Corps is fortunate to have such able and dedicated young officers as yourself. What a pity you had not completed your training in time to join us in Poland.'

'I regret that, General.'

'Don't worry, you will soon be winning your spurs on our next campaign. When the time comes, we shall have no difficulty in overrunning northern Europe. The Norwegians and Danes will capitulate at once, the Belgians have no army to speak of and a stubborn fool for a king, and the Dutch have only antiquated weapons to match our new tanks and planes. We shall steam-roller our way into France.' The general smiled at him jovially. '*Der Schritt über di Grenzen*, eh? The march across frontiers. And once we are in France we shall devour the French army.'

'And the British, sir?'

'We need not worry too much about the British. Our Intelligence tells us that their forces are poorly armed and inexperienced and their communications a disaster. Their leaders are jealous of each other and are under the command of the French who are incompetent. The British and French have hated each other for years; they do not make happy bedfellows. Best of all, their own Intelligence is non-existent. They sit on their backsides behind their sacred Maginot Line and believe that they are safe and sound. Their men are growing bored, undisciplined, careless . . . That will prove to be their greatest mistake of all.' The general smiled. 'We shall give them the shock of their lives.'

'How soon, sir?'

'Come, come, *leutenant*, such things are Top Secret. But I am pleased to see you so keen. Let us say that the Führer is just as eager as yourself, but with winter already upon us you may have to contain your impatience until the spring.' The general tapped him playfully on the shoulder. 'Not even the Panzers and their tanks are immune to the weather.'

Otto came rigidly to attention and saluted as the general left. Stephan Stange, a fellow officer, sauntered up. 'You're the blue-eyed boy, Otto. They'll be pinning medals on you next. What did the old boy say to you?'

'He believes that we shall have no difficulty taking the Low Countries. And that the French and British will not withstand a surprise attack.'

Stephan nodded. 'I think he's right.'

'I am not quite so sure about the British.'

'Well, you know them better than I. What are they like?'

'Never to be underestimated.'

Guy appeared in Lizzie's attic studio one Saturday evening in December. She was busy cleaning brushes when she heard the door open and there he was in his RAF uniform, officer's cap dangling from his hand. He looked marvellous.

'I've got a couple of days' leave and thought I'd drop by. Aunt Helen said you were up here in your eyrie, as usual.' He came over and bent to kiss her cheek. He smiled down at her and flicked her chin lightly. 'There's some paint on your chin, did you know, Cousin Lizzie? No, don't rub it off, it looks very artistic.' He tossed his cap onto the table and took a silver case from a breast pocket that had wings sewn above it. 'Cigarette? No, of course, you're much too young for vices. Shocking habit.'

She watched him as he lit up. 'Aunt Sheila told us you're flying fighters.'

'That's right. Hurricanes. I'm rather hoping to transfer to Spitfires eventually but the Hurry's not bad at all.'

She pictured him swooping through the skies; very fast, very confident, very smooth. 'Is it a difficult plane to fly?'

'Piece of cake, really.' He put his lighter away in his trouser pocket and perched on the edge of the table. 'I gather Anna's still in France. Aunt

Helen said she and your father are pretty worried about her.'

'They went over to Lille in October to try and persuade her to come back but she wouldn't. She's still hoping to arrange for her parents to get to Switzerland but she hasn't heard anything from them since the war started. Nor have my parents.'

'If she won't come back to England, then she ought to try to go to Switzerland herself. If the Germans manage to invade France she could get caught there.'

'That's what Mummy and Daddy keep telling her, but she won't listen. She says the French insist it's not possible for the Germans to invade. They wouldn't get past their defences.'

'As always, she hasn't a clue what she's talking about. On recent form, I'd say the Huns were capable of anything. She's mad to stay there. I'll get the address from Aunt Helen and write and tell her not to be such a damn fool. Not that she'll take any notice of me. In fact, on second thoughts, it'd probably make her do just the opposite. I take it you'll be staying in London, Lizzie? Not packed off to the country with all the evacuees.'

'I'm rather old to be sent away with a label tied to me.'

He smiled at her. 'Sorry, I always forget. You must be what now . . . ?'

'Nearly eighteen.'

'God, are you really! How time flies. I always think of you as that little girl with pigtails.'

'I know you do.'

'You were such a solemn, anxious little thing. I used to believe you were a bit afraid of me.'

'I was. A bit.'

'Lord, was I that bad?'

'No. You were just very *good* at everything. It was rather nerve-racking.'

'Do you think Matt's ever felt like that? In the shade, because of his arm. Mother once said something of the sort, a long time ago.'

'I'm not sure. He's never talked about it to me.'

'Well, I damn well hope not. I never thought he minded about the arm, did you? He manages incredibly well with it. Anyway, he's going to be a fantastic doctor.' He looked at his watch. 'Lord, is that the time. Sorry, Lizzie, but I've got to dash. I'm due to pick someone up to go to the theatre.' He bent to kiss her cheek again. 'You know, you really oughtn't to stay here. London won't be exactly the safest place to be if things hot up.'

'If the Germans drop bombs on us, you mean. They don't seem to be bothering to.'

'They're too far away for their fighters to be able to protect their bombers at the moment, but that could change. You'd be much safer somewhere like Tideways. Mother would have you all like a shot.'

'Daddy wouldn't leave because of his work,' she said. 'And Mummy wouldn't want to leave him. Besides she's got involved with the WVS and she's awfully busy. And I wouldn't want to leave them.'

'Well, that's that, then. I'll just have to keep the Huns at bay for you.'

'We've turned the coal cellar into a shelter – it's right under the pavement, you know. It'd be perfectly safe and we've got bunks in it so we could sleep in there all night.'

'You might have to.' He picked up his cap and bent to kiss her cheek again. ''Bye then, Lizzie. Take care of yourself.'

'You, too, Guy.'

He smiled at her from the doorway: his most charming smile. 'I always do.'

If I'd ever been silly enough to let it happen, she thought wryly, he could have broken my heart.

At Christmas they went to Tideways. Guy was somewhere with the RAF and Uncle William away at sea, but Matt had come home. He was decorating the tree in the hall when Lizzie arrived with her parents. She gave him a hand. 'Thank God you're here to cheer us up, Lizzie,' he told her. 'Mother's in a real state about Father and Guy. She's convinced herself that Father's ship's going to be sunk by a U-boat. And now Guy's squadron's been sent to France.'

She said, dismayed, 'I didn't know that, Matt. He came to the house a week or two ago – when he was on some leave – but he didn't say anything about it.'

'Probably didn't know himself, then. And anyway they're not allowed to tell anyone any details. We had a letter from him two days ago, saying he was somewhere in France. He says they're living in the lap of luxury, billeted in a commandeered château, and that the food and wine are fantastic but the weather's awful. Freezing cold and lots of snow and almost no flying. Here, you always do this one.' He gave her the beautiful glass angel with outstretched wings. She stood on tiptoe and hung it as high as she could reach. 'How long will he be there, do you think?'

'In France? I don't know. They'll need the RAF to give air cover to our troops if the Germans try anything, I imagine. Here's another one.'

'You don't think there's any chance that the Germans'll give up, now they've got what they wanted?'

'I think Hitler wants a whole lot more.' Matt fiddled clumsily with the lights. He was only using his good hand, she noticed, keeping the other one out of sight. 'I hope I'm doing these all right. Guy always used to do them.'

'They look fine.'

'Is there any news of Anna?'

'She wrote to say that she's been promised that her parents will be able to go to Switzerland very soon. It's all being arranged, apparently.'

'That's wonderful. Poor Anna! It must have been awful for her, waiting and waiting. Will she be coming back here?'

'She says she'll try to go to Switzerland if she can. To be with her parents.'

He looked crestfallen. 'I hoped she'd come back here. What a rotten Christmas! No Father. No Guy. No Anna. No Nereus.'

'What's happened to Nereus?'

'Didn't you hear, Lizzie? He died last month.'

'Oh, no . . .' Tears came into her eyes. 'Oh, Matt, I'm sorry. I'll miss him.'

'Well, he was pretty old, you know. I expect it was best for him.'

Nothing was the same. Everything was changing so fast and it was frightening. Even Christmas itself was different. There were no candles, no crackers and no charades and Aunt Sheila started crying in the middle of the lunch. On Boxing Day Lizzie and Matt walked down towards the jetty. It was bitterly cold with a sullenly overcast sky. They passed Nereus's grave, in a quiet corner beneath a tree and marked by a stone with his name on it. 'I can't remember a time without him,' Matt said. 'I keep expecting him to appear, just like he always used to. It's weird.'

'Will you get another dog?'

He shook his head. 'Mother wants to shut up the house. She says she can't stand it here on her own. I heard your mother suggesting she came to stay in London with you. I think it's a good idea. She's have some company and she wouldn't be so miserable.'

'Guy thinks the Germans might bomb London.'

'When did he say that?'

'When he called by that time. He thinks we really ought to leave London. We won't, though. We've got our shelter in the coal-hole, so we'd be quite safe.' They had reached the top of the steps leading down to the river and the jetty. 'Where's the *Rose*?'

'In the boat-house. Guy and I put her away for the winer – well, for the duration, most probably. I doubt if we'll get her out till the war's over.' They walked down the steps and out onto the jetty, their feet making hollow sounds on the planking. 'Don't tell Mother, Lizzie, but I've applied to join the army. I don't suppose they'll have me, but it's worth a try.'

She glanced at his face. 'It means a lot to you, doesn't it, Matt? That they take you?'

'Yes, it does. I can't stand the thought of being left out. I'm fit and strong and I can do most things, but they probably won't see it that way. Heavens, they turn you down for flat feet, apparently.' He gave her a quick sideways grin. 'Not a word to a soul.'

'Don't you split on me, then. I'm trying to join the Women's Air Force but they probably won't have me either because I'm not actually eighteen yet. Don't say anything, though. My parents are dead against the idea.'

'You know I won't. Why the Air Force?'

'I thought that might be easier to get into because it's new. Most girls seem to want to join the WRNS. Or the ATS.'

'I thought perhaps it might be because of Guy.' He picked up a stick off the jetty with his good hand and hurled it hard across the water. 'You never know, you might bump into him.' The stick had sailed high into the air and landed far out in the river. 'We're in the same boat then, aren't we,

Lizzie? Both praying for the chance to do something.' They watched the stick being carried fast downstream.

Anna leaned her bicycle against the wall beside the courtyard door. She tugged at the bell handle and listened to its jangle inside the house. The sound died away to silence. She pulled it again, harder this time, and the jangling went on longer. Still silence and then, after a while, the rasp of iron bolts being dragged back. The door opened halfway. His bearded face was hidden in shadow.

'What do you want?'

'You know very well, monsieur. I want the news of my parents that you promised.'

'I have no news yet. You should not come here so often. I told you that it would take time. You must have patience.'

'I've been patient for long enough.' She shoved the door hard, catching him off balance so that he staggered back. 'I insist on talking with you.'

He shrugged. 'Since you are already inside, mademoiselle . . .' She followed him down the dark passageway and into an even darker inner room, cold as a tomb but richly coloured. Oriental rugs were hung on flaking plaster walls, piled high on the stone flagged floor, draped over furniture. He was a dealer in expensive and rare carpets, an Armenian who had lived in France for many years. A Jew. She faced him.

'When I first came to see you, monsieur, you gave me your assurance that it would be a matter of weeks before my parents were safe in

Switzerland. It has been months and there is still no news.'

He spread his hands, palms up. 'There was great difficulty in finding your mother and father – I told you. Since they were no longer at the address you gave me, it took much searching before they were found. Much time was wasted.'

They had been traced to an address in a part of Vienna that she had never heard of – a poor quarter, she had been told, where they and other Jews were lying low from the Nazis. It would still be possible to help them, but it would be dangerous and it would cost more money. She had sold the necklace to a jeweller in Lille for far less than its real worth. It was too old-fashioned. Nobody wore such jewellery any longer, certainly not now that France was at war. Nevertheless it had raised enough to meet the sum necessary to pay for her parents' freedom. Half of it she had handed over to the Armenian in advance; the remainder she had kept back.

'But since they were found, what progress has been made? How and when are they to leave Vienna? Do they now have the necessary papers to enter Switzerland? What route will they take?'

He raised his hands in mock consternation. 'Always so many questions, mademoiselle. You ask things that I cannot tell you. I do not know how these things are accomplished. It must all be achieved in the utmost secrecy. Papers must be falsified, contacts made, money change hands . . . and all with much caution. My contacts are at

300

great risk from the Nazis if it should be discovered that they are helping the Jews.'

'They are well paid for it,' she said coldly. 'And it is not for love of Jews but for love of money.'

'Unfortunately, they are asking for more. It would be as well to give it to them. Part of the balance . . .'

'I told you that I am not giving another sou to them until my parents are in Switzerland. That was the arrangement.'

Another shrug. 'As you please. But I understood that the safety of your mother and father was of paramount importance to you.'

'You know very well that it is. Why else would I be here? Who are these people? They are not Jews, like we are. Are they Austrians? German? Swiss?'

'More questions, mademoiselle! Alas, I am not at liberty to tell you anything. That is the way these things work. It is all a matter of trust.'

'*Trust!* How can I trust them when I am told nothing? How can I trust *you*, monsieur? You have taken my money – a great deal of money – and yet nothing has been achieved. For all I know you are cheating me—'

'Please, mademoiselle, calm yourself. It serves no purpose to make these unfounded accusations.'

'I shall go to the police and tell them that you have taken money under false pretences.'

His eyes glittered. 'Then you will certainly never see your mother or father again.'

The words hung ominously between them.

'Very well, I will pay more. Another quarter. The final quarter I keep until they are safe.'

'I knew that you would see reason, mademoiselle. You are far too clever not to.'

She gave him the money and he followed her down the dark passageway to the courtyard door. 'I will let you know as soon as I have news, mademoiselle. It will not be long now, I promise.' The heavy bolts grated home behind her.

She rode the bicycle through streets treacherous with frozen ice and snow to Madame Gilbert's apartment on the other side of Lille. It was a gloomy warren of lofty rooms full of monstrously ugly furniture and shuttered against daylight and fresh air. And it smelled of the old woman. Anna left the bicycle outside and climbed the stairs to the door. Mademoiselle Gilbert would still be out, teaching at a school in the town, but Madame would certainly be there because she only ever went out in the mornings – and then no more than a few steps as far as the *boulangerie* or the *épicerie* or the daily market in the next street. She would hear her foot on the stair and call out in that querulous voice of hers – wanting something fetched or carried or another thing done that she was perfectly capable of doing herself. Sure enough, Anna had scarcely opened the apartment door when the old woman was screeching her name. She opened the door to the salon where a black marble clock, sombre as a headstone, ticked away the hours on the mantelpiece.

'You have a visitor. An Englishman. I told him

to wait in the *salle à manger*. He has been waiting for you for nearly an hour.'

It was Guy. He was standing there, wearing a thick grey-blue military overcoat over uniform and smoking a cigarette. A peaked cap of the same colour lay on the dining-table.

'In the name of God, what are you doing here, Guy?'

'I didn't expect you to be particularly pleased to see me, Anna, but even so, that's rather unflattering.'

In fact, she was extremely pleased to see him. He looked so very comfortingly English, familiar and safe. Also, it had to be said, very handsome in his fine uniform. After all the months of miserable worrying and waiting, she felt close to throwing herself into his arms and weeping unashamedly on his chest. 'I'm sorry – it's a big surprise. Lizzie wrote to me that you were somewhere in France with the Royal Air Force but she did not know where. She said you are already flying fighter planes.'

'Well, learning to fly at Oxford rather speeded things up. And they're rather keen on training as many fighter pilots as possible just now.'

'But how are you here – in Lille?'

'Our squadron was sent over to France before Christmas. We've been based near Reims. Lizzie's mother gave me your address when I was in London and I thought I'd nip up on the train and see how you were. Take you out for dinner, if you'd like.'

They went for champagne cocktails in the

American Bar of the Café Jeanne and then on to the Huitrière close by where they ate chicken stuffed with truffles, then lemon soufflé and finished with Napoleon brandy. The restaurant was crowded with British and French officers in uniform and smartly dressed French civilians, all laughing and enjoying themselves as though they had never heard of the war. She pointed it out to Guy. 'How can they be so unconcerned, so *nonchalants*? It's incredible.'

'We're rather doing the same at the moment, aren't we? I don't much see the point of not enjoying life for as long as we can. The fun's going to stop eventually.' He leaned over to light her cigarette. 'Everyone's very worried about you in England, you know.'

'Yes . . . They write all the time, asking when I am coming back. I write letters to them, too. I'm sorry that I worry them.'

'And when will you go back?'

'Not until the war is over. I shall go to Switzerland to meet my parents there, if I can.'

'It's definitely arranged for them, then?'

'Not exactly – no. But it will be soon. It's promised.'

He smoked his cigarette, studying her. 'And just who are these mysterious people who are supposed to be organizing it all?'

'I have met only one of them – a man here, in Lille. He doesn't actually arrange it himself. He has contacts.'

'Have you already paid him?'

'Part of the amount.'

'How much?'

'That is my affair, Guy. I sold the necklace my grandmother gave me. The one I wore for the Oxford ball.'

'I remember it well. What a pity.'

'It's not a pity to me if it saves my parents.'

'This man could be swindling you, Anna. Taking your money. Making all these promises but doing absolutely nothing.'

'He has already helped others known to Mademoiselle Gilbert.'

'Some time ago, maybe. But things are very different now. We're at war.'

'There is no need to remind me of that. Is that why you came to see me, Guy? To criticize me? To give me a long lecture?'

'No. To try and make you see sense. You're not safe here. The French could intern you at any moment – they might even take it into their heads that you're a spy.'

'The police have interviewed me. Mademoiselle Gilbert has vouched for me. They know that I am a Jewish refugee.'

'They might change their minds when things get worse. You could get stuck here in France and caught by the Germans if they invade. Do you want that to happen to you?'

'The French will stop them. They have a big army. And you are here, too – the British. The Germans would be driven back. I am not leaving yet, Guy.'

He gave an exasperated sigh. 'What are you living on?'

'I still have money left from my parents and some from the necklace, and I am giving lessons in German. There are business people in Lille who believe that it may be a wise idea to improve their German.' She smiled. 'The French are very practical. And Mademoiselle Gilbert is very kind – she does not charge me rent.'

'It's absolutely freezing in that place. Don't they ever light a fire?'

'Madame Gilbert is too mean.'

'Is she the appalling old woman who let me in?'

'Unfortunately, yes.'

'Well, she was unbelievably rude.'

'She always is. She's utterly loathsome.'

'Then why do you stay?'

'I have already told you why.'

He shook his head despairingly. 'Look, Anna, I know you don't think much of me and you've never taken a blind bit of notice of anything I've ever said, but for God's sake listen to me this time. You're in danger. You should go back to that place, pack your bags, get on the first train to Calais and take the first boat to England.'

'I can't.'

'Well, I think you're being very silly and stubborn. It's crazy to put yourself in such danger. Do you imagine that your parents would wish it? Haven't you thought about that?'

'What about the danger *they* are in? Have *you* thought about that? Do you know what they are doing to Jews in Germany and Austria? They

306

are beating them, torturing them, sending them to slave camps, killing them.'

'All the more reason for you to go back to England, where you'll be safe.'

She said coldly, 'That's a thoughtless thing to say, Guy. Would you desert your parents? Would you run away to save your own skin, if they were in danger and you might be able to help them?'

'Of course I wouldn't. But that's not the point—'

'It is for me. Exactly the point.'

'I can see it's not the slightest use arguing with you.' He glanced at his watch and stubbed out his cigarette. 'Look, I've got to get the train back . . . I'll try and come up again.'

'There's no need to trouble yourself.'

'You mean you'd much sooner I didn't.'

'Not if you are going to lecture me again.'

He looked at her steadily for a moment. 'OK, Anna, I promise not to. But for God's sake be careful.'

When she returned to the apartment Madame Gilbert screeched to her from the salon.

'What do you want, madame?'

'Janine has gone out and the clock has stopped. It must be rewound.'

'Very well.' She opened the glass, fitted the key and turned it.

'Who was the Englishman? What was he doing here?'

'He is someone I knew in England.'

'Is he your lover?' The coal eyes watched her pruriently.

'No.'

'But he would like to be. I could tell. And you would like him to be, *n'est-ce pas?*'

She reset the hands, ignoring the remark. The marble clock resumed its dreary ticking away of the minutes, the hours and the days. Soon it would be the end of March. March would become April. The bitter winter would be over; the weather would get warmer and, without a doubt, the Nazis would strike.

Chapter Fourteen

By March, Otto had been promoted to *oberleut-nant*. He knew this was due to strings being pulled rather than to any particular prowess on his own part. The winter had been spent in rigorous training but there had been no chance, as yet, to prove his ability in the field. When one did come, however, he was confident that he would acquit himself well. There had been a rumour of some action in November but bad weather had put a stop to the possibility. In January the Panzers had actually moved into position to launch an attack on the Low Countries. The Führer, it was said, would delay no longer. He had promised the German people *Lebensraum* – the space to live and grow – and they were to be given it. And then something had happened to force yet another cancellation: vital invasion documents had, apparently, fallen into Belgian hands when a Luftwaffe aircraft had made a forced landing. The attack had been abandoned. Since then the weather had been atrocious but, with the melting of the snow and the coming of spring, the rumours were starting again. The Führer was making up his mind when and where they would make their move. It was going to happen at last, and soon.

His fellow officer, Stephan Stange, who had his ear permanently to the ground, boasted inside knowledge. 'We are to attack Belgium first. We bomb Brussels and our airborne troops seize Belgian fortifications and overrun their lines of defence on the weakest stretch of the Maginot Line, to the north-west. Then we do the same to Holland. The Allies will be forced to reposition their troops while the main thrust of our armoured divisions will take place further south and where it will be least expected. Guess where?'

Otto had speculated on this many times, without reaching a conclusion. 'You may as well tell me.'

'The Ardennes Forest.'

'Impossible. The terrain would be too difficult and unsuitable for tanks. It's practically impenetrable.'

'I assure you that is what they are planning. The Führer, himself, has approved.'

'But it would take many days, weeks even, to get through and the advantage of surprise would be lost.'

Stephan shrugged. 'Don't believe me, then. I tell you, the Panzers are to spearhead the offensive. We are to plunge into the Ardennes and forge our way into France. The French have only a small force guarding that stretch of the frontier. We shall smash through them easily. Little or no resistance is expected from French civilians *en route.*' Stephan grinned at him. 'So there you have it, my friend. The long wait will soon be over and glory awaits us. French food and French wine and French women. With luck, we shall be in Paris in the spring. What could be more delightful? Why aren't you smiling?'

'It's a long way from here to Paris.'

'In our tanks it will be no distance at all. And then perhaps it will be England's turn.'

'England? Have you forgotten the sea that lies in between?'

Stephan waved a hand dismissively. 'We will bomb the British the same as we did the Poles, and just like the Belgians and the Dutch. Pound them into submission. Their Expeditionary Force will have been killed or captured in Belgium and France and we will destroy their Royal Air Force with our Luftwaffe. We have many more planes, our pilots are better and more experienced and it will be easy from French airfields.'

'We will still have to contend with the Royal Navy.'

'Pah! We will bomb their ships. Sink them all. Why are you being so pessimistic, Otto? What's the matter with you? I thought you were so confident of our victory.'

'I am confident that we shall invade France and defeat the French. I am not so certain about England and the English. I told you that before.'

'One would almost think you didn't wish it to happen.'

'I believe even the Führer has his reservations.'

'Well, I for one am not so keen either, to tell

the truth. I have always heard that English girls are cold. We shall have no worries in France on that score. And since you are the rich one, Otto, you may stand me dinner in Paris with the best wine and the best food and we will find ourselves two of the most beautiful women in the city. What do you say? Is that a deal?'

Otto smiled. 'When we are driving down the Champs Elysées in our tanks, Stephan, then you may take it as a promise.'

Guy spotted the Messerschmitt about five thousand feet below him. It had popped out suddenly from the broken cloud layer and he could see it streaking along, heading due east. It was only the second time that he'd sighted an enemy aircraft – the first had been months ago when the squadron had chased some Heinkels back over the frontier. His heart raced with excitement. It was a 109, no doubt about it. He could see its shape clearly. Christ, he'd even made a model of the damn thing! He knew all about it. Every detail. Faster than him but slightly less manoeuvrable. He could out-turn the Hun if he was clever but, on the other hand, the 109 had cannon power as well as machine-guns. He tracked it for a moment. The fighter was on its own, so far as he could tell, presumably either on photo-reconnaissance or some cheeky hit-and-run raid. OK, time to put paid to his little excursion. The Merlin engine snarled like an angry guard dog as Guy banked sharply and took the Hurricane down in a steep dive.

Either the chap was half asleep or so bloody confident that he wasn't keeping a sharp lookout because he was close enough to distinguish the black crosses on the wings, the yellow spinner and the grey and green camouflage before the Hun was aware of him. The 109 rolled suddenly into a dive and headed like the clappers for the nearest bit of cloud. Guy tore after him and opened fire at a thousand yards. The Brownings blasted his ears and the Hurry seemed to falter under their recoil. Too soon. Much too soon. He could see the tracer zipping harmlessly past the Hun's tail while the 109, gaining speed, increased the gap between them. Futilely, he fired again, and missed again. Guy swore violently as the Messerschmitt vanished into the cloud. He streaked after it but without much hope and searched, flying in and out of patches of cloud. It was like hunting among bushes: a game of hide-and-seek. He switched tanks and went on for a while longer, straining his eyes and cricking his neck before he gave up and turned for home, frustrated and furious with himself. If he'd held his fire until six hundred yards, or even closer, he might have got the blighter.

He circled the 'drome, passing over the beautiful old château where the squadron was billeted. There was still the odd white streak of snow here and there but most of it had gone. He could see yellow drifts of daffodils on the lawns, new green speckling the tall trees, the pale beginnings of blossom in an orchard and a farmer hard at work with his horse-drawn plough in a nearby field.

Instead of ground hard as iron, it would be a soft landing. He came in, side-slipping over a clump of trees, to touch down smoothly on the grass.

Lunch in the Mess – once a gilded ballroom – was well up to scratch: a superb venison pie with meltingly flaky pastry, French cheeses, cold beer. Some of the other pilots were planning a trip into town that evening and invited him along. He knew the form well. They'd pile into one of the trucks, kick off at an *estaminet* for a few drinks and then progress to one of the excellent restaurants. With the warmer weather, the tables were already out on the pavements, the parasols in place, the flower stalls opening up, the French girls in pretty cotton frocks. Spring was here and summer would soon be a-coming in. The very last thing anybody appeared to be thinking about – civilians or servicemen – was the war. Anna would find it incredible. Guy wondered how much longer the play-acting could possibly last.

Aunt Sheila had closed up Tideways towards the end of January and moved into the house in Wimpole Street. She and Lizzie's mother were kept busy with work for the WVS, helping with the children being evacuated to the country from London. Uncle William came home on leave, looking tired and grim. He and her father spent a lot of time together in the study and there was talk of Lizzie, her mother and Aunt Sheila going to somewhere like Wales. To Lizzie's relief, her mother and Aunt Sheila both flatly refused. There had been no air raids at all in spite of all the flapping, and the shelter in the coal cellar which had looked almost cosy last September was now a hell-hole. Over the winter, the bunk mattresses had grown mould and the walls and roof dripped with moisture. They had started using part of it to store coal again.

Sometimes, but not often, Matt came round for supper. One evening, near the end of April, they went up to the attic studio afterwards. There was still enough daylight left not to bother with switching on the electric light and having to do the blackout.

Matt propped himself against a high stool while she sorted out some paints. He'd been bogged down in anatomy, he told her, dissecting a leg.

'A leg? You mean from a guinea-pig or something?'

'No, actually, it's a real one. People leave their bodies in their wills. Very decent of them, considering the hash we students make of it.'

Lizzie shuddered. 'How horrible!'

'It isn't really,' he said enthusiastically. 'Everything fits together so well and works so cleverly, you see. It's an amazing thing, the human body, you know. Miraculous.'

'I'll stick to drawing it on the outside, I think.'

'Of course, you'd need to know anatomy, too. Where the muscles are, and so on. You can come and help me with my leg, if you want.'

'No *thanks*.'

'Just a suggestion. Any news from Anna, by the way?'

'I had a letter last week.'

'Is she going to come back?'

'She didn't say so.'

'Well, I wish she would.'

'We keep worrying about what on earth's going to happen to her. She still believes she can get her parents out of Austria, but I don't think there's much hope. She said she saw Guy a while ago. He turned up at the house in Lille and tried to persuade her to give up and come back. She said he gave her a real talking-to.'

'I don't suppose she took much notice of him. She never did before.'

'No, she didn't, did she? They were always fighting.'

There was a pause. Matt picked up a paint-brush and twirled it in his good hand. 'The army turned me down, by the way – because of the arm. They told me I'd be more use as a doctor, in any case.' He spoke lightly but she knew how fed up and bitterly disappointed he was about it. 'I'm very sorry, Matt. They're probably right, though. I mean, anybody can be a soldier but not everyone can become a doctor.'

'Thanks for the comforting words, Lizzie. The only trouble is that I've got another four years at least before I qualify and become useful.'

'The war might last that long.'

'Actually, I'm afraid it might. Once it gets going properly. I think the Germans have just been playing a waiting game all last winter, getting themselves ready. How about you and the WAAF? Any news – now you're eighteen?'

'Well, I passed my medical OK. They said they'd be writing to tell me when and where to report for duty. It might be several weeks before I hear, apparently.'

'Do your parents know?'

'Yes, I told them. Had to, really, as I'm still under twenty-one. They were OK about it in the end.'

'You're lucky, Lizzie. I'd give my right arm to go into the services.' He smiled ruefully. 'Well, actually, perhaps that wouldn't be such a big sacrifice.' He twirled the brush again. 'I wonder what Otto's up to? Odd to think of him on the other side.'

'I know.'

'You liked him, didn't you, Lizzie? I thought he was pretty OK too.'

'Yes, I did rather. Anna hated him, of course. Because he was German.'

'You can't blame her really.'

'I think he was probably very much in love with her, though she never knew it.'

'Can't blame *him* for that either.'

Matt loves her too, Lizzie thought. I can hear it in his voice – the way he spoke just then. The look on his face. He's always loved her. I've known that for a long time. She suspected that even Guy, for all his antipathy, was far from immune. The old envy that she had felt when she had first seen Anna standing on the station platform suddenly flooded back. Secretly, in her heart, she almost wished that Anna would never return. She shut the box of oil paints, disgusted with herself. 'We'd better do the blackout, Matt. It's getting dark.'

'So, where is your English lover, eh?' Madame Gilbert was watching her from her corner chair.

'He is not my lover.'

'So you say. When is he coming here again, that young man in his fine uniform?'

'How should I know? Probably never. He is busy.'

'He will come, though, as soon as he can. He will want to see you again, mark my words. I can tell.' She was like a witch, Anna thought. A hundred years ago they would have burned her. 'He wants you to go back to England, isn't that so?'

'No.'

'Yes, he does. He told me.' The old woman wagged a finger at her. 'You should do what he says. You are doing no good here. It is a waste of time. And when the Germans come you will cause us trouble. You will put us in danger for harbouring a Jewess. I have told Janine that you must leave very soon. If you cannot go to Switzerland then you must go back to England, before the *Bosches* come.'

'What are you talking about, madame? The French have a big army to fight the Germans.'

'With an old fool to lead them. It will be a disaster.'

'And the British are here.'

318

'Pah! *Les Anglais!* We shall see what *they* are made of when the time comes.'

What did she know of anything? She was just a crazy old woman. There was no such talk in Lille. Life was going on as normal. Everybody had faith in the armies, and she had seen for herself that neither the French nor British were in the least worried. The Germans would never break through.

'They took us all by surprise, and that's a fact. The tenth of May, it was, if I remember rightly. The Jerry gliders landed at dawn in Belgium and their Stukas backed up the paratroopers. Same time as they attacked Holland. They'd got a foothold in both countries within hours. The Belgians had been so busy trying to stay neutral they wouldn't let our troops across their border before but as soon as that happened, of course, they were screaming for us. Then Jerry bombed Rotterdam flat and the Dutch surrendered.' His pipe has gone out again, but he doesn't seem to notice. 'Even then, we didn't know how bad it was – not for a bit. The French and our lot rushed up to help the Belgians and there was all that rubbish in the newspapers about beating back the Jerries, tanks meeting tanks, nothing to worry about . . . Wasn't true, of course. And what's more, we'd walked right into Hitler's trap. He wanted us there in Belgium because that got us out of the way of the biggest part of his invasion army – the lot that went through the Ardennes.'

Chapter Fifteen

The long line of Panzer tanks rumbled slowly, nose to tail, down the forest road. Together with armoured vehicles and mobile artillery they had drawn up at the Luxembourg border in three columns that stretched a hundred miles back into Germany. At nightfall they had begun moving off through the darkness, each one following the hooded rear light of the tank ahead – something they had practised many times before. By dawn they had crossed Luxembourg and plunged into the Ardennes and daylight found them well advanced into the heart of the forest, snaking their way along the steep, winding roads.

Otto stood in the turret of his tank, one hand gripping the rim, field-glasses slung round his neck. He could remember a summer holiday spent in the forest as a child. He and his father had stayed in a hotel at Bouillon. He remembered the thickly wooded landscape well, the narrow roads linking small villages, the occasional spaces of lush pasture. The trees were not yet so green but otherwise it was all the same as in his memory, except that the birdsong was obliterated by the roar and rumble of the tanks. He searched the skies constantly through the branches above his head. It seemed extraordinary that the enemy was not attacking from the air. It would be difficult for bombers where the trees were densest, but whenever it passed through a clearing the long column was easily visible and wrecked tanks could have brought them all to a halt. Stephan had been right, though he had not believed him at the time; still could not believe that a successful breakthrough could be made. If the enemy were not going to bomb them, then they would surely attack with all the forces and fury that they could muster as soon as the tanks emerged from the forest and attempted to cross the river Meuse. The sound of aircraft made him glance up quickly in time to see three Messerschmitt 109s pass overhead. The Panzers had been given fighter cover but not even the Luftwaffe could guard the whole long length of the columns.

They had passed through several small villages without pausing and in each case the few French inhabitants visible had either fled indoors or cowered in terror. There had not been a single shot fired at them, not a single challenge, not even so much as a shaken fist. Several miles further on, along a stretch of twisting road where there were few trees, another aircraft passed overhead – this time a British bomber: a Blenheim. It made no attempt to attack and flew off. Incredible as it seemed to Otto, the Blenheim appeared to be merely on a reconnaissance mission. What fools the enemy must be to miss such a chance to crush the exposed tanks, crawling along in slow procession like slugs, and just as vulnerable.

The day was warming up, the sun shining brightly through the branches, the sky a clear blue. Again, Otto was reminded of his summer holiday long ago. It had been weather like this and he and his father had gone hiking through the forest. He had been eight years old and life had been uncomplicated. It seemed to him that after that holiday, nothing had ever been quite so enjoyable. Except, perhaps, the days he had spent at Tideways that summer in England.

The tank three ahead, belonging to Stephan's group, broke down suddenly and the column behind was halted while attempts were made to repair it. Stephan came over, grinning widely. 'What did I tell you, my friend, nothing stands in our way.'

'At the moment this tank of yours does.'

'It will be mended in a moment, or shoved aside. We shall steamroller our way right across France.'

'Unfortunately, there is the small problem of crossing the river Meuse before we can do that.'

'There are bridges.'

'Even the French may get around to thinking of blowing them up.'

'Then we shall build our own. We have the finest engineers in the world. Nothing shall stop us, Otto. Have you seen how the French are in the villages? They look at us with fear in their eyes and let us pass without a murmur. Soon they will be welcoming us as liberators. Wait and see.'

The stricken tank was taking too long to repair and was pushed off the road. The column rolled forward once more. When they were out in the open, RAF Fairey Battle bombers at last appeared to attack them. Otto counted at least fifteen of them lumbering in on their bombing runs and he watched them being shot down, one after the other – picked off easily by the anti-aircraft artillery, like so many ducks. Those that weren't brought down were winged and made off before they could do any real harm. So much for the RAF with their obsolete old machines! Beside the Luftwaffe, they were nothing. The Panzers rolled on and passed through a small French town, rumbling like thunder over the cobblestones of the square. As before, the inhabitants crouched in doorways and hid behind walls – except for a small group of girls who stood on a corner and waved as they went by. They were all pretty and all smiling and one of them threw a flower which landed on the front of Otto's tank, blooming brightly against the dusty grey paint like a good omen. He smiled back at her. Once again, Stephan had been right.

'Bandits at ten o'clock low, chaps.' Guy's squadron CO's voice crackled in his ears. He leaned forward in the cockpit and searched the skies below. Christ, there was a whole bloody swarm of them down there – looked like at least thirty Heinkels with a pack of Messerschmitt

110s behind them. The R/T crackled again. 'Close up, everyone. Tight as you can.' The squadron altered course in neat formation towards the enemy. Guy, watching wingtips as well as Huns, wished to God his squadron commander would think up a better way of flying into battle. The German fighters didn't stick to the same old formations as though they were in a bloody Hendon air pageant; they'd learned better in the Spanish Civil War. The RAF were living in the past, and paying for it. The squadron had lost three Hurricanes and their pilots two days ago, picked off, in turn, from the rear before anyone had even known there were German fighters around. The day before that fiasco, they'd escorted a squadron of Battles to their deaths at the hands of German ground-artillery fire. The bridge over the river Meuse that the antiquated Battles had been sent to flatten had remained standing while the wrecked bombers lay strewn about and smouldering on the ground. Five of the squadron's Hurricanes had been demolished by attacking 109s who had outnumbered them five to one. Since the Germans had made their assault, the RAF losses had been grim.

The R/T crackled once more. 'Line astern. Close up. Go for the bombers first, chaps.' Here we go again, Guy thought. They swooped down on the Heinkels, firing in bursts, before breaking away to go round again. Guy scored a hit on one and saw it stagger sideways, its port engine erupting smoke. He hauled back hard on the stick and opened the throttle to climb fast for another go. The bombers were returning fire but the Hurricanes' speed gave them the advantage – until the 110s joined the party. They dropped down from above like rocks, spread out wide in line abreast, and within seconds the air was a maelstrom of aircraft – the fighters on both sides screaming around the bombers who ploughed on steadily through the thick of it. A Messerschmitt hurled itself head-on at Guy. He rammed the stick forward and the Hun shrieked over his head. Another was immediately on his tail and he flung his fighter to the left and missed another Hurricane's wing by inches. Guns spitting fire, they climbed and dived, dodged and weaved for what seemed like hours but was, in reality, only a matter of minutes. Out of ammo and low on fuel, the Hurricanes left the fray – those that had survived. Every plane had been hit and damaged, including Guy's, and four of them had been shot down, against a tally of one Heinkel and none of the 110s.

They flew home to find that the Germans had visited the 'drome in their absence. The lush spring grass was dented with bomb craters and littered with smoking wreckage that included three more Hurricanes.

'Junkers 88s,' the adjutant told them. 'Six of the buggers. They got two petrol bowsers as well. Two men killed. Oh and by the way, apparently the Jerries have crossed the Meuse and taken Sedan. We've had orders to decamp north, to a place thirty kilometres south-west of Lille.'

'Retreating?' Guy enquired.

'Regrouping,' the adjutant said firmly.

Otto had expected the crossing of the river Meuse to be far more difficult than Stephan had predicted. He was proved right in one respect – the French had, indeed, blown up the bridges, leaving the Panzers stranded on the east side of the river and backed up for many miles – a wonderful target. 'If they don't attack us now,' he had told Stephan, 'they deserve to lose the war.' A few RAF bombers had come over and the French artillery on the other side of the river had put some of the tanks out of action, but no great damage had been done. And then the Luftwaffe Stukas had arrived. Wave after wave of them had dived, sirens screeching hell-fire, onto the French troops, then climbed and dived again and again and again. Under cover of the bombing, the Wehrmacht infantry had begun slipping across the river in rubber dinghies while the engineers worked to patch up the main bridge at Sedan. At dawn, on 14th May, the first tanks had rumbled across.

After that, it was almost easy. Some of the French stood their ground and put up a brave fight but the majority fled before the Panzers. Others even threw away their rifles. The tanks rolled on, unchallenged, passing the detritus of panic and disorder – abandoned tanks and vehicles, dead soldiers, jettisoned rifles, French army helmets thrown away into ditches, and, significantly, Otto noted, several dead despatch riders beside their motor cycles. Without vital communications, the enemy would be in disarray and confusion. The Panzers swept on towards the west, through French villages and towns, raising a huge cloud of dust. Everywhere there were white flags – not real flags but sheets, tablecloths, handkerchiefs – hurriedly hung out from church steeples, windows of houses and cottages and farms. At Laon, Otto's division turned north-west in the direction of the English Channel. In doing so they would surround the British and French armies on two sides. The division general had drawn a graphic picture for them, tracing it with a stick in the earth of France. The Channel ports of Boulogne, Calais and Dunkirk would be taken, in turn, while the Wehrmacht advanced through Belgium in the north-west, making the third side and leaving the British with their backs to the sea. The steel trap would then be closed.

The patched-up remains of Guy's squadron flew into their new station near Lille. Instead of a palatial château and smooth lawns, they found a rough grass field and hurriedly erected canvas tents. There were no Hurricanes left at the depot for replacements and few spare parts. On their first sortie their squadron commander bought it. Guy watched the Hurricane literally blown apart in a savage attack by half a dozen Messerschmitt 109s who had fallen on the British fighter like hounds devouring their prey. He saw the remains spinning to earth – bits of body tangled with bits of Hurricane, all splattered with crimson-red blood. The gruesome sight stayed with him as they flew back, and for a long time after.

They went on flying more sorties and losing more Hurricanes until the squadron was down to six serviceable aircraft. News came through that the German Panzers had reached Abbeville on the north-west coast. It had taken them only eleven days to cross France and now they were sweeping north towards Boulogne and Calais. To make matters even worse, as far as Guy was concerned, he was suffering from appalling toothache and the pain when he flew was agonizing. He put up with it for several days and then, in between sorties, borrowed one of the small Bedford trucks to drive into town in search of a dentist. He walked around until he found one off the main square with a brass plate on the door. In the waiting-room two elderly Frenchwomen glared at him. What was he doing there, they wanted to know. Why wasn't he fighting the *Bosches* this very moment like all the good French soldiers? Was he just going to sit there and let the Germans walk over France? He told them to go to hell in English and nursed his swollen jaw.

The dentist was more sympathetic. He was a small, middle-aged man with the same fussy little movements as old Payne in Harley Street and peered into Guy's mouth, tut-tutting at what he found. 'An abscess, monsieur, on the back tooth. A bad one. I regret I cannot save the tooth. It must be extracted immediately. With gas, of course, so you will feel nothing.' Guy stared up at the ceiling while the dentist prepared things and instruments clinked. No Georgian plaster roses to count like in Harley Street, only cracks in dingy cream paint. One, two, three, four of them. Five, six . . . 'Breathe deeply, please, monsieur.' Something was put over his nose and mouth and he slid thankfully into unconsciousness.

He was awoken by someone shaking him hard by the shoulder. The face was blurred until his vision cleared and he saw that the dentist was leaning over him. '*Réveillez-vous, monsieur!* You must wake up at once. *Wake up!*' There was an unpleasant taste of blood in his mouth and his jaw felt stiff and sore, but the pain had stopped. They must have moved him from the surgery because he saw that he was lying on a couch in a small parlour. The dentist indicated a dumpy, grey-haired woman standing behind him. 'My wife and I carried you in here, monsieur. It was necessary to give you more gas than usual . . . the extraction was very difficult. You have been asleep for a long time since.'

Guy sat up. 'How long?'

'Nearly four hours, monsieur. I am waking you because there is bad news. While you were unconscious the Germans attacked the town. They came in aeroplanes, machine-gunning the streets. We are told that their tanks will be here within a day or less.'

'Jesus Christ!' Guy struggled to his feet and staggered like a drunk. The dentist caught at his arm. 'Be careful, monsieur. You should still rest . . . if there were time.'

He stumbled out to the Bedford. There was broken window glass on the pavement and in the street and bullet gouges on walls. A dead dog lay in the gutter, its side torn open, flies feasting. He reversed the truck to turn, crashing gears in his frantic haste, and drove like fury back towards the 'drome, half expecting to run slap into German tanks at any moment. The fresh air cleared his muzzy head and halfway there he realized that he had forgotten to pay the dentist. Too late now to go back; he'd have to owe it to him. He passed several carts trundling southwards along the road – some horse-drawn, others pushed or pulled by people. The carts were piled high with stuff: chairs and tables, brass bedsteads, mattresses, pots and pans, bicycles, sacks of food, even a birdcage . . . He registered it all with disbelief as he tore by. What the hell were they doing and where the hell were they going?

One big farm cart blocked the road ahead. The owners took no notice when he blasted the horn and he had to skew and slither past them on the narrow grass verge, one wheel almost in the ditch. He reached the 'drome and skidded in through the open gate, tyres squealing, and braked hard to a stop. No guard on duty, no airmen to be seen. Not a soul. Not a sound. Just the rotten-egg stink of high explosive and a faint pall of smoke hanging in the air. He drove on further before he stopped again and stared at the sunlit scene before him – at the neat rows of bomb craters, the twisted, burned-out, smoking wrecks of Hurricanes and of lorries and bowsers and trucks. It was impossible to tell which had been destroyed by the Germans on their raid and which by the RAF before they'd pulled out.

He got out of the Bedford and looked inside a couple of the tents. The squadron had made a thorough job of it. Everything left behind that might be of any use to the Jerries had been smashed to pieces: wireless sets, headsets, telephones, tools, every single bit of equipment, and there wasn't a vehicle of any sort, even a bike, that would ever go again. He counted four Hurricane wrecks. Two of them must have got airborne and flown off, God knows where – maybe to England. Lucky, lucky sods . . . If he hadn't had that bloody abscess he might have gone with them. As it was, he was stuck here in France without a clue where the squadron had gone and with the Huns closing in.

He thought about it for a moment. He'd got the Bedford. The only thing to do was to head for the nearest port and England. He was no bloody use here without a fighter. He'd grab some kit and drive north to Lille and find Anna before the Germans did and take her with him. Maybe she'd have had the sense to leave already, but knowing Anna he doubted it. He'd probably have to drag her off by the scruff of the neck. He chucked a few things into a small suitcase – shaving gear, a clean shirt and underclothes, cigarettes, soap and towel, a pocket torch. The wrecking party had missed his revolver and he took that as well, together with his greatcoat and steel helmet. He'd got back into the Bedford, started up and scorched off before he thought to take a look at the fuel gauge. A quarter full, or three-quarters empty, depending on which way you looked at things, he thought grimly.

'The *Bosches* are coming. I told you that would happen. And you will make a lot of trouble for us.' Madame Gilbert had come to her room. She stood in the doorway, leaning heavily on her stick. Anna was putting some things hurriedly into a canvas bag – a few clothes, money, a photograph of her parents. 'If the Germans see you, they will know you are a Jewess. You are a danger to us.'

'There is no need to concern yourself, I am leaving immediately, madame.'

'The English are running away like cowards, deserting us. You should run fast, too, before they catch you.' Anna picked up the bag and made for the door. The old woman blocked her way, looking at her with glad malice in her eyes. 'I hope they do.'

She pushed her aside and went into Mademoiselle Gilbert's bedroom where she left the letter of thanks that she had written for her on the dressing-table, propped carefully against the mirror. The old woman called something else after her but she didn't listen. The bike was outside against the wall and she stuffed the canvas bag in the basket on the handlebars and rode off without any real idea of where she was going, except that it seemed better to head north. The Germans were coming from the south and east and they were not so far away. There had been gunfire in the distance, German planes in the sky. She had no map, but a signpost at the edge of town pointed to Bethune and Calais. At Calais she might find a boat crossing to England. In England she would somehow continue the fight to help her parents. She set off down the road, pedalling steadily.

'She has gone, monsieur. I am so sorry.' The woman who had answered the door was much younger than the hag that Guy remembered. This must be the daughter – the one who had taught Anna at school in England. She was looking very upset. 'She left when I was at work or I should have tried to stop her. It is not good that she is travelling all alone.'

'Do you know where she was going? In which direction?'

'I have no idea. She has taken her bicycle and so she could be far away by now. She left me a note to say that she was very sorry not to say goodbye. She thanked me for everything.' The woman gave a helpless shrug. 'I am afraid that my mother said things to her – to make her leave. Anna is Jewish, you know that?'

'Yes, I know.'

'Do you understand the danger she is in? The Germans are treating the Jews very badly. My mother was frightened of what the Germans would do to us if they came here and discovered that Anna is living with us. I would have hidden her and taken the risk, but my mother might have betrayed her. Perhaps it is better for her that she has gone. Do you see?'

'Yes,' he said. 'I see.' He would have liked to strangle that old hag.

'You are wounded, monsieur? The blood . . . ?'

He glanced down at the red blotches on the front of his shirt. 'No, I had a tooth taken out.'

'What a time to have to go to the dentist!'

'Yes . . .'

'You must hurry, monsieur. They say that the Germans are very near.' She smiled at him. 'You must be Guy, of course. Guy of the Royal Air Force. She often spoke of you. And of your brother, Matt. But it was mostly of you that she spoke.'

At the edge of town he stopped to look at the map. Anna would surely have gone north-west rather than south where the Germans were blasting their way right across France. Only she might have no idea of that . . . she could be heading straight for them without realizing it. No, surely she would have gone north by instinct – towards the Channel and England. That was by far the most likely. The coast was roughly fifty or sixty miles away – a hell of a long way on a bike and God knows what danger she'd run into. He hoped to Christ that he'd find her. He checked the map again and decided that she would have headed for Calais – the closest port to England and the one most likely to have boats still crossing.

*   *   *

'Your supper's ready on the table, Mr Ransome.' Mrs Honeywell called out from the front room as Matt passed the door on the way to the stairs. 'It's all cold tonight. A nice bit of corned beef and beetroot with some of that Heinz potato salad that I know you like.' He'd been too polite to tell her that he hated it, as much as he hated corned beef and beetroot. He started up the stairs to his room and she appeared below in the hall. 'I've just been listening to the News on the wireless. Those Germans are giving us a lot of trouble. They've gone and got to somewhere called Abbeville in France. Where's that, do you know?'

'It's on the west coast.'

She gaped at him. 'But that's over the other side. However could they have done that? Why haven't the French stopped them?'

'I don't know, but it's bad news.'

'Well, we must try not to worry. Our boys will soon drive them back again. They know what they're doing, even if those French don't.'

'Was there any news about the RAF?'

'They've shot down some more German planes. Good riddance, I say! The more the merrier.' She peered upwards. 'Your brother's over there in the Air Force, isn't he? I do hope he's all right.'

He went on up the stairs slowly. *Abbeville!* The Germans must have steamrollered right through France in a matter of days. And they were advancing through Belgium from the west. It didn't sound good at all.

*   *   *

The road ahead was clogged with refugees – old men, women and children travelling south in the opposite direction, against him, and spread over its whole width so that again and again Guy was brought to a complete stop while they streamed past on each side of the Bedford, their farm carts and pushcarts and perambulators creaking and sagging under tottering loads, dogs running after them. He could smell the garlic, the sweat and the fear. They took no notice of the horn, nor of his shouts or pleas or curses. They might have been cattle, driven by some blind herd instinct. It took him two hours to travel a few miles and yet he dared not leave the main road for fear of missing Anna, reasoning that she would have stuck to one herself. Several times he asked in French if a girl with long dark hair had been seen bicycling north but they all shook their heads or shrugged and looked at him with resentment and hostility.

He heard and saw the German fighter approaching before any of the civilians were aware of it. A 109 came streaking across the fields just over treetop height and banked to turn in line with the road. Its machine-guns chattered and blazed and bullets ripped into the macadam. The refugees scattered, screaming and running for the ditches at the sides of the road. Guy fell out of the Bedford and rolled underneath it. He watched an old woman in black peasant dress, too slow to reach the ditch, mown down; a small child of about five standing rooted to the spot with terror, mangled to a bloody mess; a horse sag to its knees; a cart explode into flames. In a pointless, futile gesture, he grabbed his revolver from his pocket and fired at the fighter. The Messerschmitt flew off and a terrible sound of wailing and sobbing began. He was shaking with horror and rage. *Murdering bastard!* Christ, if only he'd been up in his Hurricane, he'd've gone after him and blown him apart.

He crawled out from under the Bedford. The refugees were emerging from the ditches, collecting scattered belongings, righting carts. He bent over the old woman and saw that she was dead – the child, too; miraculously, they were the only victims. For the moment, there was a clear way through on the road ahead and he seized the chance to drive on fast, leaving the army of refugees behind. He drove into Armentières and stopped at a garage selling petrol. The elderly man in charge shook his head. 'There is none, monsieur. Not a drop. The army has taken all.'

'The British?'

'British and French. They have both been through here – this way and that. Nobody knows what is happening or where the Germans are.' It was a long shot, but he asked the question. The man nodded. 'She is beautiful? With long dark hair?'

'You've seen her?'

'*Mais oui.* The bike had a puncture and she asked me to repair it. She was not French, though she spoke it very well indeed. She had a bit of a German accent, just a very little, and I thought perhaps that she might be a spy. But then I said to myself a German spy would not be riding around on an old bike, getting punctures . . . Besides she was very beautiful.'

'Did she say where she was going?'

'She is probably still here, monsieur. She was very thirsty and I directed her to a café just along the road from here. That was only half an hour ago.'

She was sitting at a table on the pavement in the shade of a Martini umbrella and calmly sipping at a glass. Relief switched to anger. He parked the truck and went across and stood over the table, arms folded. 'What the hell do you think you're doing, Anna?' She looked up, startled, and then smiled. 'I might ask you the same thing, Guy. I thought you would be back in England.'

'Why did you think that?'

'There were some British soldiers here a while ago, driving through in lorries and they told me the RAF were getting out. They were quite rude about it.'

'Where were the soldiers going?'

'Towards St Omer, I think. May I have a cigarette, please?'

'Don't you ever have any of your own?'

'Only French and I hate those. I prefer English ones. Why don't you sit down and have a drink? It's very nice here.'

'Anna, you do realize that the Germans can't be more than sixty miles away? There isn't *time* for a drink. Or a cigarette either. Finish your drink. We're leaving.'

'I have not paid yet.'

He tossed some coins onto the table and jerked her to her feet. 'You have now. Come on.'

'My bag . . .' She grabbed at it. 'And my bike.' He slung the bike in the back of the Bedford. 'Get in.' They roared off out of the town, taking the road on to Bailleul.

'Where are we going?'

'To the coast. Or as near as we can get before the petrol runs out. I reckon we've got about another ten miles before that happens.'

'After that we can both ride my bike.'

'This isn't a joke, Anna. We've got to get you out of France and back to England. For Christ's sake you should have gone long ago, like I told you to do. I'm praying we can get you on a boat at Calais.'

'There is blood on your shirt.'

'I had a tooth out at the dentist's. The squadron took off when I was out for the count. Unconscious. That's how I got left behind.'

'Does it hurt still?'

'I haven't had much time to think about it.' He felt his jaw cautiously. 'It's OK.' They had to slow down for another small army of refugees. 'Poor people,' Anna said. 'Where can they all go? What will happen to them?'

'I'll tell you,' he said grimly. 'The Germans will machine-gun them from the air. They did that when I was on the road from Lille. Thank God it didn't happen to you.'

'Those pigs shoot people like these? In cold blood?'

'I'm afraid so. The more panic they create the

better for them. The refugees must be rather a useful weapon. They block the roads for the Allies very effectively. The Huns couldn't do it better themselves.'

She muttered something to herself in German. 'I should like the chance to kill at least one of them.'

They reached Bethune and drove through the town. There was a street market and women were buying fruit and vegetables, fish and meat, men standing at bistro bars, as though there was nothing whatever to worry about. Outside the town they came across a British army lorry by the side of the road, bonnet open, men at work on the engine. Guy stopped and got out of the truck and walked back. 'We've broken down, sir,' the sergeant in charge told him. 'Just our bloomin' luck.'

'Seen any RAF? I've lost touch with my squadron.'

'No, sir. You're not the only one; we got separated from our unit. It's a shambles, if you ask me.'

'What's going on?'

'Well, sir, all I know is that we've been ordered to pull back towards St Omer. Jerry's working his way along the coast. It's the tanks, sir. The Panzers. They've gone right through like a dose of Eno's. The French don't seem to know what to do next and they're supposed to be giving the orders, aren't they? We've taken a real beating and lost a lot of men. We're doing our best but it's bloody chaos.'

'Well, good luck, Sergeant. I hope you get the lorry going.'

'Thank you, sir.' The sergeant saluted. 'Good luck to you too, sir.'

They wove their way through another straggle of refugees plodding south and passed another British army lorry, leaning at a drunken angle in a ditch, its cowling left open, the engine wrecked. Further on, there was a burned-out tank and several more lorries. Then another tank and more lorries. All burned or wrecked. The situation must be even worse than he had feared.

'What is happening, Guy? Why are they leaving all these?'

'Either they ran out of fuel or they broke down. Either way, they've made certain the Germans can't use them.'

Several miles further on they came to another small village and a tin-shed garage with one petrol pump and an old man sitting on a chair beside it in the sun, black beret on his head, Gauloise cigarette stuck to his lower lip, engrossed in a newspaper. Once again, Guy was told that there was no petrol. 'The reservoir is empty, monsieur.'

Guy took his revolver out of his pocket. 'I don't believe you. Give us petrol.' He was given a look of contempt. 'There is none. You can shoot a defenceless old man, if you like, but it will not help you.' As he walked back to the truck he heard the old man spit on the ground behind him. 'I think he's lying.'

'Perhaps. They do not like you running away.'

'I'm not running away, for God's sake.'

'I know, but that is how they see it. The English are retreating and deserting them. You are a *sale Anglais*. If he had petrol, he would not give it to you.'

He tapped the fuel gauge. 'Well, I'd say we have enough left to get us another five miles, if we're very lucky.' He had been optimistic. They had travelled less than two more miles when the engine suddenly choked and died. 'Well, that's that.'

'We still have the bike.'

'One bike . . .'

'We can share it. There is a strong shelf at the back, to put parcels and things. I can sit on that.'

He hauled the bike out of the truck. His suitcase and its contents would have to be left behind but he salvaged the packets of Players and his torch and dumped the rest in the ditch. He gave Anna the cigarettes to put in her canvas bag which went in the basket. She helped him push the truck off the road and he yanked out ignition wires, removed the rotor arm and slashed the tyres with the penknife he always carried. He handed her his steel helmet. 'You'd better wear this.' He folded his greatcoat into a cushion to go on the metal ledge at the back of the bike and they set off with Anna sitting behind him, clinging on to his waist.

A huge dust cloud, miles long, marked the rumbling progress of the Panzer tanks across France. Otto wiped his field-glasses on his sleeve and took another look ahead and on each side of the long straight road. Fields, orchards in blossom, the occasional farm, but no sign of the enemy except for the equipment they had left behind – wrecked British lorries and tanks now added to the discarded French arms and armaments. The British, he noted, had been very careful to disable everything. They were retreating but they were still fighting hard, standing fast at artillery posts, attacking from unexpected quarters, picking off the unwary. One stubborn group of Tommies – no more than a dozen or so – had managed to hold them up for almost half a day, pelting them with grenades and shell-fire until they had run out of ammunition. At another point, three more Tommies with one Bren-gun between them had opened fire from the roadside in a suicidal attempt before they were quickly taken out. Further on, the entire column had halted in front of what were thought to be mines laid on the road ahead only for it to be discovered that the British had put down, not mines, but upturned dinner plates. Stephan had been highly amused.

The tanks rolled on through town and village. The French civilians watched them go by from windows and doorways, and pathetic refugees scattered from their path in terror. Their progress was unstoppable. In his own mind, Otto questioned the wisdom of advancing so fast and so far beyond the infantry and their supply lines. But it was not for him to challenge such things, only to obey orders.

The Panzer column halted briefly and Stephan strode over. 'Your British fight a good fight, I grant you, but they can't hold us back. Soon, we shall have Boulogne and Calais.' He grinned up at him through the dust caking his face. 'I have heard a rumour that the King of the Belgians is going to surrender. If that happens he will leave the way wide open for us on the enemy's flank. They will have nowhere left to go but for a swim. Imagine that, Otto! First we dine in Paris, then we shall be in London. The food and the women will not be so good, but I have always heard that the English countryside is rather pleasant, especially at this time of year. Is that true?'

'Yes, it's true.'

'Then I shall look forward to it.' Stephan extended his arm in a salute. '*Heil Hitler!*'

'*Heil Hitler!*'

The column rolled forward once more. Ten miles further on and close to nightfall, Otto's tank broke down.

It was almost dark and very difficult to see their way. The bike had no front lamp though, in any case, Guy would not have dared to use one. The Germans could be anywhere. His instinct was to press on, no matter what, but he knew that Anna was tired and it made some sense to rest while the going was so hard. Earlier, they had bought some food from a village shop. Anna had made him stay outside. 'If they see your British uniform, they may refuse us.' He had waited impatiently further down the road, smoking a cigarette, and presently she had reappeared carrying a long stick of bread and a hunk of Camembert cheese which they had stowed in the basket on the handlebars. So all that was needed now was to find a safe place for a few hours.

He turned off the main road onto a narrow lane and presently they came to a rough track leading to a farm. He could see the shape of the farmhouse and some outbuildings, including a barn which might serve the purpose. He had no intention of asking permission since no-one could be trusted. A dog barked as he wheeled the bike quietly along the track, with Anna following. They waited until the barking stopped and then skirted the house. There was a clucking and fluttering as he pushed open a small door in the side of the barn and shone his torch inside. A mothers' meeting of brown hens eyed him indignantly from a far corner. He played the torch around some more and saw a wooden ladder leading upwards. 'This is OK. We can go up in the loft.' The hens clucked again as he wheeled the bike inside and concealed it behind farm machinery. The loft was partly filled with new, sweet-smelling hay and Anna sat down and took off the steel helmet. She produced the bread and cheese and they tore the food apart with their hands and ate by torchlight.

'Now, if we only had some wine, Guy, it would be a very fine supper.'

'We'd also need a corkscrew. And glasses.'

'Not glasses – we could drink, in turn, from the bottle.'

She was pretty amazing, he thought. Cool as a cucumber. Most women in her situation would be scared to death and having hysterics. He wondered if she had a clue how serious things could be. The litter of abandoned and disabled equipment on the roadsides had told its own story. The BEF was in full retreat, fighting a rearguard action against the oncoming Germans, and, so far as he could tell, in grave danger of being totally surrounded. The army could retreat only so far – until it reached the Channel. After that it would be a question of fighting it out, backs to the sea. The only real chance still seemed to him to be to head for Calais as fast as possible. To try to go south and attempt to find a way through the enemy lines would be madness. He reviewed other facts grimly: Calais was still forty miles away, or more; they had one old bicycle for transport, a revolver with a few rounds, and the Germans could overrun them at any moment. He debated whether it would be better to stay on the main road, the most direct route, or safer to take to the country lanes and try to cut across country. The one thing they did have, after all, was a map. He realized then, with a sudden and horrible jolt, that he had left it in the truck.

'What are you thinking, Guy?'

'What the hell to do next.'

'Well, I am going to sleep.'

'You'd better have my coat to keep you warm.' He laid it over her and tucked her in carefully. Just like nanny, he thought.

'You are very kind, Guy. I never knew this. Will you sleep?'

'I ought to keep guard. Just in case.'

He switched off the torch and sat with his back to the wall smoking a cigarette. He smiled to himself. Ironic to be spending the night with her in a hayloft . . . on bloody sentry duty. Not exactly what he'd have had in mind in normal circumstances. Well, at least she thought he was kind. That was a change. A big improvement. He knew he was in love with her, which was his misfortune, because she certainly wasn't with him. For how long had he been, exactly? He wasn't sure. Perhaps since the Commem. ball. Perhaps since the very beginning, when he'd first set eyes on her. It didn't matter. Nothing to be done about it. At least, not at the moment.

The dog barked over at the farmhouse and the hens clucked softly and murmured together in the barn below. Probably disturbed by a fox. He listened hard but heard nothing more until some lunatic bird started singing somewhere nearby. It was a while before he realized that it was a nightingale. He stayed awake for a long time, leaning against the wall, and then, finally, his head drooped.

A cockerel woke him, crowing raucously outside. Daylight was filtering down through a grimy skylight overhead and he swore aloud, furious with himself. They should have been on the road an hour ago at least. He shook Anna awake. The hens were not in the barn and he saw that the small door was open, which meant that somebody from the farm was already up and about. Outside the yard was empty except for the hens and the cockerel standing on a wall, neck stretched, crowing loudly. Anna tugged at his arm and he followed her gaze. A bike was propped against the same wall – rusty and old, but serviceable, so far as he could tell. As they wheeled it away down the track he expected, at any moment, to hear angry French shouts behind them. An early-morning mist was rising off the fields and the sun was coming up behind an orchard of apple trees. Nothing could have seemed more peaceful, but as they set off down the empty road they could hear the distant boom of gunfire, coming from the west.

'Did you hear the news, Mr Ransome? The Germans have gone and captured that French port. Something beginning with B.'

'Boulogne?'

'Yes, that was it. Booloin. They won't get any further, though, will they? Our boys will soon deal with them.'

'I'm sure they will.' He saw that his landlady had no idea how desperate the situation was. The Germans were systematically taking the French ports. After Boulogne it would be Calais. They must be sweeping round to encircle the Allies and if they weren't stopped in Belgium, then pretty soon there'd be nowhere left to retreat to. Where was Guy? Not in England or they would have heard from him and there had been no letter, no word for nearly three weeks. And what about

Anna? Nobody had heard anything from her either. 'I shouldn't think there's anything to worry about, Mrs Honeywell.'

'I've got some smoked haddock for your supper today. A special treat. Just a small piece.'

'Thank you.' Matt turned to go on up the stairs.

'There was another funny bit on the nine o'clock this morning,' she went on. 'Very queer. I didn't know what to make of it. They were asking for people owning boats to come forward. *At once*, they said. Without delay. The Admiralty, I think. They made it sound ever so important. Now, why would they ask a thing like that?'

He swung round. 'Did they say what kind?'

'I don't remember. Just boats, you know. Private ones, I suppose. I wasn't really listening properly, but I thought it was rather odd. It couldn't have anything to do with the war, could it?'

He came back down the stairs. 'I'm sorry, Mrs Honeywell, but I have to go out again now. I shan't be in for supper.'

'But what about the haddock . . .'

'I'm sorry . . . perhaps you'd like to eat it.'

'Well, really! After all the trouble I went to.'

'They want every boat over thirty feet they can lay their hands on, Lizzie. That's what I found out. You realize what it means? Our army over there must be in real trouble and they're going to

350

try and bring them back before the Germans reach them. They're trapped and the only way out is the sea. That's why the Navy want all the boats they can muster. To go and rescue the army, or as many as they can before the Germans capture them. There must be thousands of men over there. And Guy must be there, somewhere, Lizzie – caught in the trap, too.'

Matt paused for breath. She looked at him in horror. 'Do you really believe it can be as bad as that, Matt? The BBC just said some troops have been brought back because they weren't engaged in fighting, that's all. It didn't sound very serious and there's been nothing in the papers.'

'It's been censored, that's why. They don't want to cause a panic.' He walked about the attic studio. 'My God, if we lose almost our entire army and all their equipment, we wouldn't stand a chance if the Germans tried to invade England.' He turned to face her. 'A lot of the boats are assembling at Sheerness at the mouth of the Thames. I'm going to take the *Rose* there, Lizzie, and hand her over to the Navy. That's what I wanted to tell you.'

'But she's too small to be much use. You said over thirty feet. She's only fourteen.'

'She could carry six or seven men – maybe even more. And she's a fishing boat. Made for the sea. She can do *something* to help.' He paused. 'So can I, Lizzie.'

'But could you handle her alone?'

He flushed. 'I'll have a damn good try.'

'The tides are awful and all those sandbanks

and currents . . . Even Guy used to say how tricky it was.'

'Even Guy . . . You don't believe I could ever do anything as well as Guy, do you, Lizzie?'

'That's not true, Matt. But I'm afraid for you. I don't want anything to happen to you. They wouldn't want you to go over to *France*, would they?'

'Not as far as I know. They just want them delivered to Sheerness.'

'Let me come with you, Matt. I could help.'

He shook his head. 'No, Lizzie.'

'It's *my* chance to do something, too.'

'I can't take you. Imagine what your parents would say.'

'I won't tell them. I'll say I'm going to stay with a schoolfriend, or something. You're not telling your mother, are you?'

'Lord, no.'

'Well, let me come and help you get *Rose* into the water, at least. That's only fair. *Please*, Matt.'

He sighed. 'OK. But that's all.'

The Dorniers droned by overhead, escorted by a pack of Messerschmitts. 'They're heading towards Calais,' Guy said. 'Probably bombing the hell out of it.' He watched the bombers disappearing into the distance, wondering, yet again, what to do. Calais was the nearest port, and they had to hope that it was still operating. It was the best hope for Anna. The best for himself, come to that. There seemed no chance of joining up with the rest of the squadron – they'd be back in

England by now, for sure. The quicker he got home, the quicker he could get back into a Hurricane; seeing the Dorniers blithely swanning past had made him boil with frustration. He wished to God he knew exactly where the Germans were now but, wherever they were, it was getting too damn close for comfort and the main road too dangerous. Refugees were still straggling south, and where there were refugees there could be 109s and Stukas diving suddenly out of the skies.

He tried to remember the geography of the region and decided that there had to be a way across country, westwards, to Calais – not so direct, but safer. The next left turn looked promising and they meandered for several miles along a narrow and dusty lane through a pleasant region of farmland and orchards and without a sign of any combat. Progress was slow because the chain on the stolen bike kept coming off and they had to keep stopping while he put it back on. Even so, Guy began to feel more confident. After several miles they came to another road – well-surfaced but minor, and deserted. So far as he could tell it must be heading roughly in the direction of Calais. He decided to risk it.

They were both soaked in sweat and suffering from thirst. A small hamlet lay ahead, no more than three or four houses lining the road, but one of them turned out to be a shop. The shabby-looking window displayed a pyramid of tins with labels so faded they were almost unreadable. Anna went inside and came out empty-handed.

'There is nobody there, Guy. Only a dog chained up.'

He looked at the other houses. There was no sign of life. 'I think this whole place is deserted. They've all gone.'

'Then we can take what we need.' He propped his bike beside hers against the window and followed her inside the shop. The dog, a half-starved small brown mongrel, was crouched miserably in a dark corner in a kitchen at the back, chained to a table leg, an empty, over-turned bowl beside it. It drew back under the table, trembling as they approached. 'Better not touch him,' Guy said. 'He looks terrified, poor chap.' They poked about among dusty bottles in the shop and found some mineral water to quench their thirst, gulping it straight from the bottle and then pouring some into the bowl for the dog. It crawled forward from under the table and gulped it down frantically. Anna gave him some more. 'He is probably very hungry too.' She went through a row of tins on a shelf behind the counter. 'We can give him beef stew. He will like that. And we can take what we like too. Beans, onion soup, herrings . . .'

'How about a tin-opener?'

'I will find one.'

They opened a tin of beef stew for the dog and were watching him wolf it down when they heard a curious rumbling sound, like distant thunder. At first Guy thought it was enemy bombers again and then, as he listened harder, he knew it was not: it was tanks. British tanks surely, this far north? Withdrawing to St Omer, probably, like the sergeant he had spoken with had said. The thunder grew louder and louder and the floor beneath their feet began to shake. No, not British, he thought, grimly. Far too many of them. He motioned quickly to Anna to get down below the level of the shop window as the leading tank rolled into view, painted dark grey, a black cross on white on the side and its number in deep yellow. It was followed by a long column of more tanks and armoured cars carrying helmeted German troops, grinding and roaring past deafeningly within feet of them. So many that it was nearly an hour before the last one had gone by and it was quiet again.

'My God, Guy . . . what are we going to do?'

He ran his fingers through his hair. 'Follow them at a safe distance for the moment and hope that the British and French will stop them at some point.'

'Stop all *those*? How can they?'

'There'll be anti-tank guns set up ahead – bound to be. The British are at St Omer and that can't be more than about fifteen miles from here. They'll do everything they can to keep them from reaching Calais.' He wiped the sweat from his brow. 'It looks like they're miles ahead of their infantry. We'll get round them as soon as we can.'

'Supposing there are more tanks coming along behind?'

'We'll be able to hear them from a long way off. Come on, let's get moving.'

They took some tins of food and bottles of water with them, as well as the tin-opener.

'What shall we do about the poor dog, Guy?'

He fingered his revolver. 'The kindest thing would be to shoot the wretched thing.'

'No, Guy. I will not let you do that.'

'Well, we can't leave it chained up to starve to death. And there's nobody to look after it.'

'But at least we could let it go free.'

The mongrel cringed as Guy undid the chain. He patted it gently. 'You've had a rotten time, haven't you, old fellow? Probably never had a kind word in your life.'

The dog followed them out of the shop and down the road. Guy shooed it back and it stopped, ears down, tail drooping, looking sadly after them. They followed in the long wake of dust left by the Panzers.

Tideways was in darkness. They had walked all the way from the station in fading light, climbed over the paddock gate and crunched up the gravel drive towards the house. Matt unlocked the front door and groped for the hall light switch which clicked uselessly. 'Mother must have turned the mains off,' he told Lizzie. He made his way to the kitchen where he found a box of matches and then some candles. Lizzie had waited in the hall and they toured the downstairs rooms by candlelight. The house was deadly silent, furniture shrouded under white dust-sheets, curtains drawn. No flowers, no music, no voices – the life gone from it. He went to find the mains switch by the back door and turned on the lights in the kitchen where the blackout had been left in place at the windows. 'I'll take a look in the larder and see if there's anything for us to eat.' He found some tins of food and they opened one of sardines and some baked beans and heated them up in saucepans on the gas stove. 'Not much like Mrs Woodgate's cooking, I'm afraid.' They ate, sitting at the kitchen table. 'We can't do anything about the *Rose* until morning. I'll get a few provisions together tonight – water and a bit of food, and so on – just in case I need them.'

'How about some hot soup, Matt? There were some tins of tomato in the larder and we could put it in a Thermos – if we can find one.'

'There'll be one in the pantry cupboard. I'll get started at first light, around four-thirty. It'll be a bit of a sweat to get her down the slipway into the water.'

'I'll help you.'

'Thanks, Lizzie.' He smiled at her. 'I really couldn't have managed without you, you know.'

'I do wish you'd let me come too.'

'I can't, sorry.'

'Why not?'

'You wouldn't have Guy to take care of you – only me. Remember what happened with *Bean Goose*.'

'That was *years* ago.'

He looked down at the table, running a finger of his good left hand backwards and forwards across the checked oilcloth. 'I'll let you into a secret, Lizzie. Something I've never told a living soul because I'm so ashamed of it. I'm scared stiff of the sea. I always have been. I absolutely hate it. It terrifies me. That's why I'm so rotten at sailing and that's why I couldn't possibly let you come with me. Now what do you say?'

'That it's incredibly brave of you to do this. The sea scares me too, so I know a bit of how you must feel.'

He drew squares on the oilcloth. 'Well, I'm not even sure I'll have the guts to go when it actually comes to it. I'll probably get as far as the mouth of the river and turn back, like a coward. But I've got to try.'

'You'll do it, Matt. I know you will.'

She reached across to touch his right arm which was resting on the table, the elbow stump with its finger and thumb protruding from the sleeve of his jersey. He stiffened and pulled down the sleeve quickly. 'Sorry, I forgot. It's a pretty revolting sight.'

'No, it's not. You never used to hide it all the time, Matt.'

'It didn't seem to matter so much,' he mumbled. 'Now, it does rather.' He stood up abruptly and started to clear away the plates.

They washed up and packed a small cardboard box with two tins of sardines, a packet of biscuits, a bottle of fizzy lemonade. Lizzie found a block of dark cooking chocolate and put that in too. 'We'll do the soup in the morning. And we mustn't forget the water.'

Matt went and fetched a chart of the Thames

estuary from his father's study and spread it out on the kitchen table, tracing a course with his left hand. 'I'll go down the river and out as far as the Buxey buoy and then across the top of Foulness Sand to the North East Maplin marker. I can follow the buoys all down the south side of Maplin Sands to the Shoeburyness buoy and go straight across from there to Sheerness.'

'How long do you think you'll take?'

'Depends. About six hours, if I get it right. Better get some sleep, I suppose.' He cleared his throat. 'Not sure if the beds'll be made up.'

'Doesn't matter.'

He switched on lights on their way upstairs through the silent house and stopped outside the spare-room door. 'This is you, then. See you in the morning.'

She said, 'Just a moment, Matt. I've got a secret to tell you too.'

'What is it?'

'I love you.'

He looked incredulous. 'Wait a minute. You love *me*? Are you joking or something?'

'No.'

'But I always thought it was Guy . . . '

'And I always thought it was Anna with you.'

'*Anna?* Good lord, no! I've always liked her an awful lot – but that's quite different, isn't it?' He stared at her. 'I've loved *you* for ages, Lizzie. Years, really.'

'Why didn't you tell me before?'

'I didn't think you'd want to hear it.'

'Because of Guy?'

'I don't exactly measure up to him, do I? And because of the way I am.'

'You mean your arm? Is that what you're talking about?'

'Well, yes. It's enough to put anyone off, isn't it?' For answer, she took hold of the misshapen fingers firmly and kissed them each in turn. He swallowed hard.

'Oh, Lizzie . . .'

He put his other arm around her.

'The dog is still following us, Guy.'

He turned round and saw it slinking along behind them at a safe distance. It stopped and stood stock-still, one paw raised warily, ready to run. The poor thing was probably expecting them to chuck stones. The light was fading fast but he wanted to press on for as long as they could – until they could no longer see their way. The evening sky ahead glowed bright crimson like a tropical sunset and he realized it must be from fires in Calais. This time there was no convenient barn and when they eventually stopped, the only shelter was in the lee of a hedge. Guy spread his greatcoat for Anna and they opened a tin of herrings and ate them with their fingers. 'Just like a picnic,' she said. 'Do you remember our picnics, Guy?'

'Of course I do.'

'I teased you about the flies. I did it to make you cross.'

'Then you were very successful.'

'I am sorry now.'

He smiled. 'I expect I asked for it.'

'The dog is here. I saw his eyes shining in the torchlight. We should give him some more food.'

'No, we shouldn't. He'll just be a damn nuisance.' They did, of course, opening a tin of the beef stew and emptying it out. The dog slunk forward and gulped down the lot. 'We'll never get rid of him now.'

'Then he can come with us – to England.'

Not much chance of any of us getting there, he thought, but he didn't say so. He stayed awake, on guard, while Anna slept wrapped in his RAF greatcoat. The dog lay down at a respectful distance. As dawn came they were on the road once more. And, at that same moment, the *Rose of England*, red sails hoisted, was turning her bows downstream towards the sea.

The old man nods to himself. 'We didn't know a thing about the true situation back in England. There was nothing in newspapers or on the wireless. They kept it quiet till they had to say something. First clue we had was when they announced a Day of Prayer – that would have been the Sunday when the evacuation started. The Archbishop of Canterbury told us to pray for our soldiers in dire peril in France. Molly said to me, "What on earth's he talking about – dire peril?" We'd thought everything was all right and that the Germans were being driven back. They kept it from us.' He sucks at the dead pipe for a moment. 'When we did find out it was a nasty shock. You should've seen the troops arriving back. Those men were dead on their feet. Filthy dirty, soaking wet, looking like a lot of scarecrows – but they were home, and that's what mattered. We treated them like heroes – same as if they'd won a big battle, not lost it. Well, there was no point in sitting moaning. We had to get on with the war. Like Churchill said, we had to fight on, whatever the cost. Mind you, I don't *think any of us realized what it was going to take or how long it was going to last.' He reaches for his tobacco pouch and starts to refill the pipe. 'Just as well we didn't.'*

Chapter Sixteen

By the time the necessary repairs had been completed to Otto's tank, he knew that they must have been left a long way behind the main column. Nevertheless, he delayed further during the hours of darkness to give his three-man crew the chance to rest. For the past twelve days there had been little time for sleep and they all were at the point of exhaustion. During the day, the heat down inside the tank had been ferocious and even standing in the turret, in the fresh air, he had experienced great difficulty himself in keeping awake. After even an hour or two of sleep, however, he felt refreshed and alert again.

The tank rolled on through open countryside: fields stretching away into the distance and few trees or undulations to give any cover to the enemy. From time to time, though, he checked through his glasses, sweeping the terrain carefully. The Allies' front line lay approximately twenty miles to his east – according to his most recent information. However, in war it was wise not to take anything for certain.

They passed through hamlets that appeared

deserted except for scavenging dogs. He noticed a herd of cows with swollen udders, milling wild-eyed by a field gateway; he could hear their pathetic lowing even above the rumbling of the tank's tracks. Huge numbers of French civilians, it seemed, had fled *en masse* which was most obliging of them. A line of trees on a bend obscured his long view for a few moments, but as soon as the tank had rounded the corner he whipped up the field-glasses again. Another village lay ahead – presumably deserted like the rest. He kept the glasses trained on it.

The British soldier lay half in and half out of the open doorway, his head in the road, his feet inside the house. He had been wounded in the chest but he was still alive. As they bent over him he looked up at them with dull eyes and his lips moved. Anna knelt down closer. 'He is asking for water, Guy. Fetch the bottle quickly.' She swatted away the flies clustering over the Tommy's face and held the bottle to his lips but he seemed too weak to swallow and most of the water ran out of the corners of his mouth and down his chin. His lips moved again. 'My mate . . . in there.' Guy went inside the house and found the dead body of another soldier lying beneath the shat-tered window in the front room. The smell was already sickening. He prised the man's rifle from his fingers and found that it was out of ammu-nition. When he went back outside he heard the sound of tank tracks in the distance and saw a cloud of dust rising above a line of trees.

* * *

Otto was not surprised to see the soldier lying at the edge of the road. He knew that many of the British had been separated from their units and were wandering about behind the lines. Some had been taken prisoner; this one had not been so lucky, except that he appeared to be still alive. He gave the order for the tank to stop and climbed down from the turret. There was not much that could be done for the man, he realized. He held his water-bottle to his mouth but he was too far gone to drink. Otto looked round. Where there was one Tommy, there could be another. He unbuttoned his holster flap and, gun in hand, stepped over the soldier into the house.

It took a moment for his eyes to adjust from the bright sunlight to the dim interior. He saw the dead body of another British soldier lying beneath the window. There was a table in the centre of the room with some chairs round it and, beyond the table, an officer in the uniform of the Royal Air Force pointing a revolver. A girl stood slightly behind the man and, at her side, there was a dog. At first he thought he must be hallucinating, that the heat and exhaustion must have affected his senses. And then his eyes adjusted completely and his mind cleared. The dog was growling deep in its throat and showing its teeth. Bluebottles were buzzing loudly over the dead body.

The officer spoke. 'Put your gun on the table.'

He shrugged and did so, laying it on the table between them. Immediately the girl snatched it up and aimed it at him. He said calmly, 'If you shoot me, Guy, my men outside will blow you to pieces. You . . . And Anna. And if I do not return to my tank in one moment, they will wonder what is wrong. You have no chance. None at all. If you surrender, you will be well treated – you have my word.'

'And how will they treat Anna?'

He looked at her again. She was dirty and dishevelled, her dress torn, her face scratched, her hair tangled; of course, it made no difference. She stared back at him without a trace of fear, holding his gun very steady. She would kill me, if necessary, he thought. If she knows how to use it, I hope that she is a very bad shot. 'What in God's name is she doing here, Guy?'

'She was in France when you invaded. In Lille.'

'But what is she doing with you?'

'I'm taking her to England.'

He smiled at that; almost laughed. 'To *England*? That will not be so easy. Did you know that your army is nearly defeated? That you are in full retreat and that we are surrounding you? How did you imagine that you would go to England? All the ports are being taken. Boulogne is already ours and Calais is under siege.' He saw by the look on Guy's face that this last part, at least, was news to him. 'It would be much better to surrender.'

'I don't happen to agree with you.'

He glanced at Anna again. He knew very well how she might be treated. 'There is one chance for you, perhaps, if it is not too late. The British and French still have Dunkirk and your Royal Navy are evacuating troops from there. You would have to find a way across country as fast as you can. It is just possible that you may be able to escape by boat before we take Dunkirk. You will need a map. Do you have one?'

'No.'

He took one from his pocket and tossed it onto the table. Guy made no move to pick it up and the revolver stayed trained on him. He knew, though, that Guy would not shoot. He might risk his own life, but not Anna's. He was not so sure about Anna. The dog was still growling at him: a thin mongrel with floppy ears and a matted brown coat. 'He is yours?'

'No.'

'He believes that he is. He is not as handsome as Nereus.' He turned to Guy. 'I must return to my tank before my crew become alarmed. May I please have my revolver back?'

'Give it to him, Anna.'

'Then he will shoot us.'

'No, he won't. Put it on the table.'

She put it down slowly and very reluctantly.

'Thank you, Anna.' He picked up the gun, looking at her once more for a moment and for the last time. He spoke to her quietly in German. As he stepped over the British soldier lying in the doorway he saw that he had died.

His crew were waiting for him outside.

'Anything in there, sir?'

He rebuttoned the flap of his holster and

swung himself on board the tank. 'Just another dead Tommy.'

They caught up with the rest of the column much sooner than he had expected. The tanks were halted and Stephan, for once, was unsmiling. 'We have been ordered to stop. Can you believe it, Otto? We have the whole British army within our grasp—only a few miles away – and now we can do nothing. General von Rundstedt has ordered this. We are to stay this side of the Canal Line until we receive further instructions. They say it has been commanded by the Führer. Has he gone *mad*?'

'What about Dunkirk?'

'The rumour is that it is to be left to the Luftwaffe. Reichsmarschall Goering apparently wishes all the glory for himself. It is insane. We are building golden bridges for the British to escape.'

They might make it, Otto thought. They have been given a good chance.

'I wish you had shot him, Guy, just like they have been murdering those poor refugees.'

'If I had, his crew would have slaughtered us. We hadn't a hope, Anna. He let us off the hook. More than that, he helped us. What did he say to you in German?'

She looked away. 'It was nothing. Nothing that I believed.'

The wind was humming loudly in the mainsail – a fair north-easterly that was helping them make good headway. There had been a mist over the river when they'd left just before five o'clock, but by the time they got to the mouth of the estuary it had cleared. Just the same, Matt knew he should never have let Lizzie come. He should have stuck to his guns instead of giving in. If the fear came back he could start making stupid mistakes.

The jib gave a warning rattle and began to flap. He shouted above the wind. 'Pull it in, will you, Lizzie.' She tugged at the sheet hurriedly. She was pea-green and he knew she was feeling sick, though it wasn't rough. He should never have let her come.

They reached the Buxey buoy and he took the *Rose* south-east across the tip of Foulness Sand towards the North East Maplin marker. He kept a close watch on the skies and on the strength and direction of the wind. So long as the moderate weather held he might manage to make a decent job of it and take them safely down to Sheerness. Once there, he would hand *Rose* over to the Royal Navy and that would be that.

From the North East Maplin they sailed down the edge of Sands, following the marker buoys, into the Thames estuary. Off Shoeburyness everything changed as they started across towards Sheerness. The wind was dead astern now and much stronger and the ebb tide, running fast out of the Thames, had the *Rose* rolling heavily and the waves slapping high over her bows. The sun had vanished behind the black clouds building up overhead and Matt could feel his stomach knotting and his hands starting to shake. If he didn't do the right thing and do it quickly they could do a standing gybe. The wind could get on the wrong side of the mainsail and the boom would crash over. It could easily break the rigging and, most terrifying of all, the *Rose* could capsize. He yelled at Lizzie who was clinging tightly to the jib sheet and gunwale.

'We're going to have to take the mainsail down. Can you manage it, Lizzie? I can't leave the tiller.'

She nodded gamely. 'Tell me what to do.'

'Make the jib sheet fast on that cleat. Then undo the main halyard and pull the sail down. You'll have to pull hard. Can you do that?'

She let go of the gunwale, struggling to keep her balance while the *Rose* plunged about. He could tell how scared she was but she did it, cleating the jib sheet and tugging the mainsail down bit by bit into a bundle on the boom. He groped for a sail tie in the stern locker and chucked it over. 'Can you put this round the boom now.'

The *Rose* was running under the jib alone and only rolling gently. There was no danger now of a gybe or capsize. His hands had stopped shaking. He grinned at Lizzie and put his thumb up. 'Thanks. We'll be OK now.'

At Sheerness the harbour was crammed with craft: cabin cruisers, speedboats, drifters, a river-excursion launch with green and white awning and slatted seats, the *Southend Queen* ferry, tugs, cockle boats, even a London Fire Brigade fire-float. They tied up alongside an old fishing trawler that reeked of its catch. In a big shed on the quayside, queues of owners waited while Royal Navy officers, seated at tables, spoke to each in turn. The elderly man ahead of Matt had brought his motor boat, *Happy Days*, all the way down the Thames from Henley. 'They don't tell you anything much, but we can all guess what they want them for, can't we? I'm going over myself, if they'll let me. I've never been to sea before but I wouldn't miss it for the world.' The man behind, who was wearing a bowler hat and pinstripe trousers, said, 'Nor would I. I'm not letting those Jerries get our lads.' When Matt's turn came, he was asked details.

'Only fourteen foot? No outboard? Sorry, but she won't be much use to us unless she's towed over with the other lifeboats and dinghies. We'd be glad to take her for that.'

He went to find Lizzie. 'Too small and no motor. They'll only take her if she's towed over. I don't want her to go like that, Lizzie. I'm going to take her myself. I don't see how they can stop me. I've been talking to some of the others and they've been told to make for Ramsgate. I'm going to tag along. They're all going across from there. To Dunkirk – that's where they're taking the men off.' He saw her expression. 'And before you even ask it, the answer's no. You're not coming too. You're staying behind. I really mean it this time.'

'Just to Ramsgate. It's not far. I'll get the train back from there.'

'No.'

'I thought you said you loved me, Matt.'

'That's exactly why I don't want you coming any further.'

'We're supposed to face things together. Or don't you believe in that? I thought you did.'

He groaned.

'Oh, Lizzie, that's not fair.'

'Just as far as Ramsgate, that's all. I promise.'

In the dusk, the farmhouse looked deserted. No lights at the windows, no sign of life. The dog kept close to Guy as he moved from building to building, revolver in hand. The place was run-down and ramshackle with tin sheds on the point of collapse, Stone Age farming tools, a stinking midden, and an ancient hand pump in the yard. He kicked open a door and looked into a kitchen: oil-lamp suspended over a wooden table, cupboards gaping, an immense black range, unlit. He went through the house cautiously. The other rooms contained only cumbersome pieces of furniture, too awkward to move: a long settle, a tall armoire, a massive oak bed. Anna was waiting for him by the gate. 'It's OK. Nobody there. They've done a bunk.'

She followed him into the kitchen, wrinkling her nose. He shone the torch round on bare shelves. 'We're out of luck. Looks like they've taken everything eatable.' A birdcage hung from a beam and Anna opened the door and peered at a pathetic bundle of yellow feathers. 'They forgot to take their bird, poor little thing.' He found a door that led down a flight of brick steps to a cellar. The torch battery was dying but he could see bottles in a corner and something on a ceiling hook, wrapped in a cloth. 'It's ham,' Anna said delightedly when he bore it upstairs. He held a grime-coated bottle aloft. 'And this is home-made wine. Now all we need is something to open it with.' He risked lighting the oil-lamp to save the torch and they hunted through drawers and found a rusty corkscrew at the back of one. He pulled the cork with ceremony and held the bottle out to her. 'You first. There's plenty more where it came from.' She tipped it back and choked. 'It's horrible! Like vinegar. No wonder they left it.' They drank it, just the same, sitting at the table and sawing hunks off the salty ham with his penknife and throwing pieces to the dog. They finished the terrible wine and smoked cigarettes. 'We'll stay here until dawn,' he told her. 'And then press on as fast as we can. We'll be in Dunkirk tomorrow.'

'Do you think there will be boats?'

'You heard what Otto said. Our Navy's evacuating our troops.'

'Perhaps he lied.'

'I don't think so. The trick will be to get on one.'

'They will take you. But not me.'

He looked at her thoughtfully. 'We'll need to find you other clothes. Beg, borrow or steal some

British uniform. I'm afraid we'll have to cut your hair.'

'There are no scissors but we can use your penknife. You do it. It's easier for you.'

He got to his feet unwillingly. 'Actually, it's harder.'

'You said it must be cut, Guy. Go on, then. I don't care. It will be much cooler anyway.' She turned her back to him.

He wiped the blade, took a hank of her hair in his hands and started to hack away, hating what he was doing. 'I'm making a ghastly job of it, I'm sorry.' He worked on doggedly until there was a shining carpet round her feet. She turned to face him. 'How do I look? Like a soldier?'

'Not remotely.'

'Then you must cut more.'

He hacked until her hair was almost as short as his own.

'How do I look *now*?'

'How you always look.' He folded the knife and put it away in his pocket. 'We ought to get some kip.'

'Kip?'

'Sleep.'

'Where can we lie? There is nowhere.'

'There's a bed upstairs. The mattress looked fairly clean. No blankets, but you can have my greatcoat again.'

'I don't want your coat, Guy.'

He met her eyes. 'What *do* you want?'

'I am not sure.'

Later on, in the darkness, he said, 'I thought you didn't like me.'

'I didn't.'

A bit later still, he said, 'Well, you've got a damned odd way of showing it.'

Lizzie watched the armada heading out towards France: big ships of the Royal Navy leading a vast fleet of smaller boats, fanned out across the sea. And, after them, smallest and last of all, ploughing her way valiantly through their wakes, came the *Rose*. She could hardly see her for the tears in her eyes.

At Ramsgate station a newspaper headline screamed at her: B.E.F. FIGHTS DOWN NARROW CORRIDOR TO DUNKIRK. Another: DUNKIRK HELD AS B.E.F MOVE BACK FIGHTING EVERY INCH OF THE WAY. Lizzie bought a cup of tea and a bun from the canteen. The woman behind the counter was making a great pile of sandwiches, spreading fish paste onto slices of bread and slapping them together at high speed. 'It's for the troops. They've been arriving all day. I can't keep up with it.'

'Do you want a hand?'

'I wouldn't say no, dear. We need all the help we can get. You can take these and hand them round when the next lot get in. Then come back for the tea. Look, here come some more.'

A long line of soldiers was shuffling and limping onto the platform. They were unshaven, filthy and hollow-eyed with exhaustion. The tougher ones perked up as she handed out the sandwiches and then mugs of strong tea, managing to smile at her. 'Ta, sweetheart . . . this'll go down a treat . . . thanks love.'

'Are there any RAF with you?' she asked one of them.

He looked bitter. 'RAF? Never seen no sign of 'em. We could've done with their help an' all.'

She stayed all day, helping to hand out sandwiches, mugs of tea, cigarettes, chocolate and sweets to the troops who poured into the station and packed the trains. At midnight they were still coming. 'Got somewhere to go to get a bit of rest?' Lily, the woman behind the counter, asked her. 'You can come and sleep at our place round the corner, if you like. It's just my mother and me.' It was a neat little house, in a row of others just like it. A framed photograph of a man in army uniform stood on the mantelpiece. 'That's my husband, Peter,' Lily said proudly. 'He's over there, too. I keep looking out for him and hoping he'll get back soon.'

The water from the pump was clear and cool. Anna worked the handle, letting the stream gush over her head and sluice her body. The dog stayed at a distance, watching her with his head on one side, his right ear pricked. He wagged his tail uncertainly. She pumped some water into a bucket and he crept closer to drink.

'Nobody has ever been nice to you. Poor thing.'

She dried herself with her dirty frock and put on a clean one from the canvas bag. Guy was still fast asleep upstairs, lying on his back with one arm outstretched. She sat on the edge of the bed, gazing at him. In spite of the three-day growth of stubble, he looked, asleep, very much like the boy of sixteen that he had been when she had first met him. He had smiled at her so confidently and so charmingly, so sure of impressing: *Terribly sorry if we startled you. I'm Guy and this is my brother, Matt. We're Lizzie's cousins. You must be Anna. Anna from Vienna*. She had not been impressed at all. Not for years. She had thought him conceited and selfish and insensitive. She had been right and, at the same time, very wrong. She reached out and touched his forehead and he stirred and opened his eyes, looked first at her, and then at his wrist-watch.

'Christ Almighty, it's almost seven o'clock! We should have gone hours ago. Why didn't you wake me?'

'You have not slept for days before this, that is why.' She shook her short wet hair at him, spraying him with droplets of water. 'I have been washing under the pump.'

He pulled her down and kissed her and when he let her go his face was all wet. He smiled up at her. 'If it wasn't for this bloody war, I'd stay here for days with you.'

The dog was waiting for them in the yard. They hacked a big chunk off the ham and filled a bottle with water from the pump and put them in the basket, together with the knife. Before they set off he took her in his arms and kissed her again. 'Just wait till we're back in England.'

The country lane was empty but the sky was not. Wave after wave of German bombers roared overhead. 'Dunkirk,' Guy told her bitterly. 'They must be bombing it to smithereens.' We have no chance, Anna thought. The Germans will make sure of that. Otto must have known it very well. He lied about that, too, just as he lied to me. I mean nothing to him. I'm subhuman. By late morning they had reached the point where the lane joined up with a main road. A great stream of soldiers, British and French, were trudging northwards on foot, mixed up with a slow cavalcade of vehicles: lorries, trucks, and tanks and cars, all overloaded with more soldiers, and more soldiers riding on tractors, dustcarts, bicycles, children's scooters, horses. She saw how shocked and appalled Guy was at the sight. The dog trotted behind the bikes, weaving his way after them. They could hear the distant booming of guns and ahead a giant cloud of black smoke rose into the skies.

She quoted aloud: ' "And the Lord went before them by day in a pillar of cloud to lead them the way. And by night in a pillar of fire to give them light." '

'Sorry?'

'It's from Exodus, Guy.'

Three hours later they came into the town of Dunkirk.

*   *   *

From Ramsgate Matt had sailed due east to the Gull and from there to the North Goodwin light. He was far behind the main convoy by then, but from time to time a motor torpedo-boat appeared, circling like a sheepdog. As he crossed the Sandettie Bank, south-east of the North Goodwins, he encountered a large paddle-steamer thrashing her way back from Dunkirk. As she approached, less than a quarter of a mile away, he could see her decks crowded with men – so many that she was low in the water. He didn't spot the German dive-bombers until they swooped down suddenly out of the skies upon her. Their bombs sent up great spouts of water round the steamer and the spray fell on him like heavy rain. There was a burst of Bren-gun and rifle fire from her decks and the three dive-bombers turned for another run to rake her with their machine-guns. Then they climbed steeply and headed eastwards in the direction of Dunkirk. Matt felt not fear, but fury. More ships passed him, returning home – a fast Royal Navy vessel, its heavy wash tossing the *Rose* around like a cork, the cross-Channel ferry, *Maid of Orleans*, a minesweeper, a car ferry – its sawn-off platform wallowing through the waves – all of them packed tightly with troops.

'Steer for the black smoke and the sound of the guns,' someone had yelled at him from the wheel of a launch at Ramsgate. 'And watch out for mines.' He'd seen no mines so far but the black smoke billowing up over Dunkirk was visible from miles away and he could hear the constant thunder of guns. As he sailed nearer and darkness began to fall, flames showed up among the smoke as leaping tongues of orange. It looked as though the whole town was on fire. From the naval ships anchored offshore came the rapid blinking of Aldis lamps and the unearthly keening of sirens, and yet more flames from a sinking ship and gun flashes from the shore. He sailed closer still and saw big ships tied up along a concrete breakwater at the eastern end of the outer harbour and long lines of troops boarding them. It would be no place for the *Rose*. Matt took her instead further east beyond the breakwater and towards the beaches.

Chapter Seventeen

The town was a mass of burning, smoking rubble; its streets a shambles of broken glass, fallen masonry and twisted girders, dangling cables and wires, wrecked military vehicles, dead soldiers, dead civilians, dead horses. The heat from the fires scorched the skin and there was a hideous stench of blood and rotting flesh and bad-eggs cordite. An ambulance klaxon had jammed and was blaring non-stop, a herd of loose French cavalry horses cantered wildly up and down, whinnying in terror. In one *estaminet* drunken Tommies sat round a bottle-filled table, singing and swaying, in another that had been drunk dry, French *poilus* were smashing shelves. A platoon of British infantry marched smartly down the street, heavy boots grinding glass to powder. Guy stopped their officer.

'What's happening? Where the hell are we all supposed to be going?'

The lieutenant eyed him caustically. 'Where've you RAF chaps been? The Navy are taking us off at the harbour. The bloody Belgians have surrendered and the Jerries aren't losing any time breaking through. Our rearguard can't hold them back much longer. I'd look sharp about getting on a ship, if I were you.' His eyes moved to Anna. 'You'll have to leave the girlfriend behind.'

As he marched his men away he called back over his shoulder, 'There're some small boats working the beaches, too. You could try those.'

More enemy bombers roared over and they ran for cover down some steps into a cellar. 'The dog . . . we have left the dog. We must fetch him.' Guy yanked Anna back as the bombs shrieked down and exploded, shaking the cellar walls. He held her tightly while all hell broke loose above. When the raid was over they crawled out of a ruin. New fires blazed and thick smoke and a worse stink of explosive choked the air. Their bikes were a mangled heap; the dog nowhere to be seen. One of the cavalry horses flopped around in the middle of the road, a hind leg blown off, the gutter running with its blood. Guy took out his revolver and shot the beast between the ears where it lay. Tears were pouring down Anna's cheeks and he put his arm round her. 'Come on.'

'The dog . . .'

'We can't waste time looking for him.'

A Tommy lay face down close to a deep crater in the road. Guy knelt and turned him over. He was a slightly built boy of no more than eighteen or nineteen – stone dead, but unmarked other than by a small gash on his forehead that had spattered his greatcoat with blood. 'We'll take his uniform.' He fumbled with buttons and began tearing the filthy clothes off. 'Get these on.' Anna recoiled. 'I can't, Guy.' 'You damn well have to. Get them on.' He was undoing laces, tugging at the army boots. 'These, too. Good job he's small.' He tore the soldier's vest into strips and used them to stuff the boots. When she was dressed he put the steel helmet on her head, the rifle in her hands and redid the tie that she'd made a hash of. 'You'll pass – in the dark, at least.'

'What about my bag? It has my photographs, my passport, my papers.'

'You can take what you can put in your pockets, that's all.'

The water-bottle was broken and they left the remains of the ham, fearing it would make them too thirsty, and started walking in the direction of the harbour, clambering over mounds of rubble and past more bomb craters and row upon row of abandoned trucks, tanks and guns. At the port, burning oil tanks poured out a great pall of dense black smoke and fires raging all round the harbour lit up the smashed docks and broken cranes, and the silhouettes of half-sunken ships – funnels and masts poking up from greasy black water. Long lines, three and four deep, of ragged soldiers were formed up, waiting patiently. 'Been here for hours,' one of them told Guy. 'The big ships can't use the docks since the Jerries clobbered them. They're having to tie up at a breakwater on the outer harbour. We can get to them along it – if Jerry doesn't put a spoke in.'

Guy went back to Anna. 'We'll try the beaches first.'

Outside the town, away from the heat and smoke and flames, what power was left in the torch battery showed forlorn holiday houses squatting behind grassy sand dunes. They climbed up onto the dunes, their feet sinking deep into soft hummocks of sand. Anna sat down. 'My feet are too sore to walk more.'

'OK, we'll stay here and wait for daylight.' At a faint sound behind him Guy swung the torch beam round sharply, and picked out two shining eyes. 'Good God, it's the dog! Come on, old chap.' The mongrel, who had waited for the invitation, came forward, tongue lolling, flanks heaving but wagging its tail. 'He likes us,' Anna said. 'He trusts us.'

He's wrong, Guy thought. We can't take him with us. Not possibly. It will be a miracle if we get away ourselves. He climbed to a higher point of the dunes and stared into the darkness. The stink of death still clung to his nostrils but now he could also smell the clean, salt smell of the sea and he could hear it in the distance – the regular shushing of waves breaking onto the shore. He listened carefully. It sounded a long way out – perhaps even as much as half a mile. Must be low tide, the depth probably very shallow, shelving gently, and not much deeper at high tide. The tides would come in very fast and go out very fast. There would be no chance of any big ships getting anywhere near this beach. Nothing drawing more than two or three feet would be able to manage it without running aground. Smaller ships – if there were any – would have to be very small and what use would that be to move an army? He went on staring into the dark. As his eyes grew more accustomed to it, he could make out thousands of tiny pinpricks of light all over the beach. He took them for fireflies until he realized that they were the lights of thousands of cigarettes being smoked by thousands of soldiers.

Matt felt the *Rose* rocking gently. In the darkness, the night before, he'd sailed along the coast and run her aground, bow on, into soft sand and sat waiting for dawn. With the incoming tide, she had refloated herself.

The pre-dawn light spreading gradually across the sky revealed sandy beaches extending for what looked like several miles, all the way west to the great mushroom of smoke over Dunkirk. He had come much further east than he'd thought or intended. As the daylight grew he could see that closer to the town, the beaches were black with troops and littered with wrecked equipment. Lines of men wound like snakes across the sands and into the water. Several big ships were anchored offshore and small craft – lifeboats, cutters and whalers – were moving between them and the men queueing at the water's edge. He hoisted the mainsail quickly and took *Rose* out seawards, bringing her about and back into shore towards the closest line of men. Those in front were standing shoulder-deep in the water, rifles held over their heads. He lowered the sail and let the *Rose* drift gently towards them. Twenty Tommies or more, in full kit – steel helmets, greatcoats, gas masks, capes – waded over and sprang at her gunwales, almost capsizing her.

'I can't take you all . . . I'm sorry. Not more than ten or she'll sink.' He dragged one on board who was too weak to manage it for himself; the rest of them hauled themselves up clumsily, weighed down by sodden uniforms and water-logged boots. 'Thanks, mate,' a corporal said to Matt, grinning as he rolled into the boat. He had a week's growth of beard and looked like a tramp. 'Start the engine.'

'Sorry, no engine. We have to row. Can you give me a hand with one of the oars?'

His face fell for a second. 'Blimey . . . You'll have to show me how.' There was hardly enough room for the two of them to wield the long, heavy oars but the corporal, who had sat facing the wrong way at first, spat on his palms and soon got the knack. They pulled towards the nearest large ship, a cross-Channel ferry. 'Here comes Jerry,' the corporal announced. 'Right on bloody time.'

The Stukas came screaming in from the eastern end of the beach. Men on the sands flung themselves to the ground or scattered to the dunes; the ones already in the water stayed put. Bombs exploded, blasting sand high into the air and sending up giant spouts of water in the sea. Messerschmitts, following on the Stukas' tails, roared over at a hundred feet, machine-gunning the length of the beach. The Stukas flew on to drop more bombs on the harbour and wheeled out to sea to attack the bigger ships. AA guns opened up furiously but a steamer took a direct hit amidships, broke up, ablaze, and began to sink. 'Reminds me of the Serpentine,' the corporal yelled above the din, pulling energetically on his oar.

They came alongside the cross-Channel ferry and the lowered scrambling nets. She was already loaded down with troops and getting ready to leave. The corporal, last to jump for the nets, hesitated and turned back. 'I'll stay, if you like, mate. Give you a hand for the next trip.'

All morning they went to and fro from the beach out to whatever large ship was there waiting to take troops on board. Some of the men were too weak or too badly wounded to manage the scrambling nets and fell off. More and more troops were pouring onto the sands, the queues growing longer, not shorter. Only the smallest of the boats could get close enough to pick the men up from the beaches, the larger ones came in as near as they dared and the men had to swim out to them. Those who couldn't swim grabbed planks of wood or pieces of wreckage and kicked their way along. Matt saw two men float past on a door, using their rifles as paddles, another sitting in an inflated tyre, propelling himself with his hands. They picked up another trying to swim out in overcoat and boots, weighed down by a large pack. The men in the queues grew more desperate – so many of them fighting to clamber on board that, again and again, they threatened to swamp the *Rose*. The corporal fended them off ruthlessly with his oar. 'Get back, you bastards. You'll sink the ruddy lot of us.' Sometimes men clung onto her gunwales all the way out to the ship, or lost their grip, exhausted, and simply disappeared. The corporal leaned out and grabbed a steel helmet floating past upside down and handed it to Matt. 'I'd put this on sharpish, mate, if I were you.' Civilians crewing other small boats were wearing enamel basins and bailers and buckets on their heads. At regular intervals, the German bombers and fighters came back to strafe the beaches. Matt learned to ignore the hail of bombs and shells and bullets – to carry on, like the corporal, without flinching. 'If one gets us, it gets us,' the corporal maintained firmly. 'No good trying to dodge 'em.' The sea grew red with blood and bodies bobbed around the *Rose*, nudging her bows as she went from ship to shore and shore to ship. Some of the dead faces were already bloated.

'What's this old girl called, then?' the corporal asked on one trip.

'*Rose of England*.'

He nodded. 'Not a bad name for her, I reckon.'

For three days they had waited impatiently for orders from High Command, expecting the advance towards Dunkirk to be resumed. Instead the Panzer divisions were directed south. Stephan was torn between frustration at being denied the chance to finish off the British and delight at the prospect of dining in Paris.

'The British are done for in any case. The Luftwaffe is already pounding them to pulp and the infantry will do the rest. It'll be no more than a mopping-up operation for them. Our talents will be better used elsewhere, don't you agree, Otto?'

'Well, it's true that the marshy terrain of Flanders is not ideal for tanks, but perhaps it would have been better to make quite sure of the British. To stop her army escaping.'

'A few of them may get away but most will not. If they are not killed, they will be captured.'

'A few?' Otto said drily. 'I heard that large numbers are being rescued and taken to England. They will live to fight another day. And we may live to regret it.'

Guy had been prepared for the sight of troops on the beaches but not for the sheer numbers of them. Black masses swarmed over the dunes and long lines wound across the sands; it looked as though some gigantic ants' nest had been stirred up. He watched the larger boats waiting offshore and smaller ones shuttling to and fro, cramming as many men as they could on board. Not naval ships, as he'd expected, but civilian ones – dozens and dozens of them, working ceaselessly all along the beaches.

He knew that, sooner or later, the Luftwaffe would come, and when they did, Junkers and Dorniers and 109s shrieking across the beach, he protected Anna with his own body, lying flat in the sand dunes, the dog crouched beside them. Men were firing their rifles in hopeless desperation, from the dunes, from the open sands, from the water, aiming wildly in the general direction of the attackers. Men were throwing themselves into the sea and thrashing about, weighed down by their uniforms. Some of the small boats had been hit and had capsized or were sinking, spilling men overboard; he could hear their cries for help. On the beach, the dead were everywhere, the wounded groaning and screaming. A soldier stood shaking his fist. 'Come down you fucking bastards and fight fair!' Jesus Christ, Guy thought, what a bloody, bloody mess.

The Germans would be back but taking refuge in the dunes would not get them a place on a boat. They joined the end of one of the long queues, the dog still following them faithfully. He had been afraid that Anna would soon be spotted but the men were too dead beat to notice or care. They stood, one behind another, leaning on their rifles, shuffling forward a few inches at a time, some asleep on their feet. 'Got any water, sir?' one of them croaked hopefully. His lips were cracked and dry and smeared with sand. 'Awfully sorry, I'm afraid not.' He was thirsty himself – so was Anna – and he cursed his stupidity in not taking proper care of the water-bottle. 'Cigarette?' he offered instead. 'No, thank you, sir. Makes it worse.'

The Germans returned, bombing and strafing the length of the beaches. Men scattered, diving under the water, flinging themselves to the sand, burrowing into the dunes. When the planes had gone the dead were covered with their greatcoats; precious little could be done for the wounded, some of them crying out in agony.

By mid-afternoon, the queue had shuffled forward a mere thirty yards. The bombers and the 109s had returned again and again. Only twice did Guy catch sight of any RAF fighters – a lone Spitfire chasing three Junkers over the harbour and despatching one of them before going down itself in flames and another, mistaken for a German and brought down by savage machine-gun fire from the dunes. All day he'd been getting jibes about the RAF and cold looks from soldiers. Wherever the RAF were, he reasoned, they would surely be concentrating on bombing enemy positions and supply lines further back, and the fighters would be trying to intercept the raiders *before* they reached their targets. It would be no help to the men on the beaches to wait until the Germans were overhead. He had tried to explain this once, but he might as well have saved his breath.

As darkness began to fall, they were a long way from the front of the queue. Boats with fouled or broken-down engines floated uselessly offshore and wrecks of those that had been sunk stuck out of the water on the falling tide. And troops were still arriving, streaming onto the sands. It was hopeless, Guy decided. They'd go back to the dunes for the night and try their luck again at the harbour at dawn. In the dunes men sprawled, sleeping the sleep of the exhausted. Someone was praying aloud: *Mother of mercy, keep me through this night* . . . somebody else playing 'It's a Long Way to Tipperary' softly and slowly on a harmonica.

'Got a fag, mate?' the corporal asked Matt.

'Sorry, I don't smoke.'

'Pity about that 'cos I'm out, an' I could do with one. Don't know about you, but I've had it.'

They were both stupid with exhaustion, flesh rubbed raw, muscles tortured. Matt had lost count of the number of trips they'd done from the beach out to the bigger ships and back. They'd rowed to and fro without stopping, the *Rose* swamped with as many men as she could possibly take. When the last of the bigger boats had left as darkness fell, Matt had tied the *Rose*'s painter to the prow of a sunken wreck halfway out. He slumped in the stern, leaning on the tiller, and watched the oil tanks blazing at Dunkirk. At the harbour men were still being loaded onto a ship but the *Rose* could do no more until the next boats arrived from England.

'What do they think of us back in Blighty, then?' the corporal asked, scooping sardines out of a tin with his fingers. 'Must think we're a right lot of useless bastards, getting kicked out of France by Jerry. My old woman's goin' to give me what for – if I ever get home again, that is.'

'They don't know much about it. It's been kept out of the papers. Most people didn't have a clue how bad it was.'

'Well, they'll soon find out when they see this lot of conquering heroes turnin' up.' He sucked the remains of the oil out of the sardine tin. 'Might as well get a bit of shut-eye.' He settled down on the *Rose*'s wet and bloody bilge-boards. 'You sail this old bucket over here on your own?'

'Yes.'

'Sooner you than me. You've done a good job, mate.' He draped his sopping greatcoat over himself. 'You can call me with a nice hot cuppa first thing. An' I take two spoonfuls.'

Matt grinned. 'I'll remember. By the way, what's your name?'

There was no answer; the corporal was fast asleep.

Guy watched for the dawn to come up. As soon as there was the faintest trace of light in the east, he woke Anna. 'We've got to get over to the harbour.' She struggled to her feet. 'What about the dog? They'll never let him onto one of the big ships.'

'We have to leave him behind. He'll be all right.'

'You know that he won't, Guy. And he trusts us. Are you going to desert him when he has come all this way?'

'We couldn't stop him.'

'Supposing it was Nereus?'

'Nereus was quite different. He belonged to us.'

'This one thinks he does too. Even Otto saw that.'

394

He looked down at the dog who was listening, one ear cocked. Poor little sod, he thought, I should have finished him off ages ago. It would have been much kinder. 'They won't let him on *any* boat, Anna – big or small.'

She said stubbornly, 'I saw a soldier taking a dog on a boat yesterday – he was carrying it under his arm. Please, Guy. Let's try. We could go all the way down to the other end of the beaches. There are not so many people there.'

'And not so many boats, either.'

'But I think we may have more chance. And when the Germans come back today they will be very sure to bomb the harbour and any big ships there – just like they were doing yesterday. They don't take so much notice of the little ships.'

There was some sense in that, he acknowledged. He looked eastwards towards the dawn. If they started walking now, they would soon see if the situation was any better in that direction, and, if it wasn't, then they could go back to the harbour. There was another factor to be considered, too: the Navy would certainly have officers in charge of boarding from the harbour breakwater and Anna was much more likely to be discovered. Even if they were prepared to let a woman on board, which seemed unlikely in the extreme, Anna's passport showed that she was an Austrian citizen – an enemy. That she was also a Jewish refugee might make no difference. 'We'll give it a try,' he agreed. 'But that's all.'

As they walked, the dog a small shadow at their heels, she said, 'Will you promise me something, Guy?'

'Depends what it is.'

'If I am not allowed to leave – if they stop me getting on a boat – that you will go, just the same.'

'Leave you behind? Don't be absurd. I'd never do that.'

'But you *must*, Guy. You must go back to England and fly fighters again for the Royal Air Force. They need you. If you don't go the Germans will capture you and put you in a camp and what use is that? I'm not afraid to stay. So, will you promise me?'

'I won't do anything of the kind.' But he knew that she was right.

She'd been wrong, though, about there being fewer troops at the eastern end of the beaches. The murky light of dawn showed the same long queues into the water, the same black clusters of men on the dunes, the same junkyard of wrecked vehicles and the same dead lying in the sand. No big ships had yet arrived offshore. Anna was throwing a stick for the dog for all the world as if they were on holiday. In summer it was probably a pretty nice place for one, Guy thought. The French families would come in August and stay in the beach houses behind the dunes and play on these sands, building sandcastles and flying kites. But not this summer. Not next. Maybe not for a long time.

Anna came back with the dog bounding

happily round her. 'Guy, there is a little boat out there. It looks like the *Rose*.'

'Lots of boats look like her.'

'No, they don't. She has a straight back.'

'Stern, you mean,' he said absently. 'Look, Anna, we're wasting time. This is no good. We ought to get back to the harbour as quickly as possible.'

'She's empty, I think. And she has a sail.'

He walked down to the water's edge. He had very good sight but, even so, it was difficult to see clearly in the poor light. The boat looked as though it was caught on the wreckage of one of the ships sunk offshore. Fourteen foot, he judged, clinker-built, gaff-rigged . . . and she did have a straight Viking stern and a stowed sail. And she did seem empty. He'd noticed yesterday how some of the boats were abandoned and left to drift once the men in them had reached one of the big ships. He gauged the distance. She was probably between four and five hundred yards out and the wind had shifted, roughing up the water. Tough for Anna, but he could help her.

'Do you think you could swim out to her?'

She looked at him in anguish. 'I can't swim, Guy.'

He couldn't believe her. 'But you told me you could. I remember.'

'I knew you wouldn't take me out in the *Rose* unless I could. I've never learned. I don't like cold water.'

'My God, Anna . . .' He stopped himself. 'We'll manage somehow. Get the boots off and the greatcoat, but leave the battledress tunic – it'll help you float. You'll have to do exactly as I say and trust me.'

They waded in until Anna was up to her shoulders. The mongrel stayed, perplexed, at the edge. 'Maybe he cannot swim either, Guy.'

'All dogs can swim. Don't worry about him. He'll follow us.' He didn't think the dog had a hope. 'Remember, you must trust me.' He swam on his back, pulling her through the water in the way that they'd practised life-saving in the swimming-baths at school. She didn't panic or struggle and he swam slowly and steadily, turning his head occasionally to check the direction. The dog was still on the shore, a small dejected figure watching him, but three other swimmers were following, splashing and kicking noisily. If any more of them see us and get the same idea, he thought, it'll swamp the boat and none of us will get away. He swam on strongly, faster now.

'Wakey-wakey,' the corporal said. 'Some blokes are coming out to visit us. Take a dekko.' Matt staggered to his feet, bleary-eyed. It still wasn't light – sea and land merged in a uniform grey. 'Where?' The corporal pointed. 'Two of them there, and another three further behind. I've got X-ray eyes, see. I always eat up my carrots.'

'We'd better start rowing and pick them up.' His blistered left hand was agony to use. They manoeuvred the *Rose* towards the two swimmers closest to them – one, he saw, was supporting the other in the water. He and the corporal shipped oars and leaned over to help them. It wasn't until they were both landed in the bottom of the boat that he saw their faces. 'You lot know each other?' the corporal enquired with interest.

They picked up the other three soldiers. 'There's a dog out there somewhere,' one of them gasped. 'Don't think he'll make it, though.'

The corporal searched the water. 'I can see him. Over there. Come on, Rover, you can do it.' The dog was paddling frantically, nose just above the water. They sculled the *Rose* to meet him and Guy reached out, grabbed hold of the mongrel by the scruff of the neck and swung him, legs dangling, on board. 'Let's get the sails up, Matt,' he said. 'Time we went home.'

Oberleutnant Karl Halder had been patrolling the Channel in his Messerschmitt 109 on the lookout for enemy boats returning with British soldiers from Dunkirk. He had already despatched a lifeboat packed with survivors from a Royal Navy destroyer sunk by von Richthofen's Stukas and attacked a pathetic old steamer and her crowded decks with some success. Now, below the fighter's wings, he sighted the burning carcass of a British minesweeper, sinking slowly by the stern. He went down lower to have a closer look but could see no boats taking to the water and no sign of life. The men must have been taken off earlier and the boat was finished in any case. Disappointed, he banked away and turned south-east, heading for his base. He was low on fuel but it would be nice to find just one more target to finish up the rest of his ammunition. He went on searching the sea – flat as a lake with not a single white horse to be seen, which had given the enemy quite an unfair advantage. He swooped low over another abandoned vessel. It had green and white awnings and slatted passenger seats and looked like a river-excursion boat – the sort that went up and down the Rhine. The British must have brought out every vessel they could find. He'd seen drifters and dredgers, barges, fishing smacks, ferries – the most extraordinary collection of craft, and with scarcely a peashooter between them to defend themselves. If it had not been that so many of the Tommies were getting away, it would have been quite comical. Really, one had to hand it to the British for ingenuity. Guts, too. Their rearguard was still managing to hold the Dunkirk perimeter – by the skin of their teeth. They were a tenacious race. He flew on, searching.

He had almost given up when he spotted a very small boat with red sails, all alone and obviously making for the English coast. He peered down, considering it for a moment. A tricky little target and hardly worth the bother, but he might as well use up the few rounds he had left.

The canteen had run out of cups and they were using jamjars to serve the tea. The never-ending stream of troops continued to shuffle and hobble through the station, some without boots, some wearing borrowed civilian clothing, others wrapped in army blankets, one dressed in a sack with holes cut for neck and arms, another with a woman's fur coat draped round his shoulders. Lizzie held a jamjar of tea for a stretcher case to drink. The Tommy, head and arms bandaged and what was left of his uniform in filthy tatters, winked at her with his one visible eye. 'Now I know I'm in heaven.' A badly wounded sergeant on the next stretcher blinked away tears as she put a cigarette to his lips and lit it for him. 'Never thought we'd get a welcome like this. We thought you'd all be blowing raspberries.' One of them asked if she'd let his mother know he was safe. She wrote down the address, promising to send a postcard. Then more of them kept asking the same. In the end she got a stack of railway labels from the booking-office and wrote AM SAFE on one side and gave them out. The men signed them and wrote their addresses on the other side and she collected them up for posting.

'Take a break, dear. You've been working non-stop all day,' Lily told her.

'What about you?'

'I'll get on with this lot of sandwiches. We're running a bit low. Besides, if I leave here I might miss seeing Peter and I wouldn't want to do that. Off you go.'

'Just for a few moments, then.'

She walked out of the station in a daze. Yet another lorry was arriving. Yet another full load of exhausted, filthy, hungry and thirsty men. It was a frightening sight. They were bringing them back in their thousands. The whole of the British army in France must be being evacuated. In the station yard, a middle-aged woman was going up to the soldiers. 'Have you seen my boy, Billy?' she kept asking, again and again, tugging at arms. 'Have you seen him? His name's Billy. Billy Rice.' They answered her gently. 'Sorry, love. Don't know. What unit's he in?' 'The Gloucesters – the 2nd Gloucesters.' All down the line helmeted heads were shaken. 'Sorry, love. Never saw any of them.'

Lizzie walked on to the old harbour. It was packed with ships, the quayside seething with troops and officials, doctors and nurses, ambulances and trucks, WVS and Red Cross. Loud hailers were bawling instructions and a military policeman barred her way. 'Sorry, miss, you can't go any further.' She stood, staring at the scene: at the processions of weary troops stumbling down gangways; at men plunging their heads into buckets of water to drink like horses and gazing round them in bewilderment as they saw the Coronation bunting and flags and the huge white sheet, daubed in black paint with the words WELL DONE, B.E.F. A band struck up, playing 'There'll Always be an England'. People were waving and cheering. A girl ran forward and kissed several soldiers on the cheek. The bewilderment on the men's faces turned to grins and some of them put their thumbs up tentatively. It was just as the sergeant on the stretcher had told her. They had all expected to be booed – to get jeers and catcalls. They couldn't believe that they were being given a heroes' welcome. A woman next to her was weeping but behind someone said acerbically, 'All very well to make a fuss of them but what are we going to do when the Germans invade *us* next. We've got nothing left to fight them with.'

'We've got this lot,' someone else retorted. 'They'll do.'

More ships were entering the port. Lizzie stood on tiptoe searching over heads for the sight of a little ship with red sails. 'Get further back, please,' another MP ordered, putting out his beefy arm like a barrier. She ducked under it. 'You can't go there,' he shouted after her as she ran towards the quayside. She fought her way through the crowds and ran on down the ranks of big ships, past the gangways and the dis-embarking soldiers to where smaller ships were berthed. No red sails. No *Rose*. A Royal Navy sailor stopped her. 'Not supposed to be here, miss – not unless you're official.'

'I'm looking for a ship – one of the little ones. I thought she might have come in.'

'What's her name?'

'*Rose of England.*'

He shook his head. 'Haven't seen her. What kind?'

'Just an old fishing boat. She's got dark red sails with patches.'

He glanced over her shoulder. 'Like this one coming in now? Looks as though she's been in a spot of trouble.'

There was a jagged tear in her mainsail and she was low in the water because of her heavy burden but she came in proudly. Thank God, Lizzie thought. *Thank God*. Matt's safe. She started to wave frantically. The mainsail came down and the *Rose* drifted towards the quayside. A soldier jumped ashore holding the painter and the sailor helped him to make it fast. He brushed past her in a hurry. 'I'll get an ambulance down here.' Lizzie stopped waving. She saw all the blood, and the dead and the wounded . . . and Guy holding one of them in his arms. There was a small brown dog at his side.

'*Escargots* to start with, I think. Followed by *Côtes d'Agneau* with *pommes nouvelles* and some *haricots verts*.' Stephan smiled charmingly at the French waitress as he handed her back the menu. 'What wine shall we have, Otto? Since you are paying, you should make the choice.'

Otto watched the waitress walking away; she had long dark hair, coiled loosely in a knot at the back of her head. 'Have whatever you wish. I don't mind.'

Stephan observed him drily. 'She's beautiful, isn't she?'

'No. Not in my opinion. Quite ordinary, in fact.'

'You are always so choosy, Otto. You miss a lot of fun.'

'Very few women are truly beautiful. I have only ever known one.'

'And who is she?'

'Nobody that you know.'

'You seem out of sorts, my friend. You should be in excellent spirits, like me. Here we are in

Paris, just as I predicted, and about to enjoy a most delicious dinner. And when we have eaten and drunk to our hearts' content, the possibilities for further amusement in this marvellous city are limitless.' Stephan passed over the wine list. 'A bottle of claret would be rather pleasant.'

Otto beckoned the *sommelier*. The elderly man hurried forward, bowing. '*A votre service, monsieur*. What do you wish to order?' He picked one of the most expensive wines. '*Merci, monsieur. Merci, merci* . . .' The wine waiter bowed several more times, retreating backwards, and scurried off. Stephan watched, amused.

'They cannot do enough for us. It's really quite funny. Do you think they imagine that we shall instantly shoot them dead if we are not satisfied? If our food is not cooked as we like, or the wine is corked? I hope your English will be as anxious to please when we are in London.'

'I doubt it.'

'They are a stubborn lot, that's true. It's a great pity that so many of them escaped. Three hundred thousand or more! One has to admire their nerve. Of course, we would have polished them off easily if we had not been halted. It was crazy to stop us. Still, in reality, they are finished. Within the space of three weeks we booted them out of France, within five we are in Paris. Their army has been defeated, their tanks and weapons lost. What can they do now? We can walk into their country whenever we choose.'

'They still have their Royal Navy. And their Royal Air Force.'

'Our Luftwaffe sank six of their destroyers at Dunkirk and our U-boats will finish off the rest. As for the RAF, they are useless. The Luftwaffe outnumbers them and our pilots and machines are vastly superior. There will be no problem. So long as I am not sent to fight against the Russians this winter, then I think I am going to enjoy this war. Ah, here is the wine.' When it was poured, Stephan raised his glass. 'To victory.'

Otto drank. He set down his glass. 'Unfortunately, because of what happened at Dunkirk, I'm not so sure that we shall ever achieve it.'

There is silence in the room as I finish speaking.
After a moment or two he says, 'Was Anna killed?'

'The bullets caught the bows of the Rose *just where she was sitting. She died later in hospital in Ramsgate. The corporal was killed outright. And two of the soldiers. Matt and Guy and the third soldier were in the stern and they were unhurt.'*

'That's the way it happens in war. In life, too. It's all luck.' He looks at me. 'You're Lizzie, aren't you?'

'Yes, I'm Lizzie.'

'I thought so. Well, what happened after that? I'd like to know.'

'Guy fought in the Battle of Britain and won the DFC. He used to spend some of his leaves at the house in Wimpole Street and we'd sit and talk up in the attic. He always blamed himself for Anna's death. And I don't think he ever really got over it. He was a squadron leader when he was killed over France at the time of the D-Day landings.'

He grunts. 'His luck ran out. I'm sorry. And Matt?'

'Matt qualified as a doctor at the end of the war and we were married soon after. I served in the WAAF as a code and cypher clerk until then.'

'And the German?'

'Otto went on to achieve high rank in the army. He was taken prisoner by the Russians in 1945 and spent ten years in a labour camp in Siberia before he was released. When he came to England to find us he was like an old man. It was sad. He died a few years later.'

'Huh. Can't feel too sorry for him myself. Fought for the Nazis, didn't he, when all's said and done? What about the cocky one – Stephan?'

'I don't know what happened to him.'

'Nothing good, I'd say. He won't have enjoyed his war as much as he thought he was going to. Did you find out about Anna's family? Whether they ever got to Switzerland?'

'Yes, they did. And after the war they went to join their relatives in America.'

'So she did save them, after all.'

'Yes, but they lost Anna.'

'Another of life's little tricks,' he says.

'The aunt and uncle who were left behind in Vienna died in Auschwitz. So did the friend, Mina, and her family. And all the Fischers. And so did the mother of Daniel. Daniel is a well-known violinist now. You may have heard of him?' He shakes his head. 'Never listen to that sort of thing.'

There is another silence. He heaves himself up out of his chair and puts the pipe on the mantelpiece. 'We'd better take a look at the boat.'

I follow him out of the back door of the bungalow and down the pathway of a neglected garden. 'Don't bother much with it these days,' he tells me. 'No reason to.'

I can see her mast sticking up at the far end of the garden. She's lying beside a rubbish dump and smothered by nettles, her open deck covered with a faded green tarpaulin. We trample down the nettles and haul off the tarpaulin. I look at the old boat. The varnish has peeled away, her planking is bleached to silver-grey and in places it has rotted. She has lost her red sails, her oars and what little she had in looks, but none of her dignity. I know at once that it's the Rose.

'I told you she was a wreck,' the old man says defensively. 'Haven't looked at her for years.' I point out where the bullet holes were repaired and the initials carved on the port bow: GR, MR, OvR, AS, EE. He runs his fingers across them. 'Never noticed them before.'

I take the plunge. 'Will you sell her to me?'

'What do you want to do with her? She's not much use. You can see that.'

'I don't want to sail her. I want to give her to a museum. As I said, she's rather special.'

He is staring at the boat. 'No, I won't sell her.' My heart sinks. 'I won't sell her,' he goes on. 'I'll give her to you in exchange for something. Do you still do painting?'

'Yes. It's my job.' I earn quite a lot doing so, but I don't say so.

'Then I'd like you to paint me a picture of her the way she was then. I'd like to have that. I'd hang it over the mantelpiece so's I could look at it when I'm smoking my pipe. That would be the payment.'

We shake hands on the deal and walk back up the path. 'Otto was quite right, to my way of thinking,' he says. 'It wasn't us that was finished at Dunkirk, it was Hitler. He let us get away and that was the beginning of the end for him. We had time to get back on our feet, we won the Battle of Britain and he lost the chance to invade us. After that, we and the Yanks could get at them with our bombers and plan for D-Day. If we'd lost our army it could have been a very different story.'

He walks with me to the car. 'Don't forget about the painting.' I give him my promise. As I get into my car, he says, 'I forgot to ask about the dog. What happened to him?'

I smile. 'Guy kept him. He took him everywhere with him, to all his postings. When Guy was killed, his parents looked after him at first until Matt and I were married and then he came to live with us. The children loved him and he lived to a ripe old age. Guy called him Valiant – from The Pilgrim's Progress.'

I drive away down the potholed track. In the rear-view mirror I can see Mr Potter still standing *by the gate, looking after me. I know exactly how I'm going to paint* Rose of England *for him. I shall paint her in oils, in all her glory and in her moment of history, rescuing men from the beaches of Dunkirk.*

Postscript

There is a Little Ship, very similar to *Rose of England*, though beautifully preserved, on display in the Imperial War Museum in London. *Tamazine* is the smallest surviving open fishing boat to take part in Operation Dynamo, mounted to attempt the seemingly impossible evacuation of the British Expeditionary Forces from France in 1940. She is clinker-built, fourteen foot and five inches long and without an engine. She went over to ferry troops from the beaches to off-lying ships and came back saturated with blood. Her owners presented her to the museum where she bears permanent witness to the miraculous deliverance.

BLUEBIRDS
by Margaret Mayhew

1939 – And in the back of a three-ton lorry, a strangely assorted group of young women bumped over the road to RAF Colston. They were the first of the Waafs.

Barmaids mixed with secretaries and debutantes. They had appalling living quarters and no uniforms. And, worst of all, the Station Commander, David Palmer, didn't want them. They were a nuisance, unable to do the work of men, and undoubtedly they would collapse and panic if the station was bombed.

Felicity Newman, the officer in charge of the girls, took the scathing criticism with a red face and in angry silence, then began to try and mould the ragtag bunch of girls into a disciplined fighting unit.

There was Anne Cunningham, who knew how to dance and have fun, but found herself peeling vegetables and skinning rabbits in the station kitchens. Winnie Briggs from a Suffolk farm – who longed to work on the aeroplanes themselves but met rigid rejection at every turn. And Virginia Stratton, who saw the Waaf as an escape from a miserable home, wanting to build a new life for herself.

As the war progressed, so the girls showed their worth – behaving heroically under fire, supporting the pilots with their steadfast strength, loyalty, and often their love – a love that was sometimes tragic, sometimes passionate, but always courageous

0 552 13910 6

THE CREW
by Margaret Mayhew

There were seven in the crew – seven very young and very inexperienced airmen who, nearly every night, flew their heavily-laden Lancaster bomber into the exploding skies over enemy Germany.

On almost their first flight Piers, the navigator, managed to get them lost and Van, the pilot, nearly crashed the plane on landing. Charlie, the rear gunner, who was only seventeen but who had lied about his age, spent his time reading poetry and trying not to spew his guts out on every flight. They were from mixed backgrounds and nationalities but somehow, heroically, the welded together into a courageous fighting unit, helping each other and desperately hoping they would survive their thirty bombing flights.

And on the ground were the women who waited. Section Officer Catherine Herbert, in love with Van but already committed to another man. And Peggy, the little waitress who found herself being ardently wooed by the aristocratic Piers. And Charlie's young and pretty mother, living right on the edge of the airfield, praying every night that her son would come back.

The heroic and incredible story of seven brave men, and the women who loved them.

0 552 14492 4

FOOTPRINTS IN THE SAND
by Judith Lennox

The Mulgraves are a rootless, bohemian family who travel the continent, staying in crumbling Italian palazzos, Spanish villas, French vineyards – belonging nowhere, picking up friends and hangers-on as they go, and moving on when Ralph Mulgrave's latest enthusiasm dwindles. Faith, the eldest child of the family, longs for a proper home. But in 1940 Germany invades France and the Mulgraves are forced to flee to England. Faith and her brother Jake go to London, while Ralph reluctantly settles in a Norfolk cottage with the remnants of his family.

In the intense and dangerous landscape of wartime London Faith finds work as an ambulance driver, and meets once again one of Ralph's retinue from those distant and, in retrospect, golden days of childhood. Through war and its aftermath it is Faith on whom the family relies, Faith who offers support and succour, and Faith who is constant and true in her love.

'Judith Lennox's writing is so keenly honest it could sever heartstrings'
Daily Mail

'A compelling story of courage, resilience and enduring love, of family bonds, hope and redemption'
Home and Country

0 552 14599 8

A SELECTED LIST OF FINE NOVELS
AVAILABLE FROM CORGI BOOKS

THE PRICES SHOWN BELOW WERE CORRECT AT THE TIME OF GOING TO PRESS. HOWEVER TRANSWORLD PUBLISHERS RESERVE THE RIGHT TO SHOW NET RETAIL PRICES ON COVERS WHICH MAY DIFFER FROM THOSE PREVIOUSLY ADVERTISED IN THE TEXT OR ELSEWHERE.

14058 9	MIST OVER THE MERSEY	Lyn Andrews £5.99
14060 0	MERSEY BLUES	Lyn Andrews £5.99
14096 1	THE WILD SEED	Iris Gower £5.99
14447 9	FIREBIRD	Iris Gower £5.99
14537 8	APPLE BLOSSOM TIME	Kathryn Haig £5.99
14566 1	THE DREAM SELLERS	Ruth Hamilton £5.99
14567 X	THE CORNER HOUSE	Ruth Hamilton £5.99
14553 X	THE BRASS DOLPHIN	Caroline Harvey £5.99
14686 2	CITY OF GEMS	Caroline Harvey £5.99
14220 4	CAPEL BELLS	Joan Hessayon £4.99
14692 7	THE PARADISE GARDEN	Joan Hessayon £5.99
14543 2	THE COLOUR OF SIN	Janet Inglis £5.99
14332 4	THE WINTER HOUSE	Judith Lennox £5.99
14599 8	FOOTPRINTS IN THE SAND	Judith Lennox £5.99
13910 6	BLUEBIRDS	Margaret Mayhew £5.99
14492 4	THE CREW	Margaret Mayhew £5.99
14499 1	THESE FOOLISH THINGS	Imogen Parker £5.99
14658 7	THE MEN IN HER LIFE	Imogen Parker £5.99
10375 6	CSARDAS	Diane Pearson £5.99
14400 2	THE MOUNTAIN	Elvi Rhodes £5.99
14577 7	PORTRAIT OF CHLOE	Elvi Rhodes £5.99
14549 1	CHOICES	Susan Sallis £5.99
14636 6	COME RAIN OR SHINE	Susan Sallis £5.99
14606 4	FIRE OVER LONDON	Mary Jane Staples £5.99
14657 9	CHURCHILL'S PEOPLE	Mary Jane Staples £5.99
14502 5	THE LONG ROAD HOME	Danielle Steel £5.99
14476 2	CHILDREN OF THE TIDE	Valerie Wood £5.99
14640 4	THE ROMANY GIRL	Valerie Wood £5.99

All Transworld titles are available by post from:
Book Service By Post, PO Box 29, Douglas, Isle of Man IM99 1BQ
Credit cards accepted. Please telephone 01624 675137,
fax 01624 670923, Internet http://www.bookpost.co.uk or
e-mail: bookshop@enterprise.net for details.
Free postage and packing in the UK.
Overseas customers allow £1 per book.